HEARTLAND

For Vermont. Keep it weird.

Heartland

A True North Novel

by
SARINA BOWEN

Tuxbury Publishing LLC

ONE

Chastity

"PLEASE BE CAREFUL, Chastity. Don't drink anything that doesn't come from a sealed bottle—unless Dylan is the one who pours it for you."

"I'll be careful, Leah," I reply. But at the same time I roll my eyes in the mirror where I'm giving myself a last-minute once-over before I leave for my first college party.

The dormitory phone has a long curly cord that stretches *just* far enough into the bathroom. So I can listen to all Leah's worries and check my look at the same time.

Squinting at my reflection, I button the second button on my blouse. But then I unbutton it again. I want to look attractive, but I don't need my top to shout: HERE ARE MY BOOBS FOR YOUR PERUSAL.

It's a fine line.

"Don't go into the basement," Leah says. "That's where all the bad ideas happen."

"What kind of bad ideas?" I ask, perking up. I don't remember Dylan's house on Spruce Street even having a finished basement. But if it did, I'd probably go into it, in spite of Leah's warning. I'm more interested in bad ideas than anyone seems to understand. And I always have been. It's just that my life hasn't afforded much opportunity to try them out.

"Just be careful. Trust your gut. There are men who would get you drunk or high just to take advantage of you."

"I'll be very careful," I promise, just because it's the fastest way to end this conversation.

Leah means well. She's only nine years older than I am, but she considers herself my guardian. Two years ago—when I was nineteen —I ran away from the cult where we both grew up.

I owe her a lot. She took me in, no questions asked, even though we're only distant cousins. Leah cares about me and my future, which is a lot more than I can say about my actual parents. If I'd stayed on the Paradise Ranch I'd be married by now to a fifty-year-old man with four other wives.

Sometimes when people hear this story they say we have a "colorful history." But it's just the opposite. It wasn't colorful at all; it was really drab. And that's why I'm standing here in a burgundy silk blouse I bought secondhand and a pair of tight jeans that would have earned me a beating at the compound.

Leah bought me my first pair of jeans two years ago. I'd put them on immediately, feeling very defiant. Then I'd looked in the mirror and thought: *whore*. Because that's what they used to call me.

I still hear their voices in my head sometimes. I was a whore to them. And all because I kissed a boy.

"Are you coming home this weekend?" Leah asks. By *home* she means her farm in Tuxbury, which is about an hour's drive from the university in Burlington.

"I think so?" I uncap my only tube of tinted lip gloss and touch up my lips in the mirror.

"Did you tell Dylan your idea?"

"Not yet." And that's one of the reasons I'm going to this party at his house.

It's Wednesday, when we have a standing tutoring date. But today he didn't show. I don't have a cell phone, which is probably why I didn't hear from him. He must have called the land line while I was out.

Dylan is a little flighty, but he's a good friend. He hasn't missed a Wednesday yet. That hour of the week is a double-edged sword for me. I love spending time with Dylan. But algebra. *Oof.* It's not my forte. I spend the whole time trying not to look either stupid or heart-sick, with varying degrees of success.

I'm probably failing at the first thing, but Dylan has no idea how I feel about him, and I plan to keep it that way.

"I hope Dylan likes your idea," Leah says. "It's got a lot of poten-tial. And the kitchen is wide open on Friday and Saturday nights. Nobody ever wants to claim those hours." Leah makes fancy cheeses, but it's a seasonal business. So she rents out the commercial kitchen in her creamery to other businesses during the winter months.

"If Dylan wants in, he'll pick Saturday," I tell her. "Fridays are reserved for his awful girlfriend."

"Shhh!" Leah hisses. "Won't she hear you?"

"No. She's not here." The biggest mistake of my college career—all four weeks of it—was asking Dylan to help me carry my things into the dormitory on move-in day.

I hadn't even asked, come to think of it. He'd volunteered. He'd driven me to school in his old truck and brought me to the housing office to pick up my keys.

And I'd been so, so grateful. Right up until Dylan carried my one box into the dormitory. I'd been so nervous I'd felt like throwing up, but Dylan had whistled a happy tune as he led me down the hallway to suite 302.

"Open 'er up," he'd said kindly. "Let's see if the housing gods were kind."

They weren't. I mean—the suite is fine. My twin bed is in a sepa-rate room from Kaitlyn's twin bed. We share a bathroom that's just ours. I have a desk and a dresser and a window. I can't complain.

I'd been hoping to be paired with a roommate who would also be a friend, but Kaitlyn had been instantly chilly to me. She'd barely glanced in my direction.

She had not, however, dismissed Dylan. You know that expression —"her eyes lit up"? Well, I've never seen anyone so obviously and instantly in lust. She was like a cartoon character with hearts in her eyes.

"Is this your brother?" she'd asked.

"Just about," Dylan had said with a chuckle. "We live on neigh-boring farms."

"That's so sweet," she'd gushed.

And then, as I'd put my meager possessions away, she'd chatted him up. I learned all about her life in Manhattan and her troubles at Barnard College, wherever that is. "There was a dalliance with a professor," she'd said with a sigh. "It didn't end well. My family is horrified." She'd given him a sexy grin. "So here I am, banished to the hinterlands to finish school."

"Welcome to Moo U," Dylan had said with a slow smile. "It's not New York City, but we have other kinds of fun."

The very next day she'd asked me for his phone number. "I had a question about which dry cleaner to use. He said to ask him anything."

"I'd be stunned if Dylan ever had anything dry cleaned," I'd said. But I gave her the number, anyway.

Big mistake.

The following week she didn't come home at all on two different nights. At first I thought this was a terrific development. I loved having our suite to myself. But then, just as I was crossing the center of campus and congratulating myself on figuring out a shortcut to the math department, I'd seen them. Kaitlyn had been standing under a tree with Dylan. And then he'd leaned in and kissed her.

No—that isn't even an accurate description. He practically *devoured* her right there between classes in broad daylight. I've never walked away from anything faster in my life.

Three weeks later, and I'm still not over it. I already knew Dylan had a lot of sex. His twin sister refers to him as "the family slut." There are always girls from his high school class hanging around the Shipley farm, riding shotgun in his truck. I'm always jealous of those girls.

But Kaitlyn? Just the idea of her with Dylan makes me insane. It doesn't matter if I express that aloud, either. Kaitlyn is almost certainly at Dylan's house right now. If it turns out that he spent our tutoring hours with her instead of me, that will sting.

But Dylan will make it up to me. He really is a good friend.

"Let me know how it goes," Leah says. "I'd better go and put Maeve to bed. I can hear her begging Isaac for another story."

"Kiss her goodnight for me," I say. "I'll call you about the weekend. I'll let you know if we need to use the kitchen Saturday night."

"Have fun tonight, Chass. Just be—"

"—careful. I know, Leah. I will."

We hang up. I give myself one more glance in the mirror, then I grab my backpack and leave the little suite behind.

I hurry down two flights of stairs, heading for the dormitory exit. It's already dark outside, and I can see my reflection in the glass door. My backpack strap has tugged the silk blouse aside, revealing a tiny glimpse of my bra.

I stop suddenly to fix it, and that's when somebody plows into my back.

We let out twin shrieks.

"Sorry!" I yelp, turning around.

"No, that was totally my fault," the other girl babbles. Her name is Ellie, I think. We're in the same English class. She holds the door open for me. "Your outfit looks fine, by the way. Stop fussing with that collar."

"Uh, thanks."

"Going on a date? Kinda fancy for a Wednesday night." We're heading in the same direction down the sidewalk. "I'm going to the library, because I'm fun like that."

"Oh, I already spent four hours there," I assure her. I don't tell her that I spent all that time waiting for Dylan Shipley to show up for tutoring. "I'm going to a party off campus."

"*Really*," Ellie says, grinning. She has a mouth full of braces. Aren't those just for kids? It's been two years since I left the cult where I grew up, but there are still a lot of things that baffle me. Twenty-four months isn't a long time to learn how the entire world works. "You have fun. I'll be trying to understand Aristotle."

"Cool." I don't know what Aristotle is, either.

She reaches for my hand and tugs it away from the second button of my blouse, which I'm fingering. "Don't fidget. That's how buttons come off."

"Right. But—" I hesitate. "Is this too much?" I wave a hand in front of my chest.

"Too much what? Too much hotness? No. If I had boobs, I'd wear them proudly. Whoever it is you're trying to impress is going to love it." She gives me a wave and trots away toward the library. "Have fun!" she calls over her shoulder.

I keep walking, still feeling uncertain. Going to Dylan's house right now is probably a mistake. I don't know why he blew off our tutoring session today. It isn't like him. On the other hand, he has a lot on his plate. And I'm the one who doesn't have a cell phone.

It's not Dylan's fault that I sat there in the library from four until seven thirty, missing dinner like a dummy. But I've always been a little dumb when it comes to Dylan.

My stomach had been rumbling by the time I'd given up on him. On my way home, I'd paused outside the convenience store, wondering what a girl could buy for two dollars. Only candy, really. I hadn't bought anything, but I had bumped into Dylan's roommate, a character named Rickie.

"Chastity!" he'd exclaimed, coming out of the store with a bag full of various kinds of chips in one hand and a bag of ice in the other. "What's up, lady? You coming over later?"

"For...?" I'd only been to their house once before. It's out of the way, which is why Dylan always meets me on campus.

"The party! Didn't Dylan tell you?"

He did not. But I hadn't let it show on my face. "I didn't catch Dylan today," I'd told him. "Do you happen to know where he went?"

"Home to Tuxbury," Rickie had said. "Shit, Chastity. He said he was going to call you. The goats got loose and ate something they weren't supposed to."

"Oh no!"

"Yeah. He got a call and there was yelling, and then Dylan got in the truck and went home. But he's back at nine for the party. Come over. I'm making mulled cider and guacamole."

My stomach had gurgled, and the decision had seemed easy.

But now, as I trudge uphill toward the old Victorian house where Dylan lives with Rickie and another guy named Keith, I'm questioning all my life choices. I'll probably have to make conversation with strangers, which isn't my strong suit.

Or they'll just ignore me, which also sounds bleak.

And then there's my algebra homework which is in my backpack still incomplete. If I turn up now, Dylan is only going to feel guilty for missing our session.

There are two things powering me uphill, though. The first is guacamole. I'd never seen an avocado until I became a nineteen-year-old runaway to Vermont, and I'd been seriously missing out. The second thing is morbid curiosity. In the four weeks since I came to Burlington U, I've had only glimpses of College Dylan. And I want to know more.

The Dylan I know from Tuxbury is Family Dylan. He milks goats and cows. He whistles in the orchard while picking apples. He takes off his shirt to stack hay. He eats third helpings at the dinner table. He spars with his siblings and takes his mother to church.

And? He's a good friend to me.

College Dylan is different, though. And—fine—even more intoxicating. College Dylan drinks and smokes pot and has (from what I can guess) a lot of sex. Some of it with my evil roommate.

None of it with me.

TWO

Chastity

THE TEMPERATURE HAS PLUNGED since nightfall, so by the time I reach the house, I'm shivering.

Still, I stand on the front walk for a minute or two, acclimating. It's a beautiful house on a treelined street. There are three floors and several roofline peaks. Dylan says he's lucky to live here. Rickie doesn't charge much rent. Tonight the house is lit up like a Halloween pumpkin, with yellow light glowing from every window.

The windows are closed, but the sound of voices—lots of them—reaches me on the sidewalk. And some music. The sounds of people enjoying themselves. The longer I stand here, the harder it gets to imagine myself walking in there. I won't know anybody besides Rickie and Dylan. And Kaitlyn, who won't talk to me anyway.

I spot Dylan in the bay window. It's not hard. I'm tuned in to the Dylan Shipley channel, and have been since the day I met him two years ago. I'd know his big frame anywhere, and his familiar head of thick, wavy hair. All the Shipleys have brown hair, but Dylan's is kissed with lighter highlights. As if the sun loves him just a little bit more than it loves everyone else.

His back is to me, so I can't see his laughing eyes. But he's gesturing as he speaks, a beer bottle waving wildly between two fingers, half forgotten. All you have to do is glance at him, and you know he's a fun person.

Fun, and also *nice*. And warm. And hilarious.

Okay. I can do this.

I march up the porch steps and open the big oak door, where I'm greeted by shiny old wooden floors and an arched doorway leading to the living room. Dylan still stands in front of the window wearing his signature outfit—worn jeans and a tight T-shirt. And since it's October, he's pulled a flannel shirt on over it, the cuffs rolled up over his muscular forearms.

"...these goats are little fucking Houdinis. Griff calls me once a day at least to complain. But today they ate all my mom's spinach and kale, so he was shouting at me when I picked up the phone." Dylan takes a sip from the beer in his hand, shaking his head. "I drove home to calm him down. As if that would even work. And when I get there he wants me to raise the height of the fence, right? So I take a look around..."

I've met the two dairy goats in question. They're wily little animals and cute as heck. Dylan loves them a lot. Maybe even more than he loves his cows.

"...and the fence is *fine*. So I asked Mr. Grumpy if by chance he brought a feed bucket into the goat enclosure earlier? And he's like —'So what if I did?' And then I ask if it had the cover on it. And he said—'How did you know?'" Dylan shakes his head, as if he can't believe the stupidity. "Well, because you're ripping me a new one even though you're the idiot who gave those little fuckers a bucket to climb up onto and *launch themselves over the fence.*"

Everybody laughs a little drunkenly. There are maybe a dozen people in the living room. There's a group on the floor passing around a small pumpkin. Someone has outfitted it with two pipes that stick out of either side. It's a pumpkin *bong*.

You're supposed to take a puff and pass it on. I never have, though. Up until last month, I'd only seen weed in movies. I'd smelled it in Dylan's truck, without knowing what it was.

College is very educational.

My gaze snags on the couch, which is also occupied. The people seated on it aren't listening to Dylan's story, though, because they're too busy making out. This wouldn't be all that interesting except there are *three* of them. Two girls and a guy. It hadn't occurred to me before that three people could kiss at the same time, but they seem to be managing just fine.

I can't tear my eyes away. The view is both beautiful and complicated. The boy's eyes are closed. I briefly spot his tongue as their lips reconfigure. His hand is up one of the girl's shirts. And that girl has her hand on the *other* girl's breast. As I watch, she passes her thumb over the nipple slowly. It's a hard peak through the T-shirt covering it.

Okay, wow. I wouldn't have thought that would turn me on, but there you go. The truth is that a lot of things turn me on. And they always have. Ever since I turned thirteen, there's been a raging battle between what I'm supposed to be thinking about and what I actually think about.

I really hope nobody can read minds.

Music throbs in the background while Dylan finishes his story about the goats. His mother is mad because they ate her garden greens. "And you practically can't call yourself a Vermont farmer without a nice patch of kale. What will the neighbors say?"

Everyone laughs. My eyes come to rest on Kaitlyn as she passes the bong after her puff. My evil roommate is looking up at Dylan with stars in her eyes.

It's hard to blame her for that, because I probably look at him the same way. It's literally the only thing we have in common.

Kaitlyn gets to her feet as he wraps up his story. She takes the beer out of his hand and takes a swig. It's a way of claiming him, I guess. It makes me want to smack her. "Come on, Dyl," she says the moment he stops talking. "You said you'd let me play something for you."

"Yeah, okay. Cool." They both take a step in my direction. That's when Dylan lifts his chin and spots me. "Chastity! Hey!" He pulls me in for a Shipley-style, full-body hug—the kind I'm never quite ready for. "God, I'm sorry about this afternoon. Rickie said you waited."

Ouch. I wish Rickie hadn't mentioned that.

"It was f-fine," I stammer as his arms encircle me. There's a quick press of his hard chest against my body. The flannel shirt he's wearing doesn't disguise the muscle underneath.

His hugs always fluster me. I count to three and then step back, so

I don't find myself awkwardly patting his back for too long. That happens sometimes.

It's been two years since I came to Vermont, and while I've figured out a lot of things—like Netflix and nail polish—these little interactions still tie me in knots. On the compound, no man *ever* hugged a girl who wasn't his wife. We didn't even shake hands.

These days I'm a decent hand-shaker and there are several people I can hug without difficulty. But Dylan isn't one of them. I'm so attracted to him that each hug makes me flush like a nervous loser.

"I called," he says.

"W-what?"

"I called the land line in your suite. Kaitlyn said she'd leave you a note."

"And I left it," Kaitlyn snaps. "On the desk. Weren't we going upstairs?" She gives Dylan a little tug.

"Hang on." Dylan untangles himself from her and puts a big hand on my shoulder. "Come into the kitchen a minute. Did you eat? Mom sent me home with lentil soup."

My stomach growls, but the party is too loud for anyone to hear, thank God. With Dylan, I turn toward the kitchen. I can almost *feel* Kaitlyn's anger radiating toward me.

It's weird, but I feel no guilt. Guilt and I are usually very close friends. But when it comes to Kaitlyn, I live for these little moments of irritating her. Probably because I know they don't matter. She has what I want, and there's a zero percent chance that I'll ever get it.

"Look who's here!" Rickie says from the stove where he's stirring a pot of steaming liquid. It smells like heaven. "The cider is ready, guys. Who's in?"

"I'd love some," I say. That's the scent of Vermont—apples and cinnamon. And weed, I guess.

"Kaitlyn?" he prompts.

"Why not?" She sniffs. "I have to, right? So long as I'm at Moo U, I guess I'll drink the cider and wear a beanie and always use the pronoun of your choice."

"You should be so lucky," Rickie says cheerfully. "Just don't burn your tongue. You're probably gonna need that later." He ladles cider into a row of mugs on the counter. "Here, Chastity. Hey—nice top. Vavoom! Love the fall-themed cleavage."

My face heats instantly. I take a big sniff of the cider to cover my embarrassment. "Smells great, thanks."

Dylan is already microwaving the soup and grabbing bowls from the cupboard. "Soup? Rickie? Kait?"

"Too carby," Kaitlyn says.

"Cider is carby," Dylan points out.

"But I can pour rum into it," she says, taking a mug.

"More for me." Dylan shrugs. "Have a seat, Chastity. Ooh, guacamole." He grabs the serving bowl and plops it onto the table with a bag of chips.

Dylan and I take opposite seats at the table. Rickie parks his hip against the kitchen counter and sips his cider, while Kaitlyn circles, visibly humming with impatience that Dylan seems not to notice.

I will never get over the two of them as a couple. Never. According to his friends and gossipy family members (never underestimate Grandpa Shipley's powers of observation), Dylan has always been a ride-or-die single guy. Until Kaitlyn ensnared him, that is.

Dylan is the kind of guy who sees the best in people. So while it's obvious to me that she's a shrew, he only sees her shiny hair. And her shiny lip gloss. And her skinny little body clad in expensive clothes.

That's the best explanation I can come up with. Not for lack of trying. And I'm not supposed to care.

Whoops.

"Chass, can we maybe do algebra at breakfast tomorrow?" he asks me now. "I don't have class until ten."

"Sure. Okay. At the dining hall?" Kaitlyn never goes to breakfast, so I won't have to deal with her. It's hard enough looking stupid in front of Dylan. I don't need her scowl, too.

"Yeah, that works." He picks up his soup bowl and drains the last bit.

"Come. On," Kaitlyn urges. "I'm waiting."

I look away, because I know what's going to happen next.

"Coming," Dylan says cheerfully. He pushes back his chair and carries his soup bowl over to the sink, where he rinses it carefully before tucking it into the dishwasher. "Back in a bit," he says to me on his way out of the room.

I dip my spoon in the soup and take another bite. It was nice of Dylan to feed me. He's a good friend. And it's hardly his fault that I want things I can't have.

A moment later, two mugs land on the table in front of me, and then Rickie takes Dylan's seat. "Those two are hard to watch, right?"

Ouch. Either I'm a terrible actress, or Rickie shares my opinion that they're an awful couple.

"She won't last," he says. "I'm sure the sex is great, but he gets easily bored."

"So I've noticed," I mumble before shoving a chip in my mouth.

Rickie flashes me a smile. I like Dylan's roommate, but he's a little intimidating. He speaks German and French, and he has an earring. His clothes aren't anything like Dylan's. Tonight he's wearing ripped jeans with black leather boots that would never stand up to farm work. His vintage dress shirt is unbuttoned practically to the navel, exposing some elaborate tattoos.

Some people make my naiveté stand out. Rickie is one of those people.

He pushes a mug of cider toward me. "So what's your story?"

"What do you mean? I'm just here for the algebra."

"Uh-huh." He uncaps a bottle of rum and pours generous dollops into both our mugs. "I mean your real story. Tell me how you got here to Moo U."

"Don't you know that part?" I just assumed that Dylan had mentioned my strange story. *Don't mind my dorky friend. She grew up in a cult and can't help it.*

"I want to hear it from you," he says.

"Well it's *your* Wednesday night. I guess you can spend it on my bullshit if you want to."

He laughs suddenly, and he looks about five years younger. "I fucking love other people's bullshit, Chastity. Lay it on me."

I pull the mug of cider closer to me, considering what I might say. "When I was nineteen, I ran away from the religious compound where I grew up out West. I could only afford a bus ticket to the New

York border. And then I walked and hiked the rest." Thank God it had been summertime, or I would have frozen to death.

"What was that place like? The compound."

"Um..." What to say? I don't talk about it that much, because it's weird and embarrassing. "Let's see. The only clothing I'd owned before I left was something called the Paradise dress. Picture Laura Ingalls in pastel polyester. Long sleeves, long skirt. With a high collar." I put my hand up to my throat. "You couldn't show any skin, because that was sinful. We wore the dresses with hiking boots from Payless."

"Oh fuck," he says, blowing on the surface of the cider in his mug. "So the place was a fashion disaster. But what was it *like?* What did you do all day?"

"I worked at home. Cooking, cleaning, and sewing. I didn't go to a real school after third grade. Nobody wanted us to be smart, anyway. They only cared about obedience. They didn't want us out in the sinners' world, wondering why we couldn't have all the things that other kids had. Too many big ideas. When I was seven, I asked for a pair of new shoes, like another girl at school had. I got a slap on the face, instead."

"Wow." Rickie watches me with obvious fascination. He has hypnotic eyes. They're gray, with a darker circle around each iris. "So they thought you might figure out that polygamy is illegal?"

"Maybe," I hedge. "But it wouldn't matter all that much if we'd known. That's what brainwashing is for. We sat in church for six hours on Sunday. The preacher spent a lot of time telling us how *special* we were." I roll my eyes, although my nonchalance is forced. Two years isn't all that long, and part of me still believes some of the things I was taught.

That's the part I can't explain to outsiders. Everything our Divine Pastor ever said was a big load of bullshit. But some of it was really appealing bullshit. I'll never go back, and I don't miss the place at all. But I *liked* hearing that I was part of a special mission from God, with a unique purpose in the world.

Say what you will, but it was easier living in a world where I knew the rules. Even if I didn't always follow them.

"How did you eventually decide to run away from this special, special place?" Rickie measures me with his serious eyes.

"Now there's a story." I let out an uncomfortable laugh. "When I was sixteen, I got in some trouble. I got into the back of a car with a boy."

"You hussy!" Rickie snorts. He's kidding, but I get tense anyway. Because the boy and I got caught, and the things they called me afterward were so much worse.

"He got thrown out," I say.

"Out of the car?" Rickie sips his cider.

"No—out of the compound."

Rickie stares. "Forever?"

"Of course. The sons can't ever be alone with the daughters. It's forbidden. But I, um, wanted to know what all the fuss was about. When they preach at you every Sunday about sin…"

I don't think I can finish the sentence. My face heats just from the memory of sitting in that garage, kissing Zachariah. His hand had been on my bare thigh. I'd *really* wanted him to take it further. And then? Disaster.

"Sin has always yelled my name, too," Rickie says with a smile. "Every stupid thing. I did it."

I can't help but smile back at him. I take a big gulp of the steaming cider. The rum gives it a sharpness I'm not used to, but I kind of like it.

"So what happened to you? After you kissed the boy?"

"Oh." I set the mug down.

This part of the story isn't much fun. After several blissful minutes, we'd been discovered by the worst possible person—my vindictive uncle Jeptha. There had been no chance of him brushing it under the rug. He'd summoned the elders…

"We were punished," I say, and it comes out as a squeak.

"Shit, Chastity," says Rickie. "I'm sorry to bring up something painful."

"Oh, it's fine," I say, but my ragged voice makes me a liar. I take a gulp of my cider. "I didn't see Zach again for three years. The worst part was wondering if he was still alive." Every night I'd lay in bed trying to imagine what a homeless Zach would do. "I knew nothing of the outside world, so I pictured things I knew from the bible—beggars at the side of the road trying to fill their bellies."

Rickie's eyes are round. "What did he do?"

"Oh—he hitchhiked to Vermont. You know the Shipley's neighbors, Leah and Isaac? He knew where they'd run away together, and it wasn't too hard for him to find them." But at the time I hadn't known this—I'd thought he was dead. "Zach says getting kicked out was the best thing that ever happened to him. And now he's one of the happiest people I know."

"Uh-huh. But what about *you*," Rickie asks. "They didn't throw you out?"

I give my head a slow shake. "I got a beating. They had to make an example out of me. If you get into the back of a car with a boy, you'll be beaten until you bleed. There were at least ten men taking turns with the strap. I didn't sit down for a week, my ass was so sore."

Rickie's eyes bulge. *"Jesus Christ."*

But I can't bear to tell Rickie the worst part—that I'd been naked for the beating. That was the real punishment, I think. The toxic cocktail of pain and total humiliation. I don't mind telling Rickie how badly they hurt my skin, but I can't talk about the sound of their laughter. *Slattern*, they'd called me. *Harlot. Whore.* I will never stop hearing those voices.

"I still have the scars," I say with forced cheer.

"And so you ran away after that?"

"Nope. I hadn't figured out that I could. But when I turned seventeen, nobody wanted me for a wife, because I was compromised."

Rickie makes a noise of disgust.

"It wasn't, uh, true. But that didn't matter. And here's where it gets interesting—I realized I was going to be a leper, basically. So I asked my stepfather for a job, and he set me up with a really unusual thing—a job off the compound. I became a cashier at Walgreens."

"Now that's living." Rickie grins.

"No—it was! I got to leave every day and spy on the rest of the world. You have no idea how much fun I had selling candy and aspirin. And magazines—I read *Seventeen* and *Allure* behind the counter. I didn't get to keep the money, though. My father deposited my checks into his account. I never saw any money until I finally learned how to steal some."

"You are a *fascinating* girl, Chastity."

"Oh, please."

"I mean it." He reaches for my empty mug. I don't even remember drinking all that cider. It was gone so fast. "What would your life have been like if none of that happened?"

"They would've married me off to an old man on my seventeenth birthday. I'd get a five-minute wedding during Sunday services. And then I'd leave my parents' home to live with whomever the elders chose for me."

"And then the wedding night." He watches me over the rim of his mug. "I'm guessing birth control was not an option, either."

I shake my head. "I'd never even heard of birth control until I started reading packages at the Walgreens where I worked. Bearing children was our number-one job. They told me that every Sunday."

What I don't add is that I'd been looking forward to it. I used to sit up straighter on the bench when our Divine Pastor spoke about wifely duties. *Lie beneath your husband and give your body to God. Accept his love. Accept his seed. Bring forth a new generation to worship at our tabernacle.*

I couldn't *wait* to lie beneath my husband and accept his seed. When I was six, I asked another little boy to practice with me. He tattled, and we both got spankings. That little boy got tossed out of the compound when we were fifteen. (Not because of me, thank goodness.)

But I still remember his smile. His name was Jacob, and he had clear blue eyes. I always liked the boys too much. Eventually I learned to conceal it, but that was my secret shame. My cross to bear.

It's still true, too. Since those kisses with Zachariah in the back of a car, no other man has touched me. But I wish one would.

Dylan, specifically.

But now I'm very tired of my own bullshit. "It's your turn, Rickie. What's your story?"

He pushes my refilled cider mug toward me with a teasing smile. "I grew up an army brat. Lived in ten places by the time I turned eighteen."

"Is that why you speak German?"

"*Das ist richtig*. And here's the part you won't even believe—I won a spot at the U.S. Military Academy. I did my first year of college there. With the buzz cut and the uniform."

"And *saluting?*" I can't picture Rickie as a soldier. I just can't.

"The whole thing." He chuckles wickedly.

"Why'd you leave?"

"I don't talk about that part."

"*Hey!*" I argue. "I told you my story."

"Did you really?" His intelligent eyes hold mine. "Or did you leave out all the shame?"

Well, heck. I guess I did. We consider each other across the small table. Then he smiles, and it's very kind. As if we understand each other. "A professor basically said the same thing to me this week. Did you take freshman composition?"

Rickie shakes his head. "Is that the one where you have to write a different essay on the same theme every week?"

"Right. The semester's theme is food. So I wrote something about the unseen miracle of microorganisms making milk into cheese. The professor hated it. He said there wasn't enough of me in there."

"I guess you're supposed to bleed for him onto the page." Rickie snorts. "Have some more rum." He holds up the bottle. And I push my mug a little closer for him.

THREE

Dylan

IN MY BEDROOM, I pour myself a drop of scotch and listen while Kaitlyn plays a new composition on her acoustic guitar. I swear she played the same thing for me last weekend, but I won't want to be a dick and point that out.

Besides—it's entirely possible that the music is just a ruse to get me alone. Kaitlyn is a crafty one.

"You sound great," I say when she finally sets down her guitar. And it's true. Classical guitar isn't something I understand very well, but she's obviously talented.

"Thank you, farm boy."

That's her little nickname for me. Since it's a reference to the greatest movie of all time—*The Princess Bride*—I should take it as a compliment. But all of Kaitlyn's compliments have a dark side. In this case, it bugs the shit out of her that I really am a farm boy. It's harvest season, and I have to go home every Saturday morning at the butt crack of dawn to help my family for the weekend.

Until this year, I was a part-time student, driving to Burlington for classes. But that had kind of sucked, so when Rickie offered me a room in his house for practically nothing, I grabbed at the chance to be a full-time student. I get better financial aid this way, so I'm saving money over the long term.

My brother hates this arrangement, though, because he's short-handed on the farm.

"Play a duet with me?" Kaitlyn asks.

"Nah," I say, because I feel too lazy to get out my fiddle and tune it up.

"Your loss." She climbs into my lap and kisses me. "I missed you earlier. We were supposed to get dinner."

"Trust me," I say, running a hand down her ribcage. She's wearing a velvet top that begs to be touched. "I would rather get dinner with you than go home to be yelled at." I push her hair off her slender neck and kiss the spot under her chin.

She shivers. Kaitlyn is always horny, just like I am. That's why I broke my No Dating rule to be with her. The sex is fantastic.

Also, she'd insisted. *We're exclusive, or we don't fuck*, she'd said the first time I got her naked. Then? She'd swallowed my entire cock to the back of her throat and sucked me dry.

And that's how I ended up half of a couple. It's not the most romantic story. It's no *Princess Bride*. But it works for us, I guess.

I take her mouth in a real kiss. This is what she's been waiting for, anyway. Forget dinner. Kaitlyn tugs my shirt out of my pants and runs her hands up my chest as I give her my tongue. She straddles me, hooking her ankles behind my body, nestling the heat of her core against my thickening cock.

It's pretty great until my friend Keith calls up the stairs. "Dylan! Come and do a shot with me!"

"Ignore him," Kaitlyn whispers between kisses.

For a moment I try. But it's only ten o'clock, and the house is full of friends that I won't get to see this weekend when I'm home selling apples.

"There's Jagermeister!" Keith tries, and I laugh as I break off from kissing Kaitlyn.

She makes a noise of irritation. "Really? You're choosing Jager-meister over me? Gross."

"It's not *over* you," I say mildly. "It's *before* you."

"Two words: whiskey dick."

"Oh, please." I lift her off my lap and set her onto the bed. "It was *one* time." Rickie got me wasted on absinthe one night last week, and

I passed out before I could fuck her. But Kaitlyn won't go unsatisfied tonight.

She knows it, too. She's just impatient.

I get up, adjusting my jeans to conceal my semi. "Come on. Bring your guitar if you want." Kaitlyn likes an audience almost as much as she enjoys being fucked.

We go downstairs together. Keith stops me in the foyer, pressing two shot glasses into my hand. I down the first one, then offer the second to Kaitlyn, who wrinkles up her nose.

"There's probably wine in the fridge," I point out.

Without a word, she disappears to go look for it.

Keith trades me the shot glasses for the bong, and I take a deep, slow puff. *Ahh.* That's when my shoulders begin to unknit. Finally.

Most people love October. This weekend the country roads will be jammed full of tourists who drive up here just to revel in October's colorful wonders.

But I hate it. The days are short, the nights are dark, and my family's business runs at one hundred and fifty percent capacity. And I can't win with anybody. My brother is pissed off at me for living in Burlington. My girlfriend is pissed off at me for running home to Tuxbury each weekend.

"Fucking October," I say as Keith hands me another shot.

"Yeah. Fucking midterms," he agrees.

It's more than that, though. October is the month my father died. It's been six years, but every October I feel raw. Like I'm bleeding out of every pore. I have a few remedies at my disposal to dull the ache: booze, home-grown pot, and sex. They're not perfect, but they're the best that I've got.

"So when are you gonna bring home some new cider?" Keith asks. "I love that stuff."

Someone cranks up the Green Day just then, so I have to shout my answer. "Don't know, man. Jagermeister is cheaper." I don't need my brother bitching at me for walking off with some of the fancy hard cider he makes. "There's the bonfire in two weeks, though. Griffin always pours a lot of cider that night. You're coming, right?"

"YEAH!" Keith shouts back at me.

Christ, it's loud. I hope they don't blow out Rickie's speakers. "Where's our fearless leader?"

Keith shrugs. He leans into the living room to look around. "Rickie's right there!" he shouts, pointing. "On the beanbag with your friend from home!"

Uh-oh. Rickie better be taking good care of Chastity. Maybe I shouldn't have left her in the kitchen. And—I can't believe this happened—it sounds like she waited around in the library for me today when I was halfway across Vermont.

I am such a dick.

Stepping into the living room, I survey the wreckage. The party has deteriorated severely in the last forty minutes. Or improved, depending on your viewpoint. The lights are low and the music is loud and everyone looks half in the bag.

Even Chastity, I realize with a start. *Hell.* She never drinks. I hustle over there and look down at where she and my roommate are sprawled out on the giant beanbag chair. "Chastity!" I shout. "Are you okay?"

She lifts her head a little unsteadily. "I'm FIIIIIINE," she yells. "Did you know there's people having sex on your couch?"

Rickie giggles. "They are, aren't they? Better be using condoms!" He shouts. "No messes!"

I'm afraid to look, but I do anyway. And, yup. Rickie's friend Igor is thrusting lazily into our friend Gretchen, who's making out with a woman I haven't met. Although now I've seen her bare tits, because she's caressing them as they kiss.

Right. "Time to go home, Chass," I say, offering a hand to my friend.

"Why?" she whines. "It's really comfortable here. Although I kind of have to pee." She burps.

"Up you go." I lean down even farther and take her hand. "Hit the bathroom and find your backpack. I'm walking you home."

"My backpack?" she slurs. "That does sound familiar." She sways a little as she turns her head to look around.

Uh-oh. I don't know if she's ever had anything stronger than the wine we drink at Thursday Dinner, the rotating party my family and hers share. "Bathroom is that way," I say, pointing toward the kitchen.

"Right." She toddles off.

I haul Rickie to his feet next. "What were you thinking?" I yell over Green Day's heavy drum beat.

"I can't hear you!"

Ugh. I tow Rickie toward the kitchen. "You can't give Chastity rum! She doesn't drink at all."

"Everybody starts somewhere," he says with a shrug.

"Not Chastity," I insist. To say that she grew up sheltered is like saying that Mussolini was a little pushy. Chastity didn't cut her hair until she was nineteen. Before then, she never even wore jeans or swore or used makeup.

"She's fine, Dyl," Rickie insists. "I would never hurt your friend. She had, like, three drinks."

"What's the problem?" Kaitlyn demands, a glass of wine in one hand and a corn chip in the other.

"Chastity got a little tipsy, and Dylan wants to call the paramedics." Rickie rolls his eyes and leaves the kitchen.

"I didn't say we needed the paramedics," I grunt. "But I have to make sure she gets home safe." I pat my pocket, finding my keys there. "Let me grab a jacket."

"Wait, why?" Kaitlyn whines. "She's a drunk college student. This town is full of them. She'll either find her way home, or she'll wake up on someone else's floor. Just like anyone else."

"She's *not* just like anyone else," I point out. "I mean, every freshman gets drunk. But they go home to a roommate who makes sure they don't die. And that's you, right?"

Kaitlyn makes a face. "My drunk freshman days are long past."

Right. That's why it's going to be me.

I go to the back hall and grab my jean jacket. Kaitlyn sips her wine and watches me. She's already a junior. Her family shipped her to Moo U after some kind of scandal in New York City. That's how she ended up in the dorms with Chastity.

I'm the same age as Kaitlyn but still officially a sophomore, since I started part time.

Chastity is actually the oldest of us all. At twenty-one, she's a year older than I am. But running away from a cult steals your teen years.

"You're making too big a deal of this," Kaitlyn says, pointing toward the living room. "Look, she's fine."

I walk to where I can see through the doorway. And there's Chastity, back from the bathroom already and dancing in a loose, crazy freeform way beside Rickie. Every third or fourth beat they bump hips and then laugh.

And now I'm smiling, because that is incredibly cute. Chastity isn't one to let go very often. She'll probably have a terrible hangover tomorrow. But right now she's having fun.

The song ends, and she and Rickie stand there breathing hard. "How do you feel about pot?" Rickie asks, his hands on his hips.

"Never tried it!" Chastity replies.

And that's my cue. "Another time," I say hastily. "Did you find your backpack?"

"Yup!" she says.

"Jacket?" I prompt.

She shakes her head in an exaggerated way. "Didn't wear one."

"Can't we take your truck?" Kaitlyn appears behind me. She's wearing her jacket, so I guess she's coming with us.

"No, I can't drive. Too much booze and pot." I'm barely tipsy, but I won't risk it. I'm a fun guy, not a stupid one. "It's a ten-minute walk at the max." I put a hand on Chastity's shoulder and guide her toward the door.

"They're *still* having sex," she breathes. "Does it usually last that long?"

Kaitlyn snorts, and Rickie chuckles. "Depends who you ask."

There's a reason that I've never invited Chastity to one of Rickie's parties. You never know what you're going to see. I open the front door and remind Chastity to watch the steps. "They're steep."

"I can handle a couple of stairs, Dyl," she says with a sigh.

"It's cold," Kaitlyn complains.

"You haven't seen anything yet," I point out. "The wind off the lake makes Burlington one of the coldest places in Vermont." I remove my jacket and lift Chastity's backpack off her shoulder. "Trade you."

"Why?" she asks as I set the jacket onto her shoulders. "You don't have to."

"I've got a flannel shirt on. And I run hot. All you've got is…" I gesture toward her pretty silk shirt. And I kick myself a little for noticing how good she looks tonight. It's not the first time I've snagged my eyeballs on Chastity's cleavage. You'd have to be blind not to see how pretty Chastity is, or how stacked.

But it's bad form to ogle your drunk friend. Luckily, Chastity accepts my jacket and buttons it, shielding that delicious cleavage from view.

We head down the street. It's a crisp, fall night. The lamps inside all the antique homes give the rooms a yellow hue. The air smells like falling leaves and wood smoke, and I associate that smell with sadness.

Because I hate October.

Chastity stumbles on a sidewalk crack, and my hand shoots out to catch her. But she doesn't actually go down, and she quickly shakes off my hand.

Beside me, Kaitlyn is silent and probably fuming. Good thing I know just how to cheer her up. You have to play to your own strengths.

I'm not the most reliable guy. But I am a good time. Sometimes it's enough.

FOUR

Chastity

THE WALK HOME sobers me up a little. One of the loud songs from the party is still playing in my brain, and every few minutes I catch myself humming. Maybe I don't know how to hold my rum, but I had a good time with Rickie. He'd been sillier tonight than I'd expected him to be.

And he didn't treat me like a child, the way Dylan does. I don't need to be walked home like a puppy. The only upside is that Kaitlyn is super annoyed right now.

I swear I'm usually a nice person, but she brings out the worst in me.

When we get to the dorm, I expect Dylan and Kaitlyn to wave goodbye from the door and return to the party. But that's not what happens. They walk inside with me. I press the elevator button because my feet are a little clumsy, and I don't feel like proving anyone's point by stumbling on the stairs.

I have to hold tightly to the remaining shreds of my dignity. Not that there are very many.

Upstairs, Dylan watches me unlock the door with slow fingers. "How's your stomach?" he asks.

"Fine," I insist.

"That's good. I'm going to find you some Advil. If you take it now, you might not feel so bad in the morning."

"Good idea," I mumble. I go into my room and find my flannel pajamas.

I'm just removing my bra when Dylan walks in. "Whoa!" He turns around in a hurry. "Brought you a glass of water, too," he says, facing the wrong direction.

"Thanks." Dylan is really so nice to me. He feeds me. He looks after me. Except in the way that I really want him to...

"If you still feel okay at breakfast, we can study some algebra," he says.

"Oh, we're totally studying algebra." I don't know why he thinks I'm going to be wrecked by a couple mugs of spiked cider. Rickie didn't think it was a big deal.

I button my top and tap him on the shoulder. "It's safe to look now." I take the glass of water out of his hand, and he smiles when he hands me the pills. "Sleep well." He leans forward and gives me a kiss on the forehead.

A kiss from Dylan. But not the kiss I'm always dreaming about. "Thank you," I say softly. "You, too."

He turns and leaves me in my room alone, closing the door quietly behind him..

Tonight was fun and also a little humiliating. That's how college is shaping up for me. I like the independence, even if Dylan thinks I can't handle it. And I can't live with Leah and Isaac forever.

I like the classes, too, even though they're hard for me. Since I didn't go to high school, I had to take the GED tests before I could apply to Moo U. Those weren't so bad. But college courses are definitely a level up.

Especially algebra. I need all the help I can get.

I swallow the pills and drink the water. When I set the empty glass down on my desk, I remember that Kaitlyn had said she'd left a note for me here. So where is it? My eyes rove the desk's surface. I don't see a note.

So it's her fault that I sat alone for hours at the library?

Just when I'm ready to give up looking, I spot it. There's a row of sticky notes on the wall just over my desk. Each note has a title and author of one of the books I'm supposed to read for my Small Business class. And on the bottom edge of one of them—in faint pencil—is scribbled: *D can't make it to lib.*

You have *got* to be kidding me. And she thinks I ruined *her* night?

Upset now, I head to the bathroom and give my teeth an angry brushing. Then I stomp back to my room, get into my bed, and shut out the light.

When I stop moving around, I can hear Kaitlyn and Dylan speaking to one another in her room on the other side of the wall. I listen, waiting for Dylan to leave with her. They'll go back to his giant bed and...

Honestly, I spend an embarrassing amount of time thinking about Dylan having sex. Does he tease her as they start to kiss? Is he smiley, laughing Dylan? Or is he just so hungry for it that he's too busy stripping her clothes off to talk or smile?

That second image really appeals to me. If I were the one in the bed with him, I wouldn't want him to joke around. I'd want it to be like a sudden storm on a summer's day. Fast-moving and dangerous, blotting out the sun and beating down its wrath upon my bare body. No time to think.

There's a reason I don't tell many people all the things inside my head.

Last week, as I passed the coffee shop, I'd seen Dylan and Kaitlyn on the other side of the plate-glass window. The coffee shop is where Kaitlyn likes to do her homework. I can't afford to buy coffee that doesn't come from the dining hall, so I never go inside that place. That day they'd been together on a purple velvet sofa by the window, Kaitlyn's head on Dylan's lap, Dylan's hand on her sleek hair. His attention seemed focused on the paperback book in his other hand.

His long fingers idly stroked her hair, and I wanted to stop and watch, fascinated. Their pose said to the world: *We're definitely having sex with each other. But not right now. First, coffee and homework!*

Nobody has ever touched me like that—with casual, sensual ownership. I have no idea how it feels to be half of a couple.

There's a squeak next door. It's the sound of a window being cranked open. It's a chilly night, so the open window probably means that they're smoking a joint. Another thing I've never tried.

Now I can hear their voices a little more clearly. Kaitlyn's is the clearest. "Why do we always have to go back to your place?" she whines. "You could stay here for once."

"Three words," Dylan's lower voice says. "Queen-sized bed."

"That's not really the reason," Kaitlyn says.

The next bit is muffled, so I find myself sliding out of bed and edging toward my own window. It's already unlatched, so all I have to do is nudge the crank and it opens an inch.

And almost immediately, I wish I hadn't.

"God forbid we're overheard. Why do you fuss over her?" Kaitlyn asks, her voice high and angry.

I sit down on the edge of my bed, my heart in my mouth.

"She's a good friend."

"You just want to watch her take off that low-cut top."

"Kaitlyn!" His raised voice is easy to hear now. "You're ridiculous. Can a single puff of weed make a person paranoid?"

"I see where your eyes go. Right down that slutty blouse."

They're fighting about *me*, and I want to die. I clutch the V of skin above the first button on my PJs, as if I could undo the evening's fashion blunder.

That top *was* too revealing. Obviously. I wanted to be nonchalant and sexy. But I achieved *slutty* instead. Slutty and drunk.

Except... It wasn't Dylan who thought I looked slutty. He doesn't notice me the way I want him to. It was Kaitlyn who noticed. And Kaitlyn who didn't like it very much.

Maybe I'm a mean drunk, because this idea makes me smile in the dark.

Now Dylan's voice goes low and soft. I can't hear their words anymore. They've probably moved away from the window. I should get up and close mine, but my comforter is warm, and I'm lazy.

I've almost drifted off when a sound from next door floats me back up to the surface of consciousness. It's a keening moan.

My eyes flip open in the dark. I listen. It takes a few seconds, but then I hear it again. "*Ohhh.*" Kaitlyn moans. "*Yes.*"

I'm instantly, catastrophically awake.

It all unfolds within earshot—the terrible, wonderful sounds of Dylan making love to someone who isn't me. At first, I only hear her whimpering moans. They soften her, actually. Each *mmm* and *ahhh* is full of unselfconscious need.

But then? I hear a low growl. The hairs on my arms stand up at the sound of Dylan's voice. I can't understand the words, but her response is a hot gasp. My heart begins to pound. I flatten myself onto the mattress, ears straining.

He murmurs to her again, and the hungry timbre of his voice reverberates inside my ribcage. I'm holding my breath now.

And then it really begins—the rhythmic sound of the bed rocking against the wall.

I break out in a sweat. He grunts, and I shiver. Every little noise he makes is gold. I close my eyes, and I could almost be the one underneath him. My heartbeat syncs to his rhythm. *Inside. Straining. More. Yes.*

"*Please,*" she moans. "*Please.*"

Her begging is the soundtrack of my life. *Please, Dylan.* For once she and I are in perfect agreement. I clench my legs together against the ache. And then I do it again.

I'm a sinner. I've always been a sinner.

Pressing myself into the mattress, I spread my legs, and I imagine his body over me. His hot skin against mine. His tongue in my mouth. His low voice in my ear. My pulse pounds, and my ears strain, and I keep forgetting to breathe.

"Grab the bed rail," Dylan growls. "With both hands."

Then the wall practically begins to shake as the rhythm rises. It doesn't stop until a rich, satisfied moan comes from the other room, chorused with my roommate's.

And now I know what he sounds like when he comes.

I don't move a muscle. If I got up to close the window, I might be overheard. If Dylan knew I was listening, I'd die of embarrassment.

But nobody is thinking about me at all right now. I hear only the low murmured voices of lovers speaking to one another from very close range—the closest range there is.

I lay still and try to think of other things. But I'm turned on and lonely, and the room is spinning gently.

It takes a long time to fall asleep.

FIVE

Dylan

"HEY, MORNING." I plunk a tray down on the dining hall table and slide into the chair across from Chastity.

"Morning," she says, her voice a squeak. She glances up at me for a split second, looking mildly embarrassed.

Ah. Must be the hangover. "How's your head?"

She blinks. "Oh. It hurts."

"Your stomach?"

"It's fine, I swear."

"Okay, you need coffee, carbs, and ibuprofen. Want to skip the algebra this morning?"

"No," she says quickly. "I can't skip it. There's a quiz coming up."

"All right." I take a deep, life-giving gulp from my coffee cup. "Let me come over there, actually." I can't see her notebook from this side of the table, so I swing around and sit down on the bench beside her. I wrap an arm around her shoulders and give her a quick squeeze. "Is this your first hangover?"

"I guess." She sighs. "It's really no big deal. I'm a big girl. A headache won't kill me."

"Right. I know." It's just that I feel guilty. Rickie's parties could make anyone regret her life choices. I should have warned her. "Tell you what. Do that first problem, okay? And I'll ask the chef for my favorite hangover cure."

"The chef?" She gives me a quizzical look.

"The cook. Whatever. That dude wearing the white hat. Just trust me on this." I drop her shoulder and bolt out of my seat again.

If you're polite, people will do anything for you. When I return to Chastity ten minutes later, I'm carrying a chocolate mocha milkshake split into two portions and a plate of french fries.

She looks startled when I set them down beside her. "That's your medicine?"

"Totally. But if you were nauseated, I'd start with popcorn and work my way up to fries. Here." I push the plate a little closer to her then grab the salt shaker and sprinkle the fries vigorously.

"Thanks. I didn't know they served fries at this hour," she says, grabbing one and dipping it in ketchup.

"Sometimes you just gotta ask."

I watch her bite the fry and then smile at me. She picks up the cold shake and takes a sip. "Wow. You do know things."

"Right?" I like feeding Chastity. I always have, ever since the first Thursday Dinner she came to, when I heard her tell my mother that she'd never had a slice of pie. Not once.

I've been feeding her treats ever since.

Chastity eats a few more fries and picks up her pencil. She's on problem number two. She sort of stares at the problem for a while and then abruptly writes the answer down. "Got it."

Oh man. She's right, and she's also wrong. "Chass, algebra is all about methodology and showing your work. If you turn it in like that, he'll mark it wrong."

"That makes no sense. If the answer is *four*, then it's four!"

I chuckle then shake my head. "Look, I want you to think of each variable as a wrapped gift. You're not supposed to just *guess* what's inside. That's not the point of algebra. You need to manipulate the other parts of the equation to *show* what's inside." I tap the page. "Try number three."

"But what if it's just obvious?" she argues. "I tried a couple of numbers, and only one of them works."

"It doesn't matter, because soon the problems will have more than one variable, and there will be more than one thing that X can be."

"That sounds dreadful," she grumbles, taking another sip of milkshake.

"It's only dreadful if you don't learn the rules. Leave the gift in the box, okay? I'm going to show you how to manipulate the package so that all the *other* information tells you what's inside."

"Okay," she says wearily. "Thank you."

"Back to number three. How can you isolate X on one side of the equals sign?"

She blinks down at the page. "Well..." Her cheeks turn pink, because this stuff doesn't come easily to her. She missed ten years of math. My older sister and I helped her pass the GED tests. I already know she's smart. But it hasn't been easy. "I could add something to both sides."

"Right! What do you want to add?"

"If only I knew."

It takes a while, but we plod along through the homework. I make her do every problem the long way, and slowly she pieces it together. And—*hallelujah*—she even does the hardest problem without any help.

"Nice!" I say, holding up a hand.

It takes her half a second to realize she's supposed to high-five me, but then our palms make a satisfying sound as they meet in midair. And there's that smile again. It warms me from the inside.

There aren't many people in my life who see the best in me, but Chastity has always been one of them. It relaxes me to spend time with her. And helping her with math problems is really no big deal.

I sit back on the bench and drain my coffee. "Good work today."

"Thanks." She unzips her backpack to put the textbook back inside. The spine is practically falling off. Chastity must be that book's hundredth owner.

"I have some packing tape at home you could use on that thing," I point out. "I can't believe the bookstore didn't throw that copy away."

"Someone did," she mutters. "I bought it off eBay for seven bucks. It's a hundred bucks new."

"Ah."

"Hey, Dyl? I need to pick your brain about something. It's a moneymaking idea with a twist."

"Yeah? I like money."

"So..." She licks her lips nervously, which is a little distracting, because Chastity is a really pretty girl, and I'm oversexed. But I snap out of it when she says, "You have all that goat's milk in the freezer, and Leah hasn't been able to use it for cheese."

"Tell me about it," I grumble.

My two goats—Jacquie and Jill—are a major point of contention at home. I bought them this past summer when Leah and Isaac—Chastity's surrogate family—said they'd like to try making goat cheese. But when I accepted Rickie's offer of a room in his house, the goats became my brother's problem five days out of the week.

Also, Leah hasn't found a goat cheese recipe she likes well enough to put into production. So Jacquie and Jill are losing the family money and driving my brother crazy.

"Would you consider another use for the milk?" Chastity asks me.

"*Any* use will do." I chuckle. "My mother made a big batch of goat's milk soap, but that will last for months. Griffin mostly pours it on his cereal and blows up my phone complaining about milking Jacquie and Jill by hand. What's your big idea?"

"Well..." She clears her throat. "Goat's milk makes really good caramel. And the only other ingredients are sugar and vanilla."

"Caramel," I repeat slowly. "Like, candy?"

"Exactly. And people buy a lot of treats during the holidays. I thought caramels would be a good seasonal product."

"Oh. Wow." Who doesn't like caramel, right? So this is a fun idea. Except for one problem. "Isn't that hard to make? Have you done this before?"

"Well, no." Chastity bites her lip. "But it's just chemistry. Not that you should make a habit of taking chemistry lessons from your friend who never went to high school. But I watched a lot of cooking videos, and those people pulled it off."

"I thought candy was tricky. Don't you need to bring it to exactly the right temperature?" I've never been known as a details man.

"What if we tried to make a test batch?" she suggests. "It's just three ingredients and a little patience. Although you probably don't have time to noodle around in Leah's creamery."

"Wait, the commercial kitchen? Doesn't she charge money for that space?"

"Usually," Chastity admits. "But there are openings when she's not making cheese and nobody else wants to rent it. She said we could use it on—" Chastity's eyes dip. "—Friday nights."

Friday nights. Now that's a problem. I usually drive home to the farm on Saturday morning, leaving the comfort of my bed before five a.m. so that I can help in the dairy barn by six thirty.

Kaitlyn likes me to be around on Friday nights. She calls it "our night out."

On the other hand, I could always use more cash. And I need to get Griffin off my back. We used to get along better. But since I moved to Burlington, he won't shut up about how much work the dairy takes.

Fridays, though. I let everybody down eventually. It's probably just Kaitlyn's turn.

I lift my coffee mug and drain it. "Interesting idea, Chass. Handmade candies are expensive. Like Leah's cheeses, right? The retail price would be pretty high. And with all the gourmet crap our families are selling already, it wouldn't be hard to get it into shops."

"Exactly." She grabs a folder out of her backpack, but hesitates before handing it over. "Don't laugh, but I wrote it all up for my Economics of Small Businesses class."

"I'm not going to laugh," I insist as she hands me the folder. In fact, I'm damned impressed when I flip it open and scan the numbers.

"Sugar is really cheap," Chastity says. "That's the second ingredient in caramel."

"See?" I have to chuckle. "You don't hate math, as long as we're making candy."

"I don't hate numbers at all," she argues. "I hate *variables.*"

"Obviously. Because this is really thorough." I scan her ingredients list, and the prices beside them. She's right. Other than the goat's milk, everything is dirt cheap. "Wow. Okay. So when do you want to try this? It's already October. We'd have to hustle if we want to sell them for the holidays."

A big smile breaks across Chastity's face. "Well, tomorrow is Friday. I could buy sugar and vanilla before Spanish class. We could make a test batch tomorrow night."

"Tomorrow." I close the folder and hand it back to her. "All right. Why not? We'd have to leave right after classes. You can ride home with me, but you'll have to stay until Sunday afternoon when I'm ready to drive back."

"That's fine with me," she says quickly.

"Okay, it's a deal. Fun project, Chass. I hope this works."

"It will," she says, looking pleased with herself. Chastity's eyes really sparkle when she's happy. "I mean—this will be my first batch of caramel ever. But I have a good feeling."

"What if it won't firm up?" I have to ask. "What if we make a whole vat of milky goo?"

"Then we'll freeze it and call it ice cream?"

"Guess what? I thought about making goat's milk ice cream. But you need big commercial freezers and those cost a lot more than a twenty-five pound bag of sugar."

"Then we better get it right on the caramels." She zips her backpack.

"Cool. I better run." I get up and drop a kiss on the top of her head. Her hair smells like lemons. "See you tomorrow. Pick you up at four?"

"I'll be ready," she says.

I carry my tray off to the dishwashing window. And as I glance her way on my way out of the room, she makes an awkward motion with her hand.

Strangely enough, it looks like a fist pump.

SIX

Freshman Composition

Section 4

Title: Hungrily
Author: Chastity Campbell

I GREW up on a cattle ranch. But I wasn't allowed to eat a steak until I was a nineteen-year-old runaway, and two thousand miles from that place.

Honestly, that's really all you need to know to understand my story. But you wanted two pages, so I'll give you the ugly details.

Where I grew up women worked in the kitchen and the men never set foot in there. When dinner was over, my stepfather got up and left the table without a backward glance at his dirty plate.

And if he ever left a scrap of something on it, one of his many children would grab it and shove it in his mouth in no time flat.

One night every year, the menfolk (we actually used that word) who worked the ranch held a steak dinner to congratulate themselves on another auction of steers. I guess that sounds normal enough until

I add that none of the wives were invited to this dinner. Or the daughters.

But—as I mentioned above—the men of Paradise Ranch don't do their own cooking. And why would they? My stepfather has five wives.

On steak night they did their own outdoor grilling. (Because that's somehow different? More manly.) But the daughters spent the day slicing potatoes and creaming spinach. And it was the daughters who carried in the steaming casseroles and the beans and the warm rolls with real butter. We set all these glorious foods on the long tables, where the men were seated with bowed heads.

And then we stood back against the walls of the dining hall while our divine pastor said his lengthy prayer. It lasted five minutes at least. Maybe ten. That's how long I stood with my back pressed to the wall, inhaling the scent of meat that I would never taste.

When he was finally done with the windy men-only prayer, the men fell on all that delicious food like a pack of wolves. And I still wasn't excused. It was my job to circle the table pouring water and refilling baskets of rolls.

And I'm ashamed to say that I actually looked forward to this annual humiliation. Because it was an honor to be chosen to serve. I was first picked to serve at fourteen, and then again at fifteen. I was so proud. And for what?

My only reward was attention. The whole time I circled that table with my icy water pitcher, refilling their cups, they eyed me the same way they looked at the food. The same way they eyed the fattened steers on the way to auction.

Hungrily.

SEVEN

Chastity

"OH MY GOD. Is your seatbelt on?" I ask Dylan. I'm gripping the steering wheel of his truck with two slightly sweaty hands.

"I'm locked and loaded over here," he says from the passenger seat. "Let 'er rip, Chass. It's only four miles."

"Okay." I take my foot off the brake and tap the accelerator gently. "For the record, this was all your idea." I turn out of the gas station and point Dylan's truck uphill.

This must be how a criminal feels when she's driving the getaway car. I've stolen Dylan away from Kaitlyn, at least for the weekend. For some reason Dylan decided I should practice my driving. I have a license but no car, so I've barely driven at all after passing the test. He offered to let me do some highway driving, too. But I refused.

Dylan looks completely relaxed, singing along with the radio as I drive us the last few miles toward home.

In the cupholder, his phone lights up with a text. Again. His phone is full of texts from Kaitlyn. She's pissed off that Dylan left town a day early. Every time his phone lights up, I feel a shimmy of victory, followed immediately by discomfort.

Because I told a lie. And I got away with it.

Dylan doesn't even glance at his phone, though. That's just his way. He'll get to you when he gets to you. But when you have his attention all to yourself? There's nothing else like it.

"Are we going to make caramel before dinner or after?" he asks me now. "You said it takes a while."

"Before," I say, steering carefully around a curve.

"I hope this isn't a disaster." He laughs. "Because when I told Griffin what we were trying to do, he got all excited. He wanted to know the cost of every ingredient by weight." Dylan shakes his head. "I told him that you were the numbers man in this business venture."

I still can't believe we're doing this. I nearly chickened out yesterday instead of sharing my idea, because I hadn't wanted to get shot down. But I'd still been hungover and still angry at Kaitlyn.

I hadn't felt like I had anything to lose. And there had been no mistaking Dylan's spark of interest. The unsold goat's milk was a problem.

Still, I didn't have to tell him that Friday was the only day available to us. I'd surprised myself by lying. Kaitlyn's awful excuse for a note pushed me over the edge, though. She'd known exactly what she was doing when she'd left me sitting in the library like a loser.

I'm aware that it's a shallow victory. Dylan is still hers. But this is the only time I've ever had something she wanted—a night in Dylan's company. I don't really deserve it. Yet here we are.

I make the last turn, and then we're cruising down the dirt road to our neighboring farms. The Shipley Farms sign comes into view first, its posts decorated with a scarecrow and a collection of pumpkins. By nine o'clock tomorrow morning, tourists' cars will be parked all over this road. They'll come in droves to pick apples, ride in the wagon, and buy cider.

Leah and Isaac are almost two miles past the Shipleys' driveway. "Next-door neighbor" means something different in Vermont than it means elsewhere. We pass a cow pasture and then row after row of the Shipleys' apple trees. Eventually, these give way to a little bungalow where Griffin Shipley lives with his wife and baby boy.

The Abrahams' place is just beyond. Leah and Isaac bought their farm five or six years ago now. It was in foreclosure, which is why a couple of runaways from a cult could save up enough money to afford it. They made their escape a few years before that, because they wanted to marry each other, and they weren't going to be allowed to.

By the time I got here, it was already a small but thriving farm. The Abrahams grow vegetables and raise a few dairy cows. But the big cash crop is Leah's artisanal cheeses. They retail for twenty-four dollars a pound.

We roll past six greenhouses with solar panels on their roofs. Greenhouses are the only way to get a reliable tomato harvest in Vermont. Every time Isaac can save up enough money, he builds another greenhouse.

Leah and Isaac are amazing people. They ran away with nothing but huge plans. And the farm isn't even the end of it. Leah is all fired up about starting a nonprofit to help other women and men who leave cults. They've helped me and Zach get on our feet, and now they want to help more people, too. So Leah spent the summer learning all she could about charitable fundraising.

If they get their nonprofit off the ground, I'll be first in line to help. They say that the best revenge is living well. If I can help some other girl with scars on her butt get out of that hellscape where I grew up? That's a double victory.

"Nice job," Dylan says as I slow down to turn into the driveway. I pass the greenhouses and roll up to the farmhouse on the left.

On the right, there's a small dairy barn, and also the state-certified Creamery Kitchen where Leah makes her cheeses.

"Oh, man," Dylan grumbles.

"Did I do something wrong?"

"No way! You did great. But Griff is here." He points at another truck parked beside Isaac's greenhouses. "I'm sure he'll find something to nag me about."

It's not very unusual for Griffin to stop by. Our two farms are intertwined in so many ways. The Shipleys sell cow's milk to Leah for cheese. And when there's a big job to do—like a sudden harvest or a greenhouse to raise—we barter our time. Dylan says he spent many of his teenage hours weeding peppers and lettuces for Isaac. And Isaac helps Griffin make cider after the veggie season is done.

I open the truck door and hop out just as Griffin comes out of the farmhouse. "I thought I heard the Ford," he says. "The engine is still knocking?"

"I'll get it looked at," Dylan says gruffly, hopping out of the truck.

"You missed the afternoon milking," Griffin says. "How convenient for you."

"It's my fault," I say as I open the back door of Dylan's truck to collect my stuff. "He had to wait for me to get out of class."

"Likely story." Griff bites into an apple he's holding.

"Got more of those?" Dylan asks. It's almost dinnertime, and he's always starving.

Griffin reaches into his jacket pocket, pulls out two apples, and offers one to me before tossing one to Dylan. "You're milking in the morning, right?"

"Of course I am. Sunday morning, too. But we head back around noon." He bites the apple.

"Did you declare a major yet?" Griff asks.

Dylan actually grimaces. "Did you think I'd have a different answer than when you asked me ten minutes ago?"

His brother just shakes his head. "Drive the horses for me tomorrow, would you?"

"Sure," Dylan grunts. "Whatever you need." His words are helpful, but his expression is shuttered.

"Good deal. Your goat's milk is in the creamery fridge," Griff says, pointing. "I got dibs on the first batch of caramels."

"A smarter man would put dibs on the third batch," Dylan says.

"But if you get it right the first time, there won't be a third batch," Griff says. "Besides, how bad could a caramel be?"

"Curdled?" I suggest. "Burnt? Don't jinx us."

Griff makes a comical grimace. "Yikes, kids. I hope this doesn't end badly."

You and me both.

"Where's the girlfriend? What's her name—Kimberly?" Griff asks.

"Kaitlyn," Dylan grumbles. "She's going to a poetry reading, and she's pissed I'm not there." He reaches into the truck for his phone and then closes the door with a bang.

"*Poetry?*" Griffin pronounces the word as if it's poison. "Bullet dodged, bro." He hurls his apple core over the chicken fence, and the hens go running for it. Dylan does the same with his, and now there's clucking and competition. "Thought maybe you were going to say you broke up."

"Why would I say that?"

"Because you never spend more than a single night with anyone." Griffin laughs.

He isn't wrong. I kick a pebble with my shoe and try to appear disinterested in this conversation. *As if.*

"Can't you grill me on my personal life later?" Dylan asks his brother. "What are you doing here, anyway? Besides giving me a hard time."

"Helping Leah with some paperwork for her nonprofit."

"Cool," Dylan says lightly. "See you in the morning, then?"

"Yeah, go on," Griff says, waving a hand toward the creamery. "I brought down three gallons of goat's milk for you. Nobody will be happier than me if you can use that stuff. Jacquie jumped the fence *three* times today! I spent lunchtime chasing her around the fucking orchard. Now there's a good time."

Dylan scowls. "Did you see how she got out?"

His brother shakes his head grumpily.

"I'll look at the fence tomorrow," Dylan says. "Maybe the water bucket—"

"It wasn't the fucking bucket," Griff snaps. "Learned that lesson already."

"They can't *fly*, Griff," Dylan returns. "It has to be something."

"Then figure it out. I got other things to worry about. Are you coming home for supper?" Griff looks at his watch. "You don't have a lot of time."

"I cooked!" comes Leah's voice from inside the house. "Dylan can eat here. Homemade mac and cheese and chicken cutlets."

"Score." Griff claps him on the back. "Good luck with the candy. Be in the barn at six tomorrow morning. Don't forget to set your alarm."

"I won't. Jesus." Dylan rolls his eyes as his brother climbs into his own truck.

Griffin leaves, finally. And Leah gives us a wave hello from the door then disappears as well.

Then it's just me and Dylan. Alone. The way I like it.

EIGHT

Dylan

EVEN A MINOR RUN-IN with Griffin puts me in a crappy mood. So I'm standing in the creamery scowling while Chastity unpacks a bunch of ingredients from a grocery bag.

It doesn't bother me so much that he calls me *kid*. And I don't mind doing farm work. But he's gotten so pushy lately about what I plan to do with my life. Like maybe he's hoping I won't follow through on farming with him after graduation.

The dude really likes to be in charge. And everyone thinks of me as the fuckup. Maybe he doesn't think I deserve to help run the place after college.

And maybe he's right.

"You okay?" Chastity asks.

"Sure. Tell me what to do," I demand, trying to shake off my bad mood. "We'll make the first batch small, right?"

"Yes, and no. We're going to cook two batches at once. But we'll pour them off at different times, at different temperatures. After it cools overnight, we'll decide which batch we like best. I only brought five pounds of sugar so we can't get too carried away."

"Still sounds like a lot."

"We won't need it all." She looks up at me with those clear blue eyes of hers and tilts her head to the side. "Ignore Griffin, okay? This is going to be fun." She plucks an apron off a row of hooks on the wall and places it in my hands.

"Don't let me screw it up," I grumble. I seem to do that a lot.

"You can't," she says. "Caramel is just basic science. You have sugar and fat. We're boiling the water out of the milk, and then the temperature keeps rising until things start to caramelize. Which has something to do with carbon. The only variable is how high to go, and when to stop."

"How do you know all this?" I ask, looping the apron over my head.

"YouTube. And the people in those videos didn't look any smarter than we are. Find the heaviest pot, would you? Look in that drawer." She points. "We'll start with two quarts of goat's milk. I had to get vanilla extract because I couldn't afford a vanilla bean."

"That's okay. We don't need to be so fancy, right?" I open the drawer and take out the largest pot. "Making money on food is all about walking the line between premium and too expensive."

"True. You can rein me in if I get too ambitious." Chastity lifts her eyes to mine, and I smile for nothing. I always have fun with Chastity. She just gets me. She doesn't look at me and see broken fences and unmilked cows and a guy who'd rather mess around on his fiddle than make a five-year-plan. She isn't always trying to change me into someone else.

Even as I form this thought, my pocket buzzes with a text. When I pull out my phone, I see Kaitlyn's name next to a long string of messages. I tuck the phone away again. I'll deal with her later. Maybe if I take her out to dinner on Sunday night she'll get over her snit.

If I'm honest, hanging out in a kitchen with Chastity is a better Friday night than listening to hipsters try to sling poetry. I like poetry just fine, but I like it to be *good*.

"Pour in the milk, okay? Two quarts." Chastity is measuring sugar into a bowl. "And we're going to need a wooden spoon."

"Sure thing."

We work in companionable silence for a while, with me stirring the milk over the flame while she adds the sugar and the salt. And then we switch jobs, with Chastity watching the temperature slowly rise on a candy thermometer, while I butter some baking pans and then wash and dry various tools and the surfaces.

"Does it matter that nothing seems to be happening in that pot?" I ask. It still looks like milk.

"Just because you don't see it doesn't mean it's not happening," Chastity says. "It takes time and heat."

"Nobody said I was a patient man." I turn on Leah's speaker and play some music from my phone. I take another turn at the stove. The kitchen is warm, and the air is beginning to smell sweet.

Leah pokes her head in the door. "Can you two stop for dinner?"

"Dylan could," Chastity says. "But someone has to stir, so it doesn't scorch."

"I could make you both a tray," she offers.

"That's a great idea," I say, passing the spoon to Chastity. "Let me help."

I follow Leah into her farmhouse. "Hi, Dylan!" her preschooler says from her booster seat at the table.

"Hey, shorty." I ruffle the little girl's hair. "How's business, Isaac?"

"Can't complain," he says from his dining chair. "Awful nice of you to help Chastity like this. We're grateful for all that you do for her."

I just shrug. "You know me, Isaac. I'm not really that nice a person. But I like caramel as much as the next guy."

He laughs, but it's just the truth.

Leah loads two plates up with chicken, homemade mac and cheese, and salad. And while she does that, she quizzes me. "Do you think Chastity is doing okay in her classes? Can she pass algebra?"

"Yeah," I say. "She probably can. It's all new material for her, but she can get it. And she loves that business class."

Leah glances toward the door, as if making sure that Chastity can't overhear her. "I shouldn't have pushed her to go full time. If it doesn't work out, I'll feel terrible."

"It's only been a few weeks," Isaac says from the table. "Give it a little time?"

"I know," Leah agrees, wiping her hands on a dish towel. "But next semester she has to take *five* courses to maintain her status as a full-time student."

"Because of her scholarship?" I ask.

Leah's head bobs. "She can't get room and board if she's part time. I should have steered her toward community college. I just got so excited about the financial aid package."

I pick up the loaded tray in two hands. "Thank you for dinner, Leah. And try not to worry, okay? She doesn't have to make the dean's list. It's all good."

"Okay." She gives my arm a squeeze. "You're a great friend, Dylan."

I thank her again and carry the tray outside and into the creamery. Chastity is humming to herself and stirring the pot slowly. It still looks like a bunch of nothing, but I won't be a dick and point that out.

I finish my food in record time, but Chastity is still stirring. "Let me do that," I say. "You eat."

She switches places with me and tucks into her food. "Oooh. I love Leah's cornbread."

"Same." And I knew that already, so I left the bigger piece for her.

"Would it jinx us to talk about our branding?" she asks.

"Probably." I look into the pot of bubbling goo and notice that the color is richening. So that's something. "What are you going to call this candy empire, anyway?"

"I have no idea."

"Naming stuff is the hardest part. How about *North Hill Caramels*? That sounds a little uptight. *Chastity's Chews*?"

"No!" Her pretty face fills with horror. "We're *not* naming them after me. I have literally the *least* sexy name in the world."

I don't know why, but this makes me snort with laughter. "There's nothing wrong with your name."

"Are you *high*? Do you know anyone younger than eighty-five named Chastity? It's a name that literally tells a guy to peddle it elsewhere."

And now I'm dying, because Chastity *never* talks about sex. But she has a good fucking point.

My phone rings, and Chastity squints at me. "Is that Kaitlyn calling?"

"Probably."

"Answer it," she says, putting down her fork. "Or she'll just call back."

I suppose that's true. I hand Chastity the spoon. "Check it out—the goo is actually getting thicker."

"Of course it is." She shoos me toward the door. "Go now while we still need ten more degrees."

I step outside and answer the second time Kaitlyn calls. "What's up, baby? Having fun?"

"I love Kahlua!" she shrieks. "I am going to marry it."

"Are you, now?" I smile into the phone. A drunk Kaitlyn is a fun Kaitlyn. "How's the poetry?"

"Horrible!" she says with obvious glee. "One guy rhymed *flipper-less* with *clitoris*."

"Oh Jesus." I laugh. "That bad, huh?"

"He was one of the better ones." She hiccups. And then she spends the next ten minutes recounting the horrors of the poetry slam. "If you come home right now you can hear Rickie try to rhyme. He says he's gonna rhyme *penis* with *zenith* just for funzies."

"Rickie won't actually rhyme anything," I point out. "He's probably so baked that it will just *seem* to him like the words go together."

"I'll take a video."

"No need." I snort. "You're taking one for the team, here."

"Come home," she whines. "Forget the poetry. You can just fuck me in the shower."

"That is a nice offer," I say gruffly. "But you know I have to be home for the weekend."

"I miss you. What are you doing right now?" she demands.

"Helping out in the kitchen." I don't tell her *which* kitchen, because I haven't told Kaitlyn about Operation Caramel. It's just an idea at this point, anyway.

"Is she there?" Kaitlyn asks.

"Who?"

I can hear her dismissive sniff through the phone. "Chastity. Be honest. You have a *thing* for Chastity."

I laugh. Where did that come from? "Buddy, that's just the Kahlua talking. I miss you, too."

"You don't. Why won't you just admit it?"

I hold back my groan. "Kaity, honey. Go listen to some bad poetry, and we'll talk later. I'll be home on Sunday afternoon."

"She's there with you, isn't she?"

"Nope." The lie just slips out. Because you can't win a pointless argument with a drunk girl, and I'm not that interested in trying.

Unfortunately, that's the exact moment Chastity calls me. "Dylan? It's getting hot!"

"*What's* getting hot?" Kaitlyn yelps. "Are you shitting me right now?"

"Listen," I grumble. "You already picked a fight with me that I can't win. There's no way to prove to you that I wish I was there tonight."

"Because you *don't* wish that!"

"I do so!" Jesus. "And you already know why I have to come home on the weekends. You have a standing invitation to come with me anytime. I invited you about four hours ago, and you turned me down."

"Your mother hates me."

"Not true." There is nobody my mother hates. No one. "Look, I have to go and finish up here so I can milk things before dawn. And then I have to sell apples and do laundry."

"You're a good time," she mumbles.

Fuck, that stings a little. "It was your idea to date a farmer. That's how it is. Now go have fun."

She hangs up without saying goodbye.

"Dyl?" Chastity calls.

I dart inside. "Sorry. Shit." Chastity is holding the giant pot off the stove, trying to keep the temperature from rising any further.

"Steady that buttered pan?"

"Sure. Got it. I hope I didn't fuck up the batch." She's been stirring it forever. I slap the buttered pan down on the counter and she immediately tips a stream of glossy, molten caramel out onto the surface. The smell is so delicious that I nearly start to drool. "Holy shit. You did it."

"Of course. I mean, if YouTube can do it."

I laugh as the smooth, shiny caramel puddles in the pan. "And this will cool into a solid?"

"Some version of a solid. That's why I'm going to cook the rest of this a little longer. So we can decide how nice and hard we like it."

There's a joke about nice and hard things in there somewhere. But I never make sleazy jokes with Chastity. "When can we taste it?" I ask instead.

"Tomorrow," she says, crushing my dreams. "Both batches have to spend a night in the refrigerator. I'll cut them into pieces tomorrow morning and bring you some."

"This really is going to work, isn't it?" I realize suddenly. "We could use up a lot of goat's milk this way. I mean, what kind of freak wouldn't want a caramel that we made?" The scent of caramel is turning me into an optimist. Who knew?

She sets the pot on the burner again, and I grab the spoon and start stirring immediately. "This will only take a couple more minutes, right? Eat your chicken."

"Watch the thermometer, would you? Keep it off the bottom of the pan."

"Yes, oh great and wise candymaker."

She gives me a smile that warms my cold little heart. "I might need a business card that says that."

"Uh-huh. Sure."

"Caramel will always be my favorite. Do you know why?"

I shake my head.

"We didn't have candy at the Paradise Ranch."

"Like, none?" She doesn't talk about that place very often. Neither does Zach, our farmhand, or Leah or Isaac.

"No candy at *all*. We didn't celebrate holidays, either. But when I was seventeen years old, I got that job at the Walgreens in town."

"Yeah. I remember."

Girls weren't supposed to have jobs at Paradise Ranch, but she was a special case, because she'd been *compromised* by kissing Zach. As if that makes any sense at all. The place where Chastity and Zach grew up was seriously fucked.

"Mostly I worked the cash register at the drugstore," she says.

"See? I knew you were quick with numbers."

She dismisses that idea with a wave of her hand. "Pay attention. So there I am standing in the den of iniquity—Walgreens—and for the first time I'm surrounded by all this stuff I've never seen before. Pantyhose. Deodorant. Snickers. Coke. But I don't have any money. So I sell to strangers all day and just wonder what it's like to buy those things."

"You didn't get paid?"

"My check went straight to my stepfather. I didn't even have a way to cash it if I'd dared. But I loved the job anyway. Any idiot can scan barcodes and make change. And I was out in the world, eavesdropping on conversations and listening to pop music on the sound system. I wasn't getting slapped around by my stepfather's wives or ironing his shirts."

Christ. That's a pretty low standard for fun.

"Then, maybe two weeks after I started working there, a kid plunges a Halloween-costume saber into a bag of Rolos. His mom was so mad. She paid for the candy but wouldn't take it, because she didn't want to reward his behavior."

"So you ate Rolos?"

"So. Many. Rolos." She grins. "I had no self-control. The manager lady thought I was hilarious. She was really nice—Mrs. Cates. The only reason I was finally able to run away was because of her."

"Really?" I park my butt against the counter because I've never heard this part of the story before.

"She was scandalized by the way I had no control over my life. Everyone who works at Walgreens for six months gets a raise, and she paid me the extra money on a Visa gift card. She wanted me to have the money."

"That's some sneaky shit right there."

Chastity's pretty smile widens. "Do you know how hard it is to hide Visa gift cards in a house where eleven people live, and nobody has locks on their doors? Nowhere is safe. Not the mattress. Not the underwear drawer. I kept them in the potato cellar under a bucket of pickling salt."

"Oh, please. Daphne learned how to pick the lock on my bedroom door when she was eight years old. All it takes is sliding a credit card into the door jamb. Seriously—when you have a twin sister, you're literally tempted to hide things in your ass crack."

"Gross, Dylan!"

We both laugh.

I check the thermometer again. "Time to pour. We're spiking over two-fifty."

Chastity turns off the burner. I line up the buttered pan, my mouth watering. "Can I at least lick the spoon when we're done?"

"Nope. You're only going to taste the finished product. So you can get the full effect."

I let out a sad little moan as she moves the sweet-smelling pot past my nose. "Are we equal partners in this venture or not?"

"Sure, but you're the one who doubted it would work."

"I was wrong. Very, very wrong."

"Heat and patience, Dylan. That's all it takes. So show me some patience."

She pours the caramel while I try not to look down her shirt. The swells of her breasts are *right* there, damn it.

But it doesn't mean I have a "thing" for Chastity. We're good friends. And I can't help that I have eyes.

"Find the sea salt?" Chastity suggests. "The first batch needs some love."

Don't we all.

I reach for the salt.

NINE

Chastity

I WAKE up at dawn in my little bed upstairs in Leah and Isaac's home. I'm wired to wake up early and not because this is a dairy farm. On the Paradise Ranch, sleeping in was the easiest way to earn a punishment. It meant a smack from my stepfather's paddle or going hungry at lunch.

Old habits die hard. And not just for me. When I walk into Leah's kitchen at six thirty a.m., she and Isaac and little Maeve are already there, too. Leah and Isaac are standing side by side at the kitchen counter, drinking tea, while Maeve—their preschooler—sits at their feet chattering to her dolls.

Leah and Isaac are the only couple I know of who ran away from Paradise Ranch together. Leah's father wanted to marry her off to a fifty-five-year-old man with three wives, and Isaac was so in love with her at seventeen that he couldn't let that happen.

So they left, picking fruit across the Midwest until arriving in Vermont, where they found year-round work. It took them years to save up enough to buy their little farm. But they did it.

I can't imagine what it would be like to have a partner so devoted to you that he'd risk everything to give you a normal life and to be your one and only.

Most of us have to save ourselves. There's honor in that, too.

Except it's lonely. Even now, I feel like an interloper as I wish them good morning.

"Hi, sweetheart," Leah says. "I have a frittata in the oven. Should only be a few more minutes."

"That sounds great." Leah is a fabulous cook. So is Isaac. When I first arrived in Vermont I was so malnourished that I weighed less than a hundred pounds. I am grateful for every meal I've eaten at their table.

But I'm also conscious of the fact that I can't sponge off them forever. They aren't my parents. It was by design that they made themselves discoverable to runaways from Paradise. When I turned up, they were ready to receive me.

That was two years ago, though. So when Leah discovered I could get a hardship scholarship at Moo U, I jumped at it.

I go to the silverware drawer and pull out forks for everyone. I'm setting the table when Maeve decides that she needs my attention. "Lemme show you my fort," she says, tugging on my hand.

"Okay, awesome." I let her drag me into the laundry room where she's draped an old set of curtains off a countertop to make a hiding place beneath.

"There's a lantern!" she says. "Lemme turn it on."

Childcare has been one of the only ways I can really help Leah. So whenever Maeve wants my attention, I'm willing to sit cross-legged on the floor in her latest hiding place, while she chatters to me about hiding from dragons and making pies to sell at the market.

Someone runs on quick feet past us, and I expect to be called to breakfast. But that's not what happens. The bathroom door is flung open and there's the sound of someone vomiting.

"Oh, heck," I whisper.

"Mama," Maeve says solemnly.

"Poor Mama." *And poor me,* I add privately. I shouldn't have come home this weekend. I can't afford to get the flu. I still get sick more often than most people, because I grew up in an isolated community without the same germs that other people learn to fight off.

"Mama gets sick every morning," Maeve says. "And sometimes at night."

"Oh no!" That's when it clicks. Leah is pregnant again.

"Oh yes," Leah says with a sigh from a few yards away.

"Wow." I push the curtain aside and climb to my feet.

"You okay, honey?" Isaac calls.

"I will be," she says as the toilet flushes. "A few months from now."

Isaac winks at me as I reenter the kitchen. "We're pretty excited, but Maeve doesn't know," he whispers under his breath.

"When?" I mouth.

"May," he says quietly.

The oven timer dings. "Will Leah eat breakfast?"

"Absolutely," he says. "Whether she keeps it down is an open question."

When Leah emerges from the bathroom, Isaac wraps her into a hug. My throat feels a little tight, and I have to swallow hard. They deserve this happiness.

I suppose we all do.

By eight, I'm at the Shipley farm up the road. That's the thing about farmers—you can visit as early as you want, and nobody thinks it's weird.

And I know just where to find Dylan. When I step into the dairy barn, I spot him kneeling on the floor, having a chat with Jacquie the goat.

"Look," he murmurs. "I need a favor. And I wouldn't ask, but it's kind of important."

Jacquie turns her pointy chin in his direction, ears flopping, and assesses him with her odd brown eyes. Goats have a strange rectangular pupil. And—unlike me—Jacquie seems unmoved by Dylan's handsome face. She returns her attention back to the alfalfa he's left for her in the feed holder.

"No, really," he argues, his big hand rhythmically squeezing her udder, releasing the last few drops of milk into a shiny stainless pail. "You have to do a better job of staying inside the fence, or Griffin is going to make me sell you. Nobody wants that. You might end up down the road at the Mittson place. And I heard there are trolls under their bridge."

Jacquie snorts, and I nearly do, too. I know that eavesdropping is rude, but he's so cute that I stand there a moment longer.

With the kind of smooth movement that's meant to keep an animal calm, Dylan covers the milk pail and then lifts Jacquie's foot off the floor. She's still munching away as he lifts the trimming shears and quickly snips the front edge of her overgrown hoof.

"That's a girl," he whispers. "You should be so lucky to get a pedicure this early on a Saturday. Other goats would be jealous."

She turns her head, considering the idea.

"Big plans for your Saturday?" he asks her. "A little foraging, and climbing on tires? Some gossip with Jill, maybe? Stay in the fence, okay? There will be lots of kids here picking apples today. Loud ones, the kind who pull on ears."

I finally clear my throat, and both Jacquie and Dylan whip around to spot me. "Sorry to interrupt," I say. And I chuckle because I can't help myself.

"Hi," he says, flashing me the kind of smile that makes me feel melty inside. "How long have you been standing there?"

"Long enough to worry about trolls down the road," I admit. "Which bridge should I avoid?"

"They don't eat humans," he says, going back to Jacquie's hooves. "Only naughty goats. How come you're up so early?"

"I'm always up this early. I already had breakfast, and I'm ready to sell apples. I'll drive the pony cart if you want."

He looks up in surprise. "Really? I hate that job."

I know that, silly. "I don't mind helping out."

"You're the best." Dylan stands up and wipes his hands on a rag. "How come you don't mind driving horses, but it makes you nervous to drive my truck? The horses are a lot more work."

"Oh, please. The horses have the good sense not to crash into trees. The truck cannot be trusted."

Dylan laughs. Then he points at my hand. "What do you have there? Is it finally time?"

"Oh, yup!" I was so busy admiring his broad shoulders that I forgot

I was holding a generous box of our caramels. "I haven't tasted them, either. I waited for you." I lift the lid off the plastic container and show Dylan the arrangement of perfectly rectangular caramels inside. "I cut them up, and it wasn't too tricky. And, look—the sea salt is adhering without melting. Doesn't this look great?" I offer him the container.

"Dude, yes." He lifts a hand and then hesitates. "I'm all goaty. Feed me one."

"Sure. This one is from the first batch. So it's a little soft. Ready?"

He opens his mouth and leans down a little.

And because I'm me, and I'm hyperaware of Dylan, I notice every little thing about this moment. When I slip a caramel past his lips, I feel his breath on my hand and the brush of his whiskers against my thumb. It gives me a shiver.

"Mmm," he says huskily, his eyes lighting up. We're standing so close together that I could trace his smile with my fingertips.

Instead, I pick up another caramel and slip it into my mouth. And —*wow*. It's nothing like a drugstore candy. A toastier, nuttier sweetness spreads across my tongue.

Dylan lets out an honest-to-God moan, and goosebumps rise on my back. "Damn! That is *intense*."

"No kidding." We end up smiling at each other again.

He licks his lips, and I instantly wonder what it would feel like if he licked mine. "Do I get to taste the second batch?"

"Of course." I pluck one of those out of the container, and Dylan swoops in, playfully capturing it before I'm ready, along with my fingertips, too. I let out a squeak of surprise at the brief sensation of his tongue on my skin.

He laughs. Of course he does. "Jesus Christ, Chass. These are amazing. We are going to rake in the cash."

Still chewing, he gives me a caramel-scented kiss on the cheek. But it's so quick that it's over before I even realize it's happening. "Come into the kitchen, okay? Griffin has got to taste this." He leans down to give Jacquie a friendly pat. "Be good, today. I mean it." Then he gives her a kiss on her floppy ear.

And now I'm jealous of a goat.

He unclips Jacquie so she can run away and hang out with Jill. "Coffee?" he asks me. "There's still a half an hour before the hordes arrive." October is a crazy month at the Shipleys. Because who wouldn't want to spend the afternoon in a sunny orchard with Dylan?

Nobody, that's who.

I follow him toward the farmhouse.

Breakfast time at the Shipley farm can be a little like standing in a gale-force wind. Everybody talks at once. This morning, they're all talking about our caramels.

"You need a name for this," Grandpa Shipley says, banging his coffee mug down on the giant table. "Gimme another one so I can think of the right name."

"May ate the last one," Dylan grumbles.

"Someone had to," she says. "Do you have a list of stores yet? I think the Onion River Co-op should sell these."

"And the gourmet shop in South Royalton," Ruth Shipley puts in. "Who needs more coffee?"

"You gotta have a name," Grandpa insists. "It has to be catchy. How about *Scapegoat's Candies*?"

"Hmm," I say slowly. "I'll think about it." Scapegoat is a fun word, but it's negative.

"*I Goat You, Babe*," Griffin suggests.

"Good one," his wife says, high-fiving him from the chair beside his. "You could put 'organic and troll free' on the label."

"I like 'troll free,'" I admit.

"Oh, fine!" Grandpa storms. "You like Audrey's suggestions. What about my needs? Will there be more flavors? The salt is nice, but I'm a chocolate man."

"Chocolate gets fussy," Audrey argues. She's a trained chef, so she should know. "That would add a lot of time to the production."

"Not to mention expense," I say under my breath. "We have to figure out packaging. There are start-up costs besides the sugar."

"I'll invest," Griffin says easily. "How much could packaging cost? Are we talking tins or boxes?"

"Tins," Dylan says at the exact moment that I say "boxes."

We look at each other with matching apologetic expressions. "Chastity and I haven't done the homework on this," he says. "I didn't believe her when she said we could make a salable product."

"It's entirely salable," Audrey says. "All the shops where Leah sells cheese should be willing to stock caramels, too."

This is a an important calculation that I've already made. Our families sell food for a living. You can walk into any gourmet shop in New England and find either the Shipleys' ciders or the Abrahams' cheeses. Hopefully, Dylan and I can hitch our wagon to their successes.

"This sounds like work, though," Griffin points out. "I hope this doesn't end like Dylan's other ideas. Remember when he told us he was going to make maple soda to sell at the farmers' market?"

"I was *nine*," Dylan sputters. "And that required refrigeration."

Griffin shrugs. "Just saying. This isn't your first big idea."

Dylan gives his older brother a grumpy look and then pulls out his phone. "Where do I look for tins or boxes?" he asks. "The other question is—do we wrap up the pieces in a square of waxed paper? Or are they nestled in individual cups?"

"Cups," Audrey says firmly. "That's more upmarket. And you have to charge a lot, okay? Whatever you think the right price is, add twenty-five percent."

"No—add fifty," Griffin says.

"You need a cute logo," Dylan's sister May insists. "You can't have a great product without a great logo. Dylan—draw a goat."

"I *will*," he says. "Give a guy a minute. What is the internet search term for those little paper cups that candies sit in?"

"Candy cups," Audrey says, taking his phone. "Here, let me look."

"Oh! A drawing. Will you really do that?" I ask Dylan. He's so artistic. No wonder Dylan can't figure out what to do with his life. If I were good at everything, I'd have trouble, too.

"Sure. Consider it done," he says.

"I could use another pancake," Grandpa grumbles. "If nobody is giving me another caramel."

"Candy cups!" Audrey squeals. "You can buy them for a hundred and thirteen dollars," she says. "Ask me how many?"

"How many?" someone says.

"Twenty-five thousand." She laughs. "That ought to do it. And now you don't have to sit around for hours twisting caramels into their wrappers."

"What does ribbon cost?" I ask. "That might look festive."

"Maybe," Dylan says. "But not if it means the boxes don't stack well on top of each other."

"Oh, heck, I wouldn't have thought of that."

He gives me a quick smile. "This family has been selling food for four generations. Figuring this shit out is literally in our blood. What are we calling these, anyway? Grandpa is right. We do need a name."

"I'll get the whiteboard," May says, exiting the dining room with a spring in her step.

"Next you'll need to make up a promo batch," Audrey points out. "You'll want finished packages of caramels to show the retailers. They need to taste the product and see the packaging."

"But they need to figure out their pricing, first," Griff argues. "That's hard because there's so many choices. Should you do eight to a box? Or sixteen? Or a whole pound? I don't know where the price point should be."

"You need market research," May adds, setting the whiteboard on the sideboard.

"What if..." Audrey breaks off, deep in thought. "If it were my project, I'd take a few caramels down to Bud at the Country Store in Weston. He likes to talk about product development, and he has a thriving mail-order business."

"Would he be there on a Sunday?" Dylan asks. "We could go tomorrow."

My heart gives a happy kick.

"I'll email him," Audrey offers. "Let's see."

"That's a good plan," Griffin says. "You can't make caramels next Friday, anyway. We have the bonfire. And the cemetery service."

"Oh," Dylan says. And then he looks at his hands.

I'd forgotten about this, too. Every year the Shipleys gather to remember August Shipley's passing. This will be the sixth time. They visit the cemetery and then hold a bonfire in his memory.

"Dylan," Ruth says gently. "Please bring your fiddle home on Friday. I want to hear you play 'St. Anne's Reel.'"

He says nothing, his expression shuttered. All he does is lean over to pluck a piece of bacon off May's plate, then shove it in his mouth.

That's when Zach walks into the dining room. "Morning, guys!"

We all look up, and various greetings are called out. Everyone loves Zach. He's always in a good mood and always ready to work. This is the man I thought I killed by kissing him in the back of a car five years ago. But here he is, healthy as an ox, married to a smart, wonderful woman who loves him.

I'm so happy for him. But I'll always feel a little twinge of guilt when I see his face.

"Need breakfast?" Ruth asks him.

"Thanks, but I'm good. Who's taking the first shift with the horse wagon? Should I go down the road and get the team from Isaac?"

"Would you?" I say, rising from the table. "Then I'll drive first shift." Tourists love to be escorted around the property on a wagon pulled by Isaac's two workhorses.

"No problem!" he says cheerfully. "It will only cost you one of those caramels everyone is raving about."

"I'll cut some more of them this afternoon and bring you some."

"Dibs on the rest!" Grandpa shouts. "Age before beauty."

Then everyone starts talking at once. Except for Dylan, who picks up his coffee mug and gives me a smile.

And I feel meltier than a batch of caramel at two hundred forty-eight degrees.

TEN

Dylan

AT THE COUNTRY STORE, I don't know why I expected to do any of the talking. Although I think of Chastity as shy, she frequently surprises me.

Like now, for instance.

"What if we did a small box and a larger box?" she asks as Bud tastes another caramel. "And maybe each candy should be smaller than these."

"Yes to all that," he agrees. "They're pretty decadent, so you could go down to a square shape. Like so." He holds up his fingers.

"Or thinner?" Chastity counters. "They'd be easier to cut neatly."

"Sure. And if you put eight of them in a small box and then twenty-four in the large…" He sighs. "They're irresistible, young lady." I'm pretty sure he means both Chastity and the caramels. "This is a great product for the holidays. Your label should have red on it somewhere. It's a subtle hint, but people respond."

"Good tip," she says. "What retail price would you put on eight of these? If they were a little smaller."

"Let's weigh a couple and think about it," he says.

I know when I'm not needed, so I just stand back and let it all happen.

"You make 'em yourself, right?" Bud asks as he places four caramels on the scale where they weigh out cheeses.

"We do!" Chastity says. "In a state-licensed commercial kitchen, of course. From organic Vermont goat's milk and organic sugar. We'll do a fifty percent wholesale discount, or maybe fifty-five percent for larger orders. What do you think about five dollars for the small box?"

"That price is a little low, honey," he says. "Might wanna mark 'em up after you charm a few more geezers like me. I think you should say eight bucks."

"Yikes, really?" Chastity is all smiles.

"Really. This is a premium product, and it's just the kind of thing people expect to find in small shops like mine."

I chime in for the first time. "My brother would say eight. He leans into the luxury market, too."

"That's right," Bud agrees. "Griffin works his tuchus off for those ciders. And he prices them accordingly. Now is not the time for imposter's syndrome."

"I don't even know what that is," Chastity says.

He laughs. "Doesn't matter. Go make some more beautiful candy. When will I hear from you to place my order?"

"Two weeks?" I suggest. "We'll need to start delivering caramels by the second week of November. We don't want to miss the holiday buyers."

"Good deal, kids." He hands me a business card. "Nice doing business with a cute couple like you. I was young once."

"Thank you, sir," I say, declining to correct him. No sense in arguing with our new customer. I glance at Chastity right as her face flushes pink. "Have a great day."

"You too, son. Can't wait to order a few dozen boxes."

Chastity looks so happy she might explode. And we zip right out of that store before he can change his mind. I hold the door for Chastity, who practically dances out into the parking lot. Before we reach the truck, I hug-tackle her, scooping her up.

She squeaks as I whirl her around. "Dylan!"

"What? I'm excited." If my goats become an asset instead of a liability, that's awesome.

I set Chastity down on her feet again, and she turns to face me, chest heaving, eyes bright. I have the terrible urge to kiss her. I don't know what's gotten into me. Maybe I've had too much coffee, or maybe it's a whole weekend of celibacy. But she looks so fresh and pretty in the yellow autumn light. She's looking up at me with wide eyes.

Does she feel it too? Is temporary insanity contagious?

I take a quick step backward. "Great work in there."

"Thanks," she says turning to open the door of my truck.

I hop in on the other side and crank the engine. "Don't take this the wrong way, but that nice old man liked chatting with you. I think it helped."

"Well." She sniffs. "Good to know. And if any of these shops are run by women, you can flex for them when you hand over the box. Maybe leave a couple of buttons open on your flannel shirt."

I let out a startled bark of laughter. "Okay. Whatever it takes. You're a shark, Chastity."

"No kidding. I'm not the nice girl everyone thinks I am."

"You're very nice. What's wrong with nice?" I'm pretty nice myself.

She doesn't answer the question. "I only have two weeks to source all the packaging and come up with an order form. We still need a name and a design."

"I'll start sketching cute little goats." Honestly, I feel gleeful about this. "Do we need any extra equipment to scale up? Bigger pans?"

"No, just time."

Ah, the most precious resource. "I'll plan accordingly."

It's a hundred miles from Weston back to Moo U in Burlington, and the drive takes two and a half hours, because the roads in Vermont don't always go where you need them to.

Chastity reads her econ textbook in the passenger's seat. I'm glad one of us can make good use of the time.

It isn't easy being Chastity. She's trying to tackle college with only a GED. Everyone wants her to make it—especially Leah and Isaac. They never got a chance to go to college.

It's a lot of pressure. I'm familiar with pressure, and I'm not a fan.

This morning when Griffin and I were milking cows together, he told me a long story about why the price of winter feed keeps going up. I nodded and said "uh-huh" in all the right places, because I already know these details.

But I worry that Griffin is trying to lay the groundwork for shutting down the dairy. He already sold off our other herd when the lease on the land got too expensive. These days we only farm on our own land. But Griffin might be sick of cows. He's probably already done the math on how many more apple trees he could plant if we didn't need to graze cows.

I always thought I'd grow up to be a farmer like my dad and then my brother. I never even questioned it. But now I wonder if there's room for me in this scenario.

And he won't stop asking me to pick a major. If I pick something that requires me to go to graduate school, I think he'd put my cows on the block the next day.

But all this deep thinking is depressing me, so I turn up the radio and ponder another question—which restaurant should I take Kaitlyn to later? I shouldn't spend money on fancy dinners, but I deserve a little splurge once in a while. And it will keep the girlfriend happy.

My phone rings just as we reach the outskirts of Burlington. "Could you put that on speaker?" I ask Chastity.

"Sure." She grabs the phone out of the cupholder and answers the call.

"Hey man," Rickie says as I slow down for a traffic light. "Good weekend?"

"Totally."

"Got a minute?"

"What do you need?"

There's a beat of silence, and then Rickie says, "I saw Kaitlyn last night."

"Yeah?" That's nothing unusual. They travel in the same circles. I take my foot off the brake and follow the traffic through the light. "And?"

"I saw her liplocked to a lacrosse player."

Chastity takes a quick breath. But it honestly takes a moment for me to realize what he's saying. "Wait, what? She was with another guy?"

"Sad, but true," he confirms.

"Where was this?"

"A party. I was in the basement of the multicultural house, smoking a bowl."

Of course he was.

"And there she is, sitting on this guy's lap. No shame."

I feel sudden pressure in the center of my chest. I'd been wondering why I didn't get any calls or texts from her last night. And mine went unanswered. "What then? Do I even want to hear this part?"

"She left with him."

My heart starts to hammer. It's actually pretty hard to get me angry, but I swear my blood is already simmering. She was in my bed on Thursday night. And in someone else's by Saturday?

"Are you *sure* it was her?" Maybe Rickie was so baked he got it wrong.

His silence says, *Really, dude?*

"But didn't she see you sitting there?" I ask. I mean—it's one thing to cheat, but it's another to do that in front of your boyfriend's roommate.

"Didn't look like she was in the mood to be subtle."

My heart drops. "What the hell? I was gone for a *weekend*."

"Which she *hates*," he points out.

"You think that makes it okay?" My voice gets all high and weird, and anger squeezes my chest.

"Did I say that?" His voice is as calm as ever. Rickie never gets riled up about anything. It's part of his charm, and it makes us easy roommates. "Sorry to drop this on you. But I didn't know where you were headed today, and I thought you needed to know."

"Thanks," I grunt. "I'll be home in twenty minutes, anyway."

"I'll put the teapot on." Rickie ends the call.

"Dylan," Chastity says. "Turn here?"

"Fuck." I almost missed the turn toward her dorm, because I'm so stuck inside my head. I put on the blinker and change lanes so quickly that the guy behind me lays on the horn.

Chastity flinches. "Are you okay?"

"*Sure*," I thunder. "Never better. This is why I don't date, though. What is the fucking point?"

She clears her throat. "Why are you dating her, anyway?"

I snort. "You probably don't want to hear the answer to that question."

"You're right," she murmurs. "I probably don't."

All the happy, optimistic thoughts I'd been feeling today are just *gone*. Fucking Kaitlyn. Making me look like an idiot just because she got a little bored when I left town.

I pull up outside the dorm and put the truck in park. Kaitlyn might be in there right now. I could try to find a parking spot and ask her what the heck happened.

Or I could go home and save myself the fifty bucks it would have cost to take her out to dinner.

"Are you okay?" Chastity asks again.

That snaps me out of my own gloomy thoughts. "Yeah, I'll be fine. Good work this weekend, Chass. See you Wednesday for Algebra? I promise I won't leave you at the library again."

"Okay," she says softly. "It's a plan. I'm sorry about..." She looks wildly uncomfortable.

"Not your problem," I grumble. "Be well. Take good notes in algebra."

"Will do." I get a flash of a smile as she climbs out of the truck.

And then? I turn the truck around and navigate back to Rickie's gingerbread house on Spruce Street. For the first time in my life, I'm living in a place where the neighbors' houses are visible from the window, and I can walk all the places I need to go.

Don't tell my family, but I kind of love it.

I park my truck in the driveway. Rickie owns the house outright—he doesn't even have a mortgage. My rent money goes to taxes and utilities. He told me he bought the house with cash from a legal settlement, but he won't say why he was owed this windfall.

That's fine with me. Rickie can have his secrets. For modest monthly rent, I get one of the semi-dilapidated house's second-story bedrooms to myself, plus a place to park my truck. And Rickie is interesting company. That's probably the best part.

When I walk in through the back door, he's sitting at the kitchen table in a silk bathrobe. His ever-present teacup is in one hand, and his other holds a volume by Goethe. In German. He lifts his big eyes, peering at me from beneath his mop of hair. Rickie has the good looks of a European model who doesn't take good care of himself.

"Sorry, dude," he says. "You know I'm not her biggest fan, but I thought you should know."

"Of course I should know." Jesus. I don't need people to tiptoe around me. I'm not fragile like that.

I carry my duffel bag over to the counter and pull out some food that my mother sent home with me. Frozen chili and a ham casserole. She thinks I eat junk in Burlington.

She's right.

"Sit a minute," Rickie says after I close the freezer.

I hesitate. I shouldn't stew over Kaitlyn. I should run upstairs and write my econ paper.

But I pull out the chair opposite him anyway. Even though sitting "a minute" with Rickie often involves starting a seemingly trivial conversation and then glancing at the clock on the oven to find that it's four a.m.

The chair creaks when I sit down, because it's from 1953. Rickie collects mid-century furniture, but not the fancy stuff. The chair is an ugly metal number with a plastic cushion printed with daisies.

He carefully marks his place in the book and then closes it. "What are you going to do about her?"

"I'm going to call her out," I say immediately. "I can't just pretend it didn't happen."

Rickie gives me a sly smile. "You actually could."

"No, I can't. I held up my end of our bargain. I'm never exclusive with *anyone*. She knows this."

"She does," Rickie agrees. "That's why she demanded that in the first place."

"Just to bend me to her will."

"Yes. Now you're getting it." He smiles like this is fun. "But you didn't bend far enough. You deserted her on Friday night, so she punished you on Saturday."

And now I feel stabby. So it's probably a mistake to take out my phone and tap Kaitlyn's number, but I do it anyway.

She answers immediately. "Hey, you home?"

"Yep," I say, quietly seething. "Just sitting here, catching up with Rickie."

There's a silence on her end.

"Did you see him last night?" I ask. "At the multicultural house?" I don't even know where that is, come to think of it.

"I did happen to notice him at one point. Yes."

"Yeah," I say slowly. "Did you also happen to notice that you were hooking up with a guy who wasn't me?"

"Dylan." She sighs. "I was hoping you'd let this go."

"Would *you?*" I demand. "The only reason we're exclusive is because you wanted it that way."

"Yeah, but it was just a stupid night. I missed you, and I was bored. So I went out looking for trouble."

Trouble. It's a strange choice of words. Although I'm definitely troubled. "Well, I wouldn't do that to you."

"Really? Who did *you* spend your weekend with? Oh wait —Chastity."

Christ, not this again. "I didn't *fool around* with Chastity. Do you *get* that there's a difference?" My voice squeaks in anger.

"You want to, though! You can't keep your eyes off her."

"She's a *friend*, Kait. I'm not attracted to her. Stop putting words in my mouth just to make yourself feel better about this."

"Dylan," she says softly. "I didn't even let him fuck me. Let's not fight."

"We won't have to," I snap. "We're finished. I'll drop your stuff off at the dorm's front desk tomorrow."

I end the call just like that. Because there's nothing left to say.

Rickie sets down his teacup and gives me a slow clap. "Well done. Clean break. You know I never liked her."

"Yeah, but I did." I feel like punching Rickie right now. And for what? Cluing me in? None of this is his fault.

"What did you like about her?" he asks.

"What does it matter now? This is why I don't date."

He gives me a pitying look. The tea kettle whistles, and I get up to pour myself a cup. "Did you really take the stage at the poetry slam?" I ask suddenly. That would have been fun to watch.

"Yes and no. I was too stoned to make something up, so I read 'she being Brand' by e.e. Cummings. That guy was a fucking genius."

"I see what you did there." We both laugh, because that poem is a thinly veiled description of sex. It was definitely the most shocking thing ever assigned in my high school English class.

After refilling both our mugs with hot water, I sit back down at the table with a grumpy sigh. "She totally played me. How did I let this happen?"

"Oh, easy," Rickie says, blowing on his tea. "But you won't like hearing it."

Rickie is—shocker—majoring in psychology. And not just for fun. It's his true calling. I don't always enjoy his analyses of me. But they are rarely wrong.

"Okay, I'll bite. How did I walk into this mess?"

"You and Kaitlyn both need to be the one who's less in love. For you, it's just a convenience. You don't enjoy clingy feelings. But Kaitlyn needs the adoration. The imbalance feeds her. She got tired of being with someone who's unavailable."

"What are you talking about? I spent tons of time with her. Every weeknight."

"But you don't need her, and she knows it."

"What does that even mean?"

"Be honest—what was the best thing about Kaitlyn."

I close my eyes and picture her devilish smile. "She was fun. She had a lot of energy. She liked to party."

"On your cock." He smiles.

"Well, sure." Kaitlyn made no secret of her enthusiasm for sex. "But what's your point? I was good to her. And she treated me like shit."

Rickie just shakes his head. "You were good to her, because that's your default setting. But you didn't love her."

"I'm twenty years old. Not exactly eager to pick out wedding invitations."

"No kidding. But yet you can't admit to yourself that she's not your type—aside from the sexual compatibility. Which, given the loud rejoicing that frequently came from your bedroom, must have been on point." He leans back in his chair, like a grand duke in the palace.

"So? I shouldn't feel badly?"

"Nah." He grins. "The girl did you a favor. She freed you up to pursue the girl who really is your type."

"Sorry?" I don't think I had enough coffee today to follow this conversation.

"Chastity."

"What about her?"

"You have a thing for Chastity."

"Oh *fuck off*."

He makes a clicking sound with his tongue, the way you'd scold a golden retriever. "You're not usually so dense."

"I'm *not* dense."

"I know. It's one of the things I like most about you."

"Do we have any chips?" I ask suddenly. If I have to listen to all Rickie's theories about me, I might as well not starve.

"I haven't been to the store."

Shocker. I reach down and unzip the front of my backpack, pulling out half a dozen apples I grabbed out of a bushel basket on my way out today.

"Ooh, tasty. What are these?"

"Esopus Spitzenburg."

"Gesundheit." He laughs and grabs an apple. "You are attracted to Chastity, and it drove Kaitlyn bonkers."

"Chastity is a lovely girl," I point out. "But it doesn't give Kaitlyn a free pass to act like a nutter. Chastity and I are just friends."

He rolls his eyes. "We have two young women, both attractive to you. One of them you don't feel much for, but you'll bang her into next Tuesday. The other one you care for a great deal, but won't touch. One wonders why you're so unhappy."

"I *wasn't* unhappy!" I practically shout. "Everything was fine until Kaitlyn fucked it up."

"Tell me Chastity doesn't get you hot."

"She..." I struggle to figure out how to put it. "She isn't the kind of girl you can bang into next Tuesday. It doesn't matter if sometimes that seems like a fun idea."

He laughs. "Why not?"

"She's..." It isn't easy to explain. "Innocent. She grew up in this cult..."

"In Wyoming. I know. Old men porking teenage wives. But that doesn't make somebody innocent. That makes them unlucky."

"But she needs time to adjust," I point out. "There are so many things she doesn't know. And she's a good friend, so I wouldn't ever go there." I know I'm not making a whole lot of sense. But she's *Chastity*. I feel evil every time I notice her curves, or have the urge to taste her smile. That's not how friends are supposed to think about each other.

Rickie shakes his head, like I'm an amusing child. "Eventually, Chastity will learn all the things you don't want to teach her. She'll be hanging out in the basement of the multicultural house, and some lacrosse player will sidle up to her. 'Hey, honey. Love the low-cut top and the innocent smile. Let's dance. In my bed.'"

Well that's a horrible image. I might actually choke Rickie if this conversation continues. I grab a second apple, lift my backpack and walk out of the room.

ELEVEN

Chastity

I AVOID Kaitlyn after I get home on Sunday night. Not like it's hard. She spends her time locked in her room, listening to angry-sounding music.

But the next evening she disappears for several hours, and I try not to think about why. Maybe Dylan doesn't care that much that she cheated.

They're probably having makeup sex, which *Cosmo* insists is the best kind.

Anyway, I'm buried in homework. I thought things would start to feel easier, but the opposite is true. I'm only taking four classes, but the work keeps piling higher. Entire books to read between lectures. Quizzes. Essays.

It's hard to just stay afloat.

Then Wednesday afternoon approaches again. It's my algebra day with Dylan, but I haven't heard from my tutor.

"Did Dylan happen to call?" I ask Kaitlyn when she emerges to use our bathroom. She's probably left me another so-called note. This one might be penciled onto the bottom of my shoe.

"No, he didn't." She stops right in front of me, her eyes suddenly angry. "And thanks so much for rubbing my face in it, you little bitch."

My first reaction is to take a fast step backward. I lived too many years in a house where people slapped faces. Except this isn't the Paradise Ranch. And that's crazy talk even for Kaitlyn.

"What *is* your problem?" I demand.

"Don't pretend like you don't know! He dumped me, so thanks for that."

"What?" I yelp. "I didn't even know. And it has nothing to do with me." *But I'll bet he has his reasons. Like your cheating.*

"You know plenty that you don't let on," she says in a deadly whisper. "Maybe Dylan can't see through you, but I totally can. And —news flash—you'll never get what you want. He's never going to look at you the way he looks at me. He doesn't go for the whole 'poor girl next door' vibe that you're rocking. If he did, you'd already have him. So dream on and enjoy your little math classes. Because he's never going to be the numerator to your denominator."

She stomps away, leaving me blinking. And for once I don't have any trouble understanding a mathematical concept. Because it's all too clear that Kaitlyn sees deep inside my hungry little soul.

I could have avoided that whole conversation, because when I turn the corner to enter the reference section of the library, I spot Dylan in our usual spot. With his elbow on the table, playing with a curl of his hair, he looks deep in thought.

My heart swells a little as I take him in. His broad shoulders look a little resigned today. And as I approach, he looks up, showing me circles under his eyes.

"Hey, Chass," he says. "You're right on time." But he doesn't smile. "Sorry I didn't call to confirm. But…" He rubs a broad hand across his chin and fails to finish the sentence.

"Are you okay?" I ask, because I can't help myself. He doesn't look okay.

"Of course," he says. "It's just…" Another unfinished sentence.

I sit down beside him on our padded bench against the wall. I think of this as our spot. But now I realize that's ridiculous. Kaitlyn was right. I meddled. And for what? Now Dylan is sad.

"October is not my favorite month," he says finally. "And that damn bonfire is this weekend."

"And the service," I add quietly. "That's the part you actually hate, right?"

He props his chin in his hand. "Is it that obvious?"

"Anyone would hate it," I point out. "It's just sad."

"Yeah, I don't really get the whole 'celebration of life' thing. Especially on that day," he says. "There are three hundred and sixty-four other less awful days for it."

"See, that's one thing the cult got right," I say. "If you die there, you get one dreary funeral, and then that's it for you. No party. No annual reminders. There's no budget for that kind of sentiment."

He barks out a laugh. "No kidding? At least they got something right."

"How old were you when he died?" I ask. "Fourteen? Fifteen?"

"Fourteen. Freshman year of high school. Right in the middle of soccer season."

"Soccer?" I try to picture a fourteen-year-old Dylan in those tall socks they wear. "I didn't know you played soccer."

He shrugs. "I never played again. That was a lost year for me. We were all in shock."

"I can imagine," I say. Although my own father was fifty-nine when I was born, and he rarely said a word to me before he died when I was nine.

"It was me who found him," Dylan says quietly.

"You..." It takes me a moment to understand what he's saying. "The day he died?"

He nods, miserable. "In the tractor shed. I was supposed to be helping him that afternoon, but I came home late. Couldn't find him. Until I did."

"*Dylan.*" My heart contracts sharply. "I'm so sorry."

Again he shrugs. "Let's do some algebra, Chass. Do you have the homework assignment?"

"Um..." I dive into my bag and pull out the algebra book. "Yep. Sorry. One sec," I babble, pulling out a notebook and a pencil, too.

And now we're both sad.

On Saturday morning, there's frost on the grass as I hurry toward Dylan's house on Spruce Street. It's nine o'clock, and the cemetery service starts at ten thirty. Last night I emailed Dylan to ask if I could ride home with him. I made up some kind of excuse about babysitting for Leah so that she could go to the bonfire tonight.

But the truth is that Dylan dreads this day, and I want to be there for him. Even if he doesn't realize it.

His truck is still in the driveway when I arrive, so I haven't missed him. The house is quiet, though. Really quiet. I knock, and nobody comes to the door. And when I walk around to the kitchen door, nobody answers my knock there either, and the kitchen light is out.

I pound on the door again, and eventually I hear footsteps.

But when the door is yanked open, it's Rickie standing there with sleep hair, half naked in a silk bathrobe. "Chastity?" he croaks. "I didn't take you for a mean person."

"Sorry to wake you, but Dylan is supposed to leave now. Is he ready?"

"Uh…" Rickie looks upwards, as if the second floor could be seen through the ceiling. "You know, I think he overslept. I could—"

I don't let him finish that sentence. Because Dylan can*not* oversleep. Not today. I push past him and march up the stairs.

"Chastity?" Rickie calls after me. "Slow down, maybe? You might not want to go in there."

But I'm already turning the knob on his door. "Dylan?" I prompt as the door swings inward. It's dark in his room, so it doesn't sink in right away when I look at the lumpy bed.

There are two people under that comforter.

My lungs seize. And I just stand there like an idiot, staring, as Dylan sits up suddenly, the comforter falling away from his bare chest.

"Chastity," he rasps. "What is it? Something wrong?"

Is something wrong. Why yes, there is.

"It's Saturday," I yelp. "The service starts in less than ninety minutes."

"What service?" says someone else.

And I swear the girl's voice makes Dylan jump a foot. "Jesus Christ." He reaches over and snaps on the lamp. Apparently that doesn't make things better, because he peers at the person lying beside him. And then he puts both his hands in front of his eyes. "What the hell did I do last night?"

"Here's a clue," the girl's voice snaps. "You didn't do *me*. I thought you were going to be a good time, but then you passed out instead." She slides out of his bed, her hair a fright. She's wearing tiny little panties, but at least the top half of her is covered in a bright pink T-shirt.

"Sorry," Dylan mumbles into his palms.

"What. Ever." She plucks a pair of faded jeans off the floor and hops into them. "I heard you were fun, but I guess I heard wrong."

"Depends who you ask." He lifts the comforter but then drops it again quickly. "Whoops. No pants."

"False advertising," his guest says, stepping into her shoes. "At least the drinks were tasty. And your friend downstairs has good taste in music. If not roommates."

"Urgh," Dylan says. "I feel disgusting. I need a shower."

"You have five minutes," I growl, embarrassed enough for all of us.

"Okay. Yeah." He sighs.

And the worst part? Even though I'm so mad right now—no, I'm *crushed* that he found a stranger to (almost) take to bed, and he's a freaking wreck, with messy hair and probably crusty eyes and bad breath—I still ache for him.

He's so beautiful to me that it hurts to look at him.

So I don't. I turn around and get the heck out of there.

TWELVE

Dylan

WHEN I WALK down the stairs and into the kitchen, I think I'm dying. If not of my hangover, then I'm dying of embarrassment.

Chastity's face is a storm cloud when she whirls around to face me. "I made coffee."

My stomach lurches at the thought of coffee.

"And…" She opens the door to the microwave. There's a bag of popcorn in there, all popped and ready to go.

The smell of carbs and fake butter wafts across the kitchen. "I could kiss you right now," I say, and then think better of it. "Not that you'd want to kiss an asshole like me."

She turns away, sparing me the look of revulsion that's probably on her face. "Can you drive?" she asks in a clipped voice.

"Yeah." I don't feel drunk, just gruesome. I grab the popcorn bag and open the top, letting the steam out. Then I pour it into one of Rickie's plastic mixing bowls. "I need—"

Chastity is already ripping paper towels off the roll, anticipating my every need. "I also made you a water bottle. Do you have a travel mug for the coffee?" She spots it even before she finishes the sentence. "Get your violin, Dylan. We have to get out of here."

Moments later, I allow myself to be herded toward the door. The fiddle goes on the back seat, and Chastity arranges various beverages in the cup holders while I warm up the engine and shove popcorn into my mouth. My wet hair is dripping on my collar, but at least I'm clean and combed.

We don't speak for the first few miles. I feel squinty and half asleep. And so, so embarrassed. That girl in my bed? I don't remember her name. That's a new low for me. I like to party, and I like my hookups. But I'm not *that* big of an asshole—the kind who doesn't bother with names.

If Chastity hadn't been standing there, I would have apologized profusely to Pink Panties for my failure to put out. But I couldn't take the chance that she'd lash out with any more of last night's details.

The last thing I remember was Pink Panties leaning over me in bed, taking my cock into her mouth.

At that, I let out a groan. Because I can't believe I fell asleep in the middle of a perfectly good blowjob. What kind of loser does that?

"Do you feel sick?" Chastity asks me quietly.

"No, just embarrassed."

She's quiet for a second, and I imagine her judging me. But then I feel a tremor of laughter coming from the other side of the bench seat. She actually giggles and claps a hand over her mouth.

"What's so funny?" I ask as I accelerate past a hay truck.

"You," she gasps. "You actually jumped."

"What? Jumped where?"

"When I woke you up? And the girl started speaking? You startled like Jacquie when she sees a squirrel."

"Oh, hell no, I did *not*," I lie. Because goats are particularly funny when they're startled. And I'm a vain motherfucker sometimes.

"You totally did," she laughs. "Should we call her and ask her?"

"Oh, stop," I say, and I find myself smiling for the first time in days. I take a handful of popcorn from the bowl between us. "So I might have forgotten she was over there. Don't rub it in, okay? My reputation is probably gonna take a hit as it is."

"Poor baby," Chastity hiccups. "The long line of girls waiting for a turn in your bed is going to be whittled down to a manageable number."

I laugh, but the comment startles me. Chastity doesn't usually go there. She doesn't talk about my sexual exploits, although I shouldn't be too surprised that she's noticed them.

And she's still good to me anyway. She doesn't judge. "You're a good friend, Chass. Seriously. Thank you for dragging my ass out this morning, so I don't miss this thing I totally dread but shouldn't blow off."

"You're welcome," she says a little stiffly.

That's when I remember something. "Hey, is my coat within reach on the seat?"

She glances over her shoulder. "Sure, why?"

"There's something for you in the pocket. The left side."

"For *me*?"

"Don't sound so surprised. It's just a little thing. Grab it, okay?" I need to leave my hands at ten and two on the steering wheel. My head is still a little foggy, and I won't take chances with Chastity's safety.

God knows I'm willing to fuck up my own life from time to time. But not hers. She's had enough trouble with idiots already.

She unclips her seatbelt and stretches back between the headrests to grab my wool coat. I glance to my right to check her progress, and I can't help but notice the smooth skin of her belly where her sweater has ridden up and the way her hips are framed by her jeans.

And, yup, I may be sober now, but I'm still an asshole. Because friends do not stare at friends' stomachs, wondering if their skin is as soft as it looks.

Luckily, Chastity quickly flops back into her seat, holding the dainty little brown box in the center of her hand. "It's adorable. And it smells like chocolate."

"Put your seatbelt back on?" I prompt. "And then open it. Maybe it's a little early in the day for treats, but…"

"It's *never* too early in the day for treats!" she says, clipping her seatbelt and then pulling the ribbon on the little box. "Oh, wow. These are adorable. Great presentation."

"Show me." She holds the box closer to me, and I take a quick look. There are four little chocolates inside, anchored in individual paper cups. "Nice. I spotted them in the bookstore. It's toffee from a candymaker in Bennington. It's a treat, but it's also market research."

"Thank you," she says softly. Then she picks up a chocolate and studies it before taking a bite. "Umm! Wow." She lets out a little moan. "These are *magic*."

"Better than Rolos?" I ask.

"They're so good. You have to have one."

"But they're for you." I definitely have a thing for feeding her. I saw those little boxes on the counter and knew they were something she'd never buy for herself.

"Market research, Dyl. Here."

She reaches up and slips one into my mouth. Soft fingertips graze my lower lip. The chocolate begins to melt on my tongue, and then I bite down. The toffee breaks immediately, with a nice crunch.

"Wow."

"Right?" She closes the box. "I'm saving the other two for when we need a lift. Can I have a sip of your coffee?"

"Of course you can. You can have the whole thing, Chass. My coffee is your coffee." And my stomach can't handle it right now. Even the chocolate was a risk.

I step on the accelerator and push on toward the cemetery in Cole-bury, where my father is buried. Thanks to Chastity, I can almost make it on time.

That will have to be good enough.

I dread this day all year long, and yet it feels even worse than I even expected. Standing here in the carefully snipped grass, gazing down at the new chrysanthemums decorating dad's grave? It never gets easier. Six times we've done this. No—seven if we're counting the funeral.

My memories of the funeral are hazy. I remember the crowds of people standing around and all the hugs I was made to withstand. An itchy tag in the collar of my shirt. And the feeling that nothing would ever be right again.

The worst part about this ritual is my mom's tears. I can't handle them.

I mean—I do it anyway, standing here with a locked jaw as Father

Peters says nice things about Dad. But I can't concentrate, because the sound of her crying is like a knife through my chest.

It's my fault, too. My father died alone, because I wasn't home where I was supposed to be.

"Dylan," Chastity whispers. A soft hand brushes mine.

I snap out of my daze to the realization that I'm supposed to play the fiddle now. It's tucked under my arm, forgotten.

Quickly, I lift it to my shoulder. Everyone is looking my way. There's Griffin, standing with Audrey and their baby boy. May and her boyfriend, Alec. Isaac and Leah are here. Even my twin sister made the trek home for the weekend from Harkness College.

They're all expecting "St. Anne's Reel," the fiddle tune my father taught me when I was nine. It was our song. He worked out a harmony part, and we played it so many times that it's part of my soul now.

It took me a year to touch my violin after he died. And I still can't play our favorite songs.

Playing "St. Anne's Reel" right now would be like slicing open my chest with Griffin's pruning knife and carving out my heart in front of the whole family. So even though my bow lands on the A string, I start playing something else—a slower fiddle song called Planxty Irwin. It's a perfectly good song, but not one that I ever played with Dad.

I don't make eye contact with anyone. I just play the tune and let them wonder. They can think whatever they want to think. Every time I touch the fiddle I bleed a little inside.

Today the wound is a gusher. I grip the bow a little too tightly and play on, wishing I was somewhere else.

THIRTEEN

Chastity

THERE's nothing like a Shipley bonfire. Beforehand, Griffin stacks the wood in a giant metal trough that was once used for watering cattle. It makes a bright, oblong fire, with plenty of access for marshmallow roasting.

He lights it at sunset, when the yellow flames will stand out against the darkening sky. There are a series of logs and stumps ringing the fire, as well as a smattering of chairs and a bench or two.

The scent of woodsmoke fills the air, while Ruth Shipley and her other children set up a buffet table a little ways off.

And that table is *stacked* with food. I'm waiting in line with Leah, plate in my hand. Even from this distance I can see pulled pork and brisket sliders (a word I'd never heard until my first Shipley bonfire.) There are twice-baked potatoes. And coleslaw and cornbread and macaroni and cheese with bread crumbs toasted on top. And pickles and olives and carrot sticks and peppers with a creamy dip.

There's a carved ham, too. And if Audrey's feeling frisky, there might be spicy Indian lentils over cumin-scented rice, or fried pumpkin fritters.

Later will come the apple pies. Ruth's will have cranberry in them. Leah's have a crumb topping. I love them both so much that it's hard to choose. I might need a small slice of each one.

"Looks pretty great, doesn't it?" Leah asks, reading my mind.

"It looks amazing." And I mean that literally. The casual abundance is shocking to me. "Do you still have food dreams?" I ask her.

She turns to squint at me. "I'm not sure what you mean?"

"Oh." Now I feel ridiculous. "At the compound I used to dream about food. And it looked sort of like this—a table heaped with good things. I still have those dreams once in a while."

And, hey, there's a nice essay topic for composition class. I'm mining all my lowest moments for that class. I hope my crappy childhood is worth an A.

Leah puts an arm around my shoulder. "It's been a long time since I was hungry. Isaac used to sneak me extra food, anyway. I didn't have the same experience. And anyway, these days my big concern is keeping it down."

"Yikes."

"Yeah." She laughs. "Enough about me. How are your classes? Is Dylan still helping with the math?"

"He is," I tell her as my gaze flits toward him on the other side of the bonfire, where he stands with Isaac and Keith, his friend from high school and Burlington housemate. They're all holding instruments. Isaac plays the banjo, and Keith plays the guitar.

"What about the rest of your classes? How are they going?"

"It's... going," I say carefully. And this isn't what I really want to spend my Saturday night discussing.

"Do you need more help?" she worries. "You could ask the Dean for some official tutoring support."

"Maybe," I stall. "But that would take up time. And I'm already pressed for time. There's so much homework and so many pages of reading."

Dylan lifts his fiddle to his chin, and I'm saved from further conversation as Isaac begins to pluck at his banjo. The three of them launch into a fast, raucous tune. A party song.

Leah and I reach the front of the line, and I fill my plate to the sound of Dylan's playing and the crackle of the big fire. I load it up, taking care not to forget a napkin or a fork.

All the seats around the fire are already taken, but I don't mind standing so long as I can hear the music.

Dylan looks happier now. This isn't the grim Dylan who played beside his father's grave earlier today. He looks loose and cheerful. It may have something to do with the weed I smelled earlier, wafting from the backside of the cider house. Or the beer in the keg that Keith hid in the blackberry bushes by the chicken coop.

Everyone is watching them play, including a row of local girls seated on a long log by the fire. They all have plates on their knees and adoring smiles on their faces. *The swarm* is how I'm used to thinking of them.

I still feel guilty for contributing to his blowup with Kaitlyn. Then again, there are always more Kaitlyns. They're drawn to him like the moths that are already flitting too near the bonfire.

Dylan and his merry crew bring a song to a raucous conclusion. Isaac lets out a whoop when it's over, his dark eyes sparkling over his bushy beard.

"More!" hollers one of the girls on the log.

"Time for eats," Keith says. "But maybe later, hot stuff."

"Why don't you two play gigs in Burlington?" asks Debbie.

She's the girl who used to show up most frequently in the passenger seat of Dylan's truck. And the backseat, too, according to the whispered gossip I used to hear.

"You could make a pile of easy cash," she says. "Anyone would hire you guys for their wedding entertainment."

This had never occurred to me, but now I realize she's absolutely right. Dylan doesn't need to make caramels. He could be making piles of money just playing that fiddle.

"Are you *kidding?*" Dylan yelps. "First of all, you have to hustle for every job, because wedding customers don't repeat. And then you're responsible for the most important day in someone's whole—" He checks his language. "—flipping *life?* Does that sound like a good job to you?"

"I would if I could play like you," Debbie insists.

"Nah," says Daphne Shipley. "That's too many details for Dylan. Too much responsibility."

Dylan shrugs like his sister's comment doesn't bother him. But I wonder if it does. He tucks his fiddle under his arm and follows Keith toward the food table.

"Dude, Debbie is right," Keith says. "What if I got us a gig or two? Please?"

"Sure, man," Dylan says absently. "Just not weddings."

"Dylan is allergic to weddings!" Debbie calls out, and all the other girls laugh.

It takes a long time for Griffin's fire to burn down to coals.

The party rolls on, although the partygoers are spread out. There are lights on in the cider house, where Zachariah has poured some samples and where Griffin cons some of his friends into taking a turn at the presses. I can hear the crank of the apple-washing machine from here.

In a little while, they'll come out and light some fireworks in honor of Mr. Shipley.

Meanwhile, I have a marshmallow on the end of a stick, and I'm toasting it slowly. I like them brown but not blackened, and it takes a while.

It also happens that this spot is conducive to some excellent eavesdropping. I've learned that Debbie hates her job at the hair salon and is reconsidering her decision to go to beauty school next year. And that she's so *over* Billie Eilish, whoever that is.

"So, did you hear about Dylan?" one of the girls asks. "He broke up with that piranha he was dating."

I feign great interest in my marshmallow and move a half step closer.

"Yep. I did hear that," Debbie says. "Supposedly she cheated on him. As if that makes any sense."

"I know, right?" her friend says with a laugh. "Maybe he cheated first?"

"That boy has a short, little attention span," Debbie mutters.

"True story. But he stayed interested in you for a while. Are you going to hit tonight? One last fun time?"

"Who says it would be the last time?" Debbie smirks. "That boy will be single forever. Nobody is surprised that the girlfriend lasted a hot second."

The other girls snicker.

"There won't be any fun with Dylan for me tonight, though," she says. "I have to get the car back before my brother gets home and sees that it's gone. But you guys gave me an evil idea."

"Really? How evil?"

She slowly removes a perfectly toasted marshmallow from her stick and then smiles. "I'm out of here. But just watch, because Dylan's gonna disappear for a while and then come back looking... less satisfied than he expected."

The girls let out a hoot. "Bitch!"

"Burn!"

"It's just payback," she insists. "The boy turned me down last month because of what's-her-name—the cheater. Now he'll realize that was a mistake."

Leaving her friends to giggle and gossip, she carries the perfect marshmallow over to where Dylan and Keith are seated on a log. She leans over Dylan and says something I can't hear.

As I watch, he opens his mouth, and she tucks that marshmallow inside. He chews, and I'm not imagining the sloppy smile on his face. Debbie leans over and whispers something in his ear. She cups his chin, giving it a stroke, and then abruptly stands up and walks away, her walk all hips and a hair toss, too.

"Oh, this could be *good*," her friend says beside me.

Debbie leaves the fire pit, stopping to chat a moment with another acquaintance. But then? She moseys past the cider house. I lose her in the shadows for a moment, but catch the sheen of her hair again as she heads for the bunkhouse, which is quiet and dark tonight.

She doesn't go inside. She walks around to the back, instead. A few moments later, she emerges on the far side. She walks quickly toward the long row of cars in the Shipley driveway, ducking onto the far side of them. Then she hoofs it down the drive, maybe toward her own car somewhere out on the road.

And that's it. She doesn't return.

I keep my eye on Dylan after that. He has glassy eyes and a wobbly smile, thanks to the flask he and Keith have been passing back and forth.

A moment later he checks his watch, subtly. But it's enough to make the girls cackle.

I pluck my marshmallow off the stick and eat it. I clean off the stick and prop it up against the empty food table. But all the time I'm watching Dylan.

After a few more minutes, he stands up, placing a hand on Keith's head, saying... I have no idea what he might be saying. *Goodnight.* Or, *I have to check on something.* Or, *I'll be back in twenty after Debbie blows me.* I don't know how casual sex works.

Either way, he stands up. Casually, he plucks a few empty cups off the ground and carries them over to a recycling bin his mother thoughtfully left nearby. Then he walks—his hands in his pockets—slowly toward the bunkhouse.

I can tell even from this distance that he's been drinking. He doesn't stagger. Just the opposite—he's taking too much care with his gait.

Retracing Debbie's steps, he steers around the bunkhouse, heading for the dark place behind it, where there's just a strip of grass before the tree line closes in.

Dylan does not emerge a minute later on the other side. He's disappeared.

And now the girls on the log are doubled over in laughter. "How long do you think he'll wait?"

My face heats up in sympathetic embarrassment. I don't *believe* this. These girls count themselves as Dylan's friends? Is that how friends behave? They enjoy your hospitality and then laugh behind your back? My pulse pounds in my throat.

Somebody's got to tell him, and I guess that somebody is me. So I stand up slowly, slipping away from the fire. I'm used to being invisible, and nobody is watching me as I become the third person to walk toward the forest's edge. I take a different route through the shadows of the cider house, out of sight from those girls.

I cut across the pitch-black lawn toward the back of the bunkhouse. It's *really* dark back here, and I feel a little skittish sneaking around near the tree line. Some horror movies begin like this.

At first I can't guess where Dylan might be waiting, but then I notice that the door to the outdoor shower is ajar. And as my eyes grow more accustomed to the dim light, I spot Dylan's Chuck Taylors under the saloon-style wall. He's whistling softly, a stray melody from one of the fiddle tunes he played earlier.

The sound is so very *Dylan*. It's patient, maybe a little lazy, but still cheerful and fun. Suddenly, there's nothing creepy about this moment. I pace toward the open door where the grass gives way to a bed of pebbles.

The crunch of those pebbles announces my presence. I'm just about to say something when the whistling breaks off. Two hands reach from the open door, seize my hips, and pull me inside. I let out a gasp of surprise as my back hits the wooden planks. Then Dylan's mouth descends toward my open one.

Oh! My gaze locks with his.

His eyes widen immediately, but it's too late. The kiss is like jumping off the Quechee bridge into the river. Once your feet leave the edge, you're going into the water whether you've come to your senses or not.

And so we jump. Together.

Dylan's firm lips collide sweetly with mine. I taste toasted marshmallows and whiskey as our breath mingles. My reaction is swift and fierce; my hands grip his shirt, and my tongue melts against his.

He makes an eager grunt, and I feel it rumble through my chest. His lips press and kiss, and then they do it again.

Dylan Shipley is kissing me. *Really* kissing me. His tongue strokes mine, and his body presses me against the wall.

My knees are Jell-O, and I don't ever need to breathe again. I'll just stay right here, thanks, while Dylan takes second and third helpings of my eager mouth.

Everything is total bliss for at least thirty seconds, until a loud *pop* startles us both.

Dylan jerks back, as if it were the firing squad coming for him. A half-second later, I recognize the sound as the first firework splitting the night sky. But the damage is done. Dylan takes a staggered step backward, chest heaving. He lifts the back of his hand to his mouth, as if sealing it off.

"Sorry," I say as a reflex. And then I immediately want to kick myself. Because I am *so* not sorry.

"No!" he stammers. "I..." He takes another step back. And another firework pops into the sky. "Shit. *I'm* sorry. That was—" He drops his hand and stares at me. "I thought Debbie was coming back here." Even as those awful words fall out of his mouth, he flinches. "I'm really drunk right now. Really. A lot. I don't know what I'm doing."

"Okay," I croak, my heart breaking. "Don't worry about it. I came back here to tell you that Debbie wasn't coming. She went home."

"Really?" He reaches out a hand, finding the stone wall of the bunkhouse. He leans against it, as if propping himself up. "She *punked* me? I shoulda seen that coming." Then he drops his heavy head and laughs. "Fuck me. I'm such a wreck."

I would happily fuck you, I think as another firework explodes. Dylan looks up at the sky. "Hey, Dad! We're lighting a bunch of shit on fire for you! How about that? I'm sorry I wasn't in the goddamn tractor shed when I said I would be. But have some fireworks instead."

"Dylan," I gasp.

"What? I can't tell the truth? On the day he died, he wanted my help taking a tire off the tractor. I didn't show up. Then he died."

"It's just a tire," I say. "He would have forgiven you."

He leans heavily against the stone wall, his chin tilted up toward the night sky. "You know how much a tractor tire weighs? Four hundred pounds. He wrestled it off himself. Somehow he got it off and leaned it against the wall. And then he had a massive, fatal heart attack on the ground next to it."

My next breath is a sob. "*Dylan.*" I try to say his name, but my voice cracks, and I swallow hard.

"I'm shit company tonight," he grinds out. "Total shit. I'm sorry."

And before I can think of what to say, he stomps past me and out into the night. The door wobbles on its hinges after him.

Another firework goes off over my head, and I blink tears from my eyes.

FOURTEEN

Freshman Composition

Section Four

Title: Heat and Patience
Author: Chastity Campbell

A FRIEND and I have a small business together making goat's milk caramels. A very small business. He has a surplus of goat's milk to use up, and after doing a bit of research I decided that anyone can make caramels.

A few YouTube videos later, I had a recipe I was ready to try.

There's very little to it. These are the ingredients: goat's milk, sugar, vanilla, heat, and patience. Also stirring. So much stirring.

Stirring constantly, you heat everything to an average temperature of 248 degrees. Then you pour it out onto a buttered pan and chill it overnight. You can add a topping—sea salt or finely chopped nuts. But that's optional.

The only thing you can't mess up is the temperature. If you heat it to less than 248, your caramels will be too soft to cut into squares. If you heat it too hot, your caramel will cool into something so hard it will pull out your teeth.

But here's the tricky part—you can't tell by looking at the caramel if the temperature is right. Precision matters, but the thermometer is your only guide.

It only took us one batch to get it right. That makes us experts in the simple art of caramel making.

But here's one complication I didn't anticipate: I'm in love with my business partner. I can't tell him, because he doesn't date, and he says he doesn't believe in love.

Except sometimes I think he does. I'll catch him looking at me with a funny smile on his face. And I wonder what love looks like if not like standing around in the kitchen on a Friday night, stirring caramel and making silly jokes.

But I don't say a word. There's no gauge for this. No rule of thumb. I have plenty of "heat," and lord knows I have patience. But if I pour my heart out in front of him, it would probably come to nothing.

FIFTEEN

Dylan

ON SUNDAY MORNING I wake up with a splitting headache and the knowledge that I'm a goddamn moron.

I can't believe I kissed Chastity. I mean—it was an honest mistake at first. But then I just went for it. I was drunk and horny and very willing to make bad choices.

Not with her, though. Never with her. She deserves so much more than a wasted guy pushing her up against the wall of an outdoor shower.

I don't even get a chance to apologize. Leah drives her back to Burlington on Monday morning, because she was heading into the city for a doctor's appointment.

Wednesday is our algebra day, though. So at least there's that.

On Wednesday afternoon I'm buying a treat for Chastity at the bookstore—this time it's a tiny box of two truffles from Lake Champlain Chocolates—when Rickie texts me. *Chastity just called the house. She doesn't need tutoring today.*

Wait, what? That's patently untrue. It's going to take all we've got to get her through this class. That's not mean; that's just the truth.

Is she okay? I text back.

She sounded fine, he replies. *Coffee shop with me instead?*

Sure. Why not.

If I don't have to coach Chastity in algebra, I might as well have cookies and gossip with Rickie.

The guy at the counter is waiting for me to hand over four dollars for the truffles in their tiny box. I give him the money and zip the box into a pocket of my book bag. I'm going to see Chastity soon, right?

I sure hope so. I hope I haven't screwed up a really great friendship.

These are my thoughts as I walk to the coffee shop. I pull open the door and scan the room, looking for Rickie. He's not here yet, and the good velvet sofa is taken by a couple of girls.

My gaze snags on a shiny head of hair bent over something on the coffee table. And I realize that the good velvet sofa has been taken by Chastity, of all people.

She doesn't look up as I walk past on my way to the coffee line. She's deep in conversation with another girl. This one is really young-looking, with braces and a girlish smile.

"That's it!" Chastity's friend exclaims. "Now reduce that fraction and you'll have it done."

I stiffen. They're doing algebra. Without me.

The coffee line moves forward, and I stew on this while the barista makes change for my ten-dollar bill. I've been *replaced*. That's what happens when you act like an asshole, I guess.

I don't like it.

"Hey, little dinosaur. Why the long face?"

Rickie has appeared beside me. I don't know how I missed him before. He's wearing studded motorcycle boots, cut-up jeans and a bonkers red velvet jacket over his black T-shirt. "Hey. Nice jacket. But I think you'd clash with the purple velvet couch."

"We can't have it anyway." He snickers, tilting his head towards Chastity. "Your girl is cheating on you."

"Ouch, man. That's a theme with me, I guess."

"I'm *kidding*. But why would she do that? It makes no fucking sense. Is she still upset about finding that strange girl in your bed? That *was* kind of ugly."

"Nah." Funny thing is, I'd already forgotten about that. And Chastity had seemed to shrug it off. "The problem is I got sloshed Saturday night, too. That's when I did the real damage."

"Uh-oh." Rickie flinches. "What happened?"

I've spent the week trying not to replay it in my head. "I accidentally kissed her."

"Accidentally?" Rickie's eyes narrow. "How does that work, exactly?"

I have to admit it's a good question. "First you get skunk-drunk. Then you let your ex-hookup trick you into thinking you're getting a blowjob behind the bunkhouse."

Rickie laughs. "I've got to see this orchard someday."

"You have a standing invitation." Rickie has never taken me up on my offer of a weekend in Tuxbury. He doesn't like to sleep anywhere except for his own bed.

"Finish the story," he prompts.

"Well..." The trouble is that I can't really understand how it happened. I grabbed Chastity, pushed her up against the wall like she was any hookup. That part was a misunderstanding. It's just that I didn't stop there. The moment my hands landed on her body, I knew who she was. And then I kissed her anyway. Several times. I just didn't want to stop. "There's no good explanation," I admit as the barista hands me my coffee. "Except to point out that I was drunk, sad, and looking for trouble."

"How much *trouble* did you get into?" Rickie asks. There's an irritating smile playing on his lips.

"It was just a few sloppy kisses," I grumble. "Then I came to my senses." Sort of. It literally took an explosion to wake me up from the madness.

Rickie's gaze flits over to Chastity on the sofa. "But what did you do *afterward*? If she's mad at you, I'd start there."

"I apologized."

"How?" he asks, retrieving his own cup of coffee from the counter.

"I don't really remember," I admit. "Haltingly. Like the bumbling fool that I am."

He flinches. "And what did she say?"

"Nothing. She just sort of stared at me like I'd suddenly grown a really bad handlebar mustache. And then I yelled at the sky like a sad sack and wandered off."

Rickie holds my eyes as he takes a sip of his coffee. "She's either mad that you kissed her, or mad that you stopped. My money is on door number two."

"What? No. Who'd want a slobbering-idiot kiss?"

"Well, I would." His grin widens. "So long as it's from the *right* slobbering idiot. Why did you stop, anyway? I practically get a contact high off your sexual tension."

"That's just the dope you're smoking," I mutter. The last thing Chastity needs is a visit from my overeager libido.

But I can't help glancing over at her. She's bent over her notebook, penciling in another equation on the page. Then she taps her eraser on the paper and shows it to her friend.

"There you go!" says the girl with the frizzy hair.

Chastity's smile is so bright that for a second I forget how to breathe.

"Hmm." Rickie says beside me. "Interesting."

"What is?"

"You, that's what. Are you going to talk to her?"

"Of course I am. I'm going to apologize again. When you're a dick to your friends, that's what you do. Besides, I have a present for her."

"Is it your dick?" Rickie asks with a snicker.

"No, asshole."

He shakes his head. "Too bad. I'm going to score us a table. At a safe distance."

"You do that."

SIXTEEN

Chastity

"I DON'T KNOW, CHASTITY," my new friend says as I start on problem number seven. "You might not be as bad at algebra as you think. I barely even helped you."

"No, you did," I insist as I solve the last problem. "My brain just doesn't bend this way. I need to be shown what to do." Sometimes three or four times.

But at least this assignment is under control. I'll survive one more week of algebra, thanks to Ellie.

A couple hours ago I'd been sitting at a computer terminal in the library, where I submitted my composition.

I'd checked my email and found a message from Dylan.

Hi C! Are we on for algebra today? If I don't hear from you I'll head for the library.
I promise to be 100% sober. I'm sorry I was so out of line this weekend. That was completely inappropriate. It won't happen again.
-Love, D.

A perfectly nice email, but it had crushed me anyway. *It won't happen again.* Did he have to make that point so loudly? Like I don't already know that?

I'm ashamed to admit that I'd felt a little teary right there in front of a borrowed Macintosh computer. I'd grabbed a paper napkin out of my backpack to dab at my eyes.

"Are you okay?"

I'd looked up to see Ellie watching me carefully from the next terminal. "Yes," I'd croaked. "I'm fine"

"You don't look all that fine."

"True," I'd admitted. "But it isn't as bad as it looks." I've never been one to complain.

"If you say so. Turning in the composition?"

"Just did."

"Same. My computer is in the shop getting the keyboard replaced." She'd let out a sigh. "It's the second time my letter E got stuck."

"Oh, I bet that's annoying." Not that I'd know. "I'm still saving up for one."

"Jesus lord, I'd die." She'd laughed. "Okay, fine. I wouldn't die. A stuck E key is a first-world problem. But I'm used to my creature comforts. I'm Ellie, by the way."

"I know. Chastity," I'd said quickly. "That's, uh, my name."

God could I *be* any more awkward?

"Do you want to get a hot chocolate after this? It might cheer you up."

I'd almost said no. I couldn't afford to buy overpriced hot chocolate at the coffee shop. But talking to Ellie was the best distraction I'd had all week. "I want to. But I'm supposed to meet my algebra tutor later."

"Which one?" she'd asked, brightening up. "I tutor math in the lab on Saturdays and Sundays."

"Really?" I knew there was a tutoring lab, but I'd never been there. Because I have Dylan. "How much do you cost?"

"Well." She'd crossed her arms. "It's one problem set? In which course?"

"Math 101."

"Well, shoot. That will cost you a hot chocolate."

I'd taken her up on it immediately. And then—because I avoid confrontation at all costs—I'd called the house on Spruce Street, knowing Dylan wouldn't be there. It had worked like a charm. Rickie had said, "No problem, hon. I'll text him."

So here I sit in the lap of velvet sofa luxury with my new friend Ellie. I'm seven dollars poorer than I was before, but both the peppermint tea I bought for myself (the cheapest thing on the menu) and the company have cheered me up.

"So why were you having a bad day, anyway?" Ellie asks. "Man trouble?"

"Not exactly. It's more like a lack of man trouble. I kissed my hot algebra tutor. And I wasn't supposed to."

Her big eyes widen. "Which hot algebra tutor? You never said."

"He doesn't work at the lab," I say hastily. "He's a friend. And he wants to stay that way."

"Oh." She looks deflated. "That is a bummer."

"Do you have a boyfriend?"

"No." She makes a face. "It would be nice, though. This year is kind of lonely. My roommate is a total bitch."

"Oh, I have one of those, too."

"Yeah?" Ellie's eyes brighten. "Does yours steal your clothes and then lie about it?"

"Um, no. She wouldn't want any of my things. We have singles, anyway. Just a common bathroom."

"Lucky! She must be easier to stand, then."

"You'd think." I take a gulp of mint tea.

"My roommate took my brand-new scarf. With the tags still on! And when I called her out on it, she tried to gaslight me."

"Gaslight?" I feel my cheeks flush like they sometimes do when I don't understand the idioms that people use.

"You don't know *Gaslight*? It's a movie from the forties."

"Ingrid Bergman," says Dylan's voice. "We haven't got around to the classics yet."

I startle, sloshing my tea over my hand. And when I look up, Dylan is *right* there. Clear brown eyes. Tousled hair. Tight, muscular body that's clothed in a nice sweater and ripped jeans. A handsome face that I finally kissed.

Pain slices through me. Because I'm never going to get over him.

There will never be a day when I look at Dylan and don't wish for more.

"Can I talk to you for a quick second?" he asks, taking the mug and grabbing a napkin off the table. He wipes the tea off my hand.

"Now is not a good time," I say quickly. Because I don't want to cry in the coffee shop in front of my only new friend.

Dylan actually rolls his eyes. "Fifteen seconds, Chass. Give a man a break."

"*I'd* talk to you." Ellie raises her hand like a school girl. "Pick me."

And that's just what I need—another girl in my life who's swooning for Dylan. Because that always turns out well.

"Fine. Fifteen seconds." I jump to my feet. Let's get this over with.

Dylan takes my arm and tows me gently over toward the bulletin board, where nobody is currently reading the flyers for meditation circles and ski equipment sales.

"Look, I'm sorry," is his opener. "You're avoiding me. Not that I blame you. I'm sorry things got so out of control."

"Which things?" I ask warily. Because I don't want an apology for fooling around with me.

"Pick one!" Dylan raises his hands. "All the things. I shouldn't have been so inappropriate."

"But..." I know Dylan was in a serious state of drunken depression when he kissed me. It's not like I was expecting to hear those kisses made him as happy as they made me. But would it kill him to be a little less patronizing? "Dylan, I'm not twelve years old. It was just a kiss or two. I don't think I'll need a full course of therapy to recover."

He blinks. "Okay. Good?"

"So did you really need to drag me over here to apologize a third time? Did you apologize to all the girls you kissed during Spin the Bottle in seventh grade?"

I heard about Spin the Bottle and Seven Minutes in Heaven only last year, by eavesdropping on Debbie and her buddies at another bonfire. I'd been transfixed by their tales of who'd kissed whom over the years and how often.

At thirteen, Spin the Bottle would have sounded like heaven to me. Seven minutes in a closet with a boy? I would have lobbied for eight. I was always the most *inappropriate* girl in the bunch.

Yet somehow Dylan sees me as some kind of innocent child.

"No. Good point." He crosses his delicious arms and smiles at me. "You are in a feisty mood today."

"Is that so wrong?"

"No." He shakes his handsome head. "Not at all. Are we going to hug it out?" He opens his big arms wide.

Oh boy. I can't resist stepping into them. And when he pulls me in, I experience the familiar hormone rush that always happens when I'm close to him. Rapid heartbeat? Check. Goosebumps? Check. My nose lands against his flannel shirt.

My mouth is mere inches from his, of course. But this time he has no interest in kissing me. It takes all my willpower to give him a squeeze and then step back.

"Be well, Chass. I'll leave you to your tutoring session, even if you're basically cheating on me right now. But we're still making caramels this weekend, right? I told Griffin we could use six gallons of goat's milk. Don't make a liar out of me."

"I won't," I say quickly. I might be slightly irritated at him, but it will blow over. My capacity to forgive him for not loving me back is basically infinite. "We'll leave right after Friday classes?"

"You got it. And this is for you. Share it with your friend." He pulls something out of his pocket. "More market research."

He puts a little box in my hand and then walks away.

As always, it takes me a second to get over my hormone rush. I stand there blinking for a long moment until I realize Ellie is grinning at me from the sofa. So I go back over to her and sit down.

"Wow..." she says, stealing a glance at Dylan's retreating back-side. "Is that hot hunk of Vermont male your algebra tutor?"

"Yes." My voice is gravel.

"And your future ex-boyfriend?"

"Nope. I'll never get that chance. He's my best friend, but..." There's no tidy explanation.

"But you want more. I would if it were me."

I nod, miserable.

"How deep in the friend zone are you?" she asks.

"What?"

"The friend zone. Does he flirt with you? Because that might be a good sign. Or are you so far into the friend zone that he farts on you for sport?"

"Ew." I shudder. "Not that last thing. But he'd never flirt with me. He only dates shiny girls. You know—slick girls with good clothes and the right makeup."

"Ah," says Ellie knowingly. "I'll bet it's not their clothes. It's probably the confidence."

"Probably," I admit. Dylan doesn't care very much about money and bling. But confidence is just as unattainable to me as money. "I think he likes sophistication."

Ellie squints. "He *is* a farm boy, right? The work boots are a tell."

"Sure."

"Then he's looking for excitement that he doesn't think he can get at home. Vermont girls need not apply."

God, I suppose she's right. Maybe it's not personal. But that doesn't make it easier. "I just wish I could shut it off. I want to stop caring."

"Or you could just tell him how you feel?"

"No!" I recoil in horror. "That's never happening."

"Too embarrassing?" Ellie tucks a frizzy bit of hair behind her ear.

At first I nod. But then I shake my head. "Embarrassment stinks, but it's not the end of the world." And I've been embarrassed a million times. "I don't want to lose him. If he pities me, or if I make it awkward, he'll back away. It's just not worth it."

"I get it." She gives me a sad smile. "He brought you a present?"

"Yeah." I look down at the box in my hand and tug on the ribbon. "We have this project where we're making candies to sell at Christmastime. So he keeps buying examples for market research." I open the box and find two perfect chocolates inside.

"Fancy," Ellie says. "No hot guy ever bought me chocolates. At least you've got that."

I offer her the box. "There's one for each of us."

"Really?"

"Sure." I take one and then encourage her to do the same.

The chocolate bursts against my tongue. It's filled with a soft, almost liquid caramel. It's delicious.

But all I really want is more of Dylan's kisses.

SEVENTEEN

Dylan

THE WEEKEND HAD BEEN sunny and bright, with a cool yellow sun warming the farm. Chastity and I had made up our big batch of samples. And I put in a lot of face time with the animals and my brother. In that order.

Having survived the anniversary of my father's death made me more cheerful and less responsive to Griffin's questions and prodding. I mostly tuned him out, even when he suggested I become a veterinarian because "the vet bill is killing us."

I told him I'd consider it, just to see what he'd say.

"It's a lot of extra years in school, though," was his response. I could almost hear him adding up the tuition bills in his head.

I don't know what that man wants from me. I really don't. He spent four years at Boston University. And how many of Dad's cows had he milked on the weekends? Zero.

But now it's Sunday evening, and Griffin is many miles in my rearview mirror. Chastity and I have spent the last six hours dropping off our caramel samples. As we approach Burlington again, ominous gray clouds roll in off Lake Champlain, and the sky is darkening in a hurry.

"The wind is really picking up," Chastity says from the passenger's seat.

"Sure is." The trees are swaying on either side of the highway. Vermont is the kind of place where nature frequently reminds you that she's the one in charge. "Griff said something about a storm." But I hadn't really been listening.

"Good thing we're almost home."

"Yeah. Just one more shop, right? And then one tomorrow? What time is that?"

"Nine thirty," Chastity says.

She's definitely the business manager, while I'm the chauffeur. I like my job, though. I've got Post Malone playing on the radio as I pull into the last stop on our agenda today—Rockie's Gourmet in Williston, Vermont.

"How many boxes shall we give them?" Chastity asks as I shut off the engine.

"One," I say firmly. "That leaves two for tomorrow, and a single box for us. We would have even more, but you let that guy in Montpelier talk you out of an extra."

"He has two stores!" Chastity cries. "It was good for business."

"Two stores, my ass," I argue, teasing her. "He gobbled them down the second we left that place."

She laughs, and I won't deny that the sound of it fills in some of the hollow places in my chest. I've been so worried. I thought I'd wrecked our friendship.

But maybe we'll be okay. It probably helped that I was the world's most eager caramel maker this weekend. I did at least my half of the labor on Friday night. I stirred for hours. I scrubbed pots. I played music and made jokes and watched the candy thermometer as closely as you'd monitor a nuclear reactor.

Chastity seems happy with our progress. Yesterday we boxed all the caramels and stashed them in my truck, and today we drove all over hell dropping off our samples and chatting up store owners.

Griffin and Leah had primed the pump ahead of time, letting some of the store owners know that we were coming. Even so, the reception of our sample boxes was warmer than I'd hoped.

In other parts of the world, Sunday might be a strange day for doing business. But Vermont shops and restaurants are busy on the weekends and often close on Monday when the tourists go home.

That's what it's like to own a family business. You're never off the clock. My family knows all about it.

Now I grab a box of caramels off the backseat and follow Chastity into the last shop of the day. After almost two dozen sales calls, we're good at this now. She spots the manager—the gray hair at his temples probably gave him away—and by the time I've caught up to her, she's already deep in conversation with him about caramels.

"…hand-made and hand-cut in our commercial kitchen in Tuxbury," she tells him. "From organic ingredients."

"Now the taste test," I say, handing over the box. "That's for you. This is our big box, but we're also making a small one, too, for impulse purchases at the cash register."

"Don't mind if I do," the manager says, opening the box. "Cute label."

"Thanks!" Chastity says. "This guy designed it." She hooks her thumb toward me.

I did a great job, too, if I do say so myself. We'd settled on the name *Nannygoat's Candies*. I'd drawn a portrait of a floppy-eared goat with her face turned toward the viewer. And the font is blocky and subtly vintage. It's very hipster.

The older man bites into a caramel, and his eyes light up. "Wow, kids." He chews. "You can bring me samples any day."

Chastity beams. We're used to the praise by now. But we still don't know how it will translate into sales. We've been scattering our order forms like cottonwood seeds in the wind, but if nobody gets back to us, then I don't have a clue what we'll do. Follow-up visits, I guess? More samples?

"This is our order form," Chastity says. "But we're happy to transact by email. Our first delivery will happen on November tenth, with weekly deliveries through the holiday season."

"I like it," he says. "And you're related to Leah, right?"

"That's right," Chastity says. "We'll probably combine our cheese and caramel deliveries. And the payment terms will be the same as Leah's."

"Good, good," the man says, patting the order form on the counter. "Let me gather my thoughts, and I'll email you when I'm ready. I get to keep the caramels?"

"Those are all for you," I assure him before we go, leaving behind another satisfied (potential) customer.

The whole stop took only ten minutes, tops, but when we go outside, it's become pitch dark. That's late autumn in the north—nightfall is as sudden as a curtain drawn across the stage.

"Well?" I say, as we head up the road into Burlington. "I think we should make a bet. How many boxes do you think we sold so far?"

"No idea," she says. "Did you look at your email?"

"Nope!" I say cheerfully. "It's too soon. If we look now, we'll only be disappointed."

"When can we look?" she demands.

"Eight o'clock," I say, choosing a number at random. *Somebody* will order caramels tonight, right? At least one person? I don't want Chastity to be disappointed. "Let's get a pizza to kill the time. I'm starving."

"You're always starving," she points out. "We haven't made any money yet, so we shouldn't splurge."

"That's not how it works. You have to celebrate when you can, because you never know when the bad times are coming." It's basically my whole outlook on life. "Let me buy us a pizza. I want ham and olives. And a six-pack of beer. *Good* beer. The kind of beer that successful candymakers drink."

"Okay. Fine." She laughs. "I will prematurely celebrate with you. Would it be awful to ask you to look at my algebra homework while we wait for it?"

"Not awful at all. What are we dealing with?"

"There's some dreadful polynomials I'm stuck on."

"Polynomials. No problem." I feel invincible tonight. October is always a suckfest, and this year is no different. But today was a good day. And sometimes that's enough.

When I reach Spruce Street, there's a firetruck blocking the road. I roll down my window. "Is there a problem?" I ask the young cop who's minding the intersection. "I live on this street."

"The wind took a tree down," he says. "And the tree took out a telephone pole. You could try going around to the other end. But there's no power anyway. Gonna be a few hours until they get the log cut up, because there's trees down all over town. And then the power company has to do their thing. Might want to go somewhere else tonight."

"Okay, thanks." Power outages are a frequent occurrence in Vermont. And I doubt Rickie has a generator. I ease the truck past Spruce Street, wondering where to go. "Change of plans. Pizza at your place?"

"Sure," she says.

"Did, uh, Kaitlyn hang around for the long weekend?" I have to ask. Tomorrow is a federal holiday, and there aren't any classes.

"Nope. She packed a bag and left," Chastity reassures me.

We lapse into silence as I drive slowly down the street, wondering where I'm going to find a parking place. At least I don't have to see Kaitlyn. Dating her was an error in judgment, and I'd rather not come face to face with her wrath if I don't have to.

She was mad at *me* for breaking up with her. Ridiculous.

"Do you miss her?" Chastity asks softly.

"No!" I say quickly. "Not really. We were a horrible couple. I miss the sex, of course." I snort. "But you don't want to hear about my constantly horny state. And sex isn't a great reason to stay with someone who's mean to you."

"I've heard worse reasons," Chastity mumbles.

I finally find a spot big enough for the truck. Thank goodness for that. After parking, I drag Chastity into a corner store for beer, and by the time we're walking toward her dorm, the wind is howling, and we're pelted by sleet.

"Gross," Chastity says as we hurry the last half block toward her door. "Do you think they'll even deliver a pizza in this?"

"Oh, hell yes. I'll beg and plead," I promise. "I'm really looking forward to it." I pull open the door to her building, and the wind tries to yank it out of my hand.

We finally get inside, where the power is still on, and it's warm and dry. Chastity unlocks the door to her suite, and we walk in to find everything dark and quiet. Thank goodness. No Kaitlyn.

I order a large pie from my favorite pizza place, and then I sit on

Chastity's bed, propping my back against the wall and patting the spot beside me. "Okay, let's see these fearsome polynomials."

Humming to herself, Chastity retrieves the book and a notebook off the desk. Then she sits beside me. "Here we go. I did the first three, but I'm not sure I did them right."

I take the notebook, scanning her work. I'm a little distracted, though, by Chastity's proximity. Her shampoo has a fruity scent that's familiar to me, probably from the night I pushed her up against a wall and kissed the hell out of her.

That was a stupid, stupid thing to do. Because now I'm thinking about it again. We fell into kissing the way I once fell off a dock into Lake Champlain. Suddenly and without warning. And even though I'd been skunk drunk when I'd kissed her, I can't forget how good it was.

"Is it that bad?" she whispers.

"What?" I look up, finding her blue eyes at close range.

"The first three problems. Did I screw up?"

"Uh..." I squint at the page again and force myself to focus. "No. You're doing fine. They're not much different than the last two week's work, but with more terms thrown in." Chastity tends to panic whenever things start to look different. "Try number four, okay? Let's see how you go about breaking it down."

She takes the notebook back with a sigh and begins to factor the expression. The first thing she tries doesn't pan out.

"No problem," I coach. "Try again."

It takes her a few minutes to warm up, but slowly we work through each new problem. And then we get to the doozey at the bottom of the page.

"Ugh, I don't know," she complains. "That one will take all year."

"Just give it a shot? If you hurry, your reward will be pizza."

She leans over the page. As I wait for her to chew through number seventeen, she taps the end of the pencil against her knee, and my eye is drawn to the hole in her vintage jeans and the smooth skin showing through. I have the unlikely urge to pass my thumb over that oval of skin and test its softness.

Okay. *Fuck.*

I close my eyes and take a slow breath. What is my problem

today? Chastity has always been a looker, but I don't usually do this. I don't usually focus on the wrong things.

Opening my eyes, the first thing I see is Chastity's cleavage. Her soft T-shirt dips into a V right where her breasts stretch the cotton fabric...

There is no safe place to rest my gaze, apparently. My brain has become confused. Confused, and also a traitor.

"Dyl?"

I snap to attention. "Sorry. What was the question?"

"Can I multiply Z like this?"

"Uh..." I take a deep breath and get another whiff of her feminine scent. I must be really hungry, because it addles my brain. "Yes. *No.* Jesus."

Chastity laughs. "Which is it?"

"Yes, you can multiply both sides by Z. But don't forget about your denominator there..."

"Oh, crap," she says, erasing what she'd just written. "Okay, I have another idea."

She scribbles away, while I lean back and try to think about my own homework. Tomorrow is a holiday, but I have a history paper due on Tuesday. I close my eyes and think deep thoughts about the industrial revolution.

This works fine until Chastity puts a hand on my leg. It's just a casual touch—her palm resting over the denim of my jeans, right above my knee. But she might as well have put her hand on my cock, because I'm way too aware of her now.

"Dylan," she says. "Tell me I've got it now. Look."

I scan her work, and it's a miracle I can concentrate on the page. But it's true—she's cracked it open and arrived at the right answer. "Nice! You're done already. Now we can eat pizza and watch stupid shit on YouTube."

She laughs, turning to me. And there it is again—that smile that flattens me sometimes. I love making Chastity smile.

But holy shit. All I can think about is kissing her again.

It hits me that Rickie was probably right. And Kaitlyn, too, unfortunately. It might be the only time they ever agreed on anything, but I am attracted to Chastity. And I don't have the first idea what to think about that.

I pull out my phone to check my texts. *We lost power*, Rickie has written. *Don't really care because I have tea and soup and my favorite herbal remedies.* He means pot, of course. *But how long does it take for pipes to freeze?*

It's only in the 30s, I reply. *The pipes are fine. If you light a fire in the fireplace make sure the flues are open. Do you need me home?*

I almost hope he says yes. I'm in a weird mood.

Nope. Already built the fire and reading Kant in my sleeping bag by candlelight.

Chastity's house phone rings. Chastity climbs off the bed to answer it. She tucks a lock of her hair behind her ear, and I find myself admiring the smooth skin of her neck. Our pizza has arrived, and the front desk is calling to let us know.

My heart is beating a little too fast as I pull out my wallet to overtip the delivery person for working during the storm.

We'll eat some pizza together. We'll watch some John Oliver. And then I'll get the heck out of here.

An hour and a half later, I'm still lying on Chastity's bed like the lazy hedonist that I really am. There's sleet peppering the windows, and this place is too cozy to leave. The room is lit only by a dim lamp on her desk. I'm on beer number four, while Chastity nurses her first one.

The pizza has been reduced to crusts and crumbs, and Chastity is laughing at an SNL skit, her head on my shoulder.

Without even meaning to, I sift my fingers through her hair. Right after she moved to Vermont, she got it all buzzed off and dyed it pink. It was her way of striking out against the assholes who never let her cut it and forced her to dress like a Victorian virgin.

It's grown out a bit now, and it's super soft and smells good. And I feel well-fed and lazy. Like a dog in the sun.

A horny dog, honestly. Kissing Chastity flipped some kind of switch on my libido, and now my friend's proximity fills me with a hum of desire that wasn't there before.

Or, at least, I never let myself acknowledge it before.

Either way, it doesn't matter. I can watch videos in a pleasantly turned-on state without making a big deal out of it. I'm not an animal.

The skit ends, and Chastity hits pause. "That was a funny one. I never get to do this."

"Do what?" *Torture me?*

"Watch TV in my room." She shrugs, and finally drains the last of her beer.

"We have got to get you a computer."

"If we sell a lot of caramel, I'll have to decide between a computer and a phone. The computer will probably win. And at least email will get easier. Hey. Speaking of email." She lifts her head. "Is it eight? You said we could look at eight."

I did say that. But Chastity is in such a good mood that I don't want to ruin it if there aren't any orders. "I'll look in a minute."

"Please?" she begs. "I need to know if all that work was for nothing."

"It wasn't," I argue. "If nobody placed an order yet, it's just because they were busy."

"Fine. I won't be disappointed if there aren't any orders. Just check, okay?"

I open my mouth to argue, but that's when the lamp on the desk cuts out. My brain ponders the reason for this just as the video seizes on the laptop screen.

And that's when I realize that the power has gone out here, too.

"Uh-oh," Chastity says.

I close the laptop, because it's not doing us any good anymore, and we're plunged into darkness. "It's a good thing we already got our pizza."

She laughs. "You could survive anything as long as there's pizza and beer, right?"

"Basically." In the silence that follows, I feel our proximity like a physical thing.

"My key card won't work in a power outage," she says. "If I leave my room I might not be able to get back in. I read that in the student handbook."

"There's no backup power?"

I feel her shake her head next to me. "Plus, they don't want people wandering around the stairwells in the dark."

"Do you have a flashlight?" I ask.

"Nope."

I fish out my cell phone, which is running low on battery power but isn't dead yet. "Here, take this. Make yourself comfortable for the night, okay? I'll let you back into your room."

"Thank you, Dylan."

She puts her hand on my leg, nudging me over so she can get off the bed. The bright phone light winks on, illuminating a narrow strip of her room. She gets a flannel nightgown out of her dresser and then leaves for the bathroom she shares with Kaitlyn.

I wait there in the dark, considering my options. Maybe it's ridiculous, but I don't feel right leaving her alone in this nearly empty building with no power and no flashlight.

It's a dorm room. Not a remote cabin in the Yukon. The power will probably be restored during the night, and Chastity doesn't like to be babied.

Still. Chastity spent most of her life with people who should have been looking out for her, but wouldn't. I think that's why I do some of the things I do for her. Because everybody needs to know that somebody cares.

There's a tap on the door a couple minutes later, and I get up and feel my way over to open it.

"The plumbing still works," she says, handing me my phone and walking over to the bed.

"Cool. I'll test it out myself."

I head to the bathroom and take care of some necessary business. As I'm tapping on Chastity's door, my phone rings. It's Leah, so I answer in spite of my dying battery.

"Hello?" I say, feeling vaguely guilty about being in Chastity's room. "You've reached the headquarters of Nannygoat's Candies. How may I direct your call?"

"Dylan!" Leah chirps. "That isn't as funny as you think, given the call I just took. Ask me how many boxes of caramel the Vermont Country Store wants. Go ahead. Ask me."

Chastity opens the door. I stumble over to the bed, and we both sit down. "Okay. How many boxes of caramel *does* the Vermont Country Store want?"

"A *gross*," she says. "A hundred and forty-four full-sized, plus some samplers."

"Oh, shit." I laugh. "Really?"

"*Really*," she says. "And you got two smaller orders, too. You're up to, say, a hundred and seventy-five boxes."

"A hundred and seventy-five boxes," I repeat slowly. Chastity lets out a little shriek beside me. "We're going to be chained to your kitchen, Leah."

."I know! But that's a good thing."

"Is it?" I wonder. "I wonder how many caramels a guy can make on a Friday night?"

"You always have Saturday," Leah babbles. "I told Chastity you could have either day. And now you need them both."

"Oh," I say slowly. "Saturday?" I turn toward Chastity in the dark. The glow from my phone is just bright enough to catch the expression on her face.

It's guilt.

EIGHTEEN

Chastity

I'M DYING inside as Dylan finishes the call with Leah. Now my little spur-of-the-moment lie is unmasked, and I feel terrible.

I'd told myself that it didn't matter, because Kaitlyn told ten lies to my one. Every day. But it *does* matter. Because I feel sick inside.

"Yeah, the power went out, first at my house and then here," he's saying. "The phone on the wall didn't ring. But she's fine. No—it isn't very cold in here yet." He glances at me, then points at the phone, asking if I want to talk to Leah.

I shake my head.

"Don't worry," he tells her. "They probably have a lot of lines down tonight. But you know they aren't going to leave the campus in the dark for long."

A few moments later he wishes her a good night. He ends the call, pockets the phone, and darkness swallows us. And so does the silence.

I think I can hear my own heart pounding.

"Saturdays, huh?" he whispers eventually. "You told me we could only have the kitchen on Fridays."

"I'm sorry," I whisper. "That wasn't true."

"You...lied?" he asks. As if it's inconceivable.

This is why my inner bad girl doesn't come out very often. Because I'm terrible at this. "I did," I admit. "I'm sorry."

He sighs. "Move over."

"What?" My heart is in my mouth.

"Move over so there's room for two."

Surprise makes me wait another beat. But then I scramble up to the head of my twin bed and pull back the covers. Dylan stands up, which makes it easier for me to slide between the sheets. My pulse jumps erratically as I wait for him to leave, or yell at me, or ask me why I lied.

But that's not what happens.

I hear the dry sound of a zipper and the clink of a belt as Dylan sheds his jeans. Clothing rustles. And then Dylan pulls back the bedclothes and gets in beside me.

I'm so surprised that it takes a minute to start breathing again. Dylan smells like mint toothpaste, as well as the woodsy scent that I associate with him. We're lying side by side on our backs, which is not how things go in my fantasies. But it's close enough to make me feel twice as wistful. And twice as guilty.

Why did I ever think lying to Dylan would improve my life?

The silence is killing me. I practice apology speeches in my head, but before I settle on a worthy version, Dylan's breathing evens out and lengthens into sleep.

It's such a sweet sound that my eyes feel prickly. The heat of his body seeps into mine. I want to roll over and take more of it. I want to mold myself to his sturdy body and breathe his woodsy scent.

But that's not allowed. And this is all I will ever have—friendship and the ache of wanting more.

It takes me a long time to fall asleep.

———

The next time I open my eyes, I'm startled to find the wall only inches from my nose.

I'm even more startled to realize that Dylan's body is shifting sleepily against my back. All of it. A hard chest and long legs. And even a hard—

His body detaches from mine in an instant, leaving cool air in its wake. Behind me, the mattress unweights as he rolls off the bed. There's a clunk and then a mumbled curse as Dylan trips across the small room and clicks off my desk lamp.

The power must have come on in the night. It's early morning, judging by the gray light that's just starting to filter in through my window.

Dylan opens my bedroom door, propping something against it, because it doesn't close all the way after he leaves. I hear a toilet flush, and then water running for a while.

I roll over as he comes through the door in his underwear and a T-shirt.

I look away quickly, instead of appreciating the way those boxer briefs lie so snugly against his strong thighs.

He sits down on the edge of the bed. "Did you sleep?" he asks in a roughened voice.

"Yeah. You?"

"Mostly. Christ, it's cold in here. I think the power just came back on."

"What time is it?"

Dylan is a farmer, so he looks at the sky instead of at a clock. "Almost seven? So it's that pivotal hour when the choice is between sleep and coffee. The dining hall doesn't open for another hour, though, because it's a holiday." He leans back against my bed and sighs.

Awake now, I scramble around him and visit the bathroom to brush my teeth. Too late, I realize I should have brought some clothes into the bathroom with me. Dylan is probably putting on his jeans right now, because it really is freezing in here.

But when I get back to my room, he's lying in my bed, the covers pulled up to his chin. When he spots me in the doorway, he moves toward the wall to make room.

There's no way I could fall asleep again. Not with my squirrel brain running in circles, wondering whether I've completely ruined Dylan's trust in me just so I could spend a few Friday evenings with him.

In spite of my worries, I can't resist the chance to be close to him.

So I kick his backpack out of the way of the door and let it fall shut. Then I climb into the bed.

We're lying on our backs again, contemplating the gray ceiling at dawn. Dylan doesn't seem to be falling asleep. He's quiet in the way a man is when he's thinking.

"I just have one question," he says eventually. "Why did you do it?"

"Why did I...lie?"

"Yeah. Was it because Fridays were for Kaitlyn? You wanted to make her mad?"

"Yes," I whisper after a beat. It really is that simple.

"Because she was such a bitch sometimes?"

"Sometimes?" I repeat, my blood beginning to simmer. I know I'm in the wrong, here. But Kaitlyn just brings out the worst in me.

He snorts. "Fine. I get it."

"Do you?" I squeak. I'm suddenly so angry. "She was horrible to me since the moment I met her. She was rude to Rickie and Keith. She was manipulative of you. And you never called her on it. Why is that? You don't let other people run over you."

"I dunno," he mutters.

His non-answer just makes me crazier. "I'm sorry, I don't buy that. You do know. You just don't want to say it. I lied about Fridays. And I am sorry. But now you're lying, too. You put up with her because she's *very* pretty. And you wanted her in your bed."

The mattress shakes gently as Dylan laughs. "Yeah, I already admitted that. Fine. I let her treat me a little shitty, because I didn't care that much that we weren't really a good match. But I'm sorry I let her treat my friends badly. She didn't give you that message, right? When you were waiting in the library?"

"No," I grumble. "She didn't. But that's just the most obvious example. She loved rubbing my nose in it."

"In what?" he asks.

My heart flails, because I realize I said too much. "Nothing."

"In *what?*" Dylan whispers, rolling onto his side to look at me.

I look up into his beautiful face. It's *right* there, just inches from mine. And those big brown eyes are regarding me seriously.

"I was jealous, okay?" I whisper. "I wanted what she had."

Dylan blinks. "You wanted a meaningless sexual relationship with me? That can*not* be true."

"There you go again," I say as my pulse pounds in my throat. "Assuming you know what I think. That I couldn't possibly want what everyone else has. I was jealous. And that night I got drunk? She gave you that whole guilt trip about how the two of you never slept in her bed?"

Dylan winces.

"Yeah, I heard the whole thing. And everything that came afterward, too. She made sure of it. She opened the *window*, Dylan. Just to treat me to an hour of what I imagine porn sounds like."

He gapes at me. "You've never watched porn?"

"That's beside the point!" I yelp. "I have the same dirty mind as everyone else. And I just want what everyone else has."

Dylan pinches the bridge of his nose, as if he can't quite believe what I'm saying. "So you lied about Fridays."

"*Yes*," I cry, raising myself up on an elbow. Now we're nose to nose. "It was a bitchy thing to do. A real Kaitlyn maneuver. I'm not proud of it." Even if she had it coming. "I don't belong up on that pedestal where you always put me. But neither do you, you know."

"Oh I *know* that," he grunts.

"You lied, too."

His eyes narrow. "When do you mean?"

"What about last weekend when you said—" I have to swallow the lump in my throat before I can finish the sentence. "—'I'm so drunk I don't know what I'm doing.' Because I think you totally knew."

His eyes flare. And then he leans back against the wall so fast that his head makes a clunk against it. "Fine. Fair enough."

"You totally knew," I repeat.

"Yeah. I fucking did." He won't meet my gaze, though.

"And you enjoyed it. But then later you made a big deal about it, apologizing. Like it was some terrible indiscretion. As if I wasn't supposed to like it."

He squeezes his eyes shut. "Did you?"

My heart is pounding so hard now that I almost can't hear myself over it. "You know I did. Drunk doesn't cut it, Dylan. You'd have to be *dead* not to see that. Don't you dare make me feel bad about it again."

"I won't. Jesus." He shakes his head. "I'm sorry I—"

"Don't be *sorry*," I gasp.

"—made a big deal about it," he finishes, reaching across the distance between us and taking my hand in his. When he wraps his long fingers around mine, I stop breathing. "But you don't want me, Chastity. I'm a fucking mess."

The words would break my heart, if only I could really hear them. But I can't, because Dylan is holding my hand. All I can do is stare at our joined hands. Everything I ever wanted is hovering here in this small space between us.

"Don't tell me what I want," I say quietly. "That's not for you to decide. But I know how it works. Some girls are the kind you're willing to tutor in algebra. And some are the pretty ones that you're willing to tutor in sex. And I know which kind I am. I already know."

"Hey." His brow furrows. "It's not that simple."

"I think it is."

I try to take my hand back, but he holds on. "It's not like I never thought about it."

"What?" All the air leaves my body. "You *did?*"

Now it's his turn to wince. Like he said too much. "Well, sure. Because I'm twenty years old, and you have perfect breasts."

I blink. "These old things?"

He gives me a wry grin. "Just…trust me. But that isn't really the point. We're friends."

"I know that."

"Yeah. Well, did you notice that all the girls I take to bed end up hating me?"

"No, they don't."

His eyebrows lift, as if to ask, *Really?*

"Okay, a lot of them do," I admit. "But that's on them."

He shrugs. "Maybe it is, maybe it isn't. But I don't go there with you, because I don't want you to end up hating me. And I don't date, Chastity. You deserve somebody who sticks around."

"This again," I grumble. "You're telling me what I need. And you don't get to do that. But if it's not going to be you, then it isn't. I'll find someone else to tutor me."

"Tutor you," he repeats. "In...?" He doesn't finish the question, probably because he doesn't believe that I really mean it.

"Sex," I say, although I'm really just saving face right now. Lord knows that I couldn't have this conversation with anyone else on Earth. I can barely manage to have it with the boy I know best. "I'm twenty-one, and I'm tired of being everybody's naive little friend. If you can't wrap your head around that, or if you don't want the job, I'll find someone who does."

His eyes darken dangerously. "Who?"

"I don't know." I shrug, hoping for nonchalance. "Someone. Maybe Rickie will have an idea. Or Keith."

Alarm crosses his features. "That's a terrible idea."

"So what? Like you've never had any terrible ideas? I'll just go to more parties. I'll wear my red silk blouse again. Kaitlyn noticed it. She said I looked *slutty*." An edge of hysteria creeps into my voice at the memory. "You didn't even correct her. Although I've never gotten the chance to try slutty out."

His face drops, and I know I've struck a blow.

"Do you know what you said instead?"

He shakes his head, his brown eyes full of sorrow.

"You told her to grab the bed rail with both hands."

"Jesus." He covers his eyes with one hand. "You're right. I was an idiot."

But I'm too worked up to stop. "So don't sit here and tell me that sex kills a friendship. Because there's lots of other ways of doing that."

"You're right. Christ." He reaches out and scoops me into a big, full-body hug.

That's what finally shuts me up—Dylan's strong arms encircling me. His hugs are always overwhelming, but we've never hugged when we've been horizontal, and I'm unprepared for the press of his hard body against mine, our feet tangling beneath the bedclothes. His brown eyes are just inches away.

He lifts his chin and presses his lips to my forehead.

And maybe it could have ended there—with a chaste peck. But

my reaction is swift and fierce, and without even thinking, I lift my hands to catch his perfectly cut jaw. I hold onto that kiss, my thumb sliding over his cheekbone, my body easing closer to his. As if I could prevent him from ever letting go.

His lips part on my skin, pausing. Uncertain. He holds me a little more tightly as he kisses the bridge of my nose. And then my cheekbone.

Time slows all the way down to zero, as I wait to see what happens next. If I were a different girl, I would just take what I wanted. I'd throw a leg over his hip and kiss him like a starlet in a Hollywood film.

But I'll never be that girl. I'm stuck being the kind of girl who waits and hopes. The best I can do is stroke my thumb sweetly across his face, tracing the perfect curve of his cheekbone. My touch is so reverent, so filled with yearning.

Maybe he can sense it, because he kisses the corner of my eye, and then the corner of my mouth.

It's like gravity, really, the way we come together. His lips feel inevitable as they slide toward mine. His breath is warm and minty as our lips finally touch. I get a glimpse of soft brown eyes before they drift closed.

He sinks into our kiss, the way you slide into a hot bath. And that's exactly how it feels—hot and wonderful and all encompassing. Heat sizzles through my body, and I part my lips helplessly.

Dylan doesn't make me wait. He tilts his head to adjust our connection, and then his tongue tastes mine so sweetly.

His *mouth*, though. I dream about it all the time. Whiskers and heat and the snick of his kiss light my poor, hungry body on fire.

I make a desperate noise. Dylan goes still for about half a second and then makes a shocked sound in reply. "Fuck." He whispers it like a prayer against my lips.

Then we're kissing again. Faster now. He takes eager sips of my mouth from several angles. I gasp in surprise as his mouth retreats, only to land on my neck a moment later.

Wet kisses on my skin feel so good that I practically levitate off the bed. One hand flies into his hair, and the other curls into the fabric of his T-shirt. He worships the tender skin of my jaw. My ear.

"Fuck," he whispers again. He swings his big body over mine, pinning me to the bed.

I can't help my low moan as I sink back onto the pillow. This is *exactly* how all my fantasies play out, with Dylan pushing me down and taking everything I'm so ready to give him.

He doesn't, though. Not yet. He's still worshiping my neck as his hard body settles over the frustratingly thick flannel of my nightgown.

He stops, lifting his head to look down at me in wonder. He smooths the hair off my face with his thumb. "Tell me to get lost," he begs suddenly. "This is a terrible idea. Tell me to fuck off."

I can only shake my head.

His eyes dip down to my chest, which is rising and falling too fast. I expect him to say something else. To argue. So I'm not prepared for the way he drops his head to kiss the exposed skin at the top edge of my nightgown.

I gasp. When my arms clamp around his strong neck, he goes still for a moment. But then? His sweet mouth drops another kiss on my skin. Slower this time. And another. Thick fingers fumble open the first button, and his kisses trail a soft path between my breasts.

I am *electrified*. My arms tighten around his head, as if I could actually keep him here against his will. He drops hot, open-mouthed kisses onto the swells of my breasts, onto skin so unexpectedly sensitive that I want to weep with pleasure.

With a sigh, he presses his body more firmly against mine. He's hard everywhere. Against my stomach. Against my thighs. Between my legs.

Then his mouth changes course, kissing up my chest and onto my cheek, and I can't hold still any longer. My shameless hands skim down his muscular form. Even his butt is rock hard. He moans when I take it in two hands.

"Fuck," he says against my jaw. "Tell me to stop."

Once again, I shake my head.

"Chastity," he whispers. His whiskers scrape the corner of my mouth as he kisses the side of my face. "Tell me. Make me stop."

But I can't. Even if he was right all along—that this was a bad idea —I don't have that kind of willpower. I have the opposite kind—the kind that tugs his T-shirt up and slides a hand underneath, exploring the smooth skin of his back.

Then I give the shirt a really good tug.

With a groan that sounds half irritated, he yanks it up and over his head. I get one fast look at that rippling chest before his mouth descends on mine, hot and hungry.

That's when I feel his self-control snap. He moans into my mouth at the first touch of our tongues. And then we're like a couple of people running too fast downhill. Tongues tangling, hands grappling. Our kisses are wet and dirty.

I love it, but it's hard to take in every new sensation at once. So I'm no help at all when Dylan tries to tug my nightgown up and off. He's not a small guy, so his elbow catches an empty beer bottle on my nightstand, sending it crashing to the floor.

Neither of us bothers to see where it landed. I finally figure out how to raise my arms so he can lift the thing over my head and then drop it on the floor. Before I can even take a breath, he's lowered his mouth to my breasts.

As the cool air hits my skin, all the heat goes right to my face. I'm so *bare* all of a sudden. My nipples are like hard, little points. It's tempting to duck for cover, but I make myself stay completely still, except for trembling. I can't control that.

"Chastity," he whispers. "Goddamn." The next sound he makes is an eager groan. And then he's pushing me back onto the pillow again, kissing and licking first one nipple and then the other.

A warm hand lands on one breast and gives me a filthy squeeze. I'm still trembling as he licks his way across the other breast.

Then his mouth closes over my nipple, and he sucks. My mouth opens on a silent moan, because I had no idea how good that would feel. Like there's a direct wire between my breast and the throbbing between my legs.

I want so many things. I want his hands on my body and his tongue in my mouth. I want Dylan to kick off his underwear and fuck me.

I can't ask, though. I won't beg. I'll give him everything. Right now. But I don't know how to offer. I need him to just *take* it.

To take me.

He slides a hand down my body, and I hold my breath. That crafty hand slides right over my panties and between my legs. It's so perfect that I moan out loud this time.

"Fuck," he murmurs against my mouth.

He toys with the elastic of my panties, and I tremble harder. "*Please*." It's barely a whisper, but somehow it came from me.

He groans and tugs the panties roughly down my legs. I'm already kicking them away. And then I'm absolutely naked beneath Dylan Shipley.

Finally.

"Fuck," he whispers again. I feel how fast he's breathing, almost as fast as I am. "Tell me you want this." He kisses my neck.

I lift my chin, giving him access. But I can't say it out loud. That's how it is with me. I have wanted this since before I even learned the words for some of the things I desired.

But a girl who was slapped just for asking for things can't just change overnight.

"Chass," he begs between kisses.

I lift his chin, aligning our mouths and drinking him in. I need him to take me back to that tongue-tangled crazy place where nobody speaks. Not with words, anyway.

"Chass," he groans against my tongue. "What do you want?"

I take a big breath. *You. I want you.* The words are stuck inside me.

When his hand catches my flailing one in his, I seize the chance. I take that hand and push it between my legs.

I cannot *believe* I just did that.

But the puff of shame is almost immediately replaced by thick fingers spreading my legs apart. They stroke, just once, and that's all it takes to make my point. Because I am unbelievably, embarrassingly drenched.

The sound Dylan makes in response is deep and desperate. We're kissing again. Our teeth click and scrape as we devour each other with a ferocity that stuns me. Dylan's finger does a slow circle through the slippery heat of my pussy and my kiss stutters beneath his mouth.

No hand besides my own has ever touched me like that, and I'm astonished by how sharp and achy my desire is. My body throbs and my breasts ache and I can't remember to breathe. "Dylan!" I whimper shamelessly. I clench my thighs together, reaching for something that isn't there.

He moans into my mouth again. And then I lose both his tongue and touch completely. I take a much-needed gulp of oxygen as he shoves his underwear down and off his body.

A moment later we're lying side by side with nothing on. Not even the sheet. Dylan looks enormous without his clothes—all bulging muscle and sun-warmed skin.

The only thing left between us is the serious look in his eyes, and all my grasping desperation.

NINETEEN

Dylan

CHASTITY REACHES FOR ME, as if she's afraid we'll lose our momentum. But I'm made of momentum right now, and I honestly need a second to calm down. So I kiss her cheekbone instead of her mouth.

Her lush body is laid out beside me, and I'm so hard it hurts. I don't really know how we ended up here, and tomorrow I'll probably regret it.

No—not tomorrow. I'll probably regret this by lunchtime. But it doesn't seem to matter. We're like a boulder rolling downhill, fast and dangerous. And I don't know the last time I felt like this—totally desperate and lost.

I turn away and fish my jacket off the floor. From a pocket, I retrieve one of the condoms I always carry. Because I'm a filthy opportunist. I hold it up between two fingers to show Chastity.

Her chin bobs in a quick nod.

I almost add, *you sure?* Except I know in my gut that she is. The reason my body is on fire right now is because my friend mauled me almost as aggressively as I mauled her. Chastity's cheeks are pink and her glorious chest rises and falls with each rapid breath.

I want what everyone else has, she'd said. Well, I'm the guy who can deliver that. Thoughtless sex and fun times are pretty much all I have to offer the world.

So I tear open the packet and roll the condom down my aching cock. This is madness. I'm ninety-eight percent sure that Chastity has never had sex before.

What am I even doing?

"Dylan?" she breathes. Maybe she's finally come to her senses. Except she's rolling onto her back, and spreading her legs on the sheets. I can't look away. And now there's literally nothing between us except a condom and the thinnest filament of my restraint.

"Yeah?" I croak.

"Don't be careful with me."

"You don't have anything to prove, Chass." It gets so quiet that I can hear my heart thumping in my chest.

I drop a hand to her bare leg, running my fingertips up to her hip. I pass my hand over the tidy triangle of hair between her legs, and my pulse kicks up a notch. Has anyone ever touched her like that?

She moans and tosses her head when I stroke her. I could almost come just from this—the view of her lush body arching into my hand and the sound of her hunger.

I lean down and trail my lips across one pale breast. Then I kiss my way across the smooth skin of her tummy, toward the honeyed center of her. At the first touch of my tongue against her clit, she lets out a hot gasp. So I drop my mouth onto her pussy and take a greedy taste.

All her muscles go rigid, and she tugs at my hair, straining against me. But a moment later she's pushing my face away. "Not like that," she pants.

"No?" I lift my head, startled. "You don't want my mouth? What do you want?"

"You," she says firmly. "I need you."

"You need me to do what?" I ask, because I cannot get this wrong. My cock is screaming, and my blood is pounding, and I don't trust myself at all.

I swing myself into position above her, so that I can look down into her flushed face and bright eyes.

This also has the effect of pinning her to the bed with my cock. Her hips strain beneath me, lifting toward my body, as if willing me inside.

"Just…" She takes a breath, and the next two words come out so quietly that I can barely hear them. "*Use* me."

Gulp.

I can't deny that my body flashes hot when she says those words. Erotic imagery assaults my overstimulated brain. I want Chastity at the edge of the bed—her hips lifted to meet me. I want her seated on my cock, while I'm encouraging her to ride me. I want her backwards and forwards and every which way.

I want. I want. I want. All of it.

But first I lean down and take her mouth again. She opens for me immediately, like an offering. I could kiss all day like this. Her tongue is sweet and willing.

Her arms wrap around my neck, and her soft tits rub against my bare chest. It's glorious. I can't resist slipping a hand between her legs to stroke her pussy. She gasps against my mouth and spreads her legs for me.

"Good girl," I groan, as her slickness coats my fingers.

I'm hard as a fencepost. I should probably be intimidated by what we're about to do. But I want it too much to care.

Use me, she'd said. Christ. I slide my arm beneath her silky leg, lifting her knee, making space for myself in the cradle of her body. I know I need to go slow. But instinct makes me tuck my cock against her pussy, sliding my shaft against her clit.

"Oh!" she moans. "Yes."

We fall into a deep kiss, grinding and desperate. I thrust against her, in imitation of fucking her. And she pushes back against me, greedy and slick.

"Please," she begs. "Now."

Right. No big deal. It's just my incredibly sexy, *virginal* best friend, naked beneath me and begging me to fuck her. So I grip my cock and line myself up. And I slide partway into her tight, wet pussy.

"Oh!" Her arms grip me, and she tenses suddenly.

"Hey," I whisper, stroking her hair with a trembling hand. "Melt for me."

Her blue eyes blink once. Then she takes a deep breath and lets it out slowly. I feel her sink back onto the mattress.

"Good girl," I rasp as I slide right inside, where everything is tight and wonderful.

She lets out a low moan that nearly undoes me. I bite my lip, holding very still. *Farm chores.* That's what I need to think about right now. Shoveling manure. Milking cows with frozen fingers in February...

"Dyl," she breathes. "Don't stop."

Easy for you to say. I lean down and kiss her neck. "You got me so fucking worked up, Chass. I almost can't stand it." I push my face into the pillow for a second, breathing deeply until the blinding need to come ebbs a little.

Chastity's hand finds mine. I weave our fingers together and take another calming breath. I'm still trembling as I pull my hips back and then slide in again.

"Yes," she breathes, tightening against me.

Slowly, I pick up the pace. It's sweet agony. With every thrust, she makes a breathy sound of pleasure. And I'm feeding off it. I break out in a sweat, trying to hold myself back.

It has to be good for her. I know Chastity really well, but I don't know this side of her. My mind is blown by the way she's clutching me and by all the sounds she's making, like she can't get enough. And the way she's staring into my eyes, like she can see all the way to my horny soul.

It's overwhelming. There's so much tension in my body right now. The good kind. But I won't stop until I give her something to cheer about.

Her hip fits so nicely in my hand. I slide into another thrust, and she moans immediately. I pick up the pace again, running when I ought to walk.

I've had a lot of sex, in every conceivable position. But I have never been this turned on before. It's not just the novelty, either. It's *everything.* Chastity's hands gripping the sheets. The sound of her ragged, hungry breaths.

It's the complete submission of her posture right now—splayed out and taking my cock like it's her only goal in life.

And giving it to her is mine. If I'm not careful, sensory overload is going to ruin me.

I slide a hand under my body, until I can fork my fingers over the place where we're joined. I pass my thumb over her clit, and she shivers.

"Yeah," I say. "Come on now. Get there for me. I need you to." I've always been a motormouth during sex.

And Chastity doesn't seem to mind. As I whisper little words of encouragement, she begins to strain back against me, her rhythm uneven and desperate. She shivers again.

"Good girl," I babble. I close my eyes and give it to her again and again.

But I'm running out of time. Desperate, I take one of her hands and stretch it over her head, until I find the bedrail. And then I do the same to the other one, until she's gripping it with both hands, wide-eyed and watchful.

"You like that?" I ask, and she's instantly trembling.

"Then hold on tight." I jerk my hips forward.

Right away she gasps. And when I thrust a second time, her whole body shudders around my cock. She drops her head back onto the pillow and sobs with pleasure.

Her climax wrecks me. It's all I can do to give one last slow-motion thrust as pleasure roars through me. And then I pour my whole self out with a soul-deep groan.

For several long seconds after that, all I can do is try to remember how to breathe. Chastity is collapsed on the sheet, her chest rising and falling at the same vicious pace as mine.

The room looks like a storm blew through. There are clothes thrown everywhere, beer bottles on the floor. And then there's us—sweaty and spent.

As gently as possible, I disengage. I place a couple of slow kisses on Chastity's neck and then sink down onto the bed, my limbs shaking.

"You okay?" I croak. My voice sounds too loud in all this silence.

"Totally," she pants. Like it's a given.

I'm not entirely okay, myself. I lift the sheet and pull it over us on the narrow bed. I've lain in bed with naked women many times before. But this time, as my hand finds the bare curve of her hip, the moment feels shockingly intimate.

But we don't talk. I'm all mixed up inside. Somehow, I was just fine with the pounding I gave her a few minutes ago, but pulling her close to my bare chest gives me goosebumps.

I make myself comfortable on her pillow, her body tilted toward mine. We lie there together a while, coming off the sexual high. "Are you sleepy?" I ask eventually.

"Not even a little," she says.

"Me neither." I kiss her cheek. "But I really need to get rid of this condom. And probably take a quick shower so I can eventually take you out for coffee and bagels."

She gives me a serious glance before looking away. "Better test to see if the water is hot yet."

"Good idea," I reply, my voice still gravelly and weird. Everything is weird. Did we really just do that?

I wait another beat. Gingerly, I get out of the bed, running a hand through Chastity's hair before I go. I hate leaving the bed, but I'm also glad that I have to.

Regret is already tickling the back of my neck as I walk naked into the bathroom. Disposing of the condom, I squint at myself in the shocking light. I see a red-faced guy who doesn't know what hit him. I guzzle some water and then quickly push back the shower curtain and turn on the water so I can clean myself up.

From sex. With Chastity.

Jesus H. I loved every second of it. No—I *craved* it. But already I feel guilty. As if I took a delicate friendship and threw it as carelessly to the floor as I did our clothes.

It doesn't help that there was a smear of pink on the condom. Just a trace, but still a reminder of Chastity's inexperience.

Luckily, the water heats quickly. I ease my body under the spray and let out a giant sigh. As the water beats down on my head, I begin to feel more like myself.

It was just epic sex with a friend, I tell myself. *Amazing. Surprising. But not life-altering.*

It's funny how recently I'd been worried about a *kiss* messing everything up. Chastity hadn't liked it that I'd overreacted. She doesn't like to be babied.

Good thing, because I wasn't babying her in the bed just now. I gave her just what she asked for. A quick lesson in clawing, desperate sex.

It's going to be fine, I reassure myself. We're adults. We can handle this.

Just as I'm finishing up my shower, the bathroom door opens.

"Hey, can I borrow a towel?" I ask as I turn off the taps. I yank the shower curtain open, looking toward the doorway for Chastity.

But it's not Chastity who's standing there.

TWENTY

Dylan

"KAITLYN!" I yelp. "You weren't supposed to be home." Even as the words leave my mouth, I know I've just made it worse.

"Right," Kaitlyn spits, fire in her eyes. "If you'd known I was here, you would have fucked Chastity at *your* place, instead. My bed was too small, huh? But hers is just right?"

"Now hang on," I look around for a bath towel. There's only a tiny hand towel on the bar.

I reach for it but Kaitlyn is faster. She grabs it and holds it to her chest. "I want to hear this."

Fuck. "We... I..." My brain is empty, from shock, confusion, and a lack of caffeine. "There's nothing to say. It's none of your business that we..." The sentence dies, because I'm not about to discuss it. Not that I'd even know what to say. I haven't processed it myself. Things with Chastity are...

Speak of the devil. I hear Chastity's bedroom door open, and then her shocked face appears in the bathroom doorway. She tosses me a towel, which I snatch out of the air.

"Let me guess." Kaitlyn folds her arms in front of her pert little chest. Kaitlyn reminds me of an ice queen sometimes. So pretty, but also cold. And then she opens her mouth again, and it gets worse. "You got drunk, huh? Had a few beers. Got horny. So now Chastity knows what beer goggles are. Did you ever hear that expression?" She turns, directing this question at Chastity. "It means he'll do anyone when he's had three or four beers."

"Hey!" I argue. "That is *not* what happened here."

Chastity goes absolutely white and grips the door frame.

Kaitlyn's not done. "You *said* she wasn't your type. You said she isn't even attractive! So it must have taken a few drinks for you to end up naked in her bed, right?"

"Kaitlyn," I holler. "Shut your *mouth*."

"Why? You didn't shut *yours*," she shrieks. "*Fuck, Chastity. Take it. Yes!* Sound familiar? You said she was like a little sister to you. Is that how you'd treat your little sister?"

Chastity gasps. Her face is now bright red.

"*Stop it*," I growl. "You're putting words in my mouth, and you're just being cruel." I dry myself off quickly. I have got to get out of this bathtub.

"Am I? Or are *you?* I called you out so many times, and you laughed it off. I *saw* it."

That slows me down for a second, because unfortunately she has a point.

"Saw what?" Chastity whispers.

"Did you know Dylan lies?" She turns on Chastity. "Either he lied to you just now, or he lied to me for several weeks straight. Which is it, Dylan? Why don't you clear it up right now? Because not even two weeks have passed since you told me you had no interest in sleeping with her. You said it so many times. You said—"

"Stop!" I holler. "You have something to say to me, you can do it privately."

"Privately?" she asks, blinking back tears. "Should I bring the condoms and the lube?" She turns to Chastity again. "Congratulations on finally getting a turn on the mechanical bull. How did you manage it? Did you ask him for a little tutoring help, maybe? *This algebra is so boring Dylan. Why don't you teach me how to ride your dick.* Did you learn it from a romcom? Did you hope he'd fall in love with you?"

Chastity's eyes go red. She takes a step backward, as if to distance herself from Kaitlyn's venom. And she can't even *look* at me.

"Just don't forget," Kaitlyn spits. "He wanted me *first*. And I didn't have to beg to see his dick."

On that horrible note, she finally leaves, striding past Chastity and heading for her room. Her door slams closed with an earth-shattering crash a moment later.

Chastity looks as shell-shocked as I feel.

"Hey…" I don't even know what to say next. *Thanks for the towel. Shall we go out for breakfast?* "I'm really sorry—"

But Chastity's hand slices through the air with surprising violence. "Do *not* apologize right now."

"Why the hell not?"

I'm clearly the dumbest man alive, therefore "I'm sorry" seems like a pretty good opener. I can't believe I let myself get caught out naked in their bathroom. It's marginally insensitive to my ex. But it's a disaster for Chastity, who still has to live with that harpy.

"Because I don't want to hear your opinion of what actually happened," she says, her voice shaking. "Just…let's forget everything." She turns and hurries into her room.

"Wait!" I finish drying off as quickly as I can. My mind is a twisted knot of anxiety. I need to take her somewhere quiet and try to explain.

But when I leave the bathroom, Chastity meets me at the doorway to her room, her arms full of my clothes, backpack, and shoes. "Here. I think you should go."

"Right now?"

"Right now," she says stiffly.

"No way," I say, my voice cracking with unhappiness. "We have to talk."

"But I don't want to," she says. And then she steps into her room and shuts the door with a horrible click.

Leaving me standing there in the hall like an idiot. A moment later I hear a sob. And I honestly can't tell which door it came from.

I lean my forehead against Chastity's door and try to think. If I could talk to her, I'd say…

Yeah, okay. So I'm not even sure what. *You're not unattractive. And I'm not the slut that Kaitlyn claims I am.*

Except that while the first thing is true, the second one is iffy.

"Chastity," I whisper against the door.

But she doesn't answer me.

After a few more minutes shivering in this hallway, I have no other choice than to throw on my clothes and go.

My head is pounding as I drive back to Spruce Street. When I get there, I reach for the backseat to grab the backpack that I tossed there.

That's when I spot the last boxes of caramels on the seat. The ones that we had an appointment to drop off at nine thirty this morning. I pull out my phone. It's 9:23.

Shit!

Rickie comes out of the house just as I have this horrible realization. "Hey, man. We're out of groceries. Want to drive me to Hannaford?"

"Get in," I say, fishing for my keys. "But we're going to City Market."

"Ooh, fancy," Rickie says, opening the passenger door. "What's the occasion?"

"Saving my ass and selling caramels."

"Can I try one, yet?" he asks.

"I guess," I grumble. "Chastity hates me already for a long list of reasons. A few missing caramels won't even hit the top ten."

"Chastity does not hate you," Rickie says, grabbing a box off the backseat as I back down the driveway and then hustle the truck through our little neighborhood.

"You don't know that."

"I sense a story here."

"Yeah, you have no idea."

"You're late," the manager of the upscale food co-op says when I locate her in an office in back.

"I know," I say immediately. "My business partner is probably going to kill me. She's the kind of person who is never late to anything. She made these candies by hand, but then couldn't be here to meet with you."

"Why not?" the woman asks, frowning. "She was so nice on the phone, she said she'd pitch to me herself."

"Because I made her life difficult." I swallow hard. *She's too busy crying to remember your appointment.* "She's probably inventing ways to kill me right now."

"Sounds like there's a story there," the woman says, lifting an eyebrow.

"That's what I said," Rickie grumbles from somewhere behind me.

I ignore him. "So could I possibly leave these with you and ask her to follow up?" I extend the boxes a little farther in her direction. And —thank goodness—she takes them.

"Sure." She cracks open the lid of the box on top. "These do look pretty fabulous. They're handmade in Leah's creamery?"

"That's right. Leah is Chastity's cousin." Distantly, anyway. Apparently everyone from the compound is related to everyone else by marriage if not blood.

She plucks one out of the box and bites into it. "Okay, wow." She chews happily for a minute. "These are delicious. And you're ramping up for the holiday season?"

"Right. Our first delivery is in two weeks. And here's the order form with all the information and pricing." I put it down on her desk before she can object. "I'll let Chastity know you got your boxes."

"Okay, kid." She shakes her head. "I hope you get your shit under control."

"Thanks," I murmur. "You have a nice day."

I leave her office and find Rickie, who's picking out a few different fancy cheeses. "These prices are pretty high," he says.

"Let's go to our regular store, then."

"No way. You brought me to good cheese. I shall dine on good cheese. And you're paying half."

"Okay." If there's one thing I've learned by now it's that fucking things up is expensive. "They have fresh bagels."

"Ooh! Get some of those. And don't forget the smoked salmon."

"It's like fifteen bucks a pound!"

"Just get a little," he insists. "We're going to eat really well while you tell me what stupid thing you've done now."

We do eat well. But the gourmet food doesn't make it any easier to explain what happened. I begin by stumbling through an outline of what transpired between Chastity and me. Not that it's easy to explain the way we went from arguing to...

My pulse jumps when I picture Chastity naked and begging me to fuck her. Did that really happen?

"I'm not half as surprised about the sex as you are." Rickie snorts as I tear my napkin into little shreds. "That was just overdue."

"Yeah, maybe, but..." I don't know how to explain it without being crude. "I wasn't *gentle*. It was wild and—" I swallow hard. *Use me*, she'd said. And now I'm worried I did that exact thing. "And before I got a chance to talk to her and make sense of it, Kaitlyn turned up."

"Oh shit." Rickie whistles under his breath.

"I think she heard the whole thing. And she did not take it well." I tell him every horrible thing she said.

"Ouch," Rickie says, getting up to pour water from the tea kettle into both our mugs. "So you're upset because Kaitlyn told the truth?"

"No! *Jesus H.*" Was he even listening? "I'm upset because Kaitlyn *twisted* the truth. I never said Chastity was unattractive. And it's not like we sat around discussing her."

"What *did* you say, then?"

"I told Kaitlyn that I wasn't attracted to Chastity. It's not the same thing at all."

Rickie carries the mugs back to the kitchen table. "It's not exactly the same, no. But it still wouldn't be that easy to hear from the guy you just handed your v-card to."

I let out a groan, because he's right. "The only reason I *ever* denied my attraction to Chastity was that Kaitlyn wouldn't shut up about it. We never would have had the conversation if she wasn't insane."

"Is she, though?"

"Yes!"

He drops tea bags into the mugs. "Are you attracted to Chastity?"

"Of course I am!" I shout, jumping out of my kitchen chair. "We just about burned her bed down last night."

Rickie pretends to duck. "Well, now we're getting somewhere." He pushes a mug of tea toward my side of the table. "Sit down, hothead. I'm only playing devil's advocate. And in this case, the devil isn't too hard to find."

"Fuck." I collapse into the chair. "I'm the one who didn't want to screw up our friendship. And now I've detonated it. But before it all went wrong, it was..." Hot? Amazing? Incredible? All those words sound flip.

I've had a lot of sex before. I like adventure, because I'm easily bored. So I've basically tried everything. But it's been a long time since I've been so *intimate* with someone, since I've had that kind of clawing, desperate sex where I'm so stuck in the moment that I hope it never ends.

But they always do. And this one ended spectacularly badly. I don't know how to come back from that. "What do I say to Chastity? If I can even get her to talk to me. Kaitlyn was so harsh."

"Kaitlyn is a bitch," Rickie agrees. "But her feelings were hurt. And she thinks this validates her world view."

"What world view is that?"

"That you were emotionally unavailable to her."

I make a noise of disgust. Her behavior today didn't exactly make me wish I'd been more open. Good lord, the girl cannot be trusted.

Rickie's tea smells hot and spicy, and it soothes me. That's the benefit of living with the campus eccentric. Good tea and constant conversation. He rarely leaves the house, and he's never too busy to talk.

"What are you going to do about Chastity?" he asks now.

"Apologize a hundred more times." Obviously.

He clicks his tongue as if I've said the wrong thing. "But then what? More sex?"

"No," I say quickly. "No way."

"But you'd like to."

I just shrug. What I'd like doesn't really matter.

"Does she want to?" he presses.

"Doubt it. Would you? Maybe she wanted more *before* Kaitlyn made the whole thing seem like a tawdry lie."

"Did she enjoy herself?"

"Absolutely," I scoff. "But it was a terrible idea. I should have said no and saved us both the anguish."

"But you said yes. Why?"

"Well, she was so—" I scramble for words. *Raw. Needy. Real.* "Honest," is the one I settle on. "I didn't know she'd ever want me. And it blew my feeble little mind. I was like a little kid on Christmas."

Rickie laughs.

"But now I know why it's a bad idea to fuck your best friend."

"Which you'd been wanting to do for a long time."

"Fine. Sure. Does it matter if it's true? It was a horrible idea. Chastity doesn't need me. She needs a guy who—" I break off the sentence, because I don't really want to imagine her having sex with someone else.

"Who—?" Rickie prompts.

"Doesn't think with his dick," I say, for lack of a better explanation.

"She needs someone who loves her," Rickie says.

"*Yes.* Right."

Rickie smiles at me. "So you have two problems. The first is that you have to figure out what the hell you want out of this."

"I want our friendship back." It's not complicated.

"Hmm," he says. "That's it?"

"Of course. What else would I want?"

He stirs his tea slowly. "A future together? It's been done before."

"Not by me," I say quickly. "I love Chastity as a friend. There's nobody better. But I don't do futures."

"Not easily," he muses, sipping his tea. "Not with your abandonment issues."

"My what?" I sputter, and then burn my mouth on the tea. "How do you drink this stuff so hot?"

"It's my superpower. That and seeing through your bullshit."

"I don't have bullshit. And I don't have abandonment issues. That's Kaitlyn's problem."

"Oh, you have a matching set. Her father doesn't care for her. And yours left you."

"He *died*."

"I'm aware. And you haven't been the same since."

"Rickie," I growl. "Don't psychoanalyze me. You didn't even know me before."

He shrugs, as if it's just so obvious. "Look—you asked me what to do. The answer is that you have to decide if you're brave enough to try out this thing with Chastity. Because a friendship can survive one night of ill-advised sex. But it can't survive denial of feelings."

"Who's doing the denying in this scenario?" I have to ask.

"You are." He laughs. "Chastity already knows her feelings."

"Do I want to hear them?"

Rickie's smile turns wry. "I don't know if you're ready."

I put my head in my hands. This conversation is getting too heavy. "You think she has a thing for me? Like really a *thing?*"

"I don't want to put words in her mouth," he says quietly. "Maybe you can ask her yourself. But first you have to win back her trust."

"By apologizing."

"Maybe," he hedges. "But here's your real issue—you did lie. You pretended you weren't attracted to her. You lied to Kaitlyn to save face. You made this mess, and her anger is entirely justified."

"Then I guess it's time to grovel. I'll call. Today."

"She won't answer," Rickie predicts.

"I can't apologize by email. That's just cold."

"Flowers?"

"Isn't that a cliché? Chastity would prefer that I spent the money on something more useful. Like our business. She needs so many things."

"Like what?"

"A computer. A phone. The right version of her textbooks." I shake my head. "This is why I can't be casual with her. I know too much. She doesn't deserve a guy who just wants to get a little drunk and screw around. She needs someone to take care of her."

"Don't we all, though?"

"Can you just stop being the philosopher king for a second and tell me I'm not an asshole?"

"You're not an asshole... usually."

"Oh, for fuck's sake."

"In this case I think you've been an asshole to three people. Chastity, Kaitlyn, and yourself, too."

"Anyone else you want to add to the list?"

"Nope, that will do."

I pull out my phone and try Chastity's land line.

It rings and rings with no answer.

TWENTY-ONE

Chastity

I SPEND the rest of Monday hiding in my room, feeling weepy and very sorry for myself. Every time I remember the things that Kaitlyn said, I just want to die.

I know she was laying it on thick—she was intentionally cruel and trying her best to wound me. But it worked. She didn't have to even try very hard, because the truth hurts. A lot.

Did you ask him to tutor you? Did you think he'd fall in love?

Check and check. I don't know when she arrived home and began to overhear. But it really doesn't matter. She saw right through me, probably from the first day we met.

That's how pathetic I really am. Because I really *did* imagine that sex with Dylan would make him return all my feelings. I hoped he'd fall in love with me. That's all I ever wanted, since the first day I met him.

And I'm obviously bad at hiding it. Given the choice, I'd hide in my room forever. Except I'd starve to death and fail my classes.

So when dinnertime arrives, I finally pick myself up off the bed and tiptoe out into the hallway of our suite. It's quiet, and Kaitlyn doesn't seem to be here.

Small mercies.

In our bathroom, though, I find that my shampoo bottle has

fallen off the tiny window ledge where we keep our products. Somehow, its top was loose, and now it's spilled all over the tub. I pick it up, but most of the five-dollar bottle is already smeared everywhere.

It could have been an accident. But it wasn't.

Worse yet, my toothbrush is in the wrong spot. And so is my toothpaste. I guess I'll be replacing those, because only the lord knows what she did with them.

And there goes another seven dollars I don't have. I didn't mean to make an enemy, but it looks like I have one.

When I'm looking as presentable as possible, I run down the stairwell to Ellie's door and knock.

She opens it immediately, then gives me a giant metallic smile. "Hi! Need help with algebra?"

I shake my head. "Not this time. I was just wondering if you were going to dinner at the dining hall."

Her smile widens, and I feel a little puff of optimism. I have never needed a friend as badly as I need one right now.

"I'll get my coat," she says.

"How was your weekend?" I ask, pushing macaroni around on my plate. It isn't as good as Leah's.

"Not bad. I went home and made apple pie with my mother."

"Where's home?"

"Brattleboro."

"So that's close?" I guess. I know it's in Vermont, anyway.

"Two hours, actually. And they have to drive me both ways. That's why I don't get away from here very often."

"Oh. I'm sorry." I set down my fork.

"What's bothering you?" she asks. "Is it the hot farmer boy again?"

"Yes," I say, because I obviously suck at lying.

"Oh no. What happened?"

I open my mouth to answer, but then close it again. I'm not ready to discuss it in detail. I don't know if I ever will be. "I did some things. I took some chances. And I'm afraid I outed myself. Now he knows what a pathetic little fan girl I am."

"Oh no," Ellie says, her giant eyes getting glassy. "I'd die."

"You wouldn't die," I say, because I know how this works. I'm a veteran of screwing up my own life and suffering through the consequences. "You'd just be embarrassed for the next hundred years."

"I'm sorry, Chastity."

"I'll be okay." At least this time nobody will *beat me* for my poor judgment. Unless it's Kaitlyn, and she'd do it if given the chance. "I'll just avoid Dylan for the rest of my three and a half years in college. No problem."

Ellie cracks up. "Does this mean you'll need more algebra tutoring?"

"Definitely." And I should have thought of that before I charmed Dylan out of his underwear. "I think the financial aid office would hook me up with a paid tutor if I asked."

"You don't have to do that," Ellie insists. "I'll help you for nothing. It's not like I get out very much."

"Why is that?" I ask.

"Because I'm..." She murmurs the rest into her milk glass.

"Sorry? You're...?"

"Seventeen."

I blink. "Years old?"

"Yup."

"But I thought you said you were a junior?"

"Oh I am. I started when I was fifteen."

"So you're, like, a genius?" I squeak.

"That's a loaded word. We say 'intellectually precocious' instead." Then she sighs. "I shouldn't have told you, right? Nobody wants to be friends with the weirdo who isn't even voting age and doesn't have a driver's license. I know all about particle physics. But I've never been kissed by a boy. Or a girl, for that matter."

"Ellie!" I shake my head. "If there was a weirdo contest here at this table, you might not win. I'm a twenty-one-year-old freshman who ran away from a cult two years ago. And everything I know about boys I learned in *Seventeen* magazine."

Her eyes widen. "You do have some weirdo cred."

"I know, right? And I don't have any friends, except for the ones at home, and the one who has no idea what to say to me after last night."

She flinches on my behalf. "I can help you with the algebra. But not the heartache."

"That's something," I say as cheerfully as I can. "But in a few days I'll have to figure out what to do about the little business venture Dylan and I started together. We're supposed to make two hundred pounds of caramel over the next two weeks. While I put on a brave face and pretend that I'm just fine."

"Two *hundred* pounds?"

"Or more. I don't know what orders have come in."

"I can't wait to try this candy."

"You can. There's an extra box in the..." It hits me then. The co-op store meeting! A bolt of terror shoots through me. "Oh, *no!* I was supposed to deliver some samples to a Burlington store this morning. Dylan was going to take me there."

"Maybe he did it?" Ellie suggests.

"God, I hope so." But Dylan probably forgot, too. "I'll guess I have to go to the library after this and check my email. I've been avoiding him."

Ellie pulls her backpack off the floor and unzips it. She pulls out a laptop and flips it open. Then she hands it to me. "Bite the bullet."

"Right now?" I yelp.

"Get it over with," she says.

With a sigh, I take her computer. "Thank you for letting me use this."

"Anytime."

I log in to campus email. Sure enough, my inbox contains four messages. The first three are from Dylan, and the fourth is from Leah.

Oh heck. Does Leah know that Dylan and I spent the night together? The subject line of her message is: *this weekend*. If he said anything to her, I'll die of shame.

I open the oldest email and find a picture of a puppy covering its face with its paws, saying *I'm so sorry*. And Dylan's request to call him.

Yeah, I don't think so.

The next email is also from Dylan. *We have to talk, okay? Kaitlyn blew everything out of proportion. Please answer your phone. Let's not avoid each other just because Kaitlyn is a miserable human.*

He makes a good point. But it doesn't really matter. Kaitlyn is miserable, but she was also right. I'm so embarrassed about asking him to sleep with me. I can't talk to him yet.

Then—thank goodness—his third email says only: *I forgot to tell you that I drove the caramels to the food co-op and gave them to that woman who manages the place. She wants you to follow up.*

"Well?" Ellie demands. "The price of using my laptop is telling me what happened. I'm dying over here."

"Dylan dropped off the samples."

"And?" she yelps. "I need more."

"He wants to talk to me about the…" I clear my throat.

"Caramels?" she guesses.

"*Sex,*" I whisper.

Ellie drops her fork, letting out a high-pitched squeak. "There was *sex?*"

"Shhh!" I look around to see if anyone is listening. "I'm not talking about that."

"Please?" she begs. "I want to live vicariously through you. I'm never having sex. I have braces, and I'm literally jail bait. Was it awesome?"

"Of course," I whisper. "But that's all I'm saying. And I have one more email to read. Sorry."

She lets out a deep sigh. "Take your time. It's not like I have a hot, naked farm boy waiting somewhere for me."

Neither do I, though.

I click on Leah's email and then quickly scan it. She wants to know if our big order means that Dylan and I plan to make caramels on both Friday and Saturday. But of course I have no idea.

And I *dread* Friday and Saturday.

At the bottom, there's something else. *Chastity, you won't believe this! I think we're going to be awarded a grant. I don't know how large yet. But my non-profit will stop being just an idea, and become a THING! We're going to help at least a few of the women and men who need us. I'm so excited I can barely stand it.*

It's a little bit of good news on an otherwise terrible day. So I tap out a reply. *Tell me how I can help.*

After all, maybe I can help another girl escape a cult so she can live a confusing life of freedom and frequent embarrassment.

I finish my email with a promise to get back to Leah about the weekend. Maybe by then I'll be over this feeling of wanting to curl up and die of shame.

Probably not, though.

TWENTY-TWO

Dylan

OVER THE NEXT three days I become increasingly anxious when Chastity doesn't answer my emails. And nobody answers the phone, either. Not even Kaitlyn.

Since begging doesn't work, I try humor. I send Chastity funny pictures of kittens. I send her a video of black bears in a backyard pool, and goats and bunnies acting silly together. I also apologize, of course. And ask her to meet me for coffee.

"She doesn't respond. At all," I complain to Rickie. "I'm used to women being mad at me, but I don't know what to do when they're silent."

"She's not mad at you, though," Rickie points out. "She's upset and embarrassed. She has no idea what to say to you. And now you're sending her the same things you'd send a six year old who was having a tantrum. Chastity hates to be infantilized."

"But I like goats and bunnies!" I argue. "It's not supposed to be infantilizing. I really am this cuddly."

Rickie laughs. "I know, buddy. I know. You're a good guy. You're a fun guy. You like to party, and you like everyone to be happy. You help little old ladies cross the street, and then you pass them the bong..."

"Do you have a point to make, or are you just amusing yourself?"

God, I'm in a grumpy mood. This thing with Chastity has me all twisted up.

"Easy," Rickie says. "I'm just saying that we can't all be like you. Consider where Chastity is coming from—men have been lying to her for years."

"Which men?"

"All of the men in that shithole where she grew up. Think about it. They told her she's a special lamb of God. But to prove it, she had to marry an old man. They told her that her body was the only thing of value. But then they told her it doesn't belong to her at all."

"It's all disgusting," I grumble.

"It is," he agrees. "But that's why Chastity doesn't have much faith in people's words. If you apologize, she can't really hear you. She'll just be waiting for the next lie."

"So what the hell am I supposed to do?"

"You have to apologize with *action*. Just be there and do what needs doing."

Unfortunately, there are plenty of things that need doing. We have caramels to make. A lot of them. And this weekend has its own complexities.

I try email one more time. The subject line is: ***200 pounds of caramels***. That would get anyone's attention.

Hey, C:
Look, I understand why you're blowing me off. Kaitlyn took a private moment and made it ugly. But it wasn't ugly. Not to me.
You obviously need a break from my company. But there's this little matter of caramel. And Griff needs to get the goat's milk out of our freezers so that he can slaughter a pig and put the meat in there.
We have two weekends to get this done. That means you have a few more days to get over being mad at me. Most people need longer than that, but we're on a deadline.
Come home with me on Friday, okay? This will be easier if we don't have to do it all at once. And this project is important to me. (So are you, by the way.) I need you to reply to this message to let me know that you're in. This is a team project. And I really want to stay on the team.

- Love, Dylan

"Nice," Rickie says, leaning in to shamelessly read over my shoulder. "It's breezy, but heartfelt. Warm, but businesslike. I give you full points for the dismount."

"It will have to do." I sigh, refreshing my inbox, already anxious for a reply even though I just hit Send.

"Oh, Dylan," Rickie says with a chuckle. "You are such a study in contrasts. A farmer who parties. A smart man who's stupid about women. The guy who likes goats and dirty sex, but not at the same time."

I put a hand on Rickie's flannel-covered shoulder and push him back toward his corner of the couch, while he laughs.

"Wait," Keith says, entering the living room. "Who thinks goats are sexy?"

"Nobody!" *Jesus.*

"Dyllie Bean! I'm just teasing you," Keith says. "Dude, I finally got us a gig! A real one. The LGBT Committee is hiring us to play one of their Guerrilla Night events."

"Wait, what?"

"You heard me! It's a ninety-minute set at a bar. It's a paid gig, Dyl. We're splitting *five hundred bucks.* And it's this Friday."

"Friday? No way. I can't."

"Why?" Keith whines.

"Because I'm showing my feelings with actions, not words."

"What? Have you two been hitting the bong without me?" Keith paces towards the sofa and sniffs the air.

Rickie laughs. "No, we're getting high on our homework. And Dylan is stressing over a girl."

Keith turns around and sits heavily down on the couch between us. Or he tries to, but he lands halfway on top of us.

I give his flannel-covered butt a nudge. "Dude. Did I invite you to cuddle?"

"Sex is the only way to get your attention. Do I have to blow you to make this gig happen? I want to play guitar for money. And there will probably be free drinks if we smile pretty."

"When did you say this was?" I ask, sliding over a few inches to make room for him.

"Friday night. Eight thirty until ten."

"Do we even have ninety minutes of music?"

"We do if we practice."

I shake my head and check my email again, just in case Chastity happens to be sitting at the library in front of a computer terminal right this second. "How much does an entry-level Netbook cost?" I ask Keith, who knows more about computers than I do.

"Three or four hundred bucks," he says. "For a piece of crap, though. You don't want that machine."

"It's not for me," I mumble as my phone rings. I grab it, in case it's Chastity.

It's not. It's my bitchy twin sister. She never calls. In fact, the last time she called me it was an accident. "Hello? Daphne? Did you butt dial me again?"

"Dylan," Daphne says. "How are you?"

"How am I? Fine. Why?"

"What do you mean why? That's how phone calls are supposed to begin."

I let out a snort. "You never call me to shoot the shit, Daph. What do you need?"

"A place to stay this weekend. In Burlington."

"I'm supposed to go home," I say immediately. "Griff would kill me. And I have to make caramels with Chastity."

"Dyl," she says in a low voice. "Please? I need this, and I already told Griffin that you weren't coming home, because I was going to visit you."

"You did?"

"Yeah. Just now."

"And Griffin said that was fine?"

"He can get Zach for some extra hours this weekend to cover you."

I sit with that a moment, trying to decide how annoyed to be. "Okay. You can stay one night, but I really do have to make caramels. Chastity is mad at me and—"

"Why?"

Oops. "That's personal. But I can't screw this up."

"Did you sleep with her?" my sister asks, because she has never respected my boundaries. Or anyone else's.

"If I did, I wouldn't tell you."

"Dylan!" she gasps. "Really? You slept with our virginal neighbor who thinks you're a God among men?"

"She does *not* think that," I argue. And then I realize I contradicted the wrong thing. "Just stop, okay? Don't pry. I have to go home for the weekend and fix this."

Daphne laughs. "What would Leah say?"

"Nothing good," I admit. "And you're not going to tell her."

"I think we can help each other," Daphne says. "I'm coming to visit. But I have no money, so I can't take you and your roommates out to dinner as payment."

"You could cook, though," I point out.

"I suppose. But I was going to offer to help you make goat's milk caramels."

"Where? We need a state-certified kitchen."

"Better get on that, then," Daphne says. "I'm coming Friday night. My meeting is on Saturday."

"Your meeting," I repeat slowly.

"See you soon," my sister says. Then she hangs up.

I let out a loud groan. "My family are the pushiest assholes in the world."

"Your family are the nicest people alive," Rickie says without looking up from his book.

"Does this mean you're playing the gig Friday night?" Keith asks. "I'll put up with Daphne if it means I can get paid."

"Maybe," I hedge. I tap my brother's number on the phone, hoping that it goes to voicemail. Or that Audrey picks up. She's more fun to talk to.

No such luck. "Dylan," my brother answers on the first ring. "To what do I owe this pleasure?"

"It's about the weekend," I say.

"Yeah, I thought I might hear from you. Daphne wants to stay with you in Burlington, right?"

"Apparently."

He grunts. "See if you can figure out what's wrong with her, okay? She sounds rough."

"Okay." Although I'm literally the last person my sister will ever confide in. "I'll try?"

"You do that. I'm counting on it."

That's my brother—always sticking his nose in everyone's business. "Talk soon."

"You bet," he says with a weary sigh. Then we hang up.

"Yesssss!" Keith says, pumping the air. "I heard every word. And now you have to play this gig with me."

And write Chastity another email saying that now we *can't* go home for the weekend. Fuck my life.

"There wasn't any yelling," Rickie points out. "There's usually more yelling when Griffin is on the phone."

"Just wait until you meet Dylan's sister. She's like the anti-Dylan. Uptight as fuck. You'll hear some yelling."

Rickie puts his feet up on the coffee table. "This is going to be a really interesting weekend."

TWENTY-THREE

Chastity

Dear C,

Well, this is awkward.

First of all, thank you for replying to my email. Even if it was only nine words (yes, I counted them) I'm glad to hear from you.

However.

Now I can't go home. Daphne has decided she needs to visit Burlington and stay with me. And for some reason Griffin thinks this is a great idea and has excused me from working this weekend.

I'm trying to figure out how to make caramels in Burlington. But without Leah's kitchen, it's not a slam dunk.

But I'm working on it. If you want a progress report, or if you want to talk, or even if you want to yell at me, please call. Anytime.

Miss you—

D.

"NINE WORDS?" Ellie asks, eyeing me in the mirror. "Cold!"

"I wasn't cold! You don't know how I agonized over those nine," I point out.

She grins. "So how many words did you use in your reply?"

"Twenty," I admit. "I wrote—*It won't be easy to make it all in one weekend. Maybe Leah will help us. We'll figure it out*."

"Brrr." Ellie wraps her arms around her chest and gives a mock shiver. "Not one warm word for our hot farm boy? You're really making him work for it."

"It's not intentional." I don't want Dylan to feel bad. But I don't know how to go back to the way we were before. "If only I hadn't had the idea for goat caramels in the first place."

Ellie rolls her eyes at me in her bedroom mirror, where we're putting on makeup. "You need to buck up and face him. Yeah, it's awkward now. But the only way to make it less awkward is to see him again."

"I'm not ready," I grumble. "And you're not ready for this party. You didn't do your lower lashes."

"I'll just get it everywhere," she complains.

"Hold still, then." I uncap the mascara and fix Ellie's makeup.

"How are you better at makeup than I am if you grew up in a puritanical cult?"

"*Seventeen* magazine, and later, *Cosmo*," I tell her. "I was a sponge for this kind of information before I ever owned a tube of lip gloss. Once, I stole my stepfather's Sharpie marker and used it as mascara. It totally worked, too."

I'd felt impossibly bold and rebellious all day long, with my darkened lashes. Luckily, nobody noticed. I would have gotten another beating for sure. Or—worse—they might have made me give up my job at Walgreens.

In my heart I've always been a rebel. It's just that my infrequent attempts to stir things up usually end in disaster.

"You're thinking about him again, aren't you?" Ellie says.

"Maybe," I grumble. "I don't think I'm ever going to stop feeling like a fool. I took an easy friendship and made it difficult."

Although for me our friendship was never easy. I've always wanted Dylan. Always. I still want him, only now he knows it.

And I just spent two days gearing up to face him again, only to read that email a few hours ago, canceling our weekend at home.

"Time heals all awkwardnesses," Ellie says. "That's what my mother says, anyway. It might take a lot of time, though, seeing as I still vividly remember every awkward thing I've ever done. Just put on some lipstick, okay? Let's go to this party."

"When does it start?" I ask, digging through my bag for my favorite tube.

"See, I'm not sure fraternity parties have a stopping or starting time. They just *are*."

"And you know this because…?"

She doesn't answer right away, because she's blotting her own lips. "Look, I don't actually know. But that's why we're doing this. To find out which things Hollywood got right and which ones are fake."

"So this is basically a science experiment?" I lean toward the mirror and purse my lips.

"I have a very analytical mind," she admits. "But I want to go out. You and I are too sheltered, and it's time we did something about it."

"But fraternities can be a little dangerous if you don't know what you're doing." That's what Leah thinks, anyway.

"We'll stick together," she insists. "Besides, I chose this one carefully. We're going to A Mu."

"A…moo? What?"

"No—Alpha Mu. Those are their letters. It's an environmental frat. Seems like a good place to get our feet wet, right? How scary could a bunch of vegans really be?"

"An environmental fraternity?" I giggle in spite of myself. "Those red plastic cups are out, right? Unless they rewash them after the party."

"We're going to find out," Ellie insists. "Do you want to call Dylan back before we go?"

For a moment I actually consider it. I miss him. But if his sister is in town, then he's probably out with his friends. He doesn't want an earnest phone call from mopey me.

"Nope," I decide. "Let's roll."

Thirty minutes later I'm standing on the slightly sticky floor of a fraternity house basement, listening to Ellie chat up one of the pledges.

She was right about one thing. This dude is not at all scary. For starters, I probably outweigh him. He's wearing a T-shirt that reads: *Keep Earth Clean, This Isn't Uranus.* And he's explaining the environmentally friendly features of the frat house to Ellie.

"We have photovoltaic electricity," he says. "A geothermal heat pump, and solar hot water, too."

"Coolio," Ellie says.

"Want another beer?" he offers.

"Well..." Ellie looks into her cup. It's made of paper, and it's compostable. "I'm not done with this one. I'm good."

I also shake my head. The beer is warm and kind of awful. I'm confused about how people accidentally get drunk on this.

"Snacks?" he asks me. "They're gluten-free. And I didn't catch your names."

"I'm Chastity," I say, offering my hand. "And this is Ellie."

"I'm Alfalfa," he says. "That's my, uh, pledge name. My real name is Angus."

"Huh," Ellie says, and I can practically see her filing away the idea of pledge names for later. "Let's dance, Alf." She actually hooks one of his skinny arms in hers and points toward where a bunch of people are already gyrating under the light of a disco ball.

Alf's face lights up, as if he's won something wonderful. Then he leads Ellie toward the dancers, taking care to stash his cup on a ledge along the wall.

Ellie does the same. "C'mon, Chastity," she hollers over her shoulder. "Please?"

I follow them, even though I don't feel like dancing. But I'm here. I'm wearing mascara and everything. And I want Ellie to have the full experience.

Also? Dancing isn't allowed on the compound. So even though I don't really know how to dance, I'm going to do it just on principle. And it goes well enough, I guess. I swing my hips and raise my arms and smile at Ellie, who beams back at me, causing sparkly light to bounce off her braces.

Alf keeps making eye contact with Ellie, and I can't help but find them adorable. Before long, another guy kind of sidles up next to me. He gives me a friendly smile and starts to dance.

He's cute. Cuteish, anyway. But he's no Dylan Shipley.

Nobody is, though. I've spent a lot of my time this week wishing I could rewind my life. I want to take back everything I said and did after eating pizza in my room.

No—I'd go back further. I'd undo the lie I told Dylan about Leah's weekend availability. And maybe he'd still be dating Kaitlyn, and I'd still be mooning over him privately.

Everything is so much worse now. Even when I manage to forget about him for an hour or two, Kaitlyn usually reappears, giving me smug looks as she passes our bathroom. Or she's leaning over to whisper to one of her friends when I pass her in the dining hall.

The first time I kissed a boy, I was beaten for it. Now I administer my own beatings. I feel achy and sad, and I don't know how to stop.

Eventually, another guy taps my dancing partner on the arm and tells him there's some problem with the composting toilets. He makes a face, gives me an apologetic wave, and goes off to deal with it.

It's just as well, though, because a slow song comes on, and I don't really want to put my arms around a stranger. So I edge toward the wall and reclaim my warm beer off the ledge. And I try to look very busy drinking it.

Ellie is slow-dancing with Alf, which she seems to enjoy. He leans in and gives her a very polite kiss. And then another one, a little less hesitantly this time.

I look away, because I don't want to be creepy. But I keep myself planted here because I'm not willing to leave her alone with him, either.

And now I feel lonely, damn it. I wonder where Dylan is. Even if he's hanging out with his twin sister, they're probably at a bar full of cute girls that he could take home to bed.

I abandon my warm beer onto the ledge again, because it's not helping.

The reason I can't face Dylan is because I feel like I forced myself on him. He had two years to kiss me, and he never did. Not until I snuck up on him in an outdoor shower. And my clothes didn't come off until I talked him into it.

You said she wasn't your type. You even said she wasn't attractive.

Those words are still bouncing around in my chest, and they probably always will.

The music picks up again, and I glance up, looking around for Ellie. Cue my panic when I can't seem to spot her. But there are more people dancing now, so she's probably in there somewhere.

I decide to count to a hundred, and if I still can't see her, then I'll really go looking. I'm in the eighties when I spy her frizzy head bouncing to the beat. I take a step to the side, so I can see her clearly.

She and Alf are half-dancing, half-talking now. He leans in and says something right into her ear. She looks up at him with no small amount of surprise. After a few more beats, she rises to her toes and makes her reply.

Then, a few beats later, she gives his skinny arm a squeeze and leaves the dance floor, coming back to me. She takes her warm beer off the ledge and takes a gulp.

"A boy kissed me!" she yells, and her face is ecstatic.

"Awesome!" I say. "You checked that box."

"Then he offered to take me upstairs to his room!" she says, her cheeks flushed. "I just turned down sex with a vegan."

"There will be other vegans. Was he nice about it?"

"Totally!" she yells over the music. "He was really nice. But I wasn't *really* attracted to him, to be honest. And it's not the vegan thing. It's just…" She gets a faraway look in her eye. "There was no magic."

I know all about magic. And I'm relieved that she didn't abandon me here. Although I wouldn't have blamed her, if there had been magic.

"Unfortunately, we kind of have to leave the party now because I turned him down, and now I have to avoid him." She winces. "I'm sorry I dragged you here, and now I want to bail. We didn't even get to try Cider Pong."

"It's fine!" I shout over the music. "Let's go."

We make our way toward the stairs, collect our coats from a pile beside the overmatched coat rack, and then head out into the night.

"My ears are ringing," I complain.

"*What?*" She laughs. "Just kidding. Mine, too. Let's not go home right away."

"Where would we go? You already checked off a few boxes."

She twirls around happily, arms outstretched. "I'm just not ready to go home yet."

"Fine by me." We walk down fraternity row, where each house is lit from within, like a series of fat yellow pumpkins.

"Omigod!" Ellie squeals when we reach the corner. "There's Hot Farm Boy!"

My stomach swoops and dives immediately. "Where?" I look around, but the only other people in view are a pack of women crossing the street.

"Right *there*. On that poster!"

Sure enough, Dylan is looking out at me from a tacked-up flyer. In the photo, he and Keith have an arm around each other's shoulders. Keith's guitar is strapped to his body, and Dylan's holding his fiddle in his free hand. The sign advertises THE HARDWICK DUO at something called Guerrilla Night at a bar nearby.

"The Hardwick Duo!" Ellie cackles. "That sounds dirty."

"It's a town. I think Keith grew up there."

"Well, let's go! This concert is tonight." Ellie pulls out her phone to check the time. "They're on right now!" She grabs my hand and tugs me down the sidewalk.

"I'm avoiding him," I remind her several times as we head for the bar. "Tonight was supposed to be about other things."

"Let's just see," she says as we cross the street toward the brightly lit place. "Can you honestly resist Hot Farm Boy playing music on a stage?"

No, I guess I can't.

Ellie leaps onto the curb, steps up to the bar's entrance, and, holding the door open, beckons me inside.

Because I'm me, I spot Dylan immediately. Not like it's hard. He's up on a small raised stage, playing a fast-paced fiddle tune, wearing his usual white tee and flannel shirt, the sleeves rolled up on his muscular forearms.

And he's *glorious*. Swaying with the beat, the orange lighting glinting off his wavy hair. The music flows from inside him in an unselfconscious way. He looks relaxed and happier than he's looked in weeks.

Gulp. I knew it would be difficult to see him again. But this is so much worse than I even predicted. The crowd leans forward, because they can feel the pull, too. It's a hundred or so really attractive… I blink. *Men.*

I'd expected to see women throwing themselves at Dylan. But it's a bunch of dudes, with very few women mixed in. Most are same-sex couples, drinking and dancing with each other.

Holy crap. Dylan is so hot and lovely that everyone in Vermont wants a piece of him. Not just the women. Every gender.

"Sorry, my dear. I'll have to ask you to leave. It's twenty-one and over only."

I tear my attention off Dylan to focus on the bearded guy who's shaking his head at Ellie, crushing her hopes.

"But he's a friend of ours," she says.

Big Beard shakes his head again. "I can't break the law, though."

Of course he can't. "It's okay," I say, my hand already on the door. "Come on." I don't have cash for a ticket, anyway. That guy is also collecting ten bucks from everyone who walks in.

Ellie groans unhappily. Seconds later, we're back outside in the cold.

I can still see Dylan through the window. Let's face it, this is how I'll always see Dylan—at a distance greater than I wish for.

"Look, you should stay," Ellie says. "You're twenty-one. Here—I have money for your cover charge!" She digs into her pocket for her wallet.

"No way," I say quickly. "This was girls' night." I never want to be that kind of friend—the kind who abandons her buddy to chase after a boy. Especially a boy who doesn't really want her.

I give Dylan one more wistful glance. That's when I spot two familiar faces in the crowd. There are two women right in front of the stage, standing close together. I *almost* missed them, mistaking them for a couple.

The taller girl is Daphne Shipley. And the other one? *Kaitlyn.*

My stomach drops hard and fast.

"What is it?" Ellie asks.

"Nothing," I say, shaking my head to clear it. I turn away from the window. "Dylan's ex is in there."

"What?" Ellie shrieks, pushing past me to peer through the window. "Who is she? Wait..." She rises onto her tippy toes. "The one with the fancy red scarf, right? She looks like the evil queen in Snow White."

I laugh, because it's not a horrible comparison. Personality-wise, anyway. "She's smug, isn't she?" I hate that she's here, even though I can't imagine that Dylan invited her. But either way, Kaitlyn outgunned me in a game of wits I'd never wanted to play.

"Fuck her," Ellie says with surprising ferocity. "Let's go. New plan. I'm buying us something to drink. But you have to flash your ID at the liquor store."

I laugh as she grabs my hand. "Okay. What do you want? I think there's cheap wine that comes in a box."

"Cider," she says firmly. "You choose the kind."

Cider reminds me of Shipley Farm. I can't sit around mooning about Dylan, drinking out of a bottle with his name on it. That's too loser, even for me. So when we reach the store I choose a four-pack of Citizen Cider, a Shipley competitor.

Take that, Dylan.

"I'm still not ready to go home," Ellie says. "Let's go contemplate life from that weird sculpture in the quad."

"Okay, sure," I say. It's cold out, but partying with Ellie is a heck of a lot more fun than moping at home.

Forty minutes later, I've forgotten to be cold. The cider has warmed up my insides, and Ellie can't stop giggling.

"What do you think this sculpture is supposed to be?" I ask, leaning back against its granite base. I raise my chin and squint up at the odd twisting shapes corkscrewing toward the sky.

"No idea what the artist was thinking!" Ellie shouts. "But I have a theory. A dirty theory."

"Really?" I eye the sculpture again. It's easily twenty feet high, but even my dirty mind can't see anything sexual there. "What do you mean?"

She pulls out her phone and unlocks it. Then she hands it to me. "Google 'duck penis.'" She burps.

"Did you say 'duck penis'?"

She pushes the phone into my hands. "Go on. I dare you."

I never could turn down a dare. So I search that term and—

"Oh. My. God. We're sitting under a giant duck penis."

"Three of them!" Ellie shouts.

"How does this even *work*?" I squint at the phone.

"The duck vagina is very strange," Ellie says with a sniff.

"And you somehow know the shape of the duck penis and vagina?" I have to ask.

"Apparently."

"That's pretty kinky for a virgin, Ellie."

She hoots with laughter. "This is the only penis we're seeing tonight."

"Apparently." Now we both giggle like idiots.

"I think it's time to go home," Ellie says.

"Are you cold?" The hand that's holding my cider is freezing.

"No but…" She makes a gulping sound.

"Ellie?"

She stands up quickly. Then she doubles over and vomits.

"Oh, shit." I stand up, too. "Are you okay?"

She heaves again. "Yeah."

I dig into my coat pocket for a tissue, and thankfully there is one. I pass it to her, and she wipes her mouth. "Let's get you home."

When I look up, there are two men approaching. Police officers.

"Ladies, is that an open container?" one of them asks. He shines his flashlight right on my freezing-cold hand.

"Um…" I say helplessly. Of course it's an open container. "Is that a problem?"

"It's against the law," Ellie says. She giggles.

"Let's see some ID, miss," the cop says. "I hope you're both over twenty-one."

"Uh-oh," Ellie says slowly. And then she bends over and heaves again.

TWENTY-FOUR

Dylan

"How do I know I'm doing this right?" Rickie asks from the stove. "You didn't put the thermometer thingie in yet."

"Just keep stirring," I say over my shoulder while measuring out sugar into a bowl for another batch. "It takes a long time. When it starts to look like caramel, then we'll need the thermometer."

"It smells good already," Keith says.

"Yup. Keep buttering those pans. Are the other bottles of milk defrosted yet?"

He peers into the giant sink where we've set the milk bottles into tepid water. "Halfway, maybe? How long do you have this kitchen for, anyway?" Keith asks. "We're not going to get busted for breaking and entering, right?"

"I don't think so," I say. "A girl I know manages this place. It's where the college makes catered meals for alumni events."

"How do you know this girl?" Keith asks with a chuckle.

"The usual way," I admit, and he laughs. Jeanine is someone I hooked up with a couple of times last year. I totally sidestep his question about how long we're going to be here. Because caramel takes time.

It's almost eleven, and my friends would rather be out drinking. I have the kitchen until six in the morning, but I keep that to myself. Hopefully, we'll be done hours before then.

Hopefully.

I'm in a very optimistic mood right now, honestly. Keith was right —that gig was a blast. We played every tune we know, and then we had to repeat a few. But the crowd was great, and he and I were on fire tonight.

Now I'm making caramels for Chastity, who's bound to appreciate it. I tried calling her to let her know what I was up to, but she's not answering. And everything came together at the last minute. Daphne swung by our farm to get the frozen goat's milk, and I was able to reach Jeanine with my outrageous request.

"Am I getting sexual favors for this?" she'd asked, only half joking.

"Sadly, no," I'd replied. A hookup is the last thing I need right now. "But you can have my undying gratitude and two boxes of fancy caramels."

That had done the trick.

"Coffee delivery!" calls a female voice from the doorway.

It's Kaitlyn. She's basically the last person I would have asked to help me tonight. In fact, I didn't ask. But she tagged along with us after the concert, sucking up to my sister, who doesn't know I'm pissed off at Kaitlyn.

"Thanks," I say a little stiffly.

"I got a grande for everyone, and I bought a quart of milk, because I think goat's milk in coffee sounds a little weird."

She would think that. Honestly, how did I ever convince myself to be her boyfriend?

At least the coffee smells good. "Just…put it anywhere." There are piles of sugar, vanilla, butter and waxed paper everywhere. It's going to be a long night. "Where's my sister, anyway?" The two of them had gone off together.

"Right here!" Daphne says, walking in. "And I brought doughnuts."

"Aw, *yes!*" Keith hollers. "I knew you were the nicer twin."

Rickie laughs and turns around to greet my sister. His eyes widen in surprise.

Daphne notices him and frowns thoughtfully.

"You two know each other?" I have to ask.

"No," my sister says. "At least I don't think so? I'm Daphne."

"I know," my roommate says with a snort. "I'm Rickie."

Her face still looks blank. "Have we met?" she asks.

"Yup." He turns around, leaving it there.

"Where?" she counters.

"You'll figure it out eventually," Rickie says, back still turned.

My sister slowly shakes her head. "Okay. Well, here are all the apple cider donuts you can buy at ten thirty on a Friday night in Burlington."

"Can I stop stirring long enough to eat a donut?" Rickie asks.

"Yeah, but if any crumbs fall into that pot I will cut you. Daphne, the hairnets are on the end of that counter. You'll need one."

"Yessir!" she says, saluting me.

"What about me?" Kaitlyn asks, coming closer. "Put me to work."

Oh, for fuck's sake. "Thanks, but we've got it. Thanks for making that coffee run."

"Dylan," she whispers, coming closer. "I'm trying to apologize."

"Then apologize," I say under my breath. "But maybe I'm not the one who most needs to hear it."

She blinks. "You mean to Chastity?"

"Of course, I mean Chastity," I hiss. "You made her feel like dirt. It doesn't matter if you were jealous. You don't get to say that shit to people."

She looks stricken. "You love her, don't you?"

"What? Don't make this about me. You went apeshit at someone who doesn't have a thick skin like you do."

She blinks. "I was angry at you."

"So what?" I demand. "That doesn't give you the right to be a bitch, Kait. You can say whatever you want to my face. We can have it out. But it's not cool to be mad at Chastity just because we..." I don't finish the sentence, because Daphne is trying her best to eavesdrop.

My life is still complicated. I'm trying to dig myself out of this hole, but it isn't easy.

"The milk is defrosted, Dyl," Keith says. "And the pans are ready."

"Okay—you stir Rickie's pot for a while, and Rickie and I will set up a second one. Daphne, can you dig out the thermometer? It's somewhere by the vanilla."

"Of course."

"What about me?" Kaitlyn asks. That's her favorite sentence.

"Grab a hairnet," I grumble. "You can stir, too."

I grab my phone and try Chastity's number one more time, but she's not answering. Maybe she's mad that I canceled our trip home. Or maybe Leah came to Burlington and took her away for the weekend.

Keith puts on some music. He never leaves home without his tunes. And I get another batch of caramel going.

The first one is just about to temperature when my phone starts ringing on a table somewhere.

"Should I answer that?" Kaitlyn asks.

"No!" I practically shout. If Chastity is finally calling me and Kaitlyn answers, I may not be responsible for my actions. "Who's calling?"

"It says *Campus Security*," she says. "That can't be good."

"Let it go to voicemail," I decide, vigorously stirring the caramel to keep it from scorching on the sides of the pot. It's funny how this process seemed like such a miracle the first time Chastity showed me how caramel gets made. And now it's just another day at the office.

Chemistry. It's very reliable.

"Is it done?" Rickie asks. "Sure looks done."

"Timing is everything," I say. "Pour it off too soon, and it won't firm up. Leave it on the flame too long, and it will turn into cement. Bring over the first pan, Keith."

"Aye-aye, captain."

The thermometer spikes to two hundred fifty degrees again, so I stir it down and turn off the flame. Then I grab two potholders and quickly lift the pan off the burner.

"Grab that spoon?" I prompt my friend. I tip the caramel toward the buttered pan, and Keith helps me scrape it out. "Stop now," I say. "We want to leave the hardening stuff on the walls of the pot."

"Oooh, can I eat it?" he asks.

"Sure, but give me a second." The caramel pools into a glossy, beautiful surface in the pan. It's basically a giant plate of heaven.

"Dude, that's impressive."

"Thank you. Chastity taught me everything I know."

"About *caramel*," Rickie says with a chuckle.

"You hush," I grumble, just as my phone trills again.

I set down the empty pot and cross the room quickly. *BVU Campus Security*, my phone's screen reads.

"Hello?" I answer, eyeing the second pot of caramel, which has begun to thicken under Daphne's watchful eye.

"Is this Dylan Shipley?"

"It is. Can I help you?"

"We're holding a student tonight for an open-container violation. She failed a breathalyzer and her friend is faring worse. They're going to spend the night here unless someone signs them out."

"Who's the student?" I ask. All my frequently drunk friends are already present and accounted for.

"Chastity Campbell."

"What? *Really?*" All my friends swivel to look at me.

"That's right, sir. She's not under arrest, but she won't leave her underage friend, who's pretty drunk. And you're listed as her emergency contact. Could you pick them both up?"

"Of course! Where are you, exactly?"

I end the call a minute later, and everyone is staring at me. "Problem?" my sister asks.

"Is it Chastity?" Rickie guesses.

"Yeah, I..." My gut says that Chastity would not want me to tell everyone in this room her predicament. "I gotta run out for a few minutes."

"Now?" Keith yelps. "Kind of bad timing, no? When will the second batch need pouring out?"

"Um..." He's right. I dragged everyone to this kitchen to help me tonight, and now I'm going to walk away from eighty pounds of ingredients?

"Go," my sister says with a wave of her hand. "I can watch a thermometer until it reads two hundred and forty-eight."

"Well..." I'm so torn. Because Chastity wouldn't want me to fuck this up. "The temperature has to spike to two-fifty, and you stir it down a couple times."

"Yeah, I saw," Rickie agrees. "Just go and come back, okay? We won't scorch your liquid gold."

"Are you sure?" I hedge. But I'm already removing my hairnet.

"No problemo," Rickie says. "I do wonder what a little weed would be like in caramels, though. Do you think it would wreck the texture?"

"*Rick!*" I threaten. "Don't even think about—"

Keith cracks up. "You're so gullible, Dyllie Bean. Go help your girl. Is she sick?"

I shake my head, because I'm not willing to say, *No, she's temporarily incarcerated. And she's not my girl.*

I grab my jacket and go.

TWENTY-FIVE

Chastity

OF ALL THE crimes that might have landed me in a jail cell, I never thought it would happen like this.

I was a teenage runaway. I hitchhiked across the country, which is supposedly illegal. Once, in New York State without a clue how I was going to make it to Vermont, I stole food out of a guy's car in the grocery store parking lot. He was returning his cart to the store when I snatched something out of his hatchback.

I often wonder what he thinks happened to that package of hot dog buns. I'd scared myself by taking it. I'd cowered between two cars with my stolen goods, sure that the police were seconds away from collaring me.

But how do I finally end up in the slammer—sitting on a holding-cell bench with my back to a concrete wall?

By giving cider to a minor.

In fairness, the bench is padded, and I'm not even sure the door is locked. The policemen who found us under the statue checked our records for priors. And when nothing came up, they turned us over to campus security instead of taking us to the police station.

"I haven't led a life of crime!" Ellie had hollered, which didn't help her case. She kept giggling like a lunatic, too.

The campus security officer has already grilled us about our "disappointing behavior" tonight. There were lots of questions about how Ellie—a teenager—came to possess the cider.

"I lied about my age, officer!" Ellie kept insisting, trying to spare me from taking the blame.

Since she looks about fifteen, though, that defense is a tough sell. Everyone knows I bought that cider. I'm just lucky campus security doesn't want to make a big deal about it.

It also helps that Ellie stopped puking. Now she's asleep, her head in my lap, while I wait to see if the campus security people will get me in any further trouble.

"We have to call Elizabeth's parents," they've already said, "because she's a minor."

"How did you get so drunk?" I asked Ellie when they finally went away to rat her out.

"Alf gave me a shot."

"Of what?"

"I think it was tequila. They had a ski with shot glasses on it."

"A ski? Like...for snow?"

"Yeah, but it was wood. And there were holes drilled into it where shot glasses fit. The point is to—" She had to stop and yawn. "—tip it and everybody drinks at the same time."

"Why?"

"Because funner," she'd said. And then she'd sacked out on my thigh.

So here I sit, questioning all my life choices. I didn't know she'd had tequila, and it explains her sudden drunkenness. I'm not sure she ate dinner tonight, either.

I wonder if I could lose my scholarships for giving alcohol to Ellie. The idea makes me feel numb. Getting almost-arrested is emotionally draining.

With my head against the concrete, I'm just nodding off when I hear someone coming down the corridor. I jerk awake just in time to see Dylan Shipley following the security officer toward me.

Just when I thought I couldn't be any more embarrassed.

"Ellie." I nudge the girl who's drooling on my jeans. "Wake up."

She sits up quickly, and then grabs her head. "Oh my God. The room is spinning."

I brace myself for her to puke again, but it doesn't happen.

"Oh!" she says instead. "Hot Farm Boy is here to save us."

Dylan cracks a smile. "Who wants to go home?"

"Me!" Ellie's hand shoots up the air like the adorable teacher's pet that she is. The second the officer opens the door, she shoots out past him. "Can we just go?" she asks, a hand on the wall to steady herself. "I think I had a coat."

Rising from the bench, I lift my chin, trying to hold on to the last shreds of my dignity. But I probably smell like Ellie's puke, and there's a spot of her drool on my jeans.

I swear it was less humiliating to work at Walgreens in my Laura Ingalls dress and uncut hair.

When I step outside the cell, Dylan folds me against his chest. I take a deep inhale, because I can't help myself. And he smells like... "Caramel?"

"Yeah, I tried to call you. But when you didn't answer, I just assumed it was because I'm still getting the silent treatment." He pats my back and then releases me.

My face heats, because he's not wrong. I have been snubbing him. But only because I don't know how to do this. I don't know how to go back to being his little buddy, now that I know exactly what he looks like when he's...

A shiver runs through me.

"Cold?" He asks, rubbing my shoulder, the touch doubling my goosebumps.

"N-no," I mutter. "I'm fine. Let's just go, okay? Did they call you?"

"I'm on your emergency contacts list. And Ellie's parents said it was okay for me to collect both of you."

"Can we go outside?" Ellie asks. "I feel drunk again."

"Let's take you home," I say, stepping away from Dylan's hotness.

"Good idea," she babbles. "I'm sorry you had to spring us out of jail, Hot Farm Boy. We were a little naughty. We went to a fraternity party."

"*Really*," Dylan says, sounding amused.

"Which one?" the security officer asks.

"I forgot," Ellie says cheerfully. She won't throw Alf under the bus, I guess. "It doesn't matter, because I turned down sex with the vegans."

"Oh, Alpha Mu," the officer muses.

"So did Chastity!" Ellie continues. Our coats are hanging from pegs just inside the front door, and I lunge for them, hoping she'll stop talking. But no. "Chastity didn't have sex with a vegan, either," she says. "But they were very interested. *Very*. Are you a vegan?" She blinks up at Dylan.

"I'm a dairy farmer," he points out. "So that would be a no."

"Good!" Ellie says, reaching up to give his biceps a little squeeze. "I think both Chastity and I are meat lovers."

"Ellie!" I yelp, and I'm cringing inside. "Let's *go*." If we could just get out of this building, I could send Dylan on his way.

Or that was my plan, anyway. But his truck is at the curb. "Climb in, ladies."

"Oh!" Ellie says. "But I smell like vomit."

"This truck has seen a few things in its day," he says easily. "Just sit by the window so you can open it if necessary."

"Great idea! And that way Chastity can sit next to *you*." She winks.

I should really make a point to choose friends who can hold their liquor.

We climb into the truck, and it's just as awkward as you'd think it would be to be sprung from fake jail by the man who doesn't love you back.

"Hey—great concert tonight!" Ellie says. "I wish I could have heard the whole thing!"

"You were there?" Dylan asks, giving me a sideways glance.

"Only for a minute," Ellie chirps. "But I don't have a fake ID, so we had to watch through the window!"

Oh, kill me already. I can't even shush her, because that would make it worse than it already is. So I just sigh, instead.

Blissfully, it's a short ride back to the dorm. "Nice chatting with you, Ellie," Dylan says as he stops at the curb.

"The pleasure was all mine!" she says, as if we were all just out at a party together.

"I need to talk to Chastity for a second, though. Would you have a seat on the bench for a sec?"

"Sure!" she says, and then wobbles over to it.

I'm already unbuckling my seatbelt and sliding toward the open door.

"Chass, wait. I really am making caramels tonight. And I'm sorry I didn't reach you in time to ask you to join us."

"Us?" I ask, meeting his eyes for the first time tonight. His are brown and bottomless. And now I remember why I've been avoiding them.

"Me, Rickie, Keith, Daphne. For some reason Kaitlyn tagged along, and I've been trying to get rid of her. But if you come with me, I'll ask her to leave."

It's tempting. I don't want to be a slacker where the caramels are concerned. But I glance at Ellie, who's playing with her bottom lip. "Didn't you tell Ellie's parents we'd look after her?"

"Yeah, I kind of did," he says, wincing.

"Well, I'm going to make sure she gets to bed okay. There was some vomiting earlier."

"I had a feeling." He smiles at me, and my chest actually aches. "You know you can't duck me forever, though, right?"

Busted. "I don't suppose I can."

He taps his fingers on the steering wheel. "I don't know what to do, Chass. I need us not to be broken."

"Broken?" I ask, even though the word resonates with me immediately.

"Complicated," he tries. "I shouldn't have been so impulsive the other night. Because look what happened. You're not answering my calls."

"That's Kaitlyn's fault," I say. But it's a lie. Kaitlyn put words to some things that I didn't want to hear out loud. True things. "She's the one who made it awkward. But it's my fault for throwing down the challenge in the first place."

He gives me a small smile. "Well, I didn't really argue."

Except he did. He's the one who said it was a bad idea. He's the one who said he doesn't date. I didn't want to hear any of that.

So if we're broken now, I'm the one who broke us. I guess I'd better figure out how to fix it. "We're going to work together next weekend," I tell him. "I promise."

"Good," he says, giving me a tentative smile. "I'm counting on it."

Yup. It's going to be torture. "I'd better take Ellie inside."

"She seems cool," he says.

"She's terrific." I glance out at the spot where she's sort of swaying on the bench. "I'm not sure cool is the right word."

"It's exactly the right word," he argues. "The cool people are the ones who like you just the way you already are. She called me Farm Boy."

"I noticed that." It was actually *Hot* Farm Boy, but I'm not going to correct him.

"Like *The Princess Bride*," he says. "Kaitlyn called me Farm Boy, too. But she meant it as a put-down. I'm serious, Chass. The cool people are the ones you don't have to try to impress."

"That's a nice way to think about it," I say quietly. "Ellie is the coolest, then. But I should take her inside now."

"I know." He leans forward and traps me in one more caramel-scented hug, while my heart beats wildly against my ribs. I will never get enough of Dylan Shipley. He is my ultimate cool person and I'm just going to have to figure out how to live with that. "You're pretty cool yourself."

"You don't have to flatter me."

"I'm not," he says, and then he drops a kiss onto the top of my head. "Call me," he says. "Before Friday."

"I will," I promise, extracting myself and then hopping off the truck's seat and onto the curb. My skin feels too hot for a cold November night.

"Call me about algebra, too?" he asks as I'm about to shut the door.

"Maybe? Might not need help this week," I lie. Then I close the door and give him a quick wave before hurrying toward Ellie, who looks about ready to pass out again.

The truck doesn't move yet, though. Dylan will wait and watch and make sure we get inside. He'll be my friend and my algebra tutor and he'll spring me out of jail.

But he won't be my boyfriend. And that's just the way it is.

TWENTY-SIX

Dylan

IT RIPS me up to watch Chastity walk away from me, and I don't know why. I can't shake the feeling that I've broken something precious.

Life is full of little moments that don't matter a whole lot, peppered by a few moments when everything is on the line. Like when your best friend gets a little carried away and asks you to tutor her in sex.

Or when your father asks you to come straight home from school and help him wrestle a tire off the tractor. And when you don't, he dies.

Some mistakes can never be fixed. But when it comes to Chastity, at least I have a shot. So I drive back to the catering kitchen, park my truck, and go back inside.

"Dyllie!" Keith shouts. "Look at this fucking beautiful caramel! Who knew I was a candy genius!" He points to a tray of cooling caramel, and I hurry over to see how he's done.

There's one crystallized bit near the corner, but otherwise it looks fantastic. "Dude, yes! Thank you. Where are we?" I pull the hairnet out of my pocket.

"We got two more on the burners, and the earliest batch is in the fridge." He yawns. "Can we call it quits after that? You're down to two quarts of milk, anyway."

"Sure," I say, wondering if that first batch is cool enough to cut yet. I might be here all night, but after the last batches come off the stove, I can let everyone else go home. "You want to wash up the measuring stuff and then bounce?" I offer. "You've been a big help to me."

"I'll stay," he says with a shrug. "It's too late to find a party, anyway."

"Thanks, man."

"You'll play another gig with me sometime, right?" he asks. "I'm kinda counting on it."

"I totally will," I promise. Because Keith is one of the cool people, too.

By three a.m. it's just me and Daphne, sitting at a table and tucking caramels into candy cups, and candy cups into boxes.

"How are you going to get all of these home?" she asks.

"Plastic bins from K-Mart," I tell her. "They're in the back of my truck."

"Impressive," she says, although it sounds grudging. Daphne doesn't like to show me any praise. She's the tiger, and I'm the slacker, and it's been this way since the day we were born.

I came out first, but that was literally the last time I outperformed Daphne at anything.

"So why are you here this weekend?" I ask now, because I promised Griffin I would. "Do you have a secret boyfriend?"

Daphne snorts. "No. I'm just here to visit with someone in my field."

That's how she speaks—like a career academic. I haven't even chosen a major yet. "Like, a professor?"

"A PhD candidate in public health," she says. "She used to be at Harkness, but she left last year."

"Oh." I tuck the last caramel into a box and then close the lid and reach for the next box. "What else is going on with you, then?"

"Nothing." She grabs another box and sighs. "Did Griffin tell you to ask?"

I laugh out loud. "Maybe."

"You'd think he'd have enough to worry about without digging around in my business."

"You'd think," I agree. "But he thinks something is up with you. Why is that?"

My sister shrugs. "It's nothing either of you can solve. But thank you for asking."

"Okay," I say quietly. "But if you change your mind, I wouldn't tattle to Griffin."

"Noted," she says. "So what's up with you and Chastity?"

"Oh, so you don't share the shitty things you do, but I'm supposed to?"

"Who says I did anything shitty?" She eyes me over the box she's folding. "Did you?"

"Well, sure. Just the usual, though—having fun without stopping to think of the consequences."

"And what are the consequences?" she asks. "You're not dumb enough to get her pregnant, right?"

"No!" I yelp. "Jesus. Bite your tongue."

"Sorry," she says, plunking caramels into the box. "So what's the problem?"

"It's…" I hesitate, because I'm not willing to violate Chastity's privacy. "She doesn't deserve a random hookup. And that's the only kind I ever have. So now it's just really awkward."

"She wants a boyfriend?" my sister asks, studying me.

"Possibly," I hedge. "We didn't, uh, actually have that detailed of a conversation."

"So you're just *assuming* you know what she wants."

"Well…" This is why I try never to argue with my sister.

"Did she ask you for the hookup?"

"Yes."

"And you went with it. You did exactly what she asked?"

"Yes, but—"

"So what's the problem?" Daphne is like a verbal bulldozer. "Maybe it's you who's making this awkward."

"She won't *talk* to me, Daph."

"Do you know why?"

"No. I don't know. She didn't, uh, hate the experience. But Kaitlyn made everything weird by freaking out and screaming at both of us. So Chastity and I never got the chance to figure out how to look each other in the eye again."

"Kaitlyn is a very interesting person," Daphne says.

"I used to think so, too."

"You lose interest in everything, don't you?" She finishes another box. "It's a good thing the caramels are only a seasonal business."

"Thank God we're almost done here. I'm allowed to get sick of things at four in the morning, right?"

"I suppose."

We lapse into silence for a minute. But when your twin sister says something mildly offensive, you can't always let it go. "I didn't *get sick of* Kaitlyn. She decided to hook up with another guy to make me jealous. And I hate games and drama, so I parachuted out of there. Learned a lesson."

"What lesson? Not to date rich girls with daddy issues?"

"Not to *date*," I correct her.

"But you have feelings for Chastity," my sister says. It's a statement, not a question.

"Yeah. Too many. That's the whole problem—I like her too much to get her naked."

My sister snorts. "And people say I'm the crazy one."

"Do they say that?" I ask. "I thought you were the smart, accomplished one."

"I wear many hats."

We both laugh. This is probably the most fun I've had with my sister in a long time. Until she asks me one more question.

"What does Chastity think about your stance on dating?"

"I don't know. Why?"

Daphne gives me a sideways glance. "Have you considered breaking your rule for Chastity?"

"No," I say quickly. "Because that never ends well. If we break up, I lose a good friend. Not to mention all the people who will hate that idea. Leah and Isaac. Griffin. Mom."

"So you won't date her because you don't want to disappoint her?"

"Yes," I say. "That's exactly why."

She grabs another box and shakes her head. "I don't know Dylan. It sounds like you already have."

Well, fuck. That's a depressing idea. "You always know what to say to a guy."

"It's my superpower," she agrees.

TWENTY-SEVEN

Dylan

I GIVE Chastity the space she needs. Until Wednesday comes and goes with no call from her, I'm a very patient man.

If by "patient" you mean irritable, grumpy and generally hard to be around.

"It's algebra night," I complain to Rickie and Keith as we eat dinner together in the living room. "She didn't call."

"I noticed that," Rickie says, shoving another bite of lentil curry into his mouth.

"You did? Why?"

Rickie shakes his head. "Because you've spent the week moping around the house, checking your phone every few minutes."

"It's making me crazy." And I mean that in so many ways. I'm worried about Chastity. I'm worried about our friendship.

But at the same time, I can't help remembering the heat of her kiss. Every time I close my eyes, I'm back in her bed, tasting her skin, hearing her moan.

Not only am I horny as fuck, but I feel like an asshole. That night turned into an experience she regrets, but my libido can't leave it alone.

I just need to see her and talk to her and calm the fuck down, whether that means going back to the way things used to be, or explaining just how naked I want us to get so we can give it another try.

She'd never want that, though.

Would she?

"That's it." I stand up, grabbing my empty plate and stepping over Rickie's feet. "I have to get out of here."

"There's people coming over," Rickie says. "I'm making a rum punch. Chill out and have some drinks. You'll feel better."

"I won't," I admit. "I got some things I need to take care of."

An hour later I'm cruising around campus on foot, a small gift bag in my hand, optimism in my heart.

But I can't find Chastity. I risked running into Kaitlyn by stopping at the dorm, asking the person at the desk to buzz upstairs. No answer. Then I checked the coffee shop, where Rickie and I ran into her that one time with Ellie.

No dice.

So now it's almost ten, and I'm running out of places to look. Desperate now, I try the library that stays open until midnight. It's starting to empty out for the night, so it's easy enough to scan the tables.

By the time I've made it up to the second floor, I've almost given up. But then I spot her. She's leaning over her notebook, pencil in hand, and Ellie is sitting opposite her, chin propped in her hand, explaining something.

They're doing algebra again. Without me.

"Whoa there, ladies," I say, dropping the bag onto the table. "Are you doing math right now?"

Both of them look up at me with big, guilty eyes. "Hi, Hot Farm Boy. Chastity has a little quiz tomorrow. That's all."

"A quiz?" I plunk down in the chair beside Chastity and look at her for the first time in days. It takes me a minute, because I can't help but drink her in. She's wearing a soft-looking blue sweater that matches her eyes, and a long skirt I've never seen before.

"I thought I was the algebra tutor," I say, and it comes out sounding bossy as fuck. "Are you firing me?"

Chastity's eyes widen. "You think I can't pass a quiz without your help?"

"Didn't say that." We're having a stare-down, apparently. "But you know I like to help."

Across the table, Ellie is shoving things into her bag. "Look how late it's gotten! I'd better go!" she chirps. "Don't skip problems thirty-one and thirty-two, Chastity. Those look like something you might see on the quiz. Night, guys!"

Two seconds later, she disappears.

"You scared off Ellie," Chastity whispers.

"I didn't *scare* her off," I correct. "I'm not intimidating. I am, however, your algebra tutor. Ellie knows this."

"It's not a permanent position," Chastity snaps. "You can't just chase away my friend."

We're still locked in eye-to-eye combat, which is really no hardship for me. I could look at Chastity all day. "Chasing away your friend was not my intention," I say softly. "And if I did, I apologize. But I came here tonight because I didn't know what else to do. Not talking to you isn't working for me. So I bought you a prepaid phone." I give the gift bag a poke. "But I guess that won't even be helpful if you won't answer it."

"You got me a phone?" Chastity squeaks.

"Yes! Which you clearly need." I reach inside the bag and pull it out. Then I hand it to her. "Consider it your early Christmas gift. This saves me the trouble of trying to figure out what to get for a really good friend who's currently not speaking to me."

Chastity gives me a guilty look. Then she runs a thumb over the shiny surface of the phone, the way most people would gaze upon a treasure. "You shouldn't have," she says softly. "Thank you."

"It's returnable, in case you really hated this idea. But it didn't cost as much as I thought, and there's no monthly bill, and…" I realize I'm arguing all the wrong points. The phone doesn't matter. "Look, I can tell that I've made you uncomfortable. But it didn't used to be like that. We weren't uncomfortable."

Chastity looks up at me. "I know."

"So that's why I came looking for you. Is it really asking too much for me to sit here and help you with a few algebra problems? Maybe we could remember what this is supposed to be like. And if we do okay at that, we can talk about our other problem."

"Our other problem?" she asks.

I'd been referring to the fact that I want her so badly I ache. But first things first. "Never mind that. Can we do some algebra?"

"Okay," she says stiffly.

"Thank you. Now finish number thirty, so we can get to the tricky ones."

She gives me a sharp look and picks up her pencil. "Yes *sir*. Is there anything else you require?"

"Uh…" I swallow suddenly. I don't think Chastity meant for that to sound sexual. But it absolutely did. "I think you should just do the problem. Time's a wasting."

She gives me one more disgruntled look, and my libido lets out a little whimper. The truth is that I like this version of Chastity a whole lot. The feisty one.

The one who says "use me" when I'm inside her.

Okay! Algebra. Focus. I watch her simplify the equation. Or I try to. But it's just dawning on me that it isn't going to go away. That's another inconvenient truth.

"You look really great in that color," I blurt as she's reducing the fraction.

"Dylan," she grumbles without looking up. "Don't do that."

"Sorry."

We lapse into silence again for a while. But things are loud inside my head. And when she's finally writing the answer to number thirty, I let out a heavy sigh.

"What? Did I get it wrong?"

I shake my head. "Nope, it's perfect. Except I promised myself that I was only going to tell you the truth from now on. So here goes. The dumbest thing I've ever done was tell Kaitlyn that I wasn't attracted to you. I said it to shut her up. But also because I felt bad for looking at you that way. Because I thought you wouldn't want to hear it."

Chastity's pencil drops onto the table.

"Yeah, I know. We already dispelled that theory. I just needed you to hear it from me. I find you attractive. So attractive that I spent the whole week thinking about it. And I'm sorry if I ever made you feel otherwise."

She turns to me. "Well, if we're apologizing for things, I'm sorry I lied about Friday nights in the kitchen."

"You already apologized for that."

"I know. But it feels like it started the whole disaster. If I hadn't done that, we wouldn't be having this little chat right now."

"Fair enough. But I'm over it now. I just want us to tell the truth to each other. Can we do that?"

She turns her head and gives me a wary glance. "I'll try. Some of my truths you don't want to hear, though."

"Let's just see how it goes. Are you going to tackle question thirty-one now?"

"I guess." She lets out a sigh. "Here's a true statement—I hate algebra."

"Yup. But you're more than halfway there. By Christmas you'll be free."

She returns to her work, picking up her pencil and attacking the problem. "God, I hope the quiz isn't made up of really long, hard ones."

There's a really dirty joke just begging to be made, here. But I let it pass. I'm very helpful until she's finished with problem thirty-one.

"How'd I do?" she asks.

"Groovy. Once you divided by Y, you didn't have any more problems."

She beams down at her paper.

"Also? You look really touchable in that sweater. Just saying."

"*Dylan*. That's off topic." She gives me a sideways glance.

"I know. You can do the last problem now. But we're telling each other the truth, so..." I shrug. "It's a great sweater. The skirt is nice, too. Makes me wonder if you're wearing tights or not. So that's fun."

"Stop distracting me."

"If you want."

She goes back to work, trying a couple of approaches to the last problem. But when she tucks her hair behind her ear, it exposes a span of skin at her neck. And I can't help but think of the sweet, sexy noise she made when I kissed her there.

Knowledge is a dangerous thing. I can't unhear that sound. I can't unknow how much chemistry we have. And I don't even want to try. "Can I tell you my other problem now?"

"I guess," she says, erasing something on the page.

Instead of speaking, I lean in and kiss her neck. It's just a brush of my lips across her skin. But I inhale the lemon scent of her shampoo, and my heart starts to pound like I'm a drug addict who's suddenly within reach of his next hit.

"Dyl," she whispers. "Maybe you should sit on the other side of the table."

"Maybe," I whisper back. "But suggesting that isn't the same as telling me to do it. Since we're on a new truth kick, do you *really* want me to go sit there?"

Chastity considers me with her big blue eyes. She closes them and slowly shakes her head.

"Ah. I didn't think so." I lean in and kiss her neck again.

"What are you doing?" she asks in a husky voice.

"I'm kissing your neck. In case it's not enough to say that I'm honestly very attracted to you, I'm totally willing to prove it. Or I can move to the other side of the table and stick to algebra. It's really your call."

Chastity inhales a shaky breath. "Talking about this is really hard for me."

"Harder than problem thirty-two?" I ask for clarification.

"Actually, yes." Her cheeks are suddenly bright pink. "I know it's inconvenient. And you're being really wonderful right now. And the whole week of silence is totally my fault. But I have reasons—a lifetime's worth of being told what not to *ever* say."

"Okay," I say quickly. But the truth is that I never considered that talking about sex might be extra difficult for her. Talking about sex is probably my fifth favorite hobby. It's definitely in the top ten.

"I already spent the week wishing I could take back all the things I said to you before."

Ouch. "You regret being with me?"

"Not at *all*. I regret—" She gulps. "*Asking* for it."

"Oh," I say slowly, as that sinks in. It's hard enough to want things. But it's even harder if you feel ashamed for naming them. "That's a tight spot you're in, isn't it?"

She gives a stiff little shrug, like it doesn't matter. But it's finally dawning on me that it really does.

"Okay." I let out a big breath. "Okay." I put an arm around her and pull her close to me. And I add a quick kiss on her temple for good measure. "Thank you for explaining that."

She relaxes against me, and I feel like I can breathe again for the first time this week.

"I don't mean to be so dramatic," she murmurs.

"You aren't. Neither of us likes drama very much, but sometimes it's unavoidable."

"But where do we go from here?"

"Well…" That is the trickier question. "First you have one more problem to solve. But then I hope you'll come home with me. I need to spend a little time with you, and I can't do that at your place."

"Come home with you," she repeats slowly. The air thickens between us. I swear her blue eyes darken as I watch.

"That's right. It can just be for drinks and a snack. Or we can work on our *other* tutoring subject. But in my bed, this time. I like this idea a whole lot, but it's still your choice. And—" I suddenly think of an innovation. "—since you prefer not to talk about certain subjects, you don't have to. You can just give me a clue."

"A clue?" she whispers so quietly that I almost can't hear it.

"Yeah." I remember Rickie telling me that Chastity prefers actions to words. "You don't have to ask for tutoring. You don't have to say a word. I'll know you're all in if you hand me your panties."

"If I *what*?" she squeaks, her eyes blazing. We're back in stare-down mode, and I love it.

"You heard me." I run a finger down her cute little sloping nose. "If you want me to take you home and lift up that skirt, all you have to do is put the panties in my hand. Simplest thing ever."

She blinks. "So now it's your turn to throw down a challenge?"

"Apparently." I give her a shrug, pretending to be casual even though all my blood has begun traveling south. We stare at each other for another long moment, and then I grin. "But don't forget to do number thirty-two, first."

She lets out a little squeak of irritation and then picks up her pencil.

I guess it's really no surprise that problem thirty-two takes an excruciatingly long time. For both of us. She has to factor the equation three different times before she gets it right.

But eventually she solves the whole thing and throws down her pencil.

"Check your units," I say mildly. Although my *unit* is as hard as a fence post right now.

She adds a dollar sign to the answer. Then she pushes back her chair, gets up, and leaves me sitting at the table.

The seconds drag by until Chastity returns a few minutes later, looking a little hesitant, her cheeks deeply flushed.

When I stand up to meet her, Chastity looks me right in the eye and then places a scrap of fabric in my hand.

"I just want you to know," I say in a serious, quiet voice, "that I've never in my life prayed for underpants until just a moment ago."

"I guess there's a first time for everything," she whispers back. "Now put those away before someone sees."

TWENTY-EIGHT

Chastity

As Dylan shoves my panties into his pocket, I'm thinking—I cannot *believe* I just did that. And I can't believe he asked me to. It's as if Dylan Shipley looked right into my dirty little heart and understood me for the first time.

It's too good to be true. I don't even know what to do next.

Dylan does, though. He grabs the gift bag off the table. "Hold this. I'll carry your backpack." He yanks that into his hands, shoving my algebra notebook inside and zipping everything up hastily.

He's in a big hurry. My coat appears suddenly at my shoulders so that I can slip my arms inside. And then a strong arm wraps around my back, as Dylan leads us toward the exit.

"Don't you have a coat?" I ask as we hurry past bookworms and sleepy students studying for midterms.

"Nope," he says. "I'm from Vermont. I run hot." Then he gives me a glance that *smolders*.

Wow. It's disorienting to finally get this kind of attention from Dylan. I hurry to keep up with his long strides.

"I have my truck," he grunts as we step outside. He steers me toward the parking lot, and in no time at all, he's opening the passenger's door and boosting me up to the seat. A blast of cool air finds my bare body beneath my skirt, and I clench my legs together with surprise.

The door slams, and Dylan reappears on the driver's side a half second later, just as I'm reaching for the seatbelt.

But I don't even get there, because two strong arms yank me against his chest. I gasp with surprise as his mouth claims mine. Impulse kicks in immediately. With a whimper, I go limp in his arms, molding my body to his, softening under his touch.

"Fuck," he grunts. "I need to be inside you. I want it so bad." His tongue invades my mouth, showing me just how urgently he needs me.

I tremble as his hand slides down my body, reaching under my skirt. As his hand skims up my thigh, I have to fight the impulse to be modest. Kissing a boy in a car is how I ended up with scars on my backside.

But I didn't run away to Vermont to be afraid. So I grip Dylan's flannel shirt in two hands and kiss him fiercely as his slow caress approaches. And then his thumb is *right* there, brushing tenderly over the mound between my legs.

He groans loudly. "I have got to get you home," he says, pulling back, his eyes bright, his face flushed. "Like, yesterday." And I'm not going to argue. "Put on your seatbelt, because my abilities are impaired right now. Good thing it's a five-minute drive." He shakes his head, as if he's trying to clear it.

My seatbelt clicks into place, despite my shaking hands. And then it's a long five minutes to Spruce Street. And quiet, because this turn of events has left me speechless. It's almost too good to be true.

Tutoring, though. It's still just a fun time for him. A tutor isn't a serious role in someone's life. It's just extra.

My algebra class ends at Christmas time. I wonder if Dylan's interest in me will last even that long.

"Fuck," Dylan hisses when we pull into the driveway. Music is blaring from the house, and I see people in the windows.

"Problem?" I ask.

"Not really. I just forgot that Rickie invited people over."

This place is a zoo. "Should I go home?" I wonder aloud.

"Oh *hell* no." He cuts the engine. "Come on. Let's sneak in the back door."

I let out a nervous giggle, but Dylan has already exited the truck. Seconds later, he's opening my door for me, shouldering my backpack again and helping me down. When he closes the truck's door, I take a step toward the house.

Dylan stops my progress, pushing me back against the side of the truck, taking my chin into one of his roughened palms and then kissing me deeply.

His kisses are still a surprise. I've had quite a few of them by now, but I'm never really prepared for the warm press of his generous lips against mine and the commanding way he parts my lips to taste me. He kisses me with focus and intense concentration.

No wonder there's always a line around the block to kiss Dylan Shipley. I get it now.

I lose his mouth after an intense minute or two, but he rests his forehead against mine for a moment. "That will have to hold me until I can get you upstairs alone. Now let's go."

As we head for the kitchen door, he takes my hand in his, which is a different kind of exciting. Is it weird that it makes me want to shout?

Dylan is holding my hand!

From the mud room where we're kicking off our shoes, Dylan pokes his head into the kitchen.

"Dylan!" Rickie shouts. "Where've you been? The punch is half gone."

"Hey, Rick," Dylan says, hanging my backpack on a hook and then taking my hand again. "Quite the party you've got here."

"Nice of you to stop by." Rickie smirks at us. His eyes dart to our joined hands. "Who wants punch?"

Dylan looks at me. "Pour you a glass?"

"Sure," I say, even though I don't really care.

He drops my hand to reach for the ladle in the punch bowl on the table. "So who's here?" Dylan asks his roommate.

"The usual suspects. But none of the music department girls, if that's what you're asking."

"Good deal," Dylan says quickly, and I relax, too. I don't think I could face Kaitlyn tonight and maintain my bravado at the same time.

"Keith's playing some music with that guy Earnest. So if you're not in the mood to jam you should probably avoid the living room."

"That is excellent advice," Dylan says, handing me a glass cup filled with a rosy red liquid. "Careful," he says. "The fruit juice covers the taste of what I can only assume is a lot of alcohol."

"Noted," I say, taking a sip. It's tart and sweet and wonderful.

He lowers his mouth to my ear. "Don't get drunk, okay? I have big plans for you." Then he pats his pocket—the same one where my underpants are.

"Okay," I breathe, and he smiles.

He grabs a beer out of a six-pack on the counter and pops it open on a wall-mounted device for this very purpose. "Come on." He puts a hand on my lower back, and I'm happy to be led toward the staircase.

"Dylan!" Keith shouts as we pass the door to the living room. "Come jam with us! And do a shot!"

"Nope!" he calls.

"What do you mean no?" Keith demands. "Get your fiddle."

Dylan pauses to stick his head into the living room. "Not tonight, honey."

There's loud laughter, and several more voices call his name. Miraculously, he ignores them and leads me up the stairs. I think we're in the clear.

Until we reach the wide landing near the top, and find even more people—two guys and two girls. They're sitting around on cushions, playing cards.

"Dylan!" they call. "It's poker night! Sit! We need you." My heart sinks. They're practically right outside his bedroom door.

And it's not like I blame all the people who want his attention. I'm the same way—a little happier every time Dylan walks into a room where I am.

"No way," Dylan says. "You just want me to play because I suck at poker."

They all laugh. "We all suck tonight because this deck is missing two cards," one of the women complains. And then she turns big, brown puppy-dog eyes on Dylan. "Come sit. We were just going to light up."

Dylan releases my hand and takes a step toward them. And now I know exactly how Kaitlyn felt at parties with Dylan. For the first time ever, I feel like I understand her.

But Dylan doesn't sit down. He crosses to a built-in bookshelf beside the window. He rummages around for a second and comes up with another deck of cards. He hands it down to the girl with the big brown eyes. "If you smoke, open a window."

Then he takes my hand again and leads me the short distance to his bedroom door. He opens it slowly, peering inside, as if he's not sure what he'll find. But then he turns around and grins at me. "I found it!"

"What?" I ask, following him in.

He shuts the door. "The only quiet place in the house. You never know with Rickie's parties. Sometimes people help themselves to my room. Come on in."

"You need a lock," I say, following him. And then my face heats at the implication.

"They'd probably just use the credit card trick. I know I would, in certain situations." He gives me a slow grin, which causes butterflies to hit my tummy.

We're finally alone, although all the urgency is gone. I take a sip of my punch, while Dylan walks over and sits down on his bed. His room is really great, with a window seat at one end, and a messy desk against the wall. "This place is bigger than your room at home," I point out.

"Right?" he agrees. "Deal of the century."

I take another sip, feeling a little unsteady. What am I supposed to do right now? "Why is punch called punch, anyway?" I hear myself ask.

Dylan chuckles. "I have no idea, Chass. Do you want me to look it up?"

His eyes are teasing me, so I shake my head. But I don't know how to get back to where we were before—that heated, impulsive place where anything seems possible.

He swigs his beer and then reaches over to set it on the nightstand.

"Come here," he says simply. Then he crooks a finger and beckons to me.

And I'm across that room in a jiffy.

He takes the cup from my hand and tastes the punch. "Nice." He sets that on the nightstand, too. "Now come closer." He tugs my hand. "That's right. All the way." Then he scoops me up off the floor.

I end up with my knees on the bed, my hands on his broad shoulders.

"That's so much better," he says, stealing a quick kiss. "It's time for our next tutoring session. I hope to cover a lot of ground tonight." He gives me a serious look. "What chapter are we on, do you think?"

"There's no textbook for this," I choke out.

"But there should be," he argues. "Last time we kind of skipped right to the advanced sections. Maybe we should flip back to the beginning and cover some of the introductory lessons."

"Okay?"

He pulls me closer. Our noses are inches apart. "Do you know how many erogenous zones there are on your body?"

"No," I whisper. "Is there going to be a quiz?"

He shakes his head. "Just lots and lots of homework."

Then he kisses me.

TWENTY-NINE

Dylan

CHASTITY'S MOUTH softens immediately beneath mine. I don't know if I'll ever get over my surprise at how responsive she is to my touch.

You *think* you know someone. You spend a lot of time introducing them to movies and pulled-pork sandwiches and frisbee. But the whole time you're laughing at *Men In Black*, you have no idea that the two of you could have sexual chemistry capable of lighting up the night.

Kissing her makes me feel wild. And just like before, I can't help escalating the situation from a kiss to a full-on make-out session. A minute later her fingers are gripping the fabric of my shirt, while my two hands are already full of her perfect tits.

I break off our kiss, because I'm in need of oxygen. But also because we're wearing too many clothes. "Chapter Three," I say in a voice that's calmer than I feel right now. "Unbutton my shirt."

She blinks at me with heavy-lidded eyes, but her hands go right to work. "So we're skipping Chapter One?"

"No." I shake my head. "Chapter One was that kiss. Chapter Two is that look you're giving me right now. Like you can't wait any longer."

She drops her eyes immediately, but she keeps up her good work with the buttons. I push away my surprise that it's Chastity who's undressing me. And I look down at her hands to watch.

"What?" she asks when she reaches the last button. "You're staring."

"I just like your hands near my body, that's all." A look of surprise crosses her features. "Now touch me."

"Where?"

"It doesn't matter. Hell." I grab her hands and put them on my bare chest. "Sometimes all of me is an erogenous zone. Right now is one of those times. So just get busy." I shrug my shirt off my shoulders to give her plenty to work with.

At first she's tentative, stroking me with light fingers. I get goosebumps immediately. But then she forgets to be shy. Her thumb traces my stomach muscles, while one of her fingers does an investigative loop around my nipple.

It's quiet in my room, if you don't count the thumping of the music downstairs. The moment feels intensely intimate, even though we're both still mostly dressed. "Now use your mouth," I suggest.

Her blue eyes flick up to mine, questioning.

"Come on," I encourage her. "You know you want to."

She leans slowly forward until her lips meet my chest. "That's right." Her lips begin to softly explore my skin, giving me chills. "Good girl."

Something changes when I say those words—Chastity relaxes. Her kisses become less tentative. I gather her hair in my hand, and guide her head. She moans against my skin. *Whoa.* The sound makes my whole body flash with heat. "You like it when I tell you what to do, right?"

She nods quickly. I'm not a smart man, but I'm catching on. Chastity wants direction—and not because she's inexperienced. She wants direction because it makes her *hot.*

"Now use your tongue," I order, just to test this theory.

Not a half second later she's licking my nipple, stroking my chest with her other hand, and clenching her thighs together needfully. When my hand tightens in her hair, she moans again.

The whole tutoring thing was meant to be a joke. But I realize now that it does something for her. She likes it when I tell her what to do. She *really* likes it.

I'm a fan, too, apparently. We've only been home for five minutes and I'm about to burst into flames. My cock is straining against the zipper of my jeans, begging for attention. "Unzip me," I order.

She must like this idea, because she pops the button on my jeans and works my zipper down in a hurry. Then she licks a line across my stomach, right above the elastic of my underwear.

I can't wait any longer—I reach down into my boxer briefs and extract my aching dick. "You know I've been hard since sitting down beside you in the library, right?"

I take one of Chastity's hands and place it on my shaft. Chastity wraps her fingers around me immediately, her touch soft and seductive. And when she drags her thumb experimentally across my cockhead, I let out a gasp of pleasure so loud that she looks up, startled.

"Yes... That's... Keep going," I stammer. It's hard to stay in character when there's so much tension coiled inside me.

I feel my self-control begin to evaporate as Chastity strokes my cock. I'm trying to be patient and go slow, but I just want to push her down on the bed like a beast.

"Good girl," I say tightly, gathering her hair in my hand again. "You know what comes next, right?" Slowly, I lower her mouth to my cock.

Chastity is an A-plus student already. She slides off the bed, sinking to her knees on the floor. Then she leans forward and takes the tip of my cock between soft lips.

I let out a helpless curse. But this time she doesn't startle. Instead, she looks up at me with heated eyes that know exactly how much I'm enjoying myself.

Yup. We're off the textbook again. Yet we're on the exact same page. "You make me crazy, you know that? I spent the whole week dreaming about your mouth on my cock."

She whimpers, then flattens her tongue against the head.

"That's right," I hiss. "Try that."

She starts experimenting—testing the feel of my cock against her tongue, and weighing my shaft in her hand. All I can do is breathe through my desire and murmur my appreciation.

Just when I think I have my control back, she finds a rhythm, using her hand to jack the shaft while sucking on the tip. And I can't shut up. "*Fuck. Yes. More.*" I don't even know what all I'm saying. I just know that I have never enjoyed a blowjob as much as I am right now, as Chastity's blue eyes lift to watch me getting wrecked by her sweet mouth.

"God, your mouth," I pant. "Stop now. I'm too close."

She considers this while giving me a slow suck. Like she can't decide which way she wants this to go.

And that makes me even hotter. "Are you seriously disobeying me right now? I'm about seven seconds away from coming in your mouth. So if you want me to lay you out and fuck you, you better give it a rest."

That gets the point across. Chastity releases me suddenly, sitting back on the floor, hair mussed, face flushed.

Jesus lord, that view. I don't even have her clothes off yet, and she's already the sexiest sight I've seen in years.

Trying to cool down, I stand up and remove my jeans and underwear. I kick off my socks. She watches me with big eyes, and it occurs to me that I might be the first naked man she's seen in real life.

Does it make me an asshole that I like this idea a whole lot? Maybe.

"Come on," I say gently, holding out a hand to help her up. "Can I undress you?"

"Yes," she whispers. "If we lock the door." She crosses the room and drops the hook into the loop on the back of my door. Then she turns off the light, too.

"Hey, now. Am I not allowed to look at you?"

"You don't have curtains, Dylan." She points at the windows, which are completely uncovered.

"So? I'm not a modest guy. Nudity is my default setting." Just to make the point, I grab my erection and wave it around until she puts a hand in front of her smile. "But I guess we can't all be this ridiculous. So I have a solution." I cross to the dresser where there's a candle I keep there for our frequent power outages. I light it and then turn around.

She's still watching me with big, hungry eyes. I don't think I'll ever get used to that look on her face. Was it always there? Did I just not see it? "Come here."

Immediately, she complies.

I tilt her face up to look at mine. "Is it dark enough for you now?"

"Yes. Sorry."

"Don't you ever be sorry," I say quietly, leaning in to give her a quick kiss. "Now what's on the syllabus tonight?"

"You choose."

I like the sound of that. Except last time I'd felt like a pushy beast. "Fine. But what's *off* the syllabus? Give me some parameters."

"Nothing is off limits," she whispers. "Not one thing."

Yowza. "But you'll tell me if I do something you don't like?"

"You won't," she says firmly. Then she lifts her sweater and shirt off in one easy motion.

And I lose my train of thought completely.

THIRTY

Chastity

DYLAN, naked and turned on, is the stuff of my fantasies. Except he also wants to *talk?* I can hardly form a sentence right now.

Apparently I made my point, though, because he's unhooking my bra and then unzipping my skirt. He yanks off my tights, too. As soon as my clothes fall away, I back toward the bed until the mattress hits my knees.

Dylan takes a detour to his bedside table, where he grabs a condom out of the drawer and tears the packet open before sliding it down his dick in a speedy, businesslike way.

Oh thank goodness. I pull back the comforter and lie down on the sheet in a big fat hurry.

Dylan follows me, wasting no time in spreading his big body out over mine. And I don't have to make any more conversation because he immediately begins kissing my neck, and then my breasts.

I sift my fingers through his thick hair and hold back a moan. His tongue on my nipples is very educational. But he presses onward, kissing his way down my stomach. I tense up as his mouth approaches my pussy.

It was me who said that he could do anything he wanted, but I'm just not sure I can enjoy his mouth down *there.*

But he parts my legs and makes a happy noise. Then he kisses my inner thighs, one at a time. His lips are soft, and the stubble on his chin is just abrasive enough to make the contrast stand out. It's pleasant. But my muscles clench anyway because I'm bracing for his next move.

"Shh," he says. "Relax."

I try. He kisses my mound. When he flattens his tongue against my clit, I practically leap off the bed, because the sensation is so intense.

Dylan actually chuckles against my pussy. He kisses me again, slowly. Then he uses two fingers to spread me open so he can lap at my sensitive flesh.

I let out a little sob of confusion. It feels so good, but everything is too focused and extreme. I feel too exposed and helpless.

He backs off, kissing my thighs, stroking a tender thumb over my core. I miss his mouth already. My nipples are hard, and my pulse is pounding at my throat.

All my cravings hurt so good.

"I could stay here for hours, you realize," he says quietly, kissing my pussy again.

"No," I mutter as my thighs clench again.

"You don't like it?"

"It's too much," I whisper. "It's better when we're..." I can't explain it. "Together."

"Mmm," he says, kissing my belly again. Then he rises up, sliding his cock inside me without warning.

I take a sharp inhale from surprise. And then I sigh and relax against the mattress. The fullness makes me feel radiant. There's nothing like it.

Dylan leans down and kisses me on the mouth. "That's what you needed, isn't it?"

My only reply is to wrap my legs around him.

He doesn't move—he just looks down at me, his brown eyes darker in the candlelight, the shadows deepening the muscles on his arms. I've never seen anyone so beautiful.

"You never answered my test question. How many erogenous zones are there?"

"Dylan," I gasp. Why is he still talking right now? I tighten my muscles and squeeze his girth inside me. I can't help it.

He closes his eyes and lets out a hum of pleasure. "That's one, for sure," he says, as if this were actually a conversation. "There's also..." He leans down and kisses my nipple. "And..." He kisses my neck. "And the small of your back, which I can't reach right now. And the soles of your feet."

"Dylan," I repeat, lifting my hips to try to get more of him. "Please."

"And here." He lifts my hand and places an open-mouthed kiss on the inside of my wrist. It's so unexpected that I shiver. "See?"

I do see. But still, I'm impatient.

"Last one," he says. "But it's a biggie. Right here." With his broad thumb, he traces a slow line across my lips.

It's exquisite. And I'm so desperate right now. I open my mouth and suck his thumb inside.

He groans. "You kill me. You know that, right?" Finally, his hips begin to thrust. He removes his thumb from my mouth so he can go about the serious business of bracing himself on the bed and fucking me. "I tried to go slow. I really tried."

I'm not even listening, because I finally have exactly what I need. I grab his shoulders and take it. My breasts begin to bounce as he picks up the pace.

He drops his head and gives me his mouth. Our kisses are bottomless, and so am I. Because this is the moment when I feel most at peace. The old Chastity was brought up to serve men. The new one is supposed to serve herself.

This is how they merge. This right here—the candlelight and the scent of heated skin and the cool sheets at my back. The rhythm of the bed squeaking in time with Dylan's thrusts.

"Can't get enough of your mouth," he murmurs between kisses. "Or the view." He raises himself to look down between us, watching the place where we're joined. He strokes his fingers across my sensitive flesh.

All that attention is making me self-conscious. I try to pull him down on top of me again. And he lets himself be led, leaning down to kiss me. I love the connection. I wrap my arms around him and stroke the long muscles in his back.

Everything is wonderful for a while until he pulls out suddenly. I let out a gasp of despair, but then he rolls me onto my side, lifts my knee and slides back into place behind me.

I arch my back and moan, because I can feel him so deeply now.

"Yeah," he breathes. "I know."

A lovely silence descends on us as we both begin to move. He's holding my knees apart, which ought to feel ridiculous. But I like the sensation of being *braced* for him. As if he's arranged my body for his pleasure.

And mine, too, I guess. Because he slides a hand down to stroke me, and this time I'm ready. His touch converges with the steady drumbeat of his cock. And I can't take it anymore. I lean my head back against his shoulder and moan as the climax rolls through me.

"*Yes,*" Dylan encourages me. He lets out a joyful curse and pushes me onto my tummy. It isn't long before he's groaning my name and shuddering behind me.

Then he collapses onto my back with the most satisfied sigh I've ever heard.

I lie there on the sheet, hoping Dylan never gets up and moves. My body feels hot and thoroughly used, in the best possible way.

But after a few minutes, Dylan disengages. He rolls over, grabs the bedclothes from where we've thrown them on the floor, and pulls them up over both of us.

"Come here," he says, tugging me toward his big body. I slide gratefully onto his bare chest. He rests two lazy hands on my back and lets out a happy sigh.

I nuzzle his chest and stay quiet. It's not every day that you get exactly the thing that you want. I still don't quite understand how we ended up here. But that doesn't mean I can't enjoy it.

We lay there together for a long time, until someone decides to puncture my perfect little world by knocking on the door. "Dyl! Come downstairs and have a beer with me!" I don't recognize the voice.

"Maybe next time!" he calls.

"Can I come in?"

"No fucking way."

The voice laughs.

We don't hear from him again, but it doesn't matter. He's pierced the bubble of being alone with Dylan.

"Take a shower with me?" he says.

I glance toward the door. "But there're people *right* outside." I feel very naked all of a sudden.

Dylan runs a finger down my nose. "You are a fascinating combination of dirty and prudish."

"Aren't I?" My face is on fire. "Sorry."

He leans down and kisses me softly. "Figuring you out is pretty fun, though. I've learned a few things already."

"Like what?" After the words come out, I wonder if I really want to know.

"Well..." He drags a finger across the swells of my breasts. "You like a lot of tongue when you kiss. You don't care so much for foreplay. You're all about the cock."

My face heats immediately. But only because it's true.

"You don't like to talk during sex—but you're truly fearless in action." He leans down and kisses me. "It's such a turn-on. I'm already inventing new things I want to try with you."

"You are?" I'm not able to keep the shock out of my voice. Because that implies we'll be doing it again.

"I don't think I'll be able to help myself," he says. And then he kisses me again.

THIRTY-ONE

Dylan

IT'S GETTING LATE, and I'm starting to yawn. Eventually, I convince Chastity that the people on the landing are too stoned to notice us tiptoeing past them. I wrap a towel around my waist and give Chastity my bathrobe for the short trip down the hallway to the bathroom I share with Keith.

The poker game is over, from the looks of things. There's only two people left on the landing, and they're discussing whether or not their lips are vibrating in tune with the universe.

Needless to say, nobody notices us or even makes a crack about our sex-tousled hair.

After cranking up the hot water in the shower, I guide Chastity under the warm spray. Then I step in after her, taking a handful of shampoo. I amuse myself by lathering up her hair and then mine.

I'm strangely joyful. Maybe it's just the endorphins, but I feel so much tenderness toward Chastity. Like our friendship has a secret door I finally discovered. A door marked *Smoking Hot Chemistry*.

And—fine—it strokes my ego that I'm the only guy she went there with. My politically strident sister had convinced me that virginity is just a social construct. She's probably mostly right. But I'm gratified that Chastity trusted me with some of her "firsts."

Is it awful that I enjoyed being the one to show her the ropes?

"Tip your head back," I say when I need to rinse her hair. I'll bet she's never showered with anyone before, either. It's weirdly intimate to wash another person.

I fucking love it, honestly. I'm such a hedonist. And it makes me happy to train her in my self-indulgent ways.

Gently, I rotate her so I can wash us both. Just to be a goof, I lower my hand to soap up her butt.

Right away, I know something's wrong. Her smooth, water-slicked skin gives way to grooves and ridges. I hastily lean back, so I can see what the hell happened there.

Deep, whitened scars. Dozens of them. Carved right into her sweet body. "What the *fuck*." The harsh words just pop out, and a wave of nausea runs through me.

Someone hurt her, and not just a little. They hurt her *badly*.

Chastity's hands shoot back to knock mine away, and she turns around so fast she slips a little.

I grab her arm to steady her, and then our gazes lock. "What *happened?*" But even as I ask the question, I realize that I already know.

"The night Zach and I got in trouble," she stammers. "We both got the lash. I know it's hideous. There's a reason I never wear bathing suits."

"Holy *shit*, Chass." I reach for her again, but she sidesteps me as best she can in the confined space. That's when I get a clue and raise my hands in submission. "I'm sorry. I won't touch it if you don't want me to."

She crosses her arms in front of her perfect chest. "Maybe we're done here?"

I wrecked it. I ruined the moment completely. "There's a towel right on the rack for you. I just need thirty more seconds."

"Thanks."

She steps out of the tub, and I quickly rinse myself. When I shut off the water, she's already gone. I grab a towel and hurry back to my room, where Chastity is donning her skirt.

"Hey, wait half a second," I say as I drip water onto the wood floor. "Where are you going?"

"I should go home," she says, securing her bra.

"No, you really shouldn't," I argue, crossing to my dresser. "It's late. And cold." I don't want to take her back to the dorm right now, but it's not just laziness on my part. I'd never send Chastity packing after what we just shared. Or anyone else for that matter. "Come on. Come to bed. I'll give you a T-shirt. When's your first class tomorrow?"

"Ten," she says, licking her lips uncertainly.

"Perfect. Me too." I pull a Shipley Farms T-shirt out of the drawer. "You can go if you want. But I'd rather you put this on and come to bed with me."

"Okay," she says after another beat. "I wasn't sure you'd want me to stay."

"Of *course* I want you to stay." But this is the tricky stuff, isn't it? This is why sleeping with good friends is scary. "Do you have something against cuddling?"

"I wouldn't know." She gives me a quick, nervous smile. "But I just assumed that you did."

"Why? Vermont is a cold state. Cuddling is one of our top five winter sports. Come here."

Just as before, she does exactly what I say. "Dylan."

"Yeah?" I take her hips in hand and tug her against my chest.

"What does the textbook say about this part?"

"Well, you wrap your arms around each other like this." I enfold her in a hug, and kiss her on the neck. Her hair is wet. She can't go outside right now. That's madness.

She hugs me back. "You know what I'm asking. With you and me, what comes after the sex? Tomorrow am I supposed to pretend it never happened? Just tell me the rules, and I'll try to follow. You don't date. I know this. So what the heck am I supposed to assume?"

Ah well. I guess we're getting right to the heart of the tricky stuff, then. But I sure don't mind her speaking up. It's so much better than dancing around the question. "First things first. We're still friends, right? That isn't up for negotiation."

"Agreed," she says, squeezing me.

"I think..." I have to stop in the middle of the sentence, because I honestly don't know what to make of all of this. "We're friends with a lot of chemistry. I didn't really see that coming. And I don't think it's going to go away too easily. So pretending it never happened is a bad strategy. We can't be like those freaks from California who come to Moo U and then try to wear their flip-flops in the snow."

She laughs against my chest. "Does that happen?"

"Yeah. You'll see." I hold her a little closer. "So we're probably going to end up doing it again, don't you think?"

"We will if I have anything to say about it."

The candor startles me, and I laugh and kiss her forehead. "Okay. So we're friends who get naked sometimes. Can we try being that?"

She tips her head back and looks up at me. "Yes, Dylan. We can try being that. Just promise me this—you won't tell our families."

"Okay?" I hadn't gotten that far. "But why?"

"I don't want to explain myself. And it's none of their business."

"That's true," I agree. I don't really want to explain myself, either. Everyone is really protective of Chastity. I don't need that lecture. "I can keep a secret."

"Okay," she says.

"But my balls are freezing off right now. So put on this T-shirt and let's cuddle. I'll find you a toothbrush if you want."

Ten minutes later I blow out the candle and hop into the bed with Chastity. The party has quieted down, and the old house settles into its usual creaks and groans.

It's peaceful here, with Chastity in my arms. I guess it should feel super strange. But it doesn't really. "I'm sorry I made you feel weird about your scars. I just had no idea how bad it was."

"I don't like to talk about it," she whispers. "It was the most humiliating day in my life. They took turns with the horse whip."

My eyes slam shut against that image. Another wave of helpless disgust makes my guts roll. "Jesus. I'd really like ten minutes alone with whoever did that to you."

"So would I," she says softly. "No—that's a lie. I never want to see them again. I just want to forget they even exist."

I sift a hand through her damp hair, and wonder if that actually works. In my experience, the harder I try not to think about something, the worse it gets. "Good thing you don't ever have to go back there."

"Good thing," she agrees.

"I can make you forget about them, you know."

"Really? How?" She props herself up on an elbow.

"Like this." I lean in for a kiss. It's supposed to be a quick one. A joke. But Chastity tastes so sweet that I go in for seconds and thirds. Her smooth hands wrap around my body, and I tangle my legs in hers.

One kiss turns into an epic make-out session. As my lips become swollen with our kisses, it occurs to me that I might be in this a little deeper than I planned.

But kissing is my favorite thing ever, so I'm not going to worry about it too much. Not tonight anyway.

I don't worry the next day, either. Or the one after that. Over the next few weeks, Chastity and I spend a lot of time together.

In the first place, we have an impressive amount of sex. It's like when I become obsessed with playing a new song. I need to play it over and over again, and the melody becomes sweeter each time I hear it.

Many late-night hours are spent in my bed, kissing until Chastity's lips are chafed and making love like we've just invented it. We sleep tangled up in each other and wake up needing more.

It's magic.

The daylight always comes, though, and keeps us busy with other things. Exams loom. There are chemistry labs to complete and papers to write.

On the weekends, I go home to milk cows, press apples, and make caramels. Chastity and I sleep in separate houses and pretend not to crave each other as we work side by side in Leah's kitchen.

The first time I tried to steal a kiss, though, we almost got caught. Chastity's hearing must be better than mine, because she broke out of my embrace and made it halfway across the kitchen before Isaac walked through the door with two mugs of coffee for us.

Chastity thanked him sweetly. And there was no damage done, thank God. But after that, she instituted a zero tolerance policy about touching on the weekends.

"But you look hot when you're stirring caramel," I'd complained. "And I'm not good at delayed gratification. Can we make a batch of caramel *sauce*? I have some big ideas for it."

"Back in your corner," she'd said. Her eyes had flashed as she'd given my chest a shove. "We're on a deadline."

And we are. Chastity is running an entire small business from a spreadsheet on my laptop, and the orders are still coming in thick and fast.

In the bedroom, I'm the one who sets the pace. But in the kitchen, it's all Chastity. "Measure that. Stir this. Pour it in here."

The only thing I'm in charge of is the music selection. And I love this setup. I do what she tells me to, all the while admiring her flushed face and bright eyes.

We've sold *so* many caramels. Griffin hasn't said a bad word about the goats in weeks. And the payments are starting to pile up in Leah's bank account.

Since our caramels are delivered by Leah on her cheese route, we're free to drive back to Burlington on Sundays around noon. I speed along highway 89 with my hand on Chastity's knee. And I don't even bother with the pretense of asking Chastity if I should drop her off at the dorm.

We drive right back to my place, exchange a few words of greeting with Keith or Rickie, and then climb the stairs to my room. Our clothes come off immediately. And then I show her just how *hard* it is to spend forty-eight hours without touching her.

It's a good life. And let's face it. If it were any other girl, I'd probably already be feeling itchy about spending so much time together. Girls inevitably want things from me that I can't deliver. They always seem to want to hear that they're crucial to my very existence. And that's where I always let them down. I'm twenty years old, and I don't make promises. If I did, they'd sound cheap to my own ears.

I can't do it. Who the fuck knows where I'll be a year from now? Or five? It's just silly to plan that far ahead. I've broken promises before, and it nearly broke me. So now I try not to make any. It's simple.

But Chastity understands me. She always has. She doesn't ask those big questions because she has a lot going on in her own life, too.

There's school, which is still hard for her. And she's made new friends, too.

Like Ellie. And Rickie, surprisingly. Those two are unexpectedly tight. So when Chastity walks through our kitchen door on a Tuesday evening in early December, I'm not actually sure who she's here to see.

I am, however, happy to see her. "Hey! I was just thinking about you."

"Really?" She looks a little taken aback. "Whatcha making?" she asks, hanging her coat on a hook. Her cheeks are pink from the cold, and I just want to gobble her up.

"I'm reheating some tomato soup. Want some?"

She shakes her head. "I already ate. Plus, Rickie is waiting for me."

"Again?" I laugh out loud. "What's the movie this time?"

"Something about a cowboy and a puppy. I forget the title." She shrugs. "You'd hate it."

"Puppies are okay," I point out. "But I could take or leave the cowboy." I really don't understand the pact that my roommate and Chastity made. They agreed to watch twenty-four Hallmark movies together before Christmas. "Can't imagine cowboys are your thing either, right? Didn't you grow up with cowboys?"

"This isn't a *real* cowboy, Dylan," she scoffs, pulling off her boots. "He'll have a shiny belt buckle and dimples. And he'll carry the Christmas tree around while his muscles bulge inside his T-shirt."

"But nobody gets naked," I clarify, just to double check. "I'm not missing any action, right?"

"There *might* be a kiss at the end."

Like I said, I don't understand it. "But I'm still getting action later, right? Come here. I need a moment with you."

As always, Chastity obeys. She crosses the kitchen to stand in front of me, flushed and happy. "What? The movie is starting."

"Before you go ogle a fake cowboy, I need a real kiss." I crook my finger. "Make it a good one."

She steps closer, and I drop the wooden spoon onto the counter and pull her in. As soon as my warm mouth joins her cool lips, she parts them for me.

And then it's *on*. There's never just one kiss with Chastity. We always get carried away. It isn't long before I've spun us around to pin her against the countertop. Her hands are in my hair, and my tongue is in her mouth.

"CHASS!" yells Rickie from the other room. "You're missing out! The cowboy just saved a kitten!"

We break apart, panting a little. "You'd better go," I say hoarsely. "Don't miss the fake puppies and kitties."

"The animals are real," she whispers back. "But very well-behaved. Unlike you."

"You don't want me to be well-behaved," I point out. "You like me naughty."

"Guilty." She lifts her chin to smile at me. "Catch up with you later?"

"You can count on it."

Chastity leaves the kitchen, and I turn off the heat under my soup. It's hot enough, and so am I. I have a chem lab to write up, but it's going to be slow going. I know I won't be able to stop thinking about her.

Last night I had her on her hands and knees until she screamed my name. I'm hard just thinking about it.

When my soup is all gone, I clean up and peek into the living room before heading upstairs. Chastity and Rickie are shoulder to shoulder on the sofa, an ugly afghan stretched over their knees. They're sharing an enormous bowl of popcorn and dissecting the movie.

"I think the sheriff did it," Rickie says. "That man is dirty, and not in a fun way."

"You can tell because he parts his hair in the middle," Chastity agrees. "I think the dog is going to rat him out."

"No, the horse. He looks smarter than the dog."

Chastity laughs, and the sound makes me smile.

I turn and walk upstairs to get a little work done. With any other girl, I'd be a little freaked out at the way she so quickly became a fixture in my life. Maybe I'm just too sexually satisfied to care.

And maybe it will all go bad. Things usually do.

Not tonight, though. Rickie and Chastity look so comfortable that it's too tempting to sit down and watch dreck just to soak up a little of their inexplicable optimism.

The holidays are coming on fast. I'm not a big fan of Christmas break. It's a lot of togetherness. Three weeks of getting on each other's nerves. And then there's the ache of spending another Christmas without my dad.

I force myself to walk away and head upstairs.

THIRTY-TWO

Chastity

ALL MY LIFE I've known that keeping secrets is hard. But it turns out that keeping secrets from Leah is the hardest.

Even from forty miles, I feel queasy about it. Sitting here in the coffee shop on the velvet sofa, I'm reading Leah's latest email on my phone. Dylan is sitting right beside me, his hand draped over my knee in that casual way I used to see it draped over Kaitlyn's.

Life is good. Really good. Except for the guilt I'm feeling as I read.

Where are you? I called last night. I know exam time must be tricky but please call me back because I'm worried about you. Also, I have news about the foundation! We're really excited over here.

I tap the reply button, but then hesitate because I don't know how to justify my behavior. In my former life, I lied all the time. Or at least I committed sins of omission. But I did it to protect myself. If anyone on the compound knew what I was thinking about during church, I would have been beaten.

And then I slipped up a couple times and proved that theory right.

But those lies were told for survival. Lying to Leah feels awful. She's been nothing but kind to me.

Still, I'm not ready to share how often I'm in Dylan's bed instead of my own. Now I'm the one who barely comes home to the dorm anymore. I keep a toothbrush and a change of clothes at Dylan's.

I've basically taken Kaitlyn's place as Dylan's sexually fulfilled, somewhat insecure girl of the moment.

Sorry Leah! I reply. *Spending a lot of time at the library. I'll try to call you tonight. I want to hear about your foundation!*

"Leah? Or Ellie?" Dylan asks without looking up from his book.

"Leah. I'd better sleep in my own bed tonight. That way I can see Ellie at dinner and call Leah."

He looks up. "You could just tell her, you know."

"Maybe." But my reply lacks conviction.

"Wouldn't that be easier?" he presses. "My mom still thinks I'm dating Kaitlyn, by the way. I haven't corrected her, but I feel like a heel."

"I'm sorry. Let me think about it," I hedge. But in my heart of hearts I know I'm not there yet. Leah won't judge me, exactly. But she'll shower me with both questions and concern. She'll ask about birth control, and she'll probably make noises about Dylan's lack of interest in relationships.

I don't want the questions, and I definitely don't want the lecture. Because I already know he isn't the kind of guy who ties himself down.

Birth control is a good idea, though. I have an appointment tomorrow to take care of that. Dylan is a faithful user of condoms, but I know I need to own my part in it.

Rickie sets a tray on the coffee table in front of us, and then flops down on the chair we saved for him. "That line! This is why I hate exams."

"*That's* your reason?" I ask. "I hate exams, because I hate exams." My hands get all sweaty just thinking about finals next week.

He shrugs. Rickie doesn't ever seem to worry about school. I don't even know if he goes to class. It's just one of the many things I don't understand about him.

"Yay, coffee," Dylan says, reaching for one of the two enormous cappuccinos on the tray. They're served in bowls instead of cups.

"That thing is huge. You're going to be up all night."

"That's kind of the point," Rickie says.

Dylan shakes his head. "No, I got this size because Chastity likes these but never orders them." He offers me the bowl. "Here. Drink some."

"Really?" I take it from him and sip from the edge. "Thank you."

"I have a kink for feeding you," he says, giving me a smile. "This is also for you." He lifts a tiny plate off the tray and offers it to me. There's a single cookie on it, but it's a work of art. It's two layers in the shape of a Christmas bell, with a gleaming pool of red jam showing through a cutout in the center.

"Oh. It's so pretty!" I feel all warm and squishy inside as I trade the bowl for the little plate. The cookie is exactly the sort of exquisite thing that I would never buy myself. I'm too practical. The coffee shop offers a tray of day-old scones and muffins at half price, and they're the only thing I've ever eaten here.

I take a bite, and after the first crunch, the buttery shortbread seems to melt against my tongue. The jam is tangy, too, like raspberries. "Wow," I say, chewing. "Try this."

He shakes his head with a smile. "I've had them. This one is all for you." Then he leans in and kisses the side of my face. "It's your reward for solving question number seventeen."

"But I haven't done that one yet."

"When you do, I'll just have to think up *another* reward." His smile turns slightly wicked.

Across the way, Rickie waves his arm in the air, as if clearing invisible smoke. "Jesus. You guys are basically off-gassing cuteness. And everyone else in here is reeking of Christmas cheer. How do you expect me to keep up my surly facade under these conditions?" He picks up his own giant coffee bowl and takes a gulp.

"Why do you hate the holidays so much?" I have to ask.

"I don't have anything against the holidays." He shrugs. "Except Burlington will be a ghost town. No fiddle tunes from Dylan and Keith. Nobody to come over to smoke pot or have sex on my couch..."

"Aren't you going home for Christmas?" I ask. "I thought you were from Hardwick." That's a Vermont town not too far from Tuxbury.

"I'll probably stop by the parents' place for Christmas dinner," he says. "I'll bring wine and make polite conversation for as long as I can stand it. My parents and I aren't close."

Dylan kicks a foot up onto the coffee table, nudging Rickie's knee with his toe. "Why don't you come to Christmas Eve at our place? It's a big party, but casual. The food is awesome. And you can watch Chastity try to ignore me from across the room."

I laugh because all of that is true. I don't know how I'm going to make it through Christmas break pretending Dylan and I are just friends. It's going to be awkward.

"That does sound like fun," Rickie says. "Will your sister be there?" He wiggles his eyebrows.

"Of course she will. Although that's not really a selling point."

"Says you."

"Please. If Festivus was a real holiday, it would be Daphne's favorite. The airing of grievances is right up her alley."

Rickie grins. "She and I have a lot in common, don't you think?"

"Absolutely," Dylan agrees. "Although I enjoy your brand of cynicism more than hers. You throw better parties and you rarely pinch me."

Rickie sips his coffee. "I might take you up on Christmas Eve."

"Stay over," Dylan says. "It's closer to Hardwick, anyway."

"I'm not an easy guest," Rickie says slowly. "You guys might not have room."

"Sure we do," Dylan argues. "I've got you covered." They exchange a glance that has more layers of meaning.

But I don't ask, because it's none of my business. I respect secrets, because I've had plenty.

"All right, then," Rickie says. "I'll bring the wine. And I'll even help you guys box up caramels if you need me to."

"No need," Dylan says, passing me the giant cappuccino again. "We'll be retired candymakers by then. In fact, we're going to run out of goat's milk this weekend. After one more set of deliveries, we'll close up shop."

None of this is news to me, but my heart gives an unhappy squeeze anyway. There's no getting around it. Jacquie and Jill are out of commission until they have their kids in the springtime.

On the positive side, the vendors' payments are piling up in

Leah's bank account. I'll have enough money to buy my books and a cheap computer, too. Nannygoat's Candies was a resounding success, even if I'll never be ready to give it up.

Or Dylan, either. But I doubt I'll have a choice.

———————————

That evening I'm in my room, writing my very last composition essay. The professor loves my stuff these days. On the last one he wrote: *This is so raw and beautiful. Great expression!* It stuns me to receive praise for all the scary ideas in my head.

The class doesn't have a final exam, either, which means my only tests will be in Spanish, my small-business econ class, and algebra.

Totally doable. My first round of finals is still scary, but I feel like I can make it through my first semester of college without failing anything.

When I get up to get a drink of water, I find Kaitlyn standing in our bathroom, using the mirror to touch up her lipstick.

"Oops, sorry," I murmur, even though I have every right to be here.

She glances at me, but I don't get the scowl I'm so accustomed to. "You can have the bathroom. I'm just going." She drops the lipstick into her purse. She also grabs her toothbrush and a contact lens case and drops those in, too. Then she glances at me. "I'm out of here for the night. So I guess you don't have to make yourself scarce."

"New boyfriend?" I ask a little too hopefully.

"Something like that," she says. "He's a hockey player. Hands off, okay?"

"Jeez, Kaitlyn." I let out a nervous laugh. "I'm not—Dylan and I were friends for a long time before, you know?" I can't stop talking, because I feel strangely guilty about Kaitlyn these days.

"Actually, I was kidding." She gives me a smirk. "Dylan always had a weak spot for you. And lord knows you're a goner for him."

I swallow hard.

"But when he moves on, you'll have to go looking for your own hockey player, you know? I don't envy you. It's hard being the person who's more in love." She snaps her bag closed and shoulders the strap. "I prefer things the other way around."

She's ready to leave, but I'm standing here with my empty cup, feeling unsettled, because she's right. I always wanted what she had with Dylan. But now that I have it, I understand her a little better. She lost him, and then she was sorry.

I'll be sorry someday, too. "How do you stop?" I hear myself ask.

"Stop what?"

"Being the person who's got it bad."

She nudges me aside, but her expression is more gentle than I've ever seen it. "If you figure it out, let me know."

After she leaves, I text Dylan. *You won't believe this! Guess who found herself a hockey player? She's out for the night. And she took her toothbrush with her.*

I'm truly happy for her. I wonder if she knows that.

Dylan interprets this news a different way. *Goody. I'll swing by later after my study group for bio. Unless you're too busy? I'll buzz from the lobby to make sure you're done studying.*

As if I'd ever turn down a visit from Dylan. And the prospect of seeing him lights a fire under my ass. I've almost finished my essay when the house phone rings.

I leap off the bed to answer it. "Hey there!"

"Hi yourself," Leah says back to me. "You sound *really* happy to hear from me."

Oh shit. A beat goes by while I try to reorient myself. "Of course I'm happy to hear from you."

Leah laughs. "Uh-huh. Who were you really expecting? What's his name, Chass?"

"*Leah,*" I gasp.

"What? It's so obvious that you met a boy. Why else would you be gone every night? Just promise me he's a nice boy, and he knows his way around a condom."

Immediately, I feel sweaty. "You're embarrassing me," I say, because it's the truth, even if it's not *all* of the truth.

"Look, I get that this isn't an easy topic for you. The Paradise Ranch is where sexual positivity goes to die. It took me years to get over my hang-ups. But I hope you know you can ask me about anything."

"Uh, sure," I say slowly. "I think I'm good." *But I'm probably going to burn in hell for lying to you.*

"Chass, seriously. I hope you do meet someone nice. Maybe it will help you get over your raging crush on Dylan."

Oh my God. "That will never happen," I admit slowly. It's another half-truth. "You should talk, though. You fell for Isaac when you were what, fifteen?"

"You're right," she says quietly. "But I was very lucky that he was all in—he didn't make me pine for him. Some men are ready to meet their forever person when they're young. And some just aren't. You could be waiting around a long time for Dylan to grow up."

Once again, she's both wrong and very, very right. I have Dylan. And yet I really don't.

"Hey, I didn't call to make you feel bad."

"You aren't," I say quickly. "Now tell me what's up with you?"

"You know I did that interview for Wyoming Public Radio?"

"Uh-huh," I say, even if I don't exactly remember. Anytime Leah brings up Wyoming, I tune it out.

"Well, something amazing happened. I got the attention of a very well-off rancher who wants to help me fund my foundation. I think this could be big. She could move my plans forward in a big way."

"That's wild!" But I shouldn't really be surprised. Nobody is more tenacious than Leah when she has a big idea. I've never seen anyone accomplish so much with so little. She was a runaway at seventeen, and has no education. But she never stops believing that big things are possible. This past summer her cheeses won an international competition. In France.

"I'm flying to Chicago this weekend to meet the rancher."

"Chicago?"

"She's there for a convention. You won't *believe* this hotel where I'm supposed to have lunch. I'm busy having a fashion crisis right now."

"I'll bet."

"Dream big, Chastity. Sometimes you get what you've asked for."

"Mmm." Does it make me shallow that I'm mostly dreaming of Dylan?

"The other thing I have to ask you is this—could I possibly buy five boxes of caramels?" Leah asks me. "I don't want to screw up your count."

"Sure. You can have them," I tell her. As if I'd say no. My entire business relies on free time in her kitchen. "Are they for the fancy rancher lady?"

"One of them is. I hope you don't mind if I also send a box to your mother."

My heart skips a beat. "Why?" I haven't seen or spoken to my mother in two years. She failed me when I needed her most. About a month before I left Wyoming, I made the mistake of telling her that I would run away if my stepdad tried to marry me off.

You ungrateful bitch, she'd said. And then she'd slapped me across the face.

When it came time to leave, I didn't bother saying goodbye.

"I thought she might want to know that you're still alive and doing okay. It would come from me and not you."

"Oh, *Leah*," the words come out in a rush. "I don't know. Someone will see." It unnerves me to think that my family would know where I am. My *former* family, that is. I used to have nightmares about getting dragged from my new bed at Leah's house and hauled back to the Paradise Ranch by my stepdad.

"I don't have to do it," she says. "But think it over."

"Okay," I say just as someone knocks on the outer door.

"It would be a nice gesture," Leah presses.

"Um..." I'm a little distracted now. I open my bedroom door just as the knock comes again.

"Company?" Leah asks.

"Uh, maybe? Could be Ellie, I guess." I stretch the curly phone cord into the short hallway and open the outer door.

"H—" Dylan starts to greet me, but I cut him off with a chop of my hand through the air.

His eyes widen.

"I'd better go," I tell Leah. "Talk to you this weekend?"

"Sure. You have to let me know when your last exam ends. I can come get you if you can't hitch a ride back with Dylan."

"I'll ask him," I say as Dylan grins at me. "Have fun in Chicago!"

"I will! Later, sweetie." We hang up.

"Leah, I guess?" he asks. "She's going to Chicago?"

"Yeah. Something about a new donor for the—" This sentence gets cut off, because Dylan yanks me against his chest and kisses me. Hard. His hands cup my ass, and his mouth claims mine with speed and authority.

Even after the best month of my life, I'm still surprised when he does that. But not too surprised to cup his face in my hands and give it right back to him.

"Hi," he says after a long, wonderful minute or two. "I missed you. Can you tell?"

"A little," I say, breathless. I hope he takes me right to bed.

"I come bearing cheap beer and YouTube. Can you take a study break?"

"Of course," I say. "My last essay is almost done."

"Can I read it?" he asks, easing past me to remove his backpack and drop his coat on my desk chair.

"No." I already know it's good. All you need to get an A is to bare the ugliest parts of your soul.

"It was worth a shot." He opens the backpack to pull out two bottles of beer and his laptop.

It's not long until we're ensconced on my bed, watching SNL replays while cuddling. The videos are funny, but I'm distracted by the woodsy scent of Dylan's skin, and the way he's resting a hand on my tummy.

I love everything about this moment. The casual ease of our time together. The sound of his laughter. Dylan is better at living in the moment than I am. He reminds me to stop and just be.

Even after all the times we've been together, I still crave him. I want that hand to unbutton my jeans and then slide into my panties. I want him to roll me to the side and kiss me again. *Right now, please.*

"Can I play a different video for you?"

"What?" I ask stupidly. My attention is shot.

"These guys. Hang on." He clicks around the keyboard and pulls up a website I haven't seen before. It's for a French-Canadian fiddle band. "They're playing in Lebanon on New Year's Eve, and I'm thinking of getting tickets. Will you come with me?"

"Well, sure. Who's going?"

"It would just be you and me."

"Like a date?" I ask, turning to look at him.

"Just like that," he whispers, his brown eyes soft. "You got better New Year's plans?"

"Of course not." That's crazy talk. "But how will we explain it?"

He shrugs. "We don't need to. We can go wherever we want together."

My chest contracts with discomfort. "It's not a good idea. Besides, I'm saving up for my computer."

"It's my idea, I'd buy the tickets," Dylan argues. "Think of it as a New Year's present."

"You already gave me a present. A big one," I point out. "And I always babysit on New Year's so that Leah and Isaac can go out."

"Oh. Okay." He looks a little deflated.

"Sorry," I say, my heart hammering. I hate saying no to him. But if I suddenly had big plans, Leah would want to know why.

Dylan plays one of the videos anyway, and I can see why he likes this band. It's funky, but the music is based in the same fiddle music that he plays.

They're really good. And now I feel like crap for turning him down. "You could go without me, you know."

"I suppose." He wraps an arm around me and doesn't say any more about it.

Curling a little more tightly toward him, I ask myself what the hell I'm doing. I should be enjoying every minute of time he wants to spend with me. I should just live it up while it lasts. Protecting my heart is a lost cause, anyway.

And now it's becoming a problem.

That night in the library, we promised each other we'd tell the truth. But every day I fail to do that. I love Dylan, and I don't think I should tell him. He might end things if I do. That's probably what would happen.

And I don't want to see his face when I say it, either. I don't want to watch him flail around trying to explain why he can't say those words back to me.

Kaitlyn was right. It's hard to be the one who's more in love. It's frequently excruciating.

The band is still playing on Dylan's screen. But all I really see is Dylan's perfect hand resting on my stomach. Tonight I just ache for him. Right before my period, I always feel... Whatever the female version of *horny* is. *Needy*, maybe. *Heated*.

It's not a new phenomenon. When I was a teenager I used to lay awake at night fantasizing about sex. I dreamt of a man's weight pressing me into the bed.

Open your body to your husband when he asks you to, the Divine Pastor used to preach. *Receive him and take his seed whenever he is restless.*

I couldn't wait. I was already restless. But I knew better than to say so. Girls were slapped just for looking too long at the boys. They were reprimanded for flirting, or for showing any skin at all. Our dresses came down to our anklebones.

And any girl who was found walking near the young men's dormitory would be severely punished. It was also forbidden to walk around with wet hair—because that was too sexual.

I still don't understand that last one. There's nothing too sexy about my post-shower hair.

Female desire was never mentioned, even by the women. I honestly believed there was something weird about me until I worked that job at Walgreens and discovered magazines. They were very educational. "Find the Big O!" "Drive Your Man—And Yourself —Wild!" "How to Tell If He's As Hot For You As You Are For Him!"

It was there in the magazine aisle that I realized I wasn't a freak after all.

None of that is helping me right now, though. The music plays on, and I roll closer to Dylan, tucking my cheek against his shoulder, wondering when we're going to take advantage of all this unexpected privacy in the dormitory.

I love him. And I also crave him.

He clicks on another song, and I privately groan. Then he gently runs his fingertips across my tummy, which only makes things worse.

"Chass."

"Hmm?" I ask, woozy with need.

"You're very quiet tonight."

"Mmm." I stroke a hand down his chest and sigh.

"You can ask for it, you know."

That wakes me up. "For what?"

He chuckles. "For whatever. A kiss. Another beer. A hard fuck. Just come and get it."

I lie perfectly still, wondering why that seems so impossible.

"Sometimes I think your tutor has failed you. And I'm not really joking right now. I feel a little bad that you don't feel comfortable initiating."

I sit up quickly, because this turn in the conversation is alarming. "Don't feel bad. That's not your fault."

He shakes his head. Then he closes the laptop, silencing the music mid-note. "It's just that I worry that you don't feel comfortable asking for what you want. I mean—I'm so *easy*. Just smile at me, and I'm ready to go." He grins, and I know he's trying to lighten the mood.

"You'd prefer if it was my idea sometimes?" My voice cracks at the end of the question.

"Yeah, but not because I need it. I just want that for *you*. The freedom of it."

"Oh," I say, taking his laptop and moving it to the floor, just to have something to do with my hands.

"There's power in it," he whispers. "Take off your shirt."

It takes me a second to realize that he just gave me an order. But when my brain gets onboard, I lift my T-shirt immediately and toss it off the bed.

"See that?" He cups my breast, stroking a thumb across the swell above my bra. "I asked for what I want. Because I don't feel any shame in wanting it."

"Right," I agree. He's right to assume that shame is an issue. My hang-ups used to be a hundred percent about shame. "I grew up thinking that boys were supposed to want it and girls weren't."

"Yeah, I get that," he says quietly. His wicked fingers are still handling my breast. I want them to handle more of me. "Tell me something you want. Even if it's a little thing."

I swallow hard. Lately my hang-ups have shifted. I used to fear my sexual impulses because they made me a sinner, and sinners were punished.

But now I'm only guarding my heart. I can't ask Dylan for what I want, because he already said he can't give it to me. So I can't ask him for sex, either. It's too revealing. I want more because I'll *always* want more. I'm an infinite loop of wanting him.

"Okay, here's my demand. Are you ready?" I ask him.

"Yeah. Hit me." His brown eyes are smiling.

"I really want you to stop talking so much." And just to make my point clear, I unhook my bra.

His laugh is carefree and happy. "Fine. Sure." He removes my bra, and, with hungry eyes, he lowers his mouth to my breast, and everything is right with the world.

THIRTY-THREE

Freshman Composition

Section Four

Title: The Root Cellar
Author: Chastity Campbell

THE HOUSE where I grew up had no real basement. But there was an old root cellar dug beneath one side of it. The only entry was via a hatchway with two slanting metal doors above it.

Some of the daughters were afraid to go down there, because they didn't like the idea that someone could come along and close up those doors.

But I was the kind of kid who always took a dare. So I didn't mind being sent to that cellar to get things that the other little girls were too chicken to fetch. I liked playing the role of the brave girl.

Besides—thirteen people lived in that house. It was as crowded as a bus station. Even if somebody had locked me into the root cellar as a prank, I could have made enough racket that passersby would hear me even before my flashlight went out.

When I was small, I asked one of my uncles why the potatoes and carrots didn't spoil so long as we kept them in a hole in the ground.

"Because the germs are too cold to eat the potato before we can," he said.

Thirteen people eat a lot of food. As time went on, I learned how to estimate the number of potatoes in the barrel with just a glance. I learned how to stretch a pot of soup by adding water and—this is crucial—more salt.

I learned how to stretch a single pound of ground beef into a triple-sized noodle casserole. And I learned not to report on the sad state of our vegetable inventory if my stepfather looked tired or crabby.

When I was sixteen, though, I did something unforgivable. I got caught kissing a boy. You may be tempted to laugh, but it was a big deal. The boy in question was excommunicated, which is a fancy way of saying that they whipped him, taped his wrists together, and threw him off of the back of a truck.

I got the whip, too. But they don't throw away the girls. They only punish them. In my case, I was put on "probation" for six months. The timeline was to make sure that I wasn't pregnant. It didn't matter if I said that was impossible.

Nobody spoke to me for six months. I wasn't allowed in the kitchen to make the noodle casseroles. I wasn't allowed to serve the men their annual steak dinner.

I was useless, really. So I asked my stepfather if there was a job I could work that was off the compound property. And because he likes money more than anything, he actually said yes. He set me up with a job at a chain pharmacy. And I was ecstatic although I was never meant to see any of the money.

Even when my months of punishment were up, the other women still didn't speak to me. It's like they just forgot how. And none of the men wanted to marry me, because they thought I was "ruined." Like a potato that nobody had stored correctly in the cellar.

The one role I never lost, though, was going down into the root cellar. For six months straight I think the only thing my mother said to me was "bring up another five pounds of carrots and taters."

I always did as she asked. Even though I missed being someone who wasn't shunned. I'd gone from being that brave girl to being that foolish one.

Eventually I figured out how to keep some of the money from my job. And that's when I learned that money and secrets keep just as well underground as root vegetables. I saved my cash. Then I ran away and saved myself.

My own bravery feeds me better than my family ever did.

THIRTY-FOUR

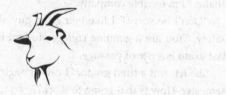

Dylan

IT ALWAYS HAPPENS THIS WAY. Every fall I drag my ass through the anniversary of my father's death. I inevitably feel relief at having survived another October.

And then the holidays come around and sock me right in the gut.

Tonight, after arriving home, I'm supposed to help my mother put up the Christmas tree. That's a job I used to do with my father. Everyone liked to hang ornaments, but just dad and I would cut down the tree and string the lights. Because I was the Shipley kid who loved Christmas most.

Not so much anymore. The next three weeks could be long ones. I'm bracing myself.

On the other hand, there's a light snow falling as I drive the final few miles toward home. It's sticking to the grasses at the side of the highway. Tomorrow, when I get up early for the milking, the distant mountaintops will probably be white. Even my damaged little heart isn't immune to all this beauty.

Or the beauty drowsing beside me in the truck. Chastity pulled an all-nighter to prep for her Spanish exam, which she finished about fifteen minutes before getting into my truck for the trip home.

I hate to wake her up. She looks so peaceful. On the other hand, this might be the last time we're alone together for a long time. So after I exit the highway, I reach over and lay my hand over hers, giving it a gentle stroke.

"I'm awake," she slurs.

"Uh-huh." I have to chuckle.

"Sorry," she says, lifting her head off the window and giving it a shake. "I'm terrible company."

"Don't be sorry." I like being the guy she trusts to get her home safely. "You are a genuine college student now. Passing out after the last exam is a rite of passage."

She lets out a tired groan. "I can't imagine taking five courses next semester. How is that going to work?"

I don't have a solution for that, so I just squeeze her hand.

"Dylan," Chastity asks. "Can I give you your present before I get out of the truck?"

"Sure." Who am I to turn down a present?

"You can't open it until Christmas."

"Why not?" I demand. "I gave you yours early."

"That was a necessity," she argues. "Mine can wait."

"Maybe you'd better hang onto it, then," I say, slowing the truck down as we reach the winding country roads. "I'm not known for my patience. You can bring it over on Christmas Eve and *slip it to me*." I make it sound nice and sleazy, because teasing Chastity is one of my favorite hobbies.

It's going to be weird pretending to be just friends for three whole weeks. I'm hoping she decides to give up on that charade after a few days of sexual frustration.

"Speaking of your impatience…" She clears her throat.

I wait. But she doesn't finish. "What? Tell me already. *Crap*. That sounded really impatient, right?"

"Yes." She laughs. "But your impatience is one of your best attributes. It's part of what makes you fun."

And there it is again—that little rush of happiness that I often have. Because Chastity *gets* me.

"So I did something," she says. "And it might lead to even more fun. The impatient kind."

"Uh-huh," I say. "Is this some kind of Chastity way of trying to talk about sex?"

"Yep," she says. "Well, birth control. That's even harder to talk about than sex. Because unlike sex, it's not very sexy. But I got some. Birth control, that is. It's an implant, and I got it a week ago, which means it's already working."

"Oh, awesome!" This is the best news ever. "Way to go." I don't spend a lot of time worrying about pregnancies. But it's nice to know that I don't have to.

"It's super-effective," she says. "So that also means that you could… You know."

"What?" I ask, because I'm taking care to watch my traction. A thin layer of new snow is the worst kind to drive on.

"Be impatient," she says. "And impulsive. With me."

I give Chastity a quick glance and note that her cheeks are pink. And then it sinks in what she's trying to say. So I apply the brake and stop the truck, right there on the dirt road. "I'm sorry, are you trying to tell me you want to go bare?" My dick is stiffening inside my jeans even as I say these words.

"Only if you want to," she says, her color deepening. "It was just a thought. We don't have to."

"Sweet baby Jesus." I tip my head back on the headrest. "And you decided to say this now? Before a three-week abstinence fest? Do you secretly hate me?"

Chastity lets out a nervous laugh. "No. I was trying to be brave about it and discuss it with you ahead of time. Like rational adults."

"Uh-huh." I put my hand between my legs, pressing the heel of my hand against my boner. "Except you mistook me for a rational adult. Right now I just want to rip off your clothes and do you. But I have to cut down a Christmas tree instead. Fuck my life."

Chastity laughs. Then puts her palm on my thigh, which solves nothing. "Sorry. Rookie mistake."

I cover her hand with mine. "I—" *love you anyway.* I stop myself just in time. "It's okay," I say instead. "I'm half teasing. But waiting for second semester just got, uh, harder."

From the other end of the road, a car appears, so I let my foot off the brake.

"Sorry," she says again, humor in her voice. "But you still have to think it over. Because it's only something we can do if we're, uh, only doing each other."

Since I'm edging over to the roadside to let my neighbor pass, I don't react right away. First, I wave at Mr. Connors and then turn to glance at Chastity. "Hang on. Let's just be clear about one thing. I'm not sleeping with anyone else. I wouldn't do that to you."

"Oh." She blinks. "Okay. Good."

I stop the truck again. "Did you seriously think I would?"

"No?" She looks uncomfortable. "But you have a lot of high school, um, friends who visit you during the holidays. And you never said..." She clears her throat. And then she falls silent.

"Okay, fair." I sit still, my foot on the brake. Here it is—the moment I most dread. The big talk. I have a way of fucking these up. "I know I'm not good at planning my life or making promises. But I'm not going to hop in bed with a high school hookup over break, Chass. We're too—" I choose my words carefully. "—close for that. I think our thing is our thing and *just* our thing until it isn't our thing anymore."

Chastity flinches.

"Okay, yep. That was the worst sentence ever composed in the English language. No wonder women get frustrated with me."

"No—" She holds up a hand. "It's honest. I'm not trying to force you into some big decision right now."

"I know you're not," I say quickly. But I'm still fucking this up. The truth is that I want us to be exclusive. And I care more for Chastity than I ever did about a hookup. Or anyone else for that matter. I care about her a lot.

I don't, however, say that. I could, but I don't. Because that would open up a lot more discussion that I don't feel ready to have.

"Okay," she says softly. "So it's just you and me for now. And you'll let me know if that changes, right?" After she asks this question, she looks out the window, and I can't see her face.

The subtext is pretty clear—she doesn't plan on being the one who calls us off.

I reach over and take her hand, because I'm better at the physical stuff than I am at talking. I don't know what to say to make this moment any less awkward. "Gonna be a long couple of weeks. Maybe we can sneak away at some point."

"To where?"

She makes a good point. It's not like we can go spread a blanket under the stars somewhere and spend time together. "We'll think of something," I mutter. It's not just the sex, either. My family is going to drive me crazy. They always do. I'm going to need a little dose of Chastity's quiet calm and happy smile just to keep me level. "Kiss me," I order.

"Right here?" She looks over her shoulder, probably wondering if I'm blocking the road for someone who wants to get by.

"It's either right now or in Leah and Isaac's driveway."

"Oh. Good point." She unlatches her seatbelt, and I put the truck in park.

I reach over and slide her body across the seat, which makes her smile. But I take my kisses very seriously. She feels good in my arms. I lean in and take her mouth with mine, and her body softens against me.

It's always like this. So good. Maybe it's the heavy talk, or her little announcement about letting my box of condoms expire, but I do not want to stop kissing her. I tilt my head and take what I want from her. She wraps her arms around me and gives it right back.

Until a car approaches. We break apart at the sound of tires on gravel. Unsatisfied, but out of options, I put the truck in gear and maneuver out of the way.

It's only three miles or so to Leah and Isaac's place. I get there way too soon.

"When am I going to see you?" I ask as I pull into their driveway.

"Tomorrow, right? Christmas Eve? Rickie will come over and amuse you, too."

"Fine. It will have to do."

She gives me a sad little smile and opens the door on her side.

I wait for her to collect her stuff out of the backseat, and when she walks away, I give her an awkward little wave.

It isn't enough. But I guess it will have to do.

THIRTY-FIVE

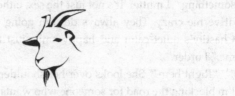

Chastity

I'M TOO TIRED to be very sociable that evening. I go to bed even before Maeve does. And then I sleep late, which is rare for me.

When I finally go downstairs, Leah is trying to grate cheese and play with Maeve at the same time.

"I'm so sorry," I say, rubbing sleep out of my eyes. "What can I do to help?"

"You can sit across from me and eat breakfast," Leah says cheerfully. "Coffee?"

"Sure. Thanks." I cross the kitchen to the pot, pour myself a cup, and then slide a slice of bread into the toaster. "Maeve? What shall we do today while Mama makes her potato tart?" This dish is legendary at holiday parties, because Leah uses fancy cheese and crispy duck confit. No potato has *ever* tasted so good.

"Clubhouse?" Maeve suggests.

"Sure," I agree.

"First, Chastity eats," Leah tells her daughter. "And I have some things to discuss with her. So why don't you watch your video early today?"

"Yay!" The little girl gets up off the kitchen floor. "Right now?"

"Right now," Leah agrees.

She disappears faster than you can say *bribery*.

"What's on your mind?" I ask Leah, taking a stool across the counter from her. "Does this have to do with your sugar mama?" That's what we're calling the rancher Leah met last week in Chicago. Apparently the meeting went great.

"Yes it does." Leah sets down her cheese grater and wipes her hands on her apron. "I know you just finished a really hard semester. But I need to tell you things are moving fast. Juni wants us to open a shelter. And she'll provide the land."

"A shelter? Like, for homeless people?"

"Exactly like that. Juni lost a daughter to a cult in Utah. She was recruited at college, of all places. She was there a year before she died of sepsis. The poor girl suffered a compound fracture in her leg, and the cult didn't believe in medical care."

"Ew!" I cry. "That sounds..." I shudder.

"She says she'll never get over it. And she and her husband have been working hard ever since to steer women away from the place where it happened. They feel like they could make sense of their daughter's death if they help shelter other women who need to get away. We could do so much good, Chastity!"

"Wow. So..." I'm trying to wrap my head around this. "Your foundation won't just provide money. But you'll have some kind of dormitory?"

"Yes. On a working ranch."

"A ranch," I say slowly. That's not what we call a farm in Vermont. "And this would be...?"

"In Wyoming," Leah says gently. "Near Laramie. That's where Juni's properties are."

"You're going to *Wyoming*?" I squeak. And I say it the same way you'd say *hell*. It's literally the last place I ever want to go. "Like, you'd *move* there?"

"Well, either in the spring or late summer," Leah says. "I know that sounds soon. But I think this could be really good for all of us. Chass, the university is right in Laramie. You could take classes at whatever pace feels right to you. And you could help make a difference at the same time."

The toast turns to sawdust in my mouth. I have to take a sip of coffee just to choke it down.

And Leah is watching me with worry in her eyes. "I can see that you're shocked."

Shocked doesn't even cover it. "I didn't think you'd move. What about your farm? You worked so hard for this place."

She bobs her head in a nod, as if that's just an afterthought. "But we can sell it. The house isn't worth much, but farmland is. Especially since the place is certified organic now."

I take another sip of my coffee and try not to feel sick. "I don't know, Leah. It sounds great, but..."

No, it doesn't sound great at all. I mean, saving people from a life of ignorance and sexual slavery is just about the highest calling there is. But I don't want to go anywhere near Wyoming. Not this summer. Not ever.

"I'm sure it's a shock," she says, reaching across the counter to cover my hand. "But it will be a little while until we really know the timing. There are two neighbors who could buy the place."

"Neighbors," I say stupidly.

"Of course. That's who cares most about what happens on this hilltop. Connors would need the farm in the springtime. Isaac won't plant anything if we're selling to him. Connors would graze beef cattle on the property."

My gaze goes involuntarily toward the window, where I try to picture strange cows in the meadow outside.

"But Griffin Shipley might be interested," Leah continues. "He cares less about the growing season, because he's too strapped for help to plant more acreage next year. He and Dylan need to have a come-to-Jesus conversation about Dylan's plans."

At the mention of Dylan's name, all the hair stands up on my arms. "Does Griff want to buy this place?"

"Theoretically," Leah says. "But only if he can figure out how to incorporate our acreage into his. He wouldn't be in a hurry. We could stay the summer if Griffin is our buyer."

"I want to stay the summer," I say quickly.

"It could happen," Leah says gently. "Let's just see. There's no need to panic. You'll have time to get used to this idea. I'm sure you'll realize what a gift we've been given."

A gift. I didn't ask for this gift. I just want to stay in Vermont and be near Dylan and figure out if I can make a go of my business degree.

Leah pats her belly, where a baby bulge is just beginning to show. She's just crazy enough to try to open a nonprofit women's shelter and have a new baby and move across country at the same time.

She needs me. It's selfish not to go and help others the way that Leah helped me.

So why do I want to lie down on the floor and weep?

It's a difficult day for me after that. Maeve is as hyper as I've ever seen her. She knows she's one day away from Santa Claus, and nothing can calm her down. Not even when I lend her my phone to draw on.

Dylan has texted me, too. *Do you miss me yet?*

He really has no idea. I feel queasy every time I think about moving away from here.

I don't return his text, because I don't even know what to say.

Meanwhile, I have to wrap the gifts I got for the Abrahams. I take Maeve upstairs with me, and I let her use too much tape on the wrapping for the hat I made for Isaac and the scarf I knit for Leah.

There's a stuffed moose on the top shelf of my closet, too. But it's hard to feel Christmas joy when my heart is breaking.

This is only my third Christmas ever. We didn't have Christmas at the Paradise Ranch. I didn't understand what a big deal it was until I worked at Walgreens and watched the entire store transform into green and red and gold a few days after the unsold Halloween stuff was carted away.

I don't want to go back there. What if I'm minding my own business in Laramie one day, and one of the Levi brothers drives down there for something? It could happen. What if they find me and decide to snatch me off campus just to teach me a lesson?

For the first time in my life I feel so *afraid*. It was never like this when I actually lived there. I evaded. I coped. Even the beating I received made me more angry than scared.

I don't want to go back. I can't.

"Chassity?" Maeve asks in her small voice. "Read me about the chipmunks?"

"Sure," I say, because I never turn her down. "Where's the book?"

She fetches it, and then we curl up on the sofa together. Maeve has a stack of Christmas books. This is the stupidest one, but also her favorite. Go figure.

We turn the pages and I read with only half my brain.

The other half is panicking.

THIRTY-SIX

Dylan

FOR TWENTY-FOUR HOURS I've smiled my way through decorating the tree. I drove my mother to the grocery store so she'd have someone to load and unload groceries. I've milked cows. I've cuddled goats. I'm basically Mr. Christmas.

Until we're standing outside the barn, where Griffin starts in with his questions about the future.

"How did that computer programming class turn out?" he asks.

"I fought for a B, but I won't be taking another one. It's not really my thing."

"Oh." His face falls. "How much time do you have left to declare that major. Two weeks?"

"Yeah, so?"

"What's it going to be?"

"It's Christmas Eve," I grumble. "Maybe give it a rest?"

"How much longer can you put off this conversation?" he demands. "I have things I need to discuss with you."

"Can we just finish up the goddamn chores and have a holiday?"

Griffin lets out a sigh. Then he retaliates by asking a favor. "This drizzle is supposed to give way to real snow," he says just as we're finishing up a bunch of chores. "Before your friend shows up, will you drive the Kubota back into the shed? I left it back by the Winesaps."

I give the farmhouse a longing glance. My fingers are just about frozen off, and I want to find a quiet spot to call Chastity. "The Winesaps? Why didn't you just park it in the next area code for fuck's sake?"

Griffin makes an angry noise. "Just do this one thing for me."

"Yeah, okay," I grumble, walking away.

"Don't come through the center meadow!" he calls after me. "Take the road!"

So I'm basically going for a long drive on a tractor that does ten miles an hour. Awesome.

I lower my head against the drizzle and trudge through the orchard. It's a long walk, so I have plenty of time to think about Chastity. That talk we had in the truck yesterday is troubling me. I should have just come out and said what I feel for her. I don't know why I couldn't.

It's a little like choosing a major. I fear being pinned down more than I fear anything else. For a guy who claims to be fun, I have a way of overthinking everything.

And I let her walk away thinking I don't care. That was cowardly of me. But it was literally the last mile before home, and I don't know how to sort out my feelings on the fly like that.

I'll call her. Soon. Maybe I can find a way to say it.

I find the Kubota. It's a small tractor that we use to mow between rows of apple trees. There's no top on it, so I'm going to be pelted by drizzle for the entire drive back.

She starts right up, so I sit down on the wet seat and begin the slow trip through the orchard. The drizzle has become more of a freezing rain at this point. My face is constantly pinged by little bits of ice.

I love Vermont. But maybe that's because I've never tried farming in California.

My hands are red and frozen by the time I pull onto the little dirt track that separates our farm from Isaac and Leah's. I can just make out their farmhouse from here, its windows lit up golden in the fading light. They have those electric candles in all the windows. It's a

New England thing—an unspoken rule that you have to put those up for Christmas.

It looks cozy there. I have the strongest urge to get off the tractor and find Chastity and kiss her until she understands that I've honestly got it bad for her.

But I have a job to do, and Rickie's going to show up any minute now at my house, so I putter along until I realize that there's a length of fencing across the road. It's a flimsy, moveable fence, but it's also electric. Isaac's chicken tractor is just inside the protective circle of the fence.

Well, that's inconvenient. I could find the electrical box, shut it off, and move the fence. But when it's raining, the poles like to fall all over the place. It's a job for two people, and I don't want to bother Isaac on Christmas Eve.

So I turn around, and—oh joy—the sleet begins to hit the other side of my face. I drive off the track and head back through the center meadow, instead. It's a shorter trip, anyway. I can get out of this weather faster.

The tractor shed is in my view and everything is going great. Until the tractor suddenly lists to the right.

I turn the wheel to try to get her out of the rut, but it doesn't work. The tractor's still leaning, and I'm also slowing down. The engine complains, so I take my foot off the gas and sort of ooze to a stop.

I'm stuck in the mud. This is about to become really embarrassing.

"Ready? Push!" Griffin roars.

I lean in and give it all I've got. We're shoulder to shoulder, trying to get her out of the mud. Daphne is sitting at the controls, ready to drive out of the rut.

"There. GO!" Griff yells.

We push again, and the tractor moves. Daphne does her best, but the damn thing is still wonky.

"Fuck!" Griffin yells. "It's the fucking tire. Look." He points at the ground, where tire fluid is leaking into the snow that's begun to accumulate.

My brother lets out a string of additional curses, and I inwardly groan. He's going to make this my fault. As if you couldn't run over a nail anywhere.

"If you'd just taken the fucking road like I asked you to—"

"Enough!" I shout. "Can we just fix this while I'm still young?" I put my hands on the rear of the tractor again, ready to push.

"A hundred and sixty-seven dollars, Dylan. That's the price of the tire if I take it in myself," Griffin rants.

"I *know*, Jesus."

"Do you?" he presses.

"Yes! I'm not happy about the goddamn tire, Griff. Let's just get the tractor home. It's Christmas Eve, for fuck's sake."

"You think I don't know that? I was trying to get it all done ahead of time. If you'd just taken the road like I asked you to—"

I let out a roar and push with every ounce of my pent-up anger. The tractor moves about a foot and a half.

"Daphne, you can go," Griffin snaps. "We'll handle this."

Oh fuck. Just what I need—more alone time with an angry Griff. And my twin—that traitor—hops off the tractor and strides toward the house. "Why'd you do that? If we get 'er out of the mud, we can drive it even on that bum tire."

Griffin shakes his head. "Let the ground freeze tonight. It will be easier to drive off it."

"Either that, or the tire will be *frozen in place*." I stand up tall, aligning my spine properly for the first time in fifteen minutes. "Can't we just fix this now? I don't want to sit through a whole night of you bitching at me over this."

"Then maybe you should have just done what I asked."

My blood boils. I feel dangerously angry. "Question—how many times have you gotten tractors stuck? A dozen? Did you give yourself a lecture, too?"

"Sure." Griffin snorts. "I don't spare myself the colorful words."

"I can't do this, Griff." I look up at the deep, cloudy sky. There's too much churning inside me right now to hold it in. "There's a reason I haven't declared a major, and I haven't decided whether my future plans include this farm. And that reason is you."

Griffin's lets out an angry grunt. "Really? You want to have that conversation now?"

"Why not? It's your favorite topic." I give the bum tire a kick.

"You act like I torture you for fun, Dyl. But nothing about this is fun. There are big decisions to make around here."

"Yeah, and you make them all. Just do me this one favor—if you're going to sell off the rest of the herd before I graduate, can you just level with me? Don't make me come home one day and be surprised."

Griffin's chin jerks up, and his scowl deepens. "You really think I'd do that?"

"You'd like to," I say slowly. "Last time, you asked all of us whether we thought you should sell the other herd. We all said no. And then you did it anyway."

"That was *necessary*. I've increased our revenue by a hundred percent! And you're still mad?"

"What I am is *tired*. It's like you forgot you were ever in college. Here's a refresher—you joined a fraternity and played football and drank beer. You didn't spend all your time trying to figure out your future on the farm."

"I don't *enjoy* nagging you," my brother growls. "But what choice do I have? There are decisions to be made. Big ones. And you claim to care about this place, so…"

"*Claim?*" I bellow. "You arrogant fuck! I care as much as you do. But I know it doesn't matter what I think, or how I feel. You're going to make all the choices, and I'm going to have to fall in line. Forever, basically. You talk as though I'm just too scattered to figure myself out."

"Aren't you?"

"No!" I roar. "I just can't picture spending the next forty years trying to make you happy. You're exhausting. So I quit. Make all the decisions you want. I'm done."

"What?" Griffin actually gasps. "No, Dyl. That's not how you make a choice."

"Save it," I bark. "I've been thinking about it a long time. I don't want to work for you."

"But you wouldn't! It's a *family* farm. We all—"

"No." I shake my head vigorously. "I know you think of yourself as the benevolent dictator, carrying on the family legacy. But who is it really for?"

"*You!*" he shouts. "Your sisters! Mom! Audrey! Gus! I work my ass off for all of you. Because it's worth it to keep it for you."

I just shake my head. "I don't want it. Not at that price. Today it's a tractor tire, right? But what if I stay on, and it goes wrong? Like, really wrong?" It's just too easy to picture this disaster. "Maybe the price of milk takes another dive. Maybe the vet bill is astronomical. I don't want to have this conversation every day until I die. I'm willing to fuck up my own life. But I don't want the hell on Earth that plays out when I accidentally fuck up yours."

Griffin's shoulders droop as I come to the end of my lengthy speech. "Don't be hasty, okay? There are big decisions to make. Let's sit down later and talk this out."

"No." I stand my ground. "I made up my mind. I finally did it. That's what you wanted, right? So why argue now?"

Griffin opens his mouth, and then he closes it again. He honestly looks defeated. That should make me happy, but it doesn't.

"And by the way?" As I say this, I start walking backwards toward the farmhouse. "Isaac's chicken tractor was in the way."

"What?" Griff looks blank.

"I was going to take the road, like you said. But he blocked it with an electric fence."

"*Fuck*, Dylan. I'm sorry."

I turn my back on him and stride toward the house. Before I even reach it, Rickie's crappy little car comes up the drive, headlights blazing in the near darkness.

He stops, kills the engine and jumps out. "Dyllie! I made it. I drove through that freezing rain. And now it's snowing."

I look up, and notice that he's right. Big, fat flakes have replaced the frozen crud. "Can you come into the barn with me? I'd like to close up before we go inside to eat and drink ourselves silly."

"Sure, dude." Rickie shuts the car door and follows me toward the barn. "Show me your tricks. I want to see all of it. Do the cows have names?"

"Of course they do. Duh." I wave him through the half-open door. "That's Millie, and this is Barbie."

"Barbie?"

"She's very blonde for a Jersey." I run a hand over Barbie's back, and she turns her head to sniff me. God, I'll miss this. If Griffin shuts down the dairy, it just won't be the same here anymore.

But I feel very clear about this all of a sudden. I meant what I said to my brother just now. I don't want to farm here if it means spending my years trying to stay out of trouble and win his approval. That's no way to live.

I make my way down the row, checking every animal and making sure nothing has gone amiss since the milking. "Rickie, serious question—do you think I could get into vet school?"

"Of course you could. But it's hard, right? Lots of years of study, and then a low-paying job afterward."

"I don't care so much about the money." Farming was never going to make me rich.

"There's no vet school at Moo U," he points out.

This is unfortunately true. "There isn't one anywhere in Vermont. I'd have to go to Massachusetts or Maine. That's not the end of the world."

"No, it's not." Rickie frowns. "But dude. Do you *want* to go to vet school? I never heard you mention it before."

"I'm not sure," I admit. "I'd rather raise animals than operate on them. But it could be good, right? I could deliver calves for a living."

"And shoot horses," Rickie points out. "And treat golden retrievers with cancer."

"You are just a ray of sunshine, aren't you?"

Rickie snickers. "Pretty much."

The cows are all tucked in for the night, so my work here is done. "See you in the morning, girls! Don't stay up too late." I shut out the light.

"Aren't you going to milk them?" Rickie asks.

"Not now. This is just a social visit. Come and meet my goats." I close the exterior door to keep the cows warm and lead Rickie through the dark toward the goat enclosure at the end of the barn. "Hi girls!"

Jacquie and Jill turn to look at me. They scamper over, probably hoping I have treats.

"Sorry to disappoint you both," I say, squatting down. Jill tries to jump on me, but I push her back and pet her instead. "It's going to snow, did you know that? Who's a pretty girl?" I croon as Jacquie tries to steal my hat.

"Honestly," Rickie says. "Viewing you in your natural habitat is very enlightening." He holds up his hands as if he's framing the picture of me with Jacquie. "I sort of get it now."

"Get what?"

"The young farmer thing. I always had a little trouble picturing you earning your diploma and then choosing a life of physical labor. But this hilltop spread is seriously cool."

I let out a sigh. "Farming means I'll never end up in a cubicle at an insurance company."

"God, no," Rickie scoffs.

"But farming is all risk. My brother is stressed out all the time. Do I really want to be responsible for whether Shipley Farms has another good decade?" It's too much pressure.

"You're a smart dude, Dylan. A farm could do so much worse than having you on it."

My roommate knows fuck-all about farming. But his words are a balm on my soul anyway. If only Griffin saw it that way, too.

But he doesn't. So I've made up my mind. And I'm done talking about it. "Are you ready to eat until you burst?"

"Yeah. I brought wine, as promised. And some funny dish towels as a gift for your mom."

"Funny dish towels?" I'm skeptical.

"Yeah. One of them says—*I love big bundts and I cannot lie.* And the other one says—*Don't go bacon my heart.*"

"You know, you'll fit right in here." I give each goat one more scratch on the chin. "Night, girls. Put your feet up. You're eating for two."

"They're pregnant?" Rickie asks.

"I hope so. The buck was brought over to stay the weekend about a month ago."

"Why don't you have your own buck? Keeping an animal whose only job was fucking should appeal to you of all people."

"Oh, Rickie." I laugh. "You make some good points. But when you only have two girls, it's too pricey keeping a buck around. He'd jump the fence and Griffin would make him into goat burgers, anyway."

I lead Rickie out the door.

"Does the drinking start now?" he asks.

"Sure, man. There's only one rule for tonight."

"No pot in the house?"

I give him a playful slap. "That goes without saying. The rule is to remember—"

"—to pretend that you and Chastity aren't doing the nasty. I won't forget. Even if that's stupid."

"It's not my idea," I say, looking around the barn for anything my goats might eat or climb on. "Let's eat some ham and drink a whole lot of wine."

THIRTY-SEVEN

Dylan

YOU'D THINK that a major fight with my brother and a major life decision would leave a guy stressed out and broody.

But it doesn't. As the house begins to fill with people, I feel more peaceful than I have in a long time. That's just how I roll. I'm sitting on a kitchen stool with Rickie when my sister May and her boyfriend Alec come through the door.

"Hey, Dyl!" May says cheerily. "Who's your friend?"

I introduce her to Rickie and accept a glass of beer that Alec has brought over. "Try this, would you? It's my oatmeal stout."

"You *made* it?" Rickie yelps. "No way. I knew this family was cool."

Alec gives us each a pint and a fist bump. And my night is shaping up.

Then the Abrahams come through the door—Isaac, Leah, Maeve, and Chastity, in that order. Rickie and I greet them all, of course. "Hey, Chass," I say, as friends do. "Happy Christmas."

"Merry Christmas," she says, but her face is like a stone. She passes by us as quickly as possible, carrying Leah's giant potato casserole into the dining room as if she's in a big hurry.

Okay. Well. I guess she plans on taking this "just friends" thing to the next level. It's a little weird. But I can take it.

"Dylan, carry the vegetables to the table," my mom says, hurrying into the room. "I'm going to carve the ham now."

"Sure, Ma." I take one more gulp of my beer.

"Can I help?" Rickie asks.

"If you want. But I've got this." I pick up a giant bowl of roasted Brussels sprouts. "Hey, Audrey!" I call to my sister-in-law. "Is there bacon in this?"

"Omigod, it's like you're *new* here," she scoffs, the baby on her hip. "Of course there is."

Rickie takes the bowl out of my hands. "I'll carry that. I don't want to let it out of my sight."

"Wait up, boy," Grandpa says, trailing behind Rickie. "I got dibs."

"Here, I have a different job for you. Hold this." Audrey passes me ten-month-old baby Gus. "If you put him down, just know that he can crawl out of sight faster than Grandpa can get at a dessert table."

"Noted."

"And he will try to grab your beer," she says at exactly the moment Gus does this very thing.

"You are a wily little fox, aren't you?" I ask my nephew as I move the beer out of his reach.

"Oopa," he says. "Bappa."

I have to smile, because Gus is a cute little beast. And his daddy hasn't taught him how to criticize me yet. So that's something.

Speak of the devil. The back door flies open and Griffin steps inside. The lower half of him is *coated* with mud. "I got it out and put it away," he says to me.

My mother makes a noise of dismay. "I don't even want to know what you're talking about. Drop those jeans and throw them on the laundry room floor. You have two minutes to clean yourself up and get to the dining room table."

"Oopa!" Gus shouts as his father disappears toward the laundry.

"Oh, he'll be back," I tell him. "Although his wardrobe choices are limited." I carry Gus into the dining room, where the table has been extended to its full holiday size. It's practically sagging under the weight of so much food. There's deviled eggs, apple chutney, Leah's decadent cheesy potatoes cooked in duck fat, the sprouts and bacon, polenta, and green beans with almonds.

I take the seat that Rickie has saved me. Gus gets a look at the table and lets out a shriek of excitement. He is a Shipley after all. The boy likes his food.

Even though it's a crime to serve anything before grace has been said, I grab the spoon in Leah's potato dish and scoop a small portion onto my plate. "Have at it, man. This is what happens when a potato dies and goes to heaven."

Gus doesn't need instructions. He uses two of his short little fingers to pluck a gooey bit of potato off the plate and shove it in his mouth.

"That is the cutest baby ever," Rickie says. "He looks like you, only fatter and more motivated."

"Oh, I'm pretty motivated. I just hide it well." I look up and see my brother in the doorway. He's standing there, holding a platter of ham, wearing a pair of my sweatpants which he obviously pulled out of the laundry bag I'd left on the floor in front of the washer.

And he's watching me and Gus with a soft expression that I rarely see on his face.

Caught staring, Griffin snaps out of it and puts the platter of ham onto the table.

"Griffin!" Isaac calls. "Come down here and tell me if you've made up your mind. Connors is blowing up my phone, but I'm holding him off."

My brother glances back in my direction, which is odd. But then he goes and takes a seat next to Isaac, and the two of them whisper quietly together for a moment.

Isaac shakes his head slowly, as if my brother has disappointed him. And then they share a one-armed man hug and a back slap that I don't really understand.

Mom rushes in with another platter, so it's time for dinner.

Audrey swoops in to take Gus, who complains about the loss of his potato feast. "Oh, there's more where that came from you little chubster," she says.

Grandpa puts his hands together and says his trademark top-speed prayer. We all say "Amen" at the same time, and then everyone reaches for a dish to pass.

We're elbow to elbow tonight as everyone digs in. Chastity is seated at the other end of the table from me, wearing a fuzzy sweater and a stricken face. I'm a little worried, honestly. Exams must have been harder on her than I thought.

I can't wait to talk to her. There are so many things I need to say. But not in this room. Who could get a word in, anyway? Everybody's talking at once. And Rickie looks as happy as I've ever seen him.

"Coming here tonight was a good decision. Mrs. Shipley and Mrs. Shipley, everything is wonderful."

"You can come back so long as you don't call me Mrs. Shipley," my mother argues. "I'm Ruth and she's Audrey."

"He's not usually polite at all," I tease. "You should just roll with it."

"Dylan, don't malign the friends who bring wine and give your mother snarky dishtowels." Mom passes the potatoes to her left. "You can bring Rickie home anytime."

Rickie gives me a smug look. "I'm beginning to see how you became the nice guy that you are. Honestly, it explains a lot."

The meal goes on and on. I spend much of it trying to catch Chastity's eye, with no luck.

Audrey brings around a tray of crackers—not the kind you eat, but those British party favors that snap loudly when you pull them apart. There's a tissue-paper crown inside, so of course we all put them on.

I give Chastity a grin down the table, and she barely musters a tight smile.

"What's up with her?" Rickie whispers.

"No idea. I guess she doesn't want anyone to know she's slumming it with me."

Rickie snorts. "Challenge. You're her favorite person in the whole entire world. She's keeping it on the down-low so she'll feel less awful when it ends."

Ouch.

"Who's ready for dessert?" my grandfather barks from the head of the table. He pushes back his chair. "I'll put the coffee on."

"I already did it, Grandpa," Daphne says. "You can just sit there looking handsome."

"You are my favorite grandchild," Grandpa says. "Somebody bring this girl a slice of pie."

"Dessert is served buffet style," Audrey says, pointing at the sideboard. "Give me two minutes, and you can both be first in line."

Chastity actually avoids me by staying in her seat until I've made my way past all the desserts. I'm a little peeved by this. But I can drown my sorrows in a slice of pumpkin bourbon pie, and a piece of bouche du noël cake.

I'm feeling fat and happy enough when Leah quiets the table by saying she has an announcement to make. She's found a donor who can make her foundation a reality. "Our plans are going forward in a big way, and since all of you have been such dear friends and neighbors all these years, I need to tell you what that means."

Half listening, I scrape frosting off my empty plate until I hear her say: "We're all relocating to Laramie in the fall."

Relocating to Laramie. Laramie...*Wyoming?*

My head snaps up and I meet Chastity's hollow eyes. And they tell me everything I need to know.

Holy shit. She's moving? That makes no sense.

"You're *leaving?*" May gasps. "Don't do that."

"It wasn't an easy decision," Leah admits, her eyes shining. "But this is important to me. And there are other benefits. Chastity can take classes at the University of Wyoming, at a pace that feels more comfortable for her. And, of course, I'm going to need her help."

I'm just trying to take this in when my evil twin chirps, "But who's going to tutor her in...algebra?"

"That's what Skype is for," my brother says, causing Rickie to choke on his wine.

"But that won't be as *satisfying,*" Daphne says with a completely straight face.

And I want to murder her. Or anybody, really. I'm suddenly so angry. I push my chair back from the table and carry my plate into the kitchen, flinging on the tap and rinsing it under the spray.

I don't know how long I stand there in front of the sink, just seething. Chastity hates Wyoming. *Hates* it. Why would she agree to go there? Was she even going to tell me?

"Hey," someone says, and I whirl around. It's only Rickie, holding out his plate. "You okay?"

"Sure," I snap, grabbing it and rinsing it off with a firehose of water. "Why wouldn't I be?"

I can feel his eyes on me. "You know, a dedicated bachelor would view this as a natural breaking-off point."

"*Natural?*" An angry noise erupts from my chest. "No, it's...stupid."

"Kidding." I hear Rickie laughing softly behind me. "Calm down. Stop trying to wash the pattern off those dishes, and go find her. I just saw Chastity put on her coat and leave the house."

"Oh." I shut the water off. I need to talk to her so badly. But I'm full of rage. It might be a bad idea.

Rickie puts his hands on me and gently steers me toward the mud room, where the boots are. "Go on. Go outside and cool down. Then find her."

I stomp toward the coats, grabbing mine off the hook and shoving my arms inside.

Unfortunately, Griffin picks that moment to show up, too. "Can I have your help with one thing? It will only take ten minutes."

"Right *now*?"

"Well, yeah. Since you have a guest, I was trying to give you Christmas day off. No milking in the morning, no chores until late afternoon. But I just need ten minutes more of your help."

"I'm not available," I grumble as my head continues exploding. Chastity can't move to Wyoming. It's the stupidest idea I've ever heard. Leah and Isaac can't either, goddamn it. Thursday dinner won't be the same.

"You made that very clear earlier," my brother says stiffly. "And I'm sure you're trying to teach me a lesson. So have at it. Go light up with your friend or whatever you were going to do. It will only take me four times as long to get the tractor tire off by myself. But you have a good time." Griffin pushes past me and stomps outside.

I'm still tugging on my boots when his words sink in. And then I can actually feel the blood leaving my extremities. That's what shock does to a body. Is he seriously going to try to lift that tire? I'll kill him myself, first.

My fingers are stupid with rage, but I manage to jerk the door open and launch myself outside, jumping off the stoop and lurching across the newly fallen snow. "Griff!"

He's already striding across the grassy circle toward the tractor shed, and doesn't bother turning around.

"Griffin! You *asshole*." I take off after him. It occurs to me to wonder where Chastity went. I don't see her anywhere. Anger propels me across the snowy yard. Even though Griffin has a head start and a long stride, I have no trouble catching up to him.

It's just that I don't slow down. I tackle him from behind, because I've forgotten how to do anything rational.

We go down hard and shockingly fast, corkscrewing a quarter turn to the side, so that my ear bounces off the snowy ground.

"Fucking hell," Griffin snarls, rolling away from me. "What the *fuck*, Dylan."

"Fuck you," I bite out, shakily sitting up. "You don't get to drop that bomb and laugh it off."

"What bomb?" he bellows, sitting up.

"A fucking *joke* about the tractor tire!" I shout. "On Christmas Eve!"

He stares back at me with the same self-righteous gaze he always wears. And I just can't take it. I'm like a grenade that bounced when it landed and has yet to explode. I lunge at my brother, knocking him back on the snow with a grunt.

Here's a tip for later—never tackle an ex-football player. Barely a half second after I watch his head bounce off the snow, the world tilts and I find myself on my back.

But I have anger on my side. I struggle with everything I've got, knocking him in the side of the head and curling my abs to try to twist free.

Ultimately, it's no good. After a quick and brutal scuffle, I'm pinned on my back, squinting up into Griffin's angry, dark eyes. "Are you on something? Serious question. Speed? Coke? What the fuck did you get into?"

That's when I hear my mother gasp from somewhere nearby. In my peripheral vision, I see Mom and Daphne and Isaac and God knows who else.

"*Nothing!*" I gasp at Griff. And all the fight suddenly drains right out of me. I flop back against the snow as Mom marches toward us. "Are you really that mean, though? Serious question. You don't get to bring up that fucking tire and turn your back on me like it's nothing."

"*Dylan.*" His voice is pure exasperation. "What *about* the tire?"

"I get that you're pissed at me. But you don't need to bring Dad into it."

"What *about* Dad?" he demands.

"Jesus Christ. He asked for my help with a tractor tire on the day he *died*. I didn't show up. You want a replay on Christmas? I guess I can't stop you."

"What?" Griffin gasps, releasing me. "Dad changed a tire? Why?"

"Because—" I put one hand down on the frigid snow and push myself up. "Because I was horsing around with Keith and missed the school bus. So he tried to do it himself. And that was it." I can't even bring myself to say the last part out loud. *He died trying.*

"Mom?" Griff asks. "Is any of that true?"

Exhaustion bleeds through me. Because of course Griffin doesn't believe me.

"No," my mother says, stunning me. "Well, Dylan missed the bus. But it didn't matter. Your father decided hours beforehand not to change the tire. He asked me to call T-Core for a service. They came at noon."

"*What?*" I gulp.

And then mom is there in the snow in front of me, on her knees in the cold, and grabbing my hands. "Dylan, it wasn't your fault. I had no idea you thought so. It was *my* fault."

"What?" I repeat. That makes no sense.

"He said he wasn't feeling well. But I didn't press. He didn't eat his lunch, and I thought that was strange. But I was busy doing the payroll and baking three pies. Pecan."

"You never make pecan," I say stupidly. Because nothing makes any sense.

"Right," she whispers, her eyes sad. "I can't look at a pecan pie anymore. That's what I was doing when your father went back to the tractor shed to listen to the baseball game on his shop radio. Alone. And I never saw him again alive."

My body must be shaking, because I hear my teeth chattering. "But the t-tire was there. When I found him." I saw it with my own eyes, leaning against the wall where he'd left it.

"Whoa. Slow down. *You* found him?" Griff asks. "Fucking hell. I didn't know that." Griffin had been away at the time, training with other would-be football stars.

"He did," my mother says, tears in her eyes. "It was a horrible thing."

"I thought…" I can't quite get the words out. "The tire was right there."

"He always kept the busted ones," Griff said. "They're useful sometimes."

My mother leans in and puts her arms around me. "The heart attack just took him," she says. "It wouldn't have mattered if you made the bus. It wouldn't have mattered one bit."

I can hear her words. But my heart can't quite believe it.

"How come Dylan doesn't already know this?" Griff asks. "The kid's been carrying this around for six years?"

The kid. There it is again. But I don't mind it so much right now.

"I didn't know," my mother says, brushing snow out of my hair. "And we're all carrying it around one way or another."

I lock my jaw to stop the shaking. And I let my mother help me to my feet.

"Griff," Daphne says. "I'll help you with the tire."

My brother glances toward the tractor shed. "Nah. It can wait. It can all wait. Let's go inside."

I glance at the group of people watching from a respectful distance. I shake my head.

"Take a minute," Mom says. "I'll say goodnight." She turns around and walks away from me and Griff.

"I'm so sorry," Griffin says gently. The way you'd speak to a baby. "I would never have said anything flip about a tire if I knew."

I shake my head again, and I realize there are tears on my face. How did they get there? I take a deep, shaky breath of cold air.

"You miss him all the time, I bet," Griff says. Like that's helping. "I do too. Every day. It used to hit me the worst when I'm in the orchard. But now it's when I'm holding the baby. I want so badly for Dad to meet him."

A sob lurches out of my chest. And I sit right down in the snow and cover my face with my hands.

My idiot brother sits down next to me. "I think you're right about me, by the way. I had this idea that I cared more about everything. You're awfully good at hiding the things that bother you. Like you're this fun guy who doesn't worry that much. It isn't true though, is it?"

I shrug. "Depends on the day of the week."

He laughs. And then he wraps an arm around me. "Come inside, okay? I still think we have a lot more talking to do. But not tonight. Come on."

I take another deep breath of the cold Vermont air, and I let myself be led.

THIRTY-EIGHT

Chastity

I'VE ALREADY WALKED down the long driveway to the road when I hear shouting.

I stop suddenly, listening. Is that Dylan's voice? It's hard to tell from this distance. And anyway, it ends after just a few seconds.

The Shipley boys can be boisterous. It kills me a little to think that they're out having fun in the snow, when I feel like my life is over.

Dylan had seemed freaked out earlier, though. When Leah spilled her news, he looked like someone had punched him. Or maybe I just wish it were true.

Leah spilled her plans before I had a chance to get used to the idea. I'm still so upset, and I don't know what to do about it.

So I'm walking home alone. It was either that or sit at the Shipley's table and cry.

A couple of minutes later, Isaac's truck ambles along, the headlights illuminating the snowy road. I step to the side and wait for him to pass.

But of course he stops. "Chastity," Isaac says after rolling down his window. "Come on, sweetie. Get in the truck."

It's cold, and I'm not wearing a hat or gloves. I open the back door, and climb in right next to Maeve, who's in her car seat. "Santa is coming!" she says. "Gotta sleep."

"That's right," I whisper. "If you're awake he might fly right past your house."

I learned about Santa when I was little. I went to a real kindergarten before our Divine Pastor decided that school was a terrible influence. The teacher read us a story about Christmas Eve. I didn't understand it, so I went home and asked my mother.

"It's just a lie," my mom said. "A lie that sinners tell their children to make them behave. There's no Santa Claus in the bible, Chastity. There's no Christmas holiday, either. If you walk the true path of Jesus, you don't need any lies."

Mom's "true path of Jesus" turned out to be full of lies too, though.

And now Maeve is getting all the things her parents were denied. There's a giant Christmas tree in her living room. Tomorrow she'll receive a pile of presents. They won't be expensive, but that's not the point.

"The only sin of Christmas is the unrecyclable plastic in these toys," Leah had told me my first year here. "My kid deserves the same red and green hype that everyone else has."

I get that. But what I don't get is why Leah wants to move back to the hellscape where we were told these lies?

I've only begun getting over all the bullshit they taught me. Two thousand miles of distance isn't enough.

After Isaac parks the truck, I remove Maeve from her car seat. Inside the house, I kiss her goodnight, and then go upstairs to my room and close the door. Heartsick, I put on my most comforting flannel pajamas and crawl into bed.

I can't sleep, though. So when Leah opens my door an hour later, I'm just staring at the darkened ceiling. "Chastity?"

"Yeah?" I croak.

She comes in and sits down near my feet. "Are you sleeping with him?"

"What?" I sputter. "Why?"

What I don't bother asking is *who*. Because I guess I'm not fooling anyone.

She lays a hand on my ankle. "I'm trying to figure out why you're so upset about the move. And that's all I could come up with. Is it true?"

I slam my eyes shut. "Will you kill him if it is?"

"Maybe." She lets out a sigh. "That isn't very fair of him."

"Why not?" I demand. Dylan has been nothing but truthful with me since we started up. "It was all my idea."

She's silent for a moment. "How does that end well?"

"It doesn't," I say flatly. "You don't have to say it."

"He's just—"

"I *know*, Leah. Everyone knows."

"Have you been careful?"

"Yes. I got an implant last week, if you must know. And they did a pregnancy test just to be safe."

"Oh." She clears her throat. "I'm sorry. This is really none of my business. I'm sorry," she repeats. "I just don't want to see you hurt."

That's pretty much a given, though.

"Can I ask you a question?"

"Sure."

"If it weren't for Dylan, how would you feel about moving to Wyoming?"

"Terrible." But after I say it, I stop and think it over. "I don't know, honestly. I like it here. But..." My head is a jumble. I can no sooner imagine Vermont without Dylan than I can imagine my own face without a nose.

"You know I can't make you go with us, right? I wouldn't do that. And you're an adult who can make her own decisions."

"Yeah. Sure." But we both know it would be really difficult for me to stay in Vermont on my own. I can't afford to.

"I feel terrible that I wrecked your Christmas. I was just so excited about the ranch."

"It's okay," I say listlessly. "I'd rather know what you're planning."

"Sleep now," Leah says. "Maeve will probably wake you up at six."

"Okay," I promise. "Night, Leah."

"Night, sweetie."

I don't sleep, though. I lay awake for hours.

At some point I get up and root around for my phone. There's a new text from Dylan. *Would you please call me?*

I'm feeling just crazy enough to do that, but now it's one in the morning, and if his phone rings, it might wake up half his house.

Another half hour passes. I finally throw off the quilt and stand up. I'm being stupid. I spent the whole day not talking to Dylan, because I didn't want everyone to know that I'm having sex with him, and that he's probably going to break my heart.

But Leah had guessed anyway and now she knows the truth. And right this second I *need* Dylan. No matter what happens later, I just want him to hold me and tell me it's going to be okay.

So I start getting dressed. Wool socks. Jeans. A turtleneck and a thick sweater. I grab my wallet and phone and tiptoe downstairs to put on my coat. On my way through the kitchen, I stop to scribble a note for Leah. *Took a midnight walk to see D.*

She won't approve, but tonight I don't care.

With a hat, boots, and mittens on, I set out into the night. The snow has stopped, and the moon has risen. If you haven't walked on a snowy night in the moonlight, you couldn't possibly understand how bright everything is.

It's only two miles, and the temperature is in the twenties. I'm not cold at all. There's not even a breeze.

I cross Isaac's cow pasture, which hooks around behind Griffin and Audrey's bungalow. It's brighter here than it would be on the road. Since the snow is new, it's completely untracked. I reach the edge of the Shipley orchards before I see evidence of another living creature, in the form of deer tracks in the snow.

It's funny how safe I feel right now. In theory, I could end up face to face with a bobcat or a pack of coyotes. But Isaac has only seen a bobcat twice in the ten years he's lived here, and coyotes are noisy.

I'm not afraid of the dark, and I'm not afraid of the nighttime. People are far more frightening. In my experience, they do their worst in broad daylight. Right to your face.

I love the silence as I plod past rows of apple trees, their gnarled branches bare, reaching up toward the sky like bony fingers. I love everything about this place. And what's more, I fought hard to be here. I got on a bus in Casper with every cent I'd saved up, and when I ran out of money in New York State, I hitchhiked the rest of the way here.

I'm not going back. It's just that simple. I'll tell Dylan. I'll ask his advice. Even if he doesn't love me, he'll still help.

We'll always be friends, right? he'd said.

I can't see the farmhouse until I get past all those apple trees. Finally, I'm crossing the meadow, passing the tractor shed, and then the barn.

Getting into the house should be easy. I know there's a key under the doormat. I also know they don't usually bother locking the kitchen door.

There's a motion-detecting light that comes on as I approach the back door. As I blink into its brightness, I have my first moment of hesitation. I know I'm welcome in this house, but not necessarily at two in the morning.

Welp. I'll just have to be very quiet. I unlatch the screen door and try the doorknob.

The door swings right open.

See? It's a sign. I quietly remove my boots, and then tiptoe through the kitchen toward the staircase.

Everyone knows that if you don't want the stairs to squeak, you have to stay at the edges. So I pick my way up the treads, my toes on the far right side.

The hallway upstairs is dark, but not too dark to find my way. Dylan's room is past the bathroom on the left. There's still a sign on the door he made when he was a kid. NO SISTERS. I can't believe it's still there, and it makes me smile.

Holding my breath, I turn the doorknob.

It doesn't move.

Okay, this is a setback I did not expect. I raise my knuckles and tap as lightly as possible.

Nothing. He's sleeping. Of course he is.

But I've come this far, and I remember him telling me how easy it is to pop the lock. I fish my wallet out of my coat pocket, remove my ATM card, and slide it between the door and the frame.

The lock pops immediately, and the door swings open.

I step inside the room, where moonlight casts shadows across the bed. Dylan is sleeping curled up on his side, which is not like him. I take a step forward to peer a little more closely at him.

That's when he rolls, leaps to his feet—arms outstretched for battle —and lets out a blood-curdling shout.

And I shriek like I'm starring in *Night of the Living Dead.*

Then several things happen very fast. First, I realize it's not Dylan on that bed. It's Rickie. I'd forgotten all about Rickie.

Second, the doorway behind us begins to fill with faces. So many faces. Daphne's, followed by Ruth's. And then Alec's and May's.

"What's happening?" someone gasps. The lights flip on.

"Chastity?" Ruth says sleepily.

Rickie gapes at me. Then he drops back onto the bed and puts a hand over his chest. "Holy crap. Did you just pop the lock on the door?"

"I—" My heart is in my mouth, and it's just dawning on me that this is going to be very embarrassing. "Where's Dylan?"

Daphne laughs. "In the bunkhouse. Is he expecting you?"

"Uh…" My face begins to heat. "Not really. I just…" …have *no* explanation for why I'm here.

"So this is just a booty call gone wrong?" Alec asks. "When I snuck into May's bedroom I was way quieter."

"Don't brag, sweetie," May says. "We can't all be born for mischief. Night, everyone."

"Later," Alec says. "The fifth stair from the bottom squeaks, by the way. For next time."

"And honey, watch out for the bunkhouse stoop," Mrs. Shipley adds. "It's made of granite and always gets icy."

"I…" I swallow hard. "Okay. Sorry."

She yawns and walks away. Daphne also melts into the shadows of the upstairs hallway, snickering as she goes.

That leaves me alone with Rickie. "Hit the light switch?" he says.

I flip if off. He lays back down and sighs. "Took a year off my life there, Chass. I actually punched the last person who snuck up on me while I was sleeping."

"I'm really sorry," I whisper. "I had no idea you'd be in here."

"S'okay," he says, tucking his cheek against the pillow. "My heart rate should return to normal by New Year's."

"Goodnight," I whisper. "Let me know how I can make it up to you."

"Just don't do that again."

I retreat, closing the door. And then I hear Rickie get out of bed to lock it behind me.

For a moment I just stand there in the hallway, trying to catch my breath. Then I make my way downstairs again, avoiding the fifth step from the bottom.

I tiptoe into the kitchen, where Grandpa is standing in the moonlit window, drinking a glass of water. "I'm sorry if I disturbed you," I whisper.

"Eh. You know what's disturbing?" he asks. "Having to piss three times every night when you're old. Enjoy being young, kid. Don't waste it."

That sounds like good advice. So I go back outside to find Dylan.

THIRTY-NINE

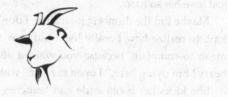

Dylan

I SLEEP FITFULLY in the bunkhouse. My body is exhausted, but my brain can't stop turning over all the things that happened tonight.

And I still haven't caught up with Chastity.

As I turn over for the hundredth time, I could swear I hear the bunkhouse door open. My eyes flip open in the dark, and I listen to the quiet footfalls of someone approaching.

"Dylan?" comes a soft voice through the door.

"Yeah?" I croak. "*Chastity?*" The door opens, and in she comes. At two in the morning! I say the first thing that comes into my head. "Holy shit, how'd you get here? And how'd you find me?"

"I walked," she says. "That was easy. But finding you was not."

"Wait." I sit up fast. "Did you knock on my bedroom door? Because Rickie is kinda jumpy—"

"Knocking would have been smart." Chastity—still in her coat—perches on the edge of the bed. "But you once told me how to pop the lock. So I scared the heck out of Rickie, terrified the both of us, and then we woke up the whole house. Now everybody knows I was trying to sneak into your room."

"Oh shit," I whisper. "Is it horrible that I'm not sorry? I need to see you."

Her eyes get wet. "I need to see you, too."

"Get in here." I pat the spot on the bed beside me. "Take off that coat. And those boots. I need to hold you."

Chastity wipes her eyes and sheds her coat. The moonlight shows me the curve of her cheek and the shine of her hair as she leans down to shed her boots. And I forget how to breathe for a second, because I just love her so hard.

Maybe I'm the dumbest man alive. I don't know how it took me so long to realize how I really feel. And now I need to tell her. "I don't mean to complain, because you walked all this way. But could you hurry? I'm dying here." I open my arms wide.

She kicks her boots aside and launches herself at me. I catch her against my chest and squeeze. All the tight places inside my chest finally loosen up. "Chastity, please don't go to Wyoming. You hate it there. And I need you too much."

A giant sob shakes her body, and her arms wrap even more tightly around me.

Don't cry, I almost say. But that's ridiculous. Sometimes you just need a good cry. So I hold Chastity against my body, rubbing her back and stroking her hair.

"I'm sorry," she sniffs. "I never cry."

"I'm just glad you're here. I really don't want you to leave."

"I can't *stand* the idea of leaving," she says with a sniffle. "But Leah really deserves my help. And I don't know how I could make it here on my own. I don't know what to do."

My heart lurches. "You're *not* on your own. Jesus. I'll help you figure it out. My family will help, too."

She takes a deep breath and lets it out slowly. "I'm sure you would. But then I'll owe you just as much as I already owe Leah."

"You won't *owe* me," I insist. "Because I love you. And I don't want you to go. I need you too much." I'm going to keep saying that until I'm sure she's heard me. "And I love you."

Chastity picks up her tear-stained face, as if she can't quite make sense of those words. "*Dylan.*"

"It's true. I promise." I wipe a tear off her cheekbone. "I'm in love with you, which is kind of inconvenient if you're leaving Vermont. But if you give me a chance, I'll make it worth your while to stay."

A beat later Chastity is still staring at me like I have three heads. I will probably have to say that a few more times before she believes me. Or—wait—Chastity needs actions, not words. So I take her face in my hands and kiss her instead.

———————————

There's a lot of kissing after that. We both need it.

Maybe I've been a little slow to figure us out. But one thing is clear —we're both very sexual people, and not just in the sense that we have a high sex drive. (Which we obviously do.) It's a key way that we communicate.

When I unzip her jeans and push them off, I'm telling her that I need to feel her skin against mine. And when she puts her palm under my T-shirt and over my heart, it's because she needs that connection.

We kiss and kiss until we can't breathe. And then we lie face to face, legs entwined. "You could spend the summer right here," I point out.

"Where?"

"Right here in the bunkhouse. If Isaac and Leah sell their place before it's time to head to Burlington in the fall, we can stay in this room together."

"I can't believe they'll sell," she whispers. "They worked so hard for everything they have."

"Wouldn't be my choice, either," I agree. "But Leah is a crusader. Her concept of home might be different from ours."

I'm still trying to figure out what home means to me, too. It's harder than I thought it would be.

"Connors wants the farm," Chastity says. "He'll put cattle in the barn."

"Isaac has a buyer already?"

"Well, yeah. Since you and Griff don't want it."

My eyes fly open again. "What?"

Chastity sits up part way. "Griffin told Isaac tonight at dinner. That you guys aren't in the position to think about it right now."

"Oh shit." I sit up, too. "Is that what Griff wanted to talk to me about?"

Chastity stares at me. "He didn't? He was supposed to."

"Um..." I think back to the fight we had over the tractor. "I told Griffin I didn't want to farm after college. I said I didn't want to work for him. But I didn't let him tell me whatever it was..." I trail off, because it's just hitting me what I turned down. "Oh fuck. Griffin was actually considering it, wasn't he?"

"I guess," Chastity flops down on the pillow. "If you don't want to farm after college, it doesn't really matter, though."

I let out a groan as I fall back on the pillow. "What a mess. I truly thought there was no room for me in this equation. But if Griffin expanded, he'd need a partner."

"It's kind of a dick move for him to decide without asking you," she says.

"Oh, it would be. It's just that I didn't give him a chance. Maybe I can fix this."

Chastity runs a hand down my arm. "Don't rush into anything."

"Will you stay in Vermont, either way?"

"Yes," she says. "Because I love you, too."

I pull her against me again, because I can't get enough. Loving Chastity isn't a big decision I made. It just happened. And as for the rest of the big decisions coming my way, they aren't as scary as they were a few hours ago.

So long as we're together, I think I can handle all the other stuff.

Chastity yawns against my chest. "We never just sleep."

"You're right." I chuckle, and her body bounces as my stomach contracts. "I have never gotten into bed with you without tearing off all your clothes first."

"It's nice," she says.

Parts of me beg to differ. But it *is* nice. I close my eyes and try to relax.

The silence stretches onward, and after a while I wonder if Chastity has fallen asleep. So I hold very still. I'm pleasantly turned on and too keyed up to sleep. But I'm too happy to care.

Chastity suddenly sits up. "Fuck it," she says. Before I can ask what she means, she rips her T-shirt over her head, allowing her breasts to bounce free.

"*Hello*," I say, startled.

She's not done. She gets up on her knees and wiggles out of her panties, and the view is right out of my best fantasies. And then? She leans down, slides a hand beneath the sheet and pulls my cock out of my pajama pants.

"Holy hell, you're initiating—" She strokes me, and I break off on a moan. "Is this real life?"

"Yes. It is. And a cute guy told me life is short." She bends down and takes my cock in her mouth. I make a noise of shock and pleasure. She pops off and says, "I mean, I still love it when you take over. But this is good, too."

"Unnngh," I say as she licks the length of me. I put my hands behind my head and let myself enjoy it.

Or that's the plan, anyway. A few minutes later, I remember that Chastity said we were cleared to have sex without condoms.

That's when I have to grab her, roll over, and press her naked body down on the bed. "Good job with Chapter Seventeen," I say, a little breathless already. "But I need to throw away the textbook again."

"Go," she says. "Do it."

Kissing her again, I do.

The next thing I know, there's a light rap on the door, and then the sound of it opening. "Dyl? Sorry to wake you but I needed to know where you put the small gage—" My brother's question breaks off suddenly. "Whoa. Sorry." The door snaps shut again.

I roll over. "The snips are on a nail on the wall of the goat enclosure," I croak.

"Should have knocked, sorry," Griff says. "Merry Christmas to you both. You might want to wake up at some point and give Mom her present."

"Will do."

When Griffin leaves the bunkhouse, I give Chastity a squeeze. At least we were fully covered by the quilt. "Sorry about that. I know you like your privacy."

"I don't think I have any of that anymore," she murmurs. "Besides, it's worth it to be here with you."

"Are you brave enough to walk into breakfast with sex hair?"

She flinches. "I don't know. Can I run home and get changed? I have to give Maeve her present."

"Of course you can. Take my truck."

"Really?" she squeaks. "Alone? There's snow on the ground."

"I'll drive you if you want. But the plow would have come by already. It's after nine. And I know you can do it."

Chastity gives me a kiss on the nose. "Dylan, do you have a black eye?"

"Maybe." I touch the sensitive spot on my eye socket. "Eh, that's nothing."

"How'd you get it?"

"It's a long story involving my big bag of crazy and Griffin's elbow."

She gives me a funny look. Then she gets up to get dressed.

When I enter the farmhouse mud room a half hour later, Griffin is there, pulling off his boots. "Sorry for not knocking earlier," he says again. "I just had no idea."

"No big deal."

"Kinda makes some sense," Griffin says, walking into the kitchen.

"What does?" I call after him. "My freak-out last night?"

He turns around, squinting at me. "No, just you in general. With Chastity. We all need someone who doesn't mind helping to carry our baggage." He turns around again.

"I don't have baggage," I say to his back as he walks away.

"Uh-huh," comes over his shoulder. "Sorry about the black eye."

"Eh. It makes me look like a tough guy. Can we talk about Isaac's farm?" I follow him into the kitchen.

He winces. "I thought you didn't want to talk about farming? I was trying not to pressure you."

"I know," I grumble. "But my timing sucks. Dad wanted that land, right? But then he didn't buy it. Do you know why?"

Griffin's face fills with surprise. "Yeah, I do. Don't you think this conversation requires coffee, though?"

"Sure." I follow him to the coffee pot, and take two mugs out of the cabinet.

"Seven years ago, the Abrahams bought their farm from—"

"—Chasternak," I supply.

"Right," Griffin agrees. "It went on the market in May, right after a nasty frost that really hurt us."

"*Oh.*" I don't remember that, but Griffin would. He's the orchard guy. He probably remembers the exact weather forecast on the day he got his first blowjob.

"Dad was worried about cash. It was one of those terrifying moments to be a farmer. There's plenty of those."

"I realize that, Griff."

He gives me a wry grin. "Sorry. I'm working on it."

"On what?"

He pours a cup of coffee and hands it to me. "It's our age difference, Dyl. When I look at you I still see a six-year-old in Spider-Man pajamas. I don't mean to patronize you. But I'm not used to thinking of you as an adult."

"Okay." I take a gulp of black coffee. The kind adults drink. "But you're working on it. So the frost convinced Dad not to buy more land?"

"Yes and no. He said it was a once-in-a-lifetime opportunity to buy adjoining farmland. But he was afraid to take on more debt when we were so cash-poor. And then Leah and Isaac showed up and made him a deal."

"Okay. That land is worth more now, though," I point out. One of our neighbors just sold a meadow we used to lease for grazing cows for a pile of money. "The parcel across the street—"

"—has million-dollar views," Griffin says, cutting me off. "But Isaac's place doesn't."

"How much is it worth?"

"Two fifty? Two sixty? But interest rates are really low right now."

"Still. That's a lot of money."

"Yes and no. Dad was right about it being a once-in-a-lifetime opportunity. But now we have a chance at it, too. Isaac might even let us finance with him. That would save us bank fees."

"Unless he already gave it to Connors," I point out.

Griffin sets his mug down on the counter. "I texted him again this morning, though. Because letting it go before I could talk to you just didn't sit well with me. The truth is that I hope you'll choose this. Not out of obligation. And not because I need more minions to kick around my dictatorship."

I flinch, and he laughs.

"Dylan, I *like* working with you. I like the art you make for the cider labels, and I like the care you take with the animals. And I like hearing you whistle in the barn. I can work on my attitude toward decision-making. If I knew you were onboard, then I'd have to get over myself a little and consider your plans."

Well, hell. My mind is blown again. "But could we afford this? If we took on Isaac's place?"

"It would be hard at the beginning," Griffin says, rubbing the back of his neck. "We might have to lease out the house to keep the cash coming in. But it's definitely possible."

Rickie enters the kitchen with an empty plate in his hand. "I don't know if I'm ever leaving," he declares. "Those pancakes your sister makes are pretty intense."

"Let's eat," Griff says. "Is Audrey around?"

"In here!" his wife calls. "Your son just ate the last pancake."

"I'll pour some more," Daphne says, coming through from the dining room. "Where's Chastity?"

The mud-room door bangs. "Right here!" Chastity calls. Then she steps into the kitchen looking flushed and happy. "Leah and Isaac say Merry Christmas."

When she moves closer, I pull her into a one-armed hug. "Did you tell them you weren't going to Wyoming?"

"I did," she whispers.

"And?"

"Leah wasn't surprised. I guess disappearing in the night kind of clued her in."

"And can I assume my truck made it back safely?"

"Of course it did."

I lean down and kiss her smile. And even though we're standing in the middle of my family, she kisses me back.

"It's weird how that doesn't seem weird," Griffin says.

"Oh, I'm used to it already," Rickie adds.

We ignore them.

Chastity steps back eventually, though. "I brought your present." She hands me an envelope.

"Thanks!" I give it a shake. "Well, it's not a puppy."

"A *puppy*," Griffin snorts. "Nobody buy him a puppy unless he's actually living in the same zip code with it."

"Just wait until Gus learns to say *puppy*," I argue. "You'll fold faster than a bad hand of poker."

Griffin grins over his coffee mug, because he knows I'm right.

I tear open the envelope and fish out two tickets to the New Year's Eve concert I wanted to attend. "Aw, really? This is awesome. You want to go with me?"

"Well, it's an easy decision *now*," she says. "But I have a hard time saying no to you. So I bought them last week."

There's even more kissing after that.

And then pancakes.

EPILOGUE

Chastity

VALENTINE'S DAY is yet another holiday I didn't have for the first nine-teen years of my life. "There were no heart-shaped candies at the Paradise Ranch," I'd told Rickie and Dylan. "Can you imagine the mayhem if every man had to romance five wives on one night?"

The idea had made me snort-laugh in a very unladylike way.

But I guess Dylan took it as a challenge. When I wake up in his bed on February 14th, I'm alone. But I can smell the coffee brewing downstairs, and when I step into the kitchen, a giant bouquet of red and silver balloons blocks my path to the coffee pot.

"Oh wow," I say, spotting Dylan's and Rickie's feet somewhere near the kitchen table. "This is so—"

"Gaudy?" Rickie supplies.

"Extravagant," I insist, pushing the balloons aside. When I locate the table, Dylan is waiting there beside a sumptuous heart-shaped box of Lake Champlain Chocolates. *And* a dozen red roses. The tag reads: *For Chastity*.

"Oh, Dylan!" I gasp. "I've never gotten roses." I step right over and sit in his lap, because there are only two chairs at the table. And because Dylan is my favorite furniture anyway.

"See?" he says, reaching over to give Rickie a poke in the arm. "Tone down the cynicism." He nudges the chocolates in my direction.

"I got this boyfriend thing all figured out." He hands me his coffee mug, and I help myself to a gulp.

He does, indeed, have this boyfriend thing figured out.

Rickie just shakes his head. "I guess you had to go big on the flowers since you can't take your girl out to a nice V-day dinner."

"That's okay with me," I say, leaning back against Dylan's bare chest. "I'm looking forward to tonight."

"There will be, like, a hundred girls drooling over your man," Rickie points out. "I predict an estrogen fest at the club tonight."

"You're coming though, right?" I demand. "Ellie is counting on you to sneak her in. How are you going to do that, anyway?"

"Piece of cake," he says. "Just wait."

The Hardwick Boys are playing their second gig ever at a Burlington bar—this one a few blocks away from the bar that Ellie and I were kicked out of in the fall. The room is packed with a Valentine's Day crowd, but I've got a plum spot near the front. Griffin made a point to drive Audrey, Leah, and Isaac into town for the evening.

"Who's babysitting?" I'd asked the moment they walked in. I feel a twinge of guilt as I ask the question. Leah and Isaac had stayed home on New Year's so I could go out with Dylan to the concert.

"We hired a high school friend of Dylan's to watch Maeve and Gus at our house," Griffin says. "Her name is Debbie? I don't know if you ever met her."

"Um, yup," I say. "I remember Debbie."

"Both kids were asleep when we drove away." Griffin shrugs. "Easy money for Debbie. Audrey and I need a night out anyway, right? And why not watch the kid play his fiddle?"

"You should stop calling him the kid," Audrey points out. "You're going to be business partners. You should refer to each other in terms of mutual respect."

"You're right, babe. Now let's watch the kid play." He points at the stage, where Dylan and Keith have appeared to hoots of applause.

"Evening!" Dylan says into the microphone. "Who wants to dance on Valentine's Day?"

There's an estrogen-fueled shriek.

"Let's do this!"

Keith counts them in, and they launch into a fast-paced tune. Keith is on an electric guitar this time, giving them a slightly grittier sound. They call their style *funkabilly*, whatever that is.

Right before he left us to tune up with Keith, Dylan announced to us that they had "a nice, tight ninety minutes" of music prepared for tonight. "It's gotten easier to put a set together."

"That must be the result of finally declaring your major," Griffin had teased.

Dylan had barely rolled his eyes. He and Griff are getting along a lot better now.

As for his major, Dylan went with agriculture and a minor in music. He and Griff are buying the Abrahams' farm. Leah and Isaac will leave for Wyoming in May.

Since I'm not going with them, they may leave even before classes are through. The farmland is leased for two years to a vegetable grower from Hardwick. This will help them pay the mortgage and some of the taxes while Dylan finishes school.

Later this spring, after Leah and Isaac leave, Griffin will try to rent out the house, and Dylan will take over cutting the lawn and looking after the place.

"Someday I think Griffin will live there," Dylan had said the other day, as we lay naked and sated in bed together. "If they have a second baby, the bungalow will get too small for them. And I bet Audrey has designs on that commercial kitchen."

"I'll bet she does, too."

"For now it will be ours to use and rent out. How many caramels do you think we can make next fall?"

"I don't know."

"What if I got two more goats?" he'd asked.

"Wait, you'd *double* the milk production?" I'd yelped.

He'd laughed. "It's just an idea. I have a lot of those." Then he'd rolled on top of me and kissed me.

Leah and Isaac are already dancing. They're pretty good at it, too. Isaac spins her, and Leah laughs.

I'm already starting to feel sad about their departure. I wish they wouldn't go. Maeve is going to be such a big girl next time I see her.

I've promised to visit the following summer. Leah would like me to stay for a couple of months, but she said I can come for a short visit if that makes me more comfortable. "It's different for you. I realize that now. Two years means it's all still raw."

She isn't wrong. I'm taking another writing class this semester, too. Because I've discovered that writing about the Paradise Ranch has helped me process my feelings about the place. And I like writing more than I expected to. So who knows what will come of that.

Griffin and Audrey start dancing, too, leaving Rickie and I standing against the wall. "T minus two minutes," he says, checking his phone.

"Are you sure this will work?"

"Baby, I was born for mischief." He swats me on the backside. "Go on. Count to sixty and then get into position, okay?"

"Sure." My heart does a little flop, though, because if we get into trouble in the middle of Dylan's performance, it's going to be embarrassing.

"I'm going," he says.

I start counting as I watch him head for the exit, where he stops to talk to the bouncer. The other man puts a stamp on Rickie's hand, probably to make it clear that he already paid the cover charge.

When I get to sixty, I head for the ladies' room. Since the music just started up, it's almost empty. There's only one woman standing at the mirror, putting on lipstick.

And that woman is Kaitlyn.

"Hi," I say, startled.

"Hi," she says without turning her face. She's busy. "You need something?"

"Well…" This is going to be awkward. "Not really." I look up at the window that's five feet off the ground. Rickie has already opened it. A hand appears on the sill. Then another one.

Ellie's face pops into the opening. "Hey there! Maybe I should be feet first?"

"Oh definitely," Kaitlyn says. "You are both a couple of amateurs." She sets her lipstick on the sink. Then she removes the plastic bag from the trash can that's standing beside the sink. She flips it over and points at it. "Feet first. We'll guide you onto this."

The other end of Ellie appears a moment later. I can hear Rickie grunt on the other side of the wall as Kaitlyn reaches for Ellie's ankles.

I'm almost too startled to help, but then I snap out of it and help lower my friend to the trash can, where she stabilizes herself and then eases her upper body through the window.

She hops down a second later and hugs me hello. "Thanks, girls! What did I miss?"

"Just one song, I think," Kaitlyn says, tossing her lipstick into her bag. "Put the trash back together, would you? And close that window." She gives an exaggerated shiver and strides out of the bathroom.

I will never really understand Kaitlyn, but she's a little nicer to me now. I give credit to her hockey player, who seems to be sticking around.

"Let's dance!" Ellie says, hurrying me toward the door. "This is my first time at a bar."

"You can't get wasted," I beg. "I don't need to hold your hair while you puke on Valentine's Day."

She laughs. "Fine. One cider. That's all I ask."

When we step out of the ladies' room, Dylan is playing a slow, romantic tune. His eyes are closed as he plays, and shivers climb up my spine as the melody swells.

This happens a lot, actually. I look at him and think, *How did I get so lucky?*

But he says the same thing to me sometimes just before we fall asleep. So I guess I'm not the only one.

"Here." Rickie is already waiting with a beer for himself and a cider for Ellie and me. "Told you it would work."

"Thank you, Rickie," Ellie says with a smile. She looks older since her braces came off over Christmas break. "You're my hero. I expect a dance after we finish our drinks."

He scowls, but we both know she'll talk him into it.

"This next song starts fast and then gets faster," Dylan says into the microphone. "So pace yourselves, ladies!" He puts his violin on his chin.

"The not-a-kid sounds great!" Griffin, says, applauding. "This is fun, baby. Thank you for making me come out tonight."

"Any time, you big grump." Audrey hugs him from behind. "Now dance with me."

Rickie and Ellie dance. We switch it up a couple of times, but the truth is that I prefer to stand still and watch. I'll always love watching Dylan play.

It's getting towards the end of the set when I hear Dylan announce, "This next song is for someone special." He smiles right at me, and my heart nearly bursts with joy.

Ellie lets out the perfect little fan-girl shriek.

"I wasn't able to take my girlfriend out somewhere alone tonight. Because I'm here with you all."

The girls in the audience all make a collective noise that sounds like *Awwww*.

"First we were friends," Dylan says, tuning up his new electric violin as he talks. "...and then we spent a lot of time together making gourmet caramel candies. So I think this whole Valentine's Day thing isn't a scam after all, you know? Because after we made all that candy together it became clear to me that I was in love for the first time in my life."

The *Awwww* is louder this time.

"That's the sound of other hearts breaking," Rickie quips.

Keith is picking up another guitar. I don't have any idea what they're about to play, but I can feel my cheeks flushing already.

"So I hope you're ready to rock, because my love song here isn't a slow one. I don't know what the songwriter was saying when he wrote this. But I think this song is about caramels and love. Let's do this!"

Keith kicks into a fast guitar riff. I don't recognize it, but then Dylan adds a riff, and it starts to sound familiar.

My pop-culture knowledge is still pretty shaky, so I have to shout a question at Ellie and Rickie. "What is it?"

"An eighties tune called 'I'll Stop The World And Melt With You'!" Rickie says. Then he cracks up. "Good one, Dyl!"

And then? Dylan lifts his chin from his fiddle and sings the lyrics. To me. Right here in this crowded room. Keith sings, too. It's magical.

The first two lines makes me blush like crazy. But, yowza. It's the most romantic thing that's ever happened to me. I'm not ashamed to say that I get tears in my eyes.

After each verse, Dylan lights up his electric fiddle. It's a super-cool cover. And the best Valentine's Day gift *ever*.

It's over too soon, and then the concert ends, too.

"I guess I was wrong," Kaitlyn says, filing past me on her way out. She has her boyfriend's hand in hers. "You did it."

It takes me a second to realize she's talking to me. "Did what?" I call after her.

She merely lifts her chin toward the stage. And I realize she means that I made Dylan fall in love with me.

I didn't, though. Nobody ever could.

All I did was lead Dylan to the kitchen where—for hours—we stirred goat's milk together with sugar.

It was just heat and patience. Those were the only ingredients.

We end up back at the house on Spruce Street, eating exquisite chocolates and drinking a bottle of champagne Rickie bought. "Because that seems right for V-day," he'd said.

Griff and the rest of the Tuxbury crew leave first. I hug Leah goodbye and promise to come home next weekend. And they're going to drop Ellie off on their way out of town.

That leaves me and Dylan and Keith and Rickie in the living room, where a fire crackles in the old fireplace.

Dylan pulls out his phone for the first time all evening. "I have a message from Daphne."

"Oh *do* tell," Rickie says, wiggling his eyebrows. "How is that hottie doing?"

Dylan gives him a weary glance. "I know you do that just to bug me. But it won't work. I don't buy it for a second."

"Daphne is hot as blazes, dude," he says with a shrug. "I don't care if you believe me."

"Uh-huh." Dylan snorts. "I just read this message four times. And it sounds like she's asking me to help her find somewhere cheap to live next year. In *Burlington*."

"Why?" I gasp. "She has two more years at Harkness." Daphne is a junior, but she's so smart that she's earning a bachelors and a masters together at the same time.

"Fuck if I know. She says, *'I have to leave Harkness. This place isn't right for me anymore.'* Whatever that means." He puts his phone away. "I'll ask her tomorrow. She's not going to tell me, though."

"Can we talk about housing for a minute?" Rickie asks.

"Sure," Dylan says, pulling me closer to him on the sofa. "Something wrong?"

"Not a thing. But you know how I don't charge you guys much rent?"

"We did, uh, notice," Keith says.

"Thing is—I have an offer to rent out the house over the summer," Rickie says. "There's some sports superstar who runs a clinic in the summertime. He wants the whole place. It pays enough money that I could make a whole year's taxes at once."

"Oh," Dylan says slowly. "You should do it. Do we need to clear out by a certain date?"

Rickie waves a careless hand. "That part is easy. The trick is that I don't have anywhere to go for the summer. Unless I turn up on your doorstep and pick apples."

Dylan hoots. "Sure man. Why not? You can have my room. Chastity and I are keeping the front bedroom in the bunkhouse." He gives me a squeeze. "We like it out there."

This was my idea. I'll be staying with the Shipleys this summer, but I'd wanted the privacy of the bunkhouse.

"I'll do a good job," Rickie says. "Just because I look like a lazy fuck, doesn't mean I don't know how to work."

"Of course," Dylan says. "We're always short-handed. And we'll have a great time."

"I appreciate it," Rickie says, crossing his legs onto the coffee table. "As a result, I can do this rental. And also your sister can live here next year if she wants to. So can Chastity, by the way. Everybody's rent will be only a hundred bucks a month, to cover heat, utilities, internet, and maintenance supplies."

"A hundred bucks?" I gasp. "That's nothing."

"You can have the other upstairs bedroom," Rickie points in the general direction of that room. "And Daphne can take the third floor if she doesn't mind living with her brother."

"Why so cheap, man?" Keith asks. "I don't get it. You could be earning a lot more rent. Or else keep the place to yourself."

"Nope," Rickie says as he gets to his feet. "Being alone is the very last thing I need. And if I had a lot more cash, I'd probably just smoke it all." He shrugs. "Night guys. See you in the morning."

He walks out of the room, and the rest of us just kind of stare at each other for a moment.

"A hundred bucks," Dylan breathes. "We're going to save so much money. This is great."

"Plus, it will be a fun summer," Keith points out. "We'll introduce Rickie to Friday nights at the Goat." He also gets to his feet. "Night guys. Good gig, Dyl. You know I'm going to ask you to do another one."

"Night!"

We're quiet for a second. "Do you think Daphne is okay?" I ask.

"God, I hope so. Because there probably isn't much I can do if she's not." He yawns. "Come to bed with me, Chass."

My tummy flips like it always does.

He takes my hand as we slowly turn out the lights and head upstairs.

"I loved the song, Dyl," I say quietly.

"I'm pretty sure it was written to mean something dark. But I don't hear it that way anymore. I hear it and think of caramel and nakedness." He kisses me on the temple. "Come to bed, and I'll show you what I think about that song."

I do. And he does, too.

THE
END

ALSO BY SARINA BOWEN

TRUE NORTH

Bittersweet (Griffin & Audrey)

Steadfast (Jude & Sophie)

Keepsake (Zach & Lark)

Bountiful (Zara & David)

Speakeasy (May & Alec)

Fireworks (Benito & Skye)

HOCKEY ROMANCE

Brooklynaire

Overnight Sensation

Superfan

Moonlighter

Sure Shot

Rookie Move

Hard Hitter

Pipe Dreams

With Elle Kennedy

GOOD BOY by Sarina Bowen & Elle Kennedy

STAY by Sarina Bowen & Elle Kennedy

HIM by Sarina Bowen & Elle Kennedy

US by Sarina Bowen & Elle Kennedy

Top Secret by Sarina Bowen & Elle Kennedy

With Tanya Eby

Man Hands

Man Card

Boy Toy

Man Cuffed

CPSIA information can be obtained
at www.ICGtesting.com
Printed in the USA
LVHW031532061120
670968LV00009B/1459

9 781942 444985